D0267786

23

MADDIGAN'S
Fantasia

MADDIGAN'S
Fantasia

MARGARET MAHY

ff

faber and faber

First published in 2006
by Faber and Faber Limited
3 Queen Square London WCIN 3AU

Typeset by Faber and Faber Limited
Printed in England by Mackays of Chatham plc, Chatham, Kent

A CIP record for this book
is available from the British Library

ISBN 978–0–571–23015–0
ISBN 0–571–23015–6

2 4 6 8 10 9 7 5 3

To Robinson and Craig . . . triumphant fathers

MADDIGAN'S
Fantasia

1

Losing Ferdy

Hello this is Garland Maddigan writing things down. I
don't know why I am writing them down because when
you write it's mostly because you're trying to tell somebody else something but right now – I'm telling myself –
me! – things I already know. Or maybe I half-know them
and writing them down finishes them off in my head so
that I know them properly. Written down things seem
true. Weird!

Stretched out among the ferns on the small tangled
hillside, her red curls burning among the green leaves
and fronds, Garland Maddigan closed the cover of
the book she had been writing in, though still holding her writing place in it with one finger. She looked at its battered blue
cover admiringly. No doubt about it. A book! A thick book of
actual pages . . . paper pages . . . empty pages. Closing her eyes
she rippled her thumb across their edges. Once, she knew, the
world had been filled with paper, but the Destruction turned
most of it to ashes. These days, even though the Destruction
and the Chaos that followed it were times of the past, even
though the world had been slowly remaking itself for years,
paper was not always easy to come by once you moved out of
the cities. And inside the cities it was often expensive. Here she

was with a whole empty book of it, found in one of those ruined houses, those empty shells twisted in gardens gone wild, lasting on in the tangled forests on either side of the road. She could move her secret thoughts from inside to outside, and then, by closing that blue cover, she could trap them before they flitted away from her. After all, soon she would be thirteen and her childhood (along with all the things that had patched her childhood together) would be fading into the past. Better write the days down before they got away from her altogether. These pages – these white spaces – were hers and hers alone. She was going to tell her secret thoughts to that mysterious reader she felt taking shape on the other side of the paper.

Down at the bottom of the hill a little plain, slightly scooped like a begging hand, reached out of a small forest of old trees stretching bare branches towards the next hill. (After all, though the sun was shining so warmly it *was* winter.) And there, on the edge of scrubby bush that fringed the true forest (trees that never lost their leaves), Garland's moving home, the Fantasia, was laid out like a strange garden set within a crescent; tents, old and sometimes patched, had the look of gallant, coloured flags. There was her home – half bus, half caravan, a crested tower pointing upward from its roof, rather as if a little castle were struggling to hatch itself out of the old van. The Fantasia dressed not only its clowns and acrobats in astonishing clothes, but turned the vehicles that carried it along the leftover tracks of the wild world into a bright and shifting village on wheels. There was the food wagon, hung with pots and pans. Bailey, the mapreader, was carefully wiping dust out of them. He turned as Maddie, Garland's mother, walked by, and shook his duster at her. It promptly turned into a bunch of flowers which he held out to Maddie. It was a trick they were both used to, but she laughed and Bailey laughed with her. The wind crept in under the canvas of the tents so that the canvas rose and fell, and the whole Fantasia looked as if it were laughing along with them. Below there, in that strange garden, people were working hard: checking the horses, practising their routines, packing and repacking, fixing the frills round the necks of the dogs, then clapping their hands for them to leap through their hoops, dance on their hind legs or spin like barking tops.

Vans and wagons were parked in a wide semicircle. Garland now saw her mother join her father, Ferdy the ringmaster, bright in his scarlet coat – not the one he wore for performances but an old one he put on when the wind was cold. The Fantasia was slow to throw anything away. She watched her parents, walking side by side, and holding hands as they checked coils of rope, or bent side by side over solid, impassive boxes, watched them pat the panting tents and laugh to one another. Yves, her father's second-in-command, walked a step or two behind them, and Boomer, that irritating boy (a sort of adopted cousin-brother), zoomed around on his small motorized bike, the treasure of his life, trying to look as if he, too, was one of the people in charge. But Boomer loved machines and perhaps machines liked Boomer. They certainly seemed to do what he told them to do. But perhaps Boomer *needed* to feel he was in charge of something. He was a Fantasia orphan, half-adopted by old Goneril the Fantasia witch who complained about him, but who made sure he had plenty to eat, and who stuck up for him when anything went wrong. And there was Goneril herself, standing outside her van which was painted with magic symbols, probably grumbling (for grumbling was her hobby). Even when the weather was fine and things were going well, Goneril always found something to grumble about. Looking down on them all, it suddenly seemed to Garland that she was watching two families . . . her own parents, of course, but also that other wider family – the Fantasia itself, that family of tumblers and grumblers related to her by wonders and work, travel and trickery . . . Maddigan's Fantasia. There they were – all of them – Tane the chief clown and a lively acrobat, Penrod who looked after the horses and flipped on the trapeze. There were Byrna and Nye the stilt walkers, there was old Goneril of course, and dreamy Bannister with one book tucked under his arm (even though he was strapping up a bundle of something), and another in his back pocket. Books, books, always books with Bannister. And there, of course, was Ferdy – descended directly from the first Maddigan, Gabrielle – walking with her mother, Maddie, who was not only a mother but an acrobat, and a knife thrower as well (though her knives had blades like stars or new moons). There they were, all those special people, laid out like pieces in a bright game . . . and beyond them, all around them, the damaged land that held still while you looked at it, but which seemed to spin and shift and tangle, turning tricks of its own once you looked away.

Garland flipped her book open again and began her writing. Funny that scribbling things down like this should be making her feel so altered . . . so powerful. The short stub of pencil, hard to hold but carefully sharpened, left its silver track across the page.

Ok . . . perhaps there is someone on the other side of the page who is reading what I am writing. Hey you! Hello there! Who are you? I suppose you'll have to read all this in a backwards way, like Alice in that Looking Glass story which my mother read to me. I'll start off telling you who I am. I am Garland Maddigan . . . a true-born Maddigan . . . part of Maddigan's Fantasia . . . the greatest circus in the world. We travel most of the year from place to place, joking, dancing, doing a thousand tricks. We cross the nowhere – the hundreds of nowheres – that lie between the camps and communities and towns and left-over cities of the world. I am twelve, well, almost thirteen, and I have red hair, a true Maddigan colour. I can do a bit of magic, but my true power is walking the tightrope. I can even turn flips on it, and that's a true Maddigan power – the power to do tricks I mean. We're a trickster family.

Garland paused, then began writing again.

I don't know if the world counts as the world any more, not since the poisonings and then the wars of the Destruction which all took place ages ago ... back before the days of Gabrielle Maddigan who counts as our first Maddigan in a way, though there must have been Maddigans before her. I know that once upon a time there used to be a great world made up of different lands with oceans between them. I know that people sailed across the oceans and even flew through the air. But then the world growled like a mad dog, and tore itself to pieces (which was what we call the Destruction). And then for a while there were the plagues and a sort of dissolving of everything (which was what we call the Chaos), and for another while after that there was almost nothing ... well, there must have been something, but nothing that was written down or saved. It was like that for years and years. And then, just before our own time, the Remaking began, when things began to come together again.

Anyhow we are the left-over people going between the left-over places ... place to place ... place to place ... on and on and on ... and as we go everything alters. Old paths twist and swallow themselves. Some roads stay put, but others just seem to disappear. Lucky us! We have our maps, even though they are falling to bits, and we have Bailey our mapreader. He's very clever. It almost seems he can read words that have fallen off the paper and read the minds of roads and tracks too, so when they strangle themselves and vanish (as they often do) Bailey knows exactly where they'll pop up again. And we all have the names of the towns in our heads. After a while I think our heads actually turn into maps, and when the roads do reappear again I think it is because the Fantasia has dreamed them back into being real.

I love being part of the Fantasia but sometimes I love spending time on my own – like now – when I'm working things out and asking myself questions. Like will I ever grow up properly? Will there be room out there for a grown-up me? Will I ever get married? Of course I'll never leave the Fantasia but there's no one in the Fantasia I could marry. Well, there is Boomer of course. But I could never fall in love with Boomer – he's only a kid, and anyway he'd only love me if I was a clockwork girl with wheels instead of feet. There's Bannister, maybe, but he's way older than I am, and anyhow he's already in love. In love with books and people in stories, so . . .

'Garland!' someone shouted urgently. She knew her father's voice. Garland looked up sharply

'Garland,' came a chorus of echoing voices. Some of them were real echoes, but among them she could make out Boomer's voice and the piping cry of Lilith, the bossy daughter of Yves, her father's right-hand man. None of them were voices she wanted to hear just then, for it was just great being a runaway hidden high on a hillside and looking down on the Fantasia . . . being a true, pure self without a couple of kids dancing around her, trying to get her attention. But her father had called her in a voice she could not ignore.

'Garland!' he was calling again, shouting and looking left and right, and this time she knew for sure that something had gone wrong.

'Garland! Quickly!' screamed yet another voice, Maddie's voice. 'Now! Oh lord, they're coming!' No way out of it! She must go. Go now!

She leapt up, sliding the book into the front of her coat and pushing the pencil stub back into her pocket. And it happened again.

The air between her and the Fantasia below rippled as if wind from another world were blowing through it . . . and a shape, coming out of nothing, seemed to struggle towards her . . . a silvery-grey shape as if an unseen pencil were drawing on the air in front of her.

Several times over the last year Garland had seen the air ripple like this in front of her, had seen that shivering mist struggling to take on some shape but always dissolving back into nothing. Garland stared at it, a little frightened, but curious too.

'What are you?' she cried aloud. 'OK! What do you want to *tell* me.' She'd asked this before but there had never been any answer.

'Garland!' screamed the voices down below.

'Look! I've got to go!' she said. 'I've got to go!'

No time to worry about any mere ghosts! She must run right through them . . . run through silver mist, and the scrub and duck in under the trees

'Garland! Now! Now!' Maddie was shouting, and really there was nothing to do but to run.

Below her the Fantasia was seething. The horses were being drawn in among the caravans and all vans were being swung around. The Fantasia must stop being a village and become an armed fort, for it was being attacked, and it was too late for Garland to join them. Ferdy, racing from one van to another, looking desperately up at the hillside as he ran, saw her and pointed her out to Maddie.

'Down! Down!' yelled Maddie and Ferdy together, both swinging their arms, flattening the air in front of them, and Garland obediently flattened herself among the tussock and the broom bushes that grew on the lower slopes of the hillside, panting a little and staring between the brown-green stems, trying to work out just what was happening. She heard them before she saw them of course – the snarling of motorbikes as they were kicked into life – the roar of their attack.

Road Rats! She should have guessed. Road Rats! And by the sound of it a big gang of them.

Up from the river, out from the scrubby bush to the right of the Fantasia they came, the bikers first, gunning their machines to make a confusing sound, winding and zigzagging as they burst in on the Fantasia. After them came more men jogging ruthlessly, slung with bows, spears and occasional guns, straggling but quick and ferocious, determined to steal whatever they could get their hands on. Often Road Rats used clearer pieces of road as bait, knowing that an easy road would lure travellers, making it easy to trap and rob them. But the Fantasia was always alert, armed and ready for Road Rats. There came the peppering fire of guns. Penrod had a gun and Goneril had one too. She was a good shot. The rest of them depended on bows and arrows.

The Road Rats engaged with the front line of the Fantasia, a furious, confused struggle. Hand-to-hand combat now! Garland saw her mother's wild red skirt flying out, saw her dealing blows right and left. She saw Yves embracing one of the Road Rats, a man with a crown tattooed around his bald head, as if they were long lost friends. But there, on the roof of the food van, Bailey suddenly collapsed and then slid sideways. Then, peering through the broom bushes Garland saw her father Ferdy bending at the knees, taking a staggering, sideways step, and toppling forward. Even from where she was, hidden in the scrub on the slope, Garland could see he had an arrow in his chest.

'No!' she screamed, leaping to her feet, dancing among the broom bushes, not caring in the least if the enemy saw her red curls like a fire suddenly blazing up in the broom. Maddie straightened, spun, and threw one of the silver stars she used in her juggling act. It flew through the air – a shooting star – shining and spinning and struck a Road Rat, biting deep into his neck. But the Road Rats were already in retreat . . . a slow double retreat since, off to one side a group of them had successfully closed in around the food van. Some of them had managed to scramble into the van. Its motor roared. It was being driven away while other Road Rats fought a rearguard action. She heard, as if from a great distance, the rattle of the pots and pans. As the van pulled away the Road Rats were already unhooking the noisy pots and flinging them off into the tussock. There was no way that the Fantasia people could get to their van without leaving themselves open to Road-Rat attack. But that was the skill of these attackers. One group would distract travellers with battle while another group, skirmishing off to one side, would steal what they could find and run for it. Though they were thin and weedy people – though they were less well-armed they greatly outnumbered the men and women of the Fantasia.

Two of their men, injured and left behind, crawled for cover, but all the Fantasia people cared about – all Garland could see – was her father . . . her fallen father.

'No!' she screamed again, as she began pelting down the hillside, briefly losing sight of the Fantasia as she twisted down into the trees, feeling them stretch out branches to catch and claw at her. She could hear the sound of those motorbikes roaring away into an unknown distance, and imagined Maddie and Yves gently drawing Ferdy back into the shelter of the caravans. Other men and women would be running to protect them, even though the Road Rats were skilfully melting away. As for their stolen van – it was already becoming part of the world beyond the road. Ferns would be leaping up around it like green jagged flames, and no one would be giving pursuit, for the Fantasia people would be too overwhelmed by Ferdy's fall. And Bailey had fallen too. She must not forget Bailey.

'Thieves! Mongrels!' she screamed, sliding and stumbling down the slope, imagining the Road Rats, now lost in the shelter of the bush, transforming, turning into twigs and leaves, stretching towards the sky or melting into the earth. And, as these pictures rushed incoherently through her mind, something struck her violently. Her feet slid from under her and her head exploded with zigzagging lights.

Just for a moment she could feel dead leaves under her hands and under her cheek as well. In her panic she had smashed blindly into the low branch of a tree. She got up. One step forward . . . another step . . . then out of the bush and into the cupped hand of the little plain. But she was going to fall. Her head was whirling and singing a strange wild song that was all its own. Pitching forward Garland knew she must rest – she absolutely *must* – rest her ringing head on the ground.

As she lay there, staring sideways and struggling to hold the dizzy darkness at bay, something strange happened somewhere to her right. A thin line of light, sharp and shining as the blade of a polished knife, cut the world in half. Two figures stepped through the gap . . . a tall boy, not just fair-headed like Boomer, but golden-haired like the prince in a fairy tale, and a smaller boy who looked like a child of the trees, wild and brown and tangled. The taller boy was holding a great doll. No! That doll was waving its hands. It must be a baby. Electric streaks seemed to dance around them. Garland tried to push herself up on one elbow, but then conquering darkness swept in over her, and she collapsed down into the leaves and twigs once more.

'Garland!' a voice was exclaiming. 'There! Garland! You're waking up, aren't you?'

Garland was indeed waking up. But even before opening her eyes she knew she had been rescued. She had been found and carried back into the inner circle of the Fantasia. She could smell it. She could *feel* it. Byrne, one of the stilt walkers, was kneeling beside her, and she was embraced by the magic circle of the Fantasia vans and tents. She was safe – as safe as was possible for any member of a Fantasia travelling the dissolving road. Men were still guarding the slots between one van and another. Other men stood around behind the women who were bending over the fallen figures of Ferdy and Bailey the mapmaster. Garland could see her father's blue shirt and her mother's red skirt as she kneeled beside him. She could see old Goneril kneeling there too, directly opposite her mother, touching Ferdy's chest, then his forehead, then looking up and shaking her head. She could not see her mother's expression but she heard herself crying out yet again. 'No! No!' as she swung herself over onto all fours, forced herself up onto trembling legs, and then, supported by Byrne, who understood her urgent mood, staggered towards her mother.

Maddie turned, then held out one arm to her. Under her streaking tears her face was calm.

'Garland!' she said, 'Garland! I know! I know! But we've got to be tough. Tough! We've got to hold in there. It's what he would want. This is Maddigan's Fantasia and we – you and me, that is – we are Maddigans.'

Garland flung herself against her mother, as if she might push right into her – as if they might somehow become the one person with the one grief. She couldn't be bothered with being brave and wept for Ferdy Maddigan, lying there dead, while the rest of Maddigan's Fantasia stood around being tough just as Ferdy would have wanted them to be.

A voice broke in on her grief. It was Yves, standing tall behind Maddie, though stained with blood from a knife wound that had cut down his left cheek and across his chest.

'Move on,' he said urgently. 'We must move on. If we move on now we can make the Horseshoe by nightfall. We'll have a bit of space there – space to bury them.'

'Mum . . .' cried Garland again but, though her mother's arm tightened around her, Maddie was looking away from Ferdy, past Garland and nodding at Yves. When she spoke her words were plain and determined but her voice was shaking.

'And Bailey's hurt . . .' she began. Her voice trembled then faded. Garland could feel her taking a deep breath, making herself strong.

'And Bailey's hurt, too,' she repeated, turning to look over at Goneril, now busy with Bailey. 'He won't be able to read the maps, will he?' Goneril shook her head. 'So! Who'll read the maps?'

'The road holds true as far as the Horseshoe,' Yves said. 'At least it used to. We'll think about directions then.' The Horseshoe – if it was still there – some miles down the road, was a place where they could camp in against a bank and would be partly protected by the curve of the land.

'Get there first and then we'll stop, take a breath and work things out,' said Yves, and once again Maddie nodded her agreement. Tears were still running down over her cheekbones, but the face under those tears was stern and determined. She was trying to be a true Maddigan. Garland knew this. She knew Maddie had to be calm and strong. Yet at the same time she wanted to see Maddie crumpling and crying so that she could crumple and cry along with her. 'Get there first!' Maddie repeated, patting the horses, which snorted and shifted uneasily, probably disturbed by the scent of Ferdy's blood Garland thought, and then thought, 'Horses care more than people do.' She pulled a scarf up over her head and climbed up into the seat beside the driver's seat . . . beside her mother . . . knowing she was an entirely different girl from the girl she had been only a few minutes earlier. As they moved on she looked back over her shoulder thinking she would never forget that place . . . the hill, those broom bushes, the trees which had struck her down, that begging hand of a plain at the bottom of the hill and the tangled forest which had hidden the Road Rats and had then swallowed them once more.

And suddenly there they were again. She had imagined they must be dreams but they were real after all . . . that tall golden-headed boy holding the baby, and the smaller brown one, scruffy and wild. Longing to be distracted, Garland stared at them and took a breath, planning to point them out to Maddie. But then the two shapes . . . the tall one and the smaller one stepped back and disappeared into the scrub and there was nothing to point out to anyone else, and nothing to distract Garland from her savage sadness, which seemed as if it would be devouring her forever.

2
Secret Watchers

Crouching on the hillside, on that unshaven chin of land, rough with scrub and wiry grass, looking down across the trees that clustered at the bottom of the slope two boys stared after the retreating vans of the Fantasia – one about fifteen years old, the other about eleven. The older boy carried a small child, little more than a baby, riding in a sling that held the child against his chest, while the younger was encumbered by a curious pack slung across one shoulder, and a belt so hung about with things it looked as if he had wrapped a kitchen shelf around his waist. He held a book open with his left hand, while the forefinger of his right moved carefully across the page in front of him.

'The words have changed,' he said incredulously. 'They've changed since last time.' He read aloud, pointing as he read. *'He is dead . . . my father is dead. The Road Rats came out of nowhere and attacked us. They wounded Yves just a little and Bailey quite badly. But they killed my father. Writing this down I feel as if I am making up a story, but it is true. Ferdy is dead.'*

The boy looked up from the page. 'It didn't say that this morning.'

'Dead!' said the older boy. 'We've arrived at the wrong time. If he's already dead we can't save him.'

'If we'd worked it out better . . . if we'd got here earlier . . .

do you think we could have altered things?' asked the younger boy. The older one shrugged.

'I don't know,' he said. 'I mean, face it! We don't really know what we're doing.'

'Yes, we do,' said the younger one. 'We've shifted through time. We rode through on a time pulse. We wanted to change things back here so they'd work out well for us in our own time. But we've got it wrong. Can we go back to our own time and have another go?'

'Eden!' exclaimed the older boy impatiently. 'Wake up! We've been through all that. We can't just walk through times as if they were rooms. It's too dangerous. We've got to line things up and . . .'

'Timon!' said the younger boy, copying his brother's impatient voice. 'Wake up! It looks more dangerous *here* than it was *there*.'

'It's our job to . . . *hide* I suppose . . . to protect the Talisman,' said the older one. 'Back in our own time we wouldn't be able to do that . . . we'd be run to ground . . . torn to bits by the Nennog.'

'But we're not even sure what the Talisman *is*,' said the younger boy, Eden, speaking in a half-hearted way as if he did not quite believe what he was saying. 'Talisman is just a word for something – something powerful.' As he spoke his hand crept up to the medallion that hung around his neck. Timon nodded.

'Right!' he said. 'We know the Talisman is something our mother gave us and she gave you *that*. So that's what I *think* it is. What I think it might be. But what we do know for sure is that the Nennog is determined to get that Talisman, and he doesn't care what he does as long as he gets it. He wants all the power in the world and the Talisman is powerful. We do know that. And we do know that even if we've got here at the wrong time we're still — we're *safer* here.' He leaned forwards and touched the medallion gently. 'It strengthens you, doesn't it?' Eden nodded. 'We don't know how, but it does. We don't know just what powers are locked into it, but we *do* know that we mustn't let the Nennog get his claws on it. So let's follow that circus down there. I mean — a circus always needs tricksters, and you're a definite trickster. We might just edge ourselves in with them.'

'All right,' said Eden. 'After all we've got to hide somewhere. And even if they move on a bit faster than we can they'll still leave signs won't they?'

'Yes, they'll drip blood and leave echoes of people laughing,' said Timon in a dark voice. Eden looked at him apprehensively. But then Timon laughed himself. 'Joking! Joking! Only joking!' he cried and Eden nodded, echoing his laughter rather uncertainly.

He looked down at the book and shook his head in wonder, then held it out to his brother.

'Look!' he said. 'Changing. Always changing.'

Eden bent towards the book.

Dear Ferdy, he read, *Everyone behaves as if you have gone, but I know you're still here. I know you're still with me. I can feel you inside this page waiting for the words I'll be putting down on it. I know you want me to tell you everything that is going on with Maddigan's Fantasia, and if I write it all down you'll know it too. In some funny way you'll soak it into yourself.*

'She's going to tell him everything,' Eden said. 'I suppose it's, like, a way of keeping him alive.'

'Let's go,' Timon said, carefully sliding that strange shifting version of Garland's diary into one of the packs that hung over his brother's shoulder.

So, as the Fantasia made off down the road, the two boys began to follow its slow but determined tracks, while the baby

Timon was carrying stretched out her hands to the sunlight, trying to pull brightness out of the air, laughing as her fingers were stained with gold.

The world had changed. The sky, the trees, the road – everything was still in its usual place but, looking around the tumbled, temporary camp they were setting up there in the semicircle of the Horseshoe bank Garland felt alteration in everything . . . everything she saw no matter how huge . . . everything she touched no matter how small. Mostly she felt alteration in herself. She was no taller, no older – still twelve almost thirteen. People were still calling her by the same name, but she was not the girl she had been a few hours ago. No way! So who was she now? Who was she *really*? The Fantasia children – Boomer – Lilith – other children too – were looking at her sideways with serious expressions . . . looking at her as if they no longer knew what to say to her.

They had wrapped Ferdy in one of the Fantasia flags so that when they shovelled earth over him his face was hidden. And then he was gone. A fold of the flag showed through the dirt for a moment and then that was gone too. It was strange how quickly he had disappeared. Disappeared forever. Standing beside Maddie, with Maddie's arm around her, Garland watched him vanish under the earth. Gone. Definitely gone. Yet, as they moved away she caught herself feeling he might leap up at them at any moment, scattering the earth and leaves around him and laughing ('Fooled you that time!') before shouting orders ('Move those vans further out. We're going to need more room.'). But of course there was no leaping up and out. Not this time. Never again! The Fantasia had changed, and she must change with it.

'Hey! Sorry!' said Boomer, in a strange gruff voice, touching her arm as he brushed by. It wasn't much to say or do, but she knew he meant it. After all, a few years ago Boomer had lost both his parents although he did not remember them in the way she would always remember Ferdy. Perhaps he would have tried to say more, but they had to hurry. 'Life hasn't stopped for us,' said Maddie, using that new, tough voice. 'Ferdy's gone. Bailey's injured and – well – it looks as if he might not recover. We have to plan what to do next. I mean we'll certainly need a new mapreader – a good reading man because the maps we have are so old and battered. They're coming to bits and they take a bit of untangling. But right now we have to have a Fantasia parley.'

A parley was the name given to the meetings when all the Fantasia people collected around the fire in the centre of the circle of vans and tents and talked about what they would do next. The fires were already burning up, and there they were – all fifty of them, wrapped in coats and scarves for, in spite of the fires, the night wind had frost in its breath. She could see her very best friends, Goneril, Penrod, Tane, Byrna, Nye, old Shell and Bannister with a book tucked under his arm as if he might lose interest in the parley and need to do a bit of secret reading. There was Maddie with Yves at her elbow and all the others too. Everyone! Everyone except . . . Garland looked down at the ground as Yves stepped forward, being the man-in-charge, taking a stand in the middle of the circle, acting as a sort of Ferdy. She hated the fact that he was moving so quickly – so easily – into Ferdy's place.

'We've got to move on,' Yves was saying. 'No break-up! No dissolving! Maddigan's Fantasia must hit the road – what road there is, and, of course, as you all know, our map reader isn't – isn't feeling so great. Of course we're going to have to change our plans, because Road Rats have stolen our store van which means we're short of things we're going to need – food mainly – so either we'll have to swing out sideways, or we might have to cut this trip and go back again. Back to Solis! What do you think?'

Solis! Just for a moment Garland found herself longing for that city . . . the city that counted as her home city, a city where everything was closed in, safe and comfortable. All roads ran to Solis, which was far too strong to be attacked by mere Road Rats.

'We *can't* go back,' said another voice. Maddie. Everyone looked at her. Some faces were pitying; some were questioning. 'Even Solis has its problems,' said Maddie. 'How much power do you think it takes to run a city like Solis?'

People immediately began guessing . . . echoing the question, then muttering as if they were secretly working things out. Maddie spoke out again.

'It takes a lot of power, I'll tell you that. They get power from the wind. They get it from the river – that dam across it generates electricity. But not enough for what Solis is becoming. They need power from the sun too . . . if they can get it, that is.'

'How can you get power from the sun,' cried Byrna. 'I mean the sun's up there and we're down here. And it *is* winter.'

'In the old days – those days before the Destruction – back before the world fell to bits – they had ways of turning sunlight into power – taking it in, then somehow compressing the energy of the light and then compressing it again – saving it in cells and then saving the cells in batteries.'(Maddie sounded as if she were a storyteller telling them an old tale.) 'The batteries are energized by what they call a "converter" and then, little by little, the power is changed into a form people can use in a whole lot of ways. There are people in Solis working their way towards learning about the whole process, but in the meantime they have to buy the cells in from the place that *does* have part of the secret . . . from Newton. Remember Newton? The people there call themselves a city of scientists. Well, we're not scientists, but we're the ones who stitch the land together . . . we're the ones who carry the news . . . the ones who unravel the roads, who make people laugh and feel at ease with the world, even if it is only for a single afternoon or evening. And this time – *this* time we've been given the job of calling in on Newton and buying a converter and then carrying it back to Solis.' She looked from face to face, seeing a kind of suspicion written there over and over again. 'Look! Solis sent off a committee of its own a few months ago to wheel and deal with the Newton people. But . . .' Maddie stopped again.

'So?' Tane asked.

'Well, you know how it is for people who don't know the ways of the road. Those men have never been heard of again. But we *do* know the ways of the road, don't we? There's no one able to come and go like Maddigan's Fantasia.' She fell silent again.

'Oh wow! Send in the clowns,' said Tane.

'Well, why not?' asked Maddie. 'Look! If Solis gets a converter it will be able to make its own solar cells, and if someone doesn't bring a converter back to Solis, it seems part of the city will begin to close down. We've been given the job of bringing that converter back to Solis, and if we don't – well, I'm not sure that we'll ever be welcome in Solis again. We can't go back without trying. We just can't.'

There was yet another moment of silence. Then the whole Fantasia began talking . . . exclaiming, arguing . . . all discussing what Maddie had just told them. Some people wanted to go back to Solis and face the music. Others said the Fantasia must go on to Newton immediately. Some people did not care about Solis ('Solis can look after itself. It can send another committee.'). Garland watched Maddie, leaning forward and gesturing just as if she were practising one of her acts. *How can she?* Garland found herself thinking. *What does it matter whether we come or go. What does anything matter? Ferdy is dead. My father . . . my father is dead.* The voices surged around her in a curious sea of sound, but she was alone on her shore of sadness.

'How long is it until the power begins to fail in Solis?' Yves was asking.

'The summer solstice is a deadline,' Maddie said. 'Ferdy promised we'd deliver the converter by then. That's why we're setting off in the winter.'

'How could he promise anything like that?' cried old Shell. 'You know what Fantasia life is like. Everything's uncertain for us.'

They argued on and on, frowning, discussing, nodding and shaking their heads.

Maddie did not know – Garland did not know – none of the Fantasia knew – that they were being watched and followed.

3

Secret Followers

Not far behind them, standing on a tussocky rise, the boy Eden was watching the Fantasia.

'What are they doing?' he asked his older brother, Timon, who was changing the baby's nappy, and frowning as he did so. 'Why are they spending all this time talking?'

'Wake up,' said Timon. 'They were attacked. Their ringmaster has just been killed – maybe some others along with him. Didn't the book mention someone called Bailey? *And* they've had some stuff stolen. They have to decide what to do next.'

'Let's try them out,' said Eden. 'Let's see if they will make room for us. Give us work! Because I've got the power . . .'

He made a gesture with his closed fist . . . then spread his fingers. Flowers fell from his opened hand. 'Zaaa!' he cried, and made a triumphant gesture.

'Don't do that,' said Timon. 'You know you have to pay for every trick. You'll get too tired to carry on.'

'If we go down there and try to join in with that lot I'll be able to do my spells and then ride in a van,' said Eden. 'And maybe the Nennog won't know where we are or what's happened to us. We might just – you know – blend in with the rest of them.'

'The Nennog will know all right,' said Timon. 'But he can't travel the way we can. He's made himself powerful in a lot of ways, but he's made himself too – too specialized I suppose. He can send his ghost back. He can haunt us through other people I think, but, really, he's pinned into our own time, even if he can put out feelers. And anyhow when you travel the way *we* do, things change. We've proved that. The words on the page all altered, didn't they? And the Nennog doesn't want alteration.'

'He wants some alterations – the alterations that suit him,' said Eden, and Timon sighed.

'Well, sure, he wants more power. He wants the Talisman.' Timon sighed again and shrugged. 'But OK! Let's go down there and see if we can melt into that lot . . . see if we can't get things to work *for* us, not against us . . .'

'. . . and save the world!' said Eden eagerly.

'Right! We've got to save the world,' Timon agreed, grinning rather reluctantly. 'Mind you, I don't think that lot over there will be able to help us much. Right now they look as if they need help even more than the world does.'

'But we're going to need help in some ways,' said Eden, 'Like, we'll run out of nappies for Jewel and she'll get a sore bum. And there might be frost or even snow. And I'm starving. Let's close in on them and see how we go.'

Garland could not stand it any longer. She could not bear to see Yves holding the ringmaster's whip or to see Maddie standing there beside him.

'Listen, you lot!' she was shouting. 'I'm the one in charge now. I married into the Maddigans. I took the vows. I'm a true Maddigan, and I say we support Solis. So that means we must press on to Gramth and stock up on food, which is what we were going to do anyway, and then on to Newton.'

'We'll need to stock up on food before that,' said Yves.

'Right!' said Maddie. 'So we'll have to call in on one of those little communities and trade what we can. Where's Bannister? Bannister! You must be our mapmaster until Bailey gets better.'

'If he does get better,' said Yves. 'Goneril says . . .'

'I say, and I *know*,' said Goneril, interrupting him. 'I've seen it all before. For years now I've been loaded with the sick ones and the babies . . . for years my van's been treated as a dumping ground for people who can't look after themselves. And I've kept quiet about it for years, but . . .'

'Kept quiet? You're always on about it,' cried Nye. 'Moan! Moan! Moan!'

'Shut up, Nye,' said Tane. 'A woman's got a right to express herself.' He sounded rather sarcastic though.

'Well – we'll see about all that,' Yves was saying, 'the thing is, I know the way to the nearest community. At least I think I do. No one can be sure of anything in this neck of the woods but they may have a bit of spare food to trade. It's worth a try. So! Let's go!'

'Let's go!' said a piping voice – his bossy little daughter Lilith, her looped pigtails sticking out like handles. She would be delighted to see her father there in the centre of the circle, telling everyone else what to do.

These voices chased after Garland like hunting hounds as she moved quietly away. She had to break away from all the discussion and argument. Garland thought she had heard enough. She loved the Fantasia but she needed space . . . she needed silence.

However, she was only a few steps away from the parley circle when strangeness seized her. The air in front of her billowed and twisted as if something were trying to break through from the other side. At first Garland thought her tears were changing the shape of the world, as tears do. Then she saw – there was no doubt about it – those silver marks on the air once more, but this time they were taking on a definite shape . . . something that could be recognized. Suddenly Garland was looking at a silver girl, a girl round about her own age, who seemed to be looking straight back at her and beckoning her forward.

Garland stared. The silver lines moved, as if, like smoke in the wind, the girl might break up and vanish. But it wasn't just the air that was moving. That silver girl was beckoning and pointing to the right. Her lips were moving, though no sound, no silver voice, came through them.

All the same there *was* a sound. Somewhere a baby had begun to cry and Garland now saw, a little to the right of the silver girl (the *fading* silver girl for the shape was already trembling and dissolving as if, having given some message, it was free to fade), the shapes of two boys, advancing out of the wild scrub, one of them strung with mysterious boxes, the other one (the bigger one . . . the one with the golden hair) carrying a crying baby in front of him.

'Friends!' cried the smaller boy, waving at her over his boxes. And then he added, 'Are you Garland?'

The bigger boy nudged him as if he were commanding him to be quiet.

'Who are you?' Garland asked. 'How do you know my name?'

'Guessing. Only guessing,' the younger boy said quickly.

But how could anyone just guess a name like 'Garland'?

'Go on guessing!' Garland shouted. 'And leave me alone. We've just buried my father and nobody really cares but me.'

Then she wheeled around and ran back towards the parley she had just left. It seemed so unfair that she should be so unhappy and frightened at the same time. It seemed unfair that she should have to cope with strangers, and such *strange* strangers too. Her mother saw her darting for cover, and moved quickly to cut her off.

'Garland!' shouted Maddie. 'None of your runaway games. We're on the road again.'

'I saw her again. And I saw them,' Garland cried back, knowing as she heard her own words that what she was saying sounded like nonsense. 'I mean . . .'

'You're not to wander away,' yelled Maddie, taking no notice whatever of what Garland was saying. But then she grabbed her and hugged her, yelling all the time. 'Back then . . . back then . . . just for a moment or two I thought I'd lost you too. I thought . . . oh my darling girl. You'll have to give up on your runaway habits. Don't keep *vanishing*! It makes me feel that someone somewhere has pulled out a black plug in the world, and all the precious things in my life are draining away into nowhere. It makes me feel I'm losing everything.'

'Let's get going,' Yves was calling impatiently. 'It's just down the road – not a town so much as a crossroads. But it'll still take time to get there. And if we are going to trade we'll have to perform. And you . . .' he pointed his finger at Garland . . . 'you might have to be one of the performers. We mightn't be able to rig the tightrope or the trapeze, so we'll probably need a magician. Your dad taught you a few tricks, didn't he?'

'But I'm really a tightrope walker!' cried Garland.

'Tonight you might have to be a magician as well as an acrobat,' Yves said. 'We're going to have to do the best we can.'

Garland looked up at her mother. Maddie nodded.

'The best we can,' she repeated. 'It's what Ferdy would have wanted. Right?'

And hearing her mother talk about Ferdy in the past tense suddenly made Garland feel she was losing him all over again.

It did not take long for the Fantasia to get going once more. After all, they had not even turned the horses and dogs loose. Mounted on her own white horse Samala, Garland rode beside the leading van, feeling that she was the one who was guarding it.

The road they now followed was nothing more than a line of

dirt with weeds and grass growing down the middle of it, and potholes so large it seemed as if the whole Fantasia might tumble into one of them and be lost forever. They crept on, wheels turning as, little by little, the dirt track vanished under mats of wet grass. Every now and then Samala put her head down trying to snatch a mouthful.

'Keep on!' cried Bannister, who was also riding on horseback beside Maddie's van, frowning as he peered down at the unfolded map, trying to read it and ride at the same time. 'Keep on . . . I think.' Which was something Bailey would never have said. But, after a mile or so of grass and tussock, with forest closing in around them, the road came to life again, shrugging off the grass and looking suddenly much more sure of itself, crossed with wheel marks and edged with footprints. Within another mile they had arrived at a crossroads very much where Maddie had told them it would be. Here was the timber town of Milton. Houses and huts rose nervously over the scrub. Gardens, little straggling orchards and small fields of sheep and goats spread out between the four roads. Green sheds, filled with long racks of timber, linked houses and roads together.

'Get the band going,' Garland heard Yves commanding. 'A bit of music sets a good mood.'

And it seemed strange to see Bannister flourishing his trombone, Tane getting out his saxophone, Nye his pipe and Boomer struggling into the shoulder straps of his great drum when Ferdy was not there to hear them. It was almost as if the music would never be complete again without Ferdy as a leader and listener. Nevertheless the old songs began and they marched along, singing those songs just as they had always done.

The Fantasia found it was expected. Someone had seen them and had run on ahead to tell the crossroads people, and the crossroads people had all turned out to see them arrive.

Whenever it came to a big town the Fantasia was always greeted with cheers and cries of welcome but places like Milton often greeted them with silence, uncertain just who was calling in on them – uncertain if it was the same Fantasia that had visited them the last time around or some treacherous imitation. People were curious but guarded, waiting to see what would happen next. Yves now jumped from the front of the leading van and began to beckon the Fantasia around him, shouting and waving his arms. 'Here we are! Here we are again! The show of wonders! The amazement of the world.' The acrobats cartwheeled beside him. Tane the clown passed his saxophone to a young man called Lattin, then leapt and tumbled and somersaulted. Bannister reluctantly slipped a book into his belt and began showing off his muscles. Children from the crowd and even some of the men tried lifting the weight at his feet. Bannister let them try, watching and smiling, then lifted that weight high, almost casually, using only one arm. Wonder began to work on the watchers as it always did. The blank and sometimes challenging faces began to soften and change. The head man came forward. Maddie moved to Yves's side. They were going to bargain. The Fantasia would perform, but the Milton must pay for a show of wonders . . . pay with food this time . . . pay with goats' milk, bread and cheese. Pay with apples? Maybe, though perhaps there were not many apples left at this time of the year. However Milton could afford a ham or two and some fresh greens. And they had eggs to spare.

'Not the whole show,' Maddie said, reporting back to the Fantasia people. 'The tumblers, the horses, the clowns and the dogs. They remember the magician . . . they've asked for him.' And then she stopped because Ferdy had been their magician and he had vanished as magicians do – but this time he was gone forever. 'They're almost demanding a magician,' she said helplessly.

'I know a few tricks,' Garland reminded her.

'Right! We'll try you,' Maddie said, but looking very doubtful. 'No choice.'

'I'll go and practise,' Garland cried. *I remember the tricks Ferdy taught me*, she was thinking. *And now I'm actually going to be Ferdy. He'll come alive again through me.* Even though it was only a small show this time, the Fantasia began its usual seething . . . partly with its own people, partly with Milton people wandering around and wondering, staring at the vans . . . at the coloured tents, unfolding and rising. Garland drew away from the crowd and set up her father's magician's table, laid out the boxes and the scarves, the coins in an orderly fashion. The cabinet of vanishment had been unloaded and stood, slightly tilted, beside her, but she did not know its secrets well enough as yet to make people disappear. ('How do you do it?' she had nagged Ferdy, but he had only laughed and had told her he must keep a few mysteries to himself.)

'You telling me you're going to be a magician?' someone asked behind her. 'That's a boy's thing to do.' Garland did not need to turn her head to know who it was. Boomer! There he was, fair, freckled, winking at the world with those bright green eyes as if he was trying to work out just what was driving it along. But Boomer was always trying to work out how things worked . . . clocks and watches . . . his noisy little motorbike . . . and of course the Fantasia vans. When something went wrong with one of them and Tane had to bend into them or slide under them Boomer was always beside him, sometimes being helpful but quite often simply getting in the way.

'Go and practise your drum,' Garland told him. 'It's simple just *hitting* something – boom, boom, boom! A ten-year-old can do it. Even *you* can do it. Right now I need to concentrate.'

'I'm *eleven*,' said Boomer indignantly. He hated it when Garland pretended to think he was only ten. 'I can almost do magic

tricks. Hey, I'll help you,' he offered. 'Maddie helps Ferdy –
she used to help Ferdy that is . . .' his voice trailed away.

'Get out!' cried Garland. 'Leave me alone.'

'It won't work,' said another voice. A childish one! Lilith
again! 'You're not good enough yet. You need to practise for
years. Years and years.' She pranced beside them, black-haired,
brown-eyed, trying to be cleverer than Garland as she always
did.

'Get out of the way, you kids! I'm going to practise for an
hour!' cried Garland. 'Just leave me alone to do it.'

She did not think they would leave her, but (perhaps because
the Fantasia was struggling there at Milton) they did. After all,
they were all children of the Fantasia and when the Fantasia
succeeded, they succeeded themselves. Garland struggled on,
palming the coins, shuffling the cards. Deep down she knew
she was not really good enough – but she might – she *might* (if
things went well enough) be good enough for a timber town at
a wild crossroads.

'What are you doing?' asked someone beside her, sounding
almost like Boomer, but not quite like Boomer.

'Leave me alone. I'm working at it!' she cried.

'Working at what?' asked the voice. She understood the
words easily, but found she still did not quite recognize the voice
itself . . . and not just the voice. There was a strange quality to it
as if the speaker were somehow breathing a different air. Garland
turned.

And there they were. There they were again – the same two
boys she had seen on the hillside. One (the taller of the two) balancing that little child on his hip this time, the other smaller
one, a thin rather delicate-looking boy, was still strung around
with those boxes including a curious black box . . . a camera
perhaps. Garland had seen cameras in the museum in Solis and
knew that, once upon a time, those boxes had somehow been

able to blink and that pictures of the world would peel up out of them. The boy's jacket bulged as if he had something hidden in the front of it. And, back there, when they first met, these boys had known her name even though they had never met before.

'Are you following us?' she asked.

'Listen! Just listen!' said the older boy in a soft, urgent voice. 'My name is Timon. My brother is called Eden and the little one here is Jewel. We're . . .' (he seemed to stop and think what to say next). 'We're friends of Solis,' he said at last as if he were experimenting with words. 'And we're – we're lost – well, half-lost. We're hungry. We need food. But we're not just begging. We'll work for it.'

Garland hesitated. They did look tired and hungry . . . and of course the Fantasia always needed workers, to load and unload, to haul on the ropes and, later, to help with the folding, the lifting, the stowing, and the checking of the wheels. And they needed trackers to guide the vans over the rough pieces of the road or places where the road vanished altogether. She was about to suggest they talk to Yves or Bannister . . . when the older boy, glancing sideways, suddenly stiffened.

'Oh no!' he said softly, and nudged the smaller one. 'Maska and Ozul!' He turned to Garland. 'We've got enemies following us. Can you hide us?'

The world was unreliable. It always had been and always would be. There it was, up to its tricks again. Garland shook her head, not understanding what was going on, but, even as she shook her head, she was opening the door of Ferdy's cabinet of vanishment with one hand and pointing into it with the other.

'In there!' she said.

'No time to tell you,' muttered Timon, scrambling obediently into the cabinet, holding one hand over the baby's head, protecting it from accidental bumps.

'This could be a sort of trap,' mumbled Eden, scrambling in after him. But Garland shut the door on them and, hands shaking, tried to palm a coin, and then to flick a card (which broke away from her indignantly, flying out, then down, trying to escape from her unpractised fingers). Who were those boys? What were they hiding from? Only a moment later she knew.

Two strange men were looking down at her from the back of two black horses . . . not Fantasia horses. Garland knew all the Fantasia horses well. They were part of her family. The men themselves had a strange, freshly polished look, as if their clothes were all new and their skins had been washed and oiled only minutes ago. What had that tall boy called them? Ozul and Maska? But which was which?

'You!' said one of the men. 'You were talking to those boys just now.'

Garland shrugged boldly. Then, looking up at the man's face she felt suddenly frightened, for his face did not look like a proper face . . . a face grown from a true childhood. It somehow looked as if it had been invented by some mad scientist back before the Remaking, before the Chaos . . . during the Destruction perhaps . . . back in some time when the wars were raging around the world like savage plagues. His companion looked rather more ordinary, but all the same there was nothing reassuring about him, and when he spoke his soft reasonable voice sounded strange coming out, as it did, between such pointed teeth and from such a grim mouth.

'We're trying to find those boys, you see. They're relations of mine . . . my nephews and my dear little niece. We're worried about them, and need to find them and bring them home again. They're too young to be wandering around in a wild world like this.'

'Why did they run away?' asked Garland. She did not for a

moment believe that a man who looked so cruel could be a loving uncle . . . in fact she found it difficult to believe he could be an uncle of any kind.

'Oh well . . .' he was saying, and somehow Garland knew he was inventing a story, snatching it out of nowhere. 'They had a fight with their mother . . . my sister. You know how it is. Sometimes there are fights even in the happiest families.'

Garland certainly knew that there could be fights in happy families. Sometimes she and Ferdy had argued fiercely with one another. All the same she did not believe this man had anything to do with any sort of happy family. And the man seemed to see in her expression that she did not believe him. His eyebrows tilted downwards across the bony bridge of his nose.

'Come on now!' he said, his voice darkening. The cruelty she had read in his face began to edge into his voice. 'Where did they go?'

'They asked me for food, but I haven't got any. The Road Rats stole our stores. So the boys just took off . . .' she waved her hand vaguely. 'Perhaps they saw you coming.'

But the man who had spoken to her first swung himself down from his horse and advanced on her. He flicked one hand at Ferdy's table, and the carefully arranged cards and coins and scarves and boxes leaped away into the wet grass as if they were terrified. Then, without asking, the man reached past her, seized the door of the cabinet of vanishment and wrenched it violently open. Garland cried out, partly in warning but in fear as well.

The cabinet was totally empty. Garland sighed with hidden relief. Those boys must have solved the mystery of the cabinet and must have managed to hide themselves in the secret spaces somewhere in the walls.

And then, before anything more could be said, Yves was suddenly upon them asking what was going on. Garland had never imagined she would ever be glad to have Yves closing in on her . . . standing between her and the rest of the world. The second man turned to meet him, smiling and using his soft and reasonable voice – explaining that he was looking for his nephews and his little niece – declaring once again that there had been a family fight, and the boys had run away leaving a mother who was, by now, desperately worried about them. As the second man talked glibly on, the first man stared around as if he might suddenly see some clue in the air.

'And there *is* a reward,' the second man was adding slyly. Garland saw Yves blinking and thinking about the reward. Moving forward, he peered into the cabinet himself, then touched the hidden lever. The inside of the cabinet throbbed. Bits of it moved away from the rest of it. The false back folded up. The false sides slid across one another. The boys would be revealed, for they must – they absolutely *must* be hiding in there. Garland held her breath but, incredibly, the secret spaces were empty. The boys had truly vanished. Somehow they had not only solved the trick of the cabinet's secret spaces, but had worked out some other escape as well, and had crawled and wriggled away, no doubt, into the flapping forest of tents beyond.

'We'll have a look around along here perhaps,' said Yves, and moved off with the two riders, now leading their horses and picking their way after him. Garland lifted the magician's table back onto its legs and began gathering up the coins and cards.

What's happened to the world? she was thinking. *Everything has turned terrible . . . and the bits that aren't terrible have gone mad. I don't understand anything any more.*

4
Flowers from the Air

'Everything's coming to bits,' Boomer cried later like a tame echo at Garland's heels. They had lost their ringmaster, and then their food wagon, and now they were having to perform with no time to catch a breath. Their dogs and their strong man all knew their acts by heart, their clowns were word-and-tumble-over perfect, but, peering in past the spectators, Garland could feel that the Milton people were not altogether happy with what they were being shown. Perhaps they had seen it all before. Perhaps they were hungry for some new revelation. She heard people exclaiming derisively to one another.

It's not going to work, she thought. *They won't trade us food. They'll throw rotten apples at us and drive us away.*

'*You* can't go on,' Boomer said, echoing her thoughts once more. 'The stars aren't right.'

'What do you know about it?' asked Garland, changing her mind within a moment. She was cross that Boomer might be able to read what she was thinking. 'I've practised all afternoon.'

Yves was pacing backwards and forwards, wearing Ferdy's ringmaster jacket. Though it was a little too big for him, it seemed to Garland he was falsely swelling himself out in an effort to fill it, strutting around and using the very same jokes that Ferdy had used. She hated it when some of the crowd laughed. She did not want to have Yves introducing her . . . yet if she did not perform it would be like yet another death for Ferdy. This was Maddigan's Fantasia and there must be a Maddigan magician in the ring.

All the same she felt actually sick as the performance stumbled on. She was not the only uncertain one. Clotilde, one of the jugglers, spun, stumbled and dropped the stars she was juggling. There was a scornful murmur in the crowd. Someone jeered.

It's up to me, Garland was feeling both heroic and terrified as Yves quickly pointed in her direction. On she ran, waving, trying to dance her way to the centre of the circle, while Tane, Morris and Tonto the clowns carried on the magician's table and trays with the cards and the coins. The rough, jeering voices fell silent. The people from Milton, longing to be amazed in spite of themselves, waited to see what would happen next. Garland looked out at her audience. Women and children sat in the front on the wooden seats, some men sat on the grass, others stood, arms folded behind the women. They looked at Garland with curiosity . . . without any great friendship but without any hostility either.

'Come on you! Surprise us!' someone yelled.

Garland heard her own voice begin shouting out at them, and her first trick went well. The children laughed and pointed. The women and some of the men smiled and shook their heads, happy to be mystified. The second trick went well too. But the third . . .

She moved too slowly. Her distraction did not work. Suddenly they were all shouting and pointing. Garland felt her hands begin to tremble, and knew that unless she could stop that shaking the fourth trick would not work either.

'Come on! Surprise us!' that rough voice yelled again. And the jeering came at her in a ragged chorus. 'Sur*prise* us! Sur-*prise* us!'

But then, as she stood there fiddling frantically, the jeering stopped abruptly. From the side, through the restless crowd, the cabinet of vanishment came trundling on, the tall blonde prince Timon pushing it. Garland could see Yves stop and step back at this unexpected entrance, could see Boomer and Lilith and other friends and enemies of hers peering after it. There beside her, Timon came to a standstill. He winked at her.

'Open the door!' he hissed, gesturing towards the door himself. Almost automatically (for after all she *was* a Maddigan) Garland flung her arms wide – then, turning, flung the door open with a flourish. Pink mist billowed out of it. A dark shape formed somewhere in the mist, and Eden stepped out, dressed, goodness knows how, in scarlet tights sparkling with stars. His clothes had none of the worn look of many of the Maddigan costumes. Eden looked as if everything he was wearing was brand new. He swept off his tall black hat to bow to the audience, and a whole flock of little balloons flew out from under the brim and into the early evening sky, seeming to dissolve, almost at once, into the air around them. When Eden clapped his hands, the world changed. Thunderclouds rolled over, lightning flashed. But then, within seconds, before the audience had time to work out what was happening and run for cover, the darkness rolled back and a rain of flowers began to fall around, perfect in the air but once again dissolving amongst the grass and into the ground.

The whole Milton mood changed. The little children began to run around, holding out their hands to catch the dissolving flowers . . . even the men turned their faces, transformed by wonder, towards the sky. At last, at last Maddigan's Fantasia was filling the world around them with mystery and amazement.

Maddie came out and touched Yves on the arm.

'Finish it,' Garland heard her say. 'Tie it off now, while we're ahead.'

'Yes! Right!' she heard Yves reply. 'But who are they?'

'I don't care!' said Maddie. 'They've saved us. Finish it!'

Behind Maddie Garland could see Goneril holding the baby girl, and for once looking blissfully contented. The magical act was almost finished. Timon stepped forward and gestured towards Eden. The Milton people waved too and cheered, before moving forward to mix with the Fantasia, still looking on with smiling astonishment. Garland was about to join them, but hesitated. She saw that Eden was sitting down now. He still held one arm high, but his head was bowed, and as she watched his arm sank limply to his side. She went to kneel beside him, planning to ask him just how he had done his astonishing tricks, but found herself asking him if he were all right instead.

'He's worn out,' said Timon. 'It's hard, what he does. Particularly when there's a crowd like this, and he has to touch every mind.'

Somewhere the band began to play. There they went . . . Bannister and Tane, a brassy duet, marching in front . . . Boomer coming behind, beating on his drum.

And from the very back of the crowd, hidden by the gathering dusk, the two men on horseback watched unsmiling. They had not wished to join that crowd of people, talking and laughing together and looking up into the sky as if more flowers might appear. Any Fantasia people who noticed them thought these two riders must be men of Milton. Milton people, if they were aware of them, imagined they belonged to the Fantasia.

'I would say they've worked their way into this gang of wanderers,' said the grimmer of the two men. 'What do you think, Ozul?'

'Oh yes,' said the other. 'And a crowd like that won't let them go easily. There's too much profit in them. But don't worry! They may have made a lucky chance for themselves, but our turn will come. We'll stay in this crazy time until we can steal them out of it without twisting the time lines too much – and steal the Talisman with them. We'll be patient and cunning. That chance will come and we'll seize it when it does. And then the Nennog himself will reward us. Oh yes! Wait and see.'

Dearest Ferdy, we're doing just what you would want us to do. We're travelling on.

And now we have two new members of the Fantasia. Two boys! Strange boys, though nobody but me knows just how strange they are. One is a magician and I promise you he is really good. None of us can work out just how he does his tricks, but they are really truly amazing. And the other boy – well, he is just ordinary, I think, except that he looks really cool. They're clever but weird. I mean most people will tell you a bit about themselves, but these two – well, it's as if they came out of nothing and might go back into it at any moment.

The other thing is that they are being followed. There are two men who came into our camp asking about them, but we didn't give them away. For one thing the men who were doing the asking were really horrible, and for another the magician-boy, Eden, is really useful to us, so of course we want to keep him for ourselves. Right now we're on the road again, pressing on. But you'd know all about that. It's something we always do. And those two men they're pressing on too . . . following us. Every now and then I catch a glimpse of them back on the road behind us.

Once again the Fantasia was weaving itself along a puzzle of tangled tracks. Those tracks made it seem as if somehow the mysterious world around them had clapped its hands together and had then drawn them apart revealing a whole cat's cradle of strings stretching between its fingers.

Sitting up on the front seat of the van wagon – sitting beside her mother who was driving just as her father used to drive – Garland looked around, then bent over her diary. She frowned, struggling to record her distrust of the strange boys who had appeared out of nowhere – the boys Yves had taken into the Fantasia so easily. Who were they? Where had they come from?

Now you've gone, I am the only born thoroughly Maddigan Maddigan left, so I ought to be the one in charge. After all the first leader of the Fantasia was a woman, wasn't she? Gabrielle Maddigan was the one who got it all going before she took off again leaving her Fantasia behind.

Garland paused, staring rather sternly at the road, which seemed determined to lead them into a wilderness, then bent over her book again and pressed her pencil firmly against the page.

Maybe you're in touch with Gabrielle! If you are ask her why she disappeared, and let her know I am protecting the Fantasia

The van jolted and her pencil shot across the page as if it were trying to cross out what she had just written.

'How can you write like that?' a voice asked. Garland frowned accusingly at her pencil, and she looked sideways to find that Timon and Eden were walking beside the van, looking up at her through the open window and both smiling, Timon with his longish blond hair hanging around his face, Eden slender and brown almost like a stick-boy walking around in the world of skin-and-bone people.

'I've asked her that over and over again,' Maddie said, bending forward and half-shouting across Garland, just as if she wasn't there to answer for herself. 'Her words must go in every direction. They looked as if they flew right off the page just now.' The van jolted again.

'They did . . . I mean I think they do. The words. Fly off the page, I mean,' said Eden. Both boys were staring with interest, almost as if they could see her diary, and Garland hastily closed it, bending forward to slide it into her shoulder pack, which was slouching down beside her van seat.

'You boys!' said Maddie. 'I think you saved our skins back there a bit. It was a great show you put on.' She looked at the road ahead, such as it was, then sideways at the boys once more. 'I can't help wondering . . . where's your luggage? How do talented creatures like you come to be wandering around on your own, with nothing but the clothes you stand up in?'

'You know how it is!' Timon shouted back, smiling.

'We did have work,' said Eden, 'but the one we worked for was a bit rough on us so we ran off. And now he wants us back, but we don't want to go.'

'I suppose I shouldn't ask,' said Maddie, with something of a groan. 'And on the other hand I suppose I should. Listen! You haven't got any parents or loving relatives or anyone like that waiting for you back wherever you came from, have you? I don't like to think that you might have a distraught mother somewhere . . .'

'I absolutely promise we haven't,' Timon replied quickly. 'No family, near or far.'

'Orphans,' Eden exclaimed, as if he had just invented the word. 'Orphans with no relations.'

'And who taught you to do tricks like the ones you did last night?' asked Maddie.

Eden looked from side to side rather anxiously.

'It's his gift,' Timon said quickly. 'It's more of a – more of a talent than a trick. He brings dreams out of himself and shares them around . . . not that it's easy. I mean he does it for twenty minutes and then he needs to lie down.' He looked down at his brother who shrugged, still refusing to look directly at Garland or Maddie. 'It makes him all shy,' Timon went on. 'You know! Being odd often makes people shy!'

Garland felt it was time she had something to say and turned to Maddie.

'Stop for a moment! Stop! I need to stretch myself,' she commanded, and Maddie laughed and signalled out through the window to let the vans behind her know that she was about to slow down.

Garland slid down to walk with the boys. Usually she rode Samala beside the van but on this occasion she really did need to stretch herself and, besides, even in these strange days after the Remaking, even when the world was full of unexpected meetings, there was something particularly mysterious about this one. The Fantasia had willingly taken the boys in, but they did not belong with the Fantasia or with the wild country rolling out around them. Yet nobody else seemed to feel this strangeness about the two boys . . . this quality they had of not truly belonging anywhere in the world around them.

'What were you writing?' Timon asked her, and though it was a perfectly ordinary question it somehow filled Garland with immediate suspicion. He smiled at her . . . an open easy smile. Garland liked his smile and his ruffled blond hair, but there was no way she wanted to tell anyone what she had been writing in the book with the battered blue cover.

'Hey! You!' shouted another voice, cutting in before she needed to answer, and there was Boomer – that pain of a Boomer – zooming around on his bike and waving his arms. He skidded to a stop beside them, cutting the little motor and sliding his heels in the grass. 'You brought a baby with you. Is it your kid?'

'She's our sister,' Eden said. 'She's called Jewel?'

'Where is she?' asked Boomer. 'Have you dumped her somewhere?'

'The old woman in the van back there offered to look after her,' said Timon. 'It's better for Jewel to have a bed and a place to crawl in than to be carried all the time.'

'You're passing your sister over to *Goneril*,' said Boomer derisively. 'Great! Goneril hates little kids.'

'But she offered to look after her!' exclaimed Timon.

Then he and Eden walked on, looking ahead of them. Garland grinned sideways at Boomer, and Boomer, encouraged, started his bike once more, zoomed around in a wide circle, closed in on the boys and began again.

'What's that *necklace* you're wearing?' he asked, and Garland noticed, for the first time, a glint of silver metal at Eden's neck. He was wearing a chain, most of which hung down under his shirt.

'It isn't really a necklace, is it?' she called after them.

It was Timon who answered, looking back over his shoulder.

'It's a good luck charm,' he said. 'We all need good luck, don't we? Well, we do. We can do with heaps of good luck.'

From somewhere ahead Yves shouted. Time for a break! There were trees in front of them so there would certainly be shade and probably dry wood. Grass too. Maddie's van began to swing to the right in a wide curve. Other vans and riders on horseback followed her.

'Looks like a great place to stop,' Maddie called down to them. 'Was it here last time? I don't remember?'

Garland shook her head. She did not remember either, but there was nothing surprising about that. Since the Chaos the world shifted continually, even though their own time (the Remaking) was becoming more and more reliable, which was a good thing, particularly when Bailey was still lying, unconscious, in Goneril's wagon, back behind them. Garland hoped that the baby Jewel was not distracting Goneril from what she should really be doing – caring for Bailey and getting him well enough to read the maps once more.

It was a wonderful relief being able to stretch and run around. And after stretching, after running and jumping (just to remind herself that she could still run and jump) Garland did what she always did. She turned a few cartwheels, then she collected her bow and arrows from the slot beside the door of the van and set off on her own, making for the trees. Carefully choosing an angle which meant that even a misfired arrow would not fly off sideways into the camp, she stood back from one particular tree and chose a target – a pale streak where the bark had peeled away. It was almost as if the tree were challenging her by flashing a secret inner skin.

There was a great pleasure in fitting the arrow to the string and drawing it back. When she let it fly it seemed that part of her flew along with the arrow, cutting the air and biting into the tree with satisfaction.

There was an exclamation at her elbow.

Garland spun around.

Timon and Eden had followed her . . . but Eden was stumbling a little as if he was not sure just which foot to put forward next. Timon held his arm, trying to straighten him out.

'Come on!' he was muttering. 'Come on!' He looked apologetically at Garland. 'He feels things most people don't,' he said. 'It's part of his gift . . . part of his magic.'

'But I didn't hit *him*,' Garland cried, suddenly anxious on Eden's behalf, yet cross with herself for caring. 'I wasn't anywhere near him.'

'Your arrow,' Eden muttered. 'It struck home. It's twisting the lines of power.'

Garland felt her own face twisting with puzzlement.

· 46 ·

'What lines of power?' she cried impatiently. 'What are you on about?'

'The tree,' murmured Eden. 'You hit the tree.'

'But it's only a tree,' said Garland. 'It's not a person.'

'It's not a person, but it is a bit like a person,' said Eden, straightening, and looking, as he often did, like some sort of mysterious creature, half-tree himself. 'It has power flowing through it. It connects with the great soup . . .'

'Shhh!' hissed Timon in his ear. 'Don't start on all that great-soup-of-existence stuff. Just shut up.'

Garland stepped back. She took a breath.

'Look!' she cried. 'Who are you? What's going on? I mean life is getting a bit too weird. First I start seeing silver in the air, which turns into a weird silver girl . . . and then I see you coming out at me through a sort of fiery crack in space. And *then* you actually turn up, doing magical tricks – which was great – but who are you *really*. *What* are you? I mean you might be some sort of ghosts left over from times before the Remaking. You might be . . .'

'We're not ghosts,' said Timon. He looked sideways at his brother. 'Well, not exactly ghosts!' And then a thoughtful expression crept over his face. He looked like someone playing with a new idea: he pinched himself and laughed a little. 'Though I suppose we might be half-ghosts in one way. But we have been following you. Because we're travellers.'

'There are a lot of travellers on these roads,' Garland said. 'But you don't feel like ordinary travellers – you feel too weird to be ordinary.' Her words seemed inadequate, but Eden raised his head.

'We *are* travellers,' he said. 'And I suppose we might feel weird because we *are* weird. We're travellers in time. We come from somewhere on ahead of you. We've had to fight – really fight – to get back. And it's all mixed-up because we've had to get back *here* to save ourselves in the future.'

5

Time Travellers

arland stared at them . . . at their solid boots, their jackets, at the scratch on Eden's hand and the smudge on Timon's cheek which might be dirt or might be a bruise.

'Time travellers!' she exclaimed derisively, turning away from Eden to look at his brother once more. 'Yeah right! I suppose that's why you're called Timon. Tick! Tick! Tick! Tock! Time off!'

'No! Listen!' said Timon. He shrugged and then his shoulders relaxed. 'I might as well try to explain, even if you don't believe me. You set out from the city of Solis, didn't you?'

'Yes,' said Garland. She couldn't help boasting about Solis. 'It's the greatest city since the Remaking. We set out from Solis . . . and we're going back there. We've come and gone over and over again, but this time we've got a mission.'

'So have we,' said Timon, 'because we come from Solis too, only not *your* Solis . . . Listen! Eden's told you, so I have to tell you too. I can put it better than he can.'

'She still won't believe you,' put in Eden.

'Our Solis is in your future,' said Timon. 'There! It's the same city and it's not the same city. You'd recognize a lot of it mind you . . . some of the buildings that is . . . .the street corners

. . . but it's not your Solis. It's ruled by the Nennog and our Solis belongs to him in most ways.'

'The Nennog?' cried Garland incredulously. 'What Nennog? What are you on about?'

'He's our great great-uncle,' said Eden, 'and he was probably all right once upon a time. He began by being the Duke of Solis.'

'The Duke of Solis!' Garland exclaimed, but Timon flapped his hand at her.

'He began in *your* time,' he said. 'But he *did* change. He somehow learned to drain energy out of the world. And he went on and on and on and turned into a monster. And he wants . . .'

'He wants to eat the whole city. He wants to eat the whole world,' interrupted Eden. 'And he wants to eat us! We're all energy, and a man who wants to live forever needs energy.'

Timon flapped his hand again, but this time it was Eden he was flapping at, telling him not to interrupt. Then he turned back to Garland again.

'We escaped him. We were helped. We rode a time pulse and travelled back because we . . .'

'OK! Stop there,' said Garland. 'I just don't believe any of this. I can't!'

'We came back to save your father . . . to save Ferdy Maddigan,' said Eden desperately. 'We thought that would displace the flow of things . . . alter our own time . . . because you see we worked out that if Ferdy had lived he would have brought back the converter from Newton to Solis. And then he would have grown in power in Solis, and somehow replaced the Duke and then – well, I can't explain it all but . . .'

'. . . but the calculations were wrong,' said Timon rather wearily. 'We got here too late and now we've got to wait for another time-slot so that we . . .'

Garland leapt to her feet.

'Just shut up!' she cried, furious because, though she did not quite believe them, she so very nearly did. 'It's all rubbish!' she shouted. 'It has to be.'

'No! We can prove it!' Eden cried back, but Timon grabbed his brother's arm.

'Forget it,' he said. 'She won't believe us, and it's not her fault. No one will believe us. They can't understand. It's . . . it's . . . too hard for them.'

Garland's fury grew.

'We're not stupid!' she said, yelling now. 'You're the mad ones . . . making out you could have saved my dad . . . making out you're so great! Making out you can feel what trees feel.'

She fled, determined to get out of the range of these two peculiar strangers who, for some reason, were making out they were even stranger than she had imagined them to be in the first place. In her mind she could see her own hand with the pencil in it moving across a page in her battered blue diary. *They must think I'm a real idiot – telling me a story like that and thinking I'll just gasp with amazement and then begin worshipping them. Time travellers! Rubbish! Rubbish! Rubbish!*

But as she imagined herself writing this down and underlining the last word, she was being careful to run alongside the winding progress of the Fantasia. And suddenly, as she jumped wildly over the tussock, feeling the cold bite of the wind as it struck her face and twisted in her red curls, she saw the air ahead of her writhe and shine and there – there once more – was the silver girl.

Garland came to a standstill so sharp her teeth rattled. Just as she was telling herself, over and over again, that there was no such thing as magic, something very like magic was happening in front of her. But this was nothing to do with two strange boys, claiming to come from another time. This was her own magic.

The silver arm rose . . . it gestured. The silver girl certainly seemed to be trying to tell her something but there was no way of knowing what she was trying to tell. Was she warning her off . . . or beckoning her on? As Garland stared, fascinated and confused, the silver girl played her usual trick. She rippled, broke up, faded and vanished.

A little ahead of her Garland suddenly heard a bell ring out. She knew what that bell meant. Maddie and Yves must have decided to have a Fantasia parley. Garland took a deep breath. Whatever mad tales the strange boys might have to tell her, no matter what the silver girl's strange gestures might mean, Garland was a Maddigan. That was the one thing that must hold true. She must not run off into the wild when the Fantasia was struggling. And then she found herself thinking yet again of that first great Maddigan, Gabrielle, and imagining that she might pull Gabrielle out of the past air and somehow put her on like a wonderful cloak. Gabrielle would not believe rubbishy, time-travelling stories. Garland began to weave back across the tussock, back to the Fantasia, which also meant facing up to stories as wild as the twisting roads that the Fantasia followed, as it struggled to make its fortune.

Everyone else was there already, the mothers holding the little children, the older children lined up in the front row. Panting slightly, Garland edged herself in beside Maddie (for after all Maddie was her mother), Timon and Eden joined in too, standing hesitantly behind everyone else, like people who have arrived late and must stand patiently in a queue. Their little sister Jewel looked back at them from the front row, peering over Goneril's shoulder, shouting and laughing, waving her hands as if she were casting a spell.

'Why is it I'm the one that gets stuck with babies?' Garland could hear Goneril grumbling her usual grumble. 'Babies and sick ones. I've got no time for babies and yet if there's a baby within spitting distance it's me that has to look after it.'

Timon must have heard her. He began winding quickly towards her, but she must have seen him from the corner of her eye. She flung out a hand, palm outward.

'Just leave it!' she shouted at him. 'I'm not complaining, just asking a question. How is it that people always think I'm the one to baby-sit their kids? But I'm resigned to it.'

Many parleys had a pattern to them. In the past Ferdy had talked first, laying out the argument. Then the leaders of the Fantasia . . . Maddie, Yves, Bannister, Tane, and others would speak out. Old Goneril would give nagging opinions, criticizing everyone and, following this, other people would offer ideas and opinions. Now Yves led the parley once more. He praised Ferdy ('He was a Maddigan of Maddigans!') then said, glancing modestly down at his feet, that Maddie and Tane and Bannister had asked him to take over the work that Ferdy had always done.

This was what everyone expected. Garland looked at him darkly but did not argue. Yves was the tallest . . . he had a head full of words . . . could reason and deal and make announcements. And Yves's first official announcement was a sad one.

'Bailey!' he said. 'Our mapmaster . . . ' He looked around at them, and suddenly everyone knew why he had called them together. 'Bailey's dead!' he said. 'Well, we knew it was probable, didn't we? All the same there's the shock of it being made so final. Ferdy one day! Bailey the next.'

Garland did not know what to say . . . perhaps there was nothing that could be said. She looked around and saw the bowed heads, felt the new wave of grief edging through the Fantasia.

Maddie began to talk. 'It's hard,' she said, her voice quivering, 'but we are who we are. We move on.' Direction, she told them. They must have direction. Back at Milton they had been paid with food – they had enough for a few days. But now they must make for Gramth. They must perform and build up their stores so that they would have enough to carry them all the way through to Newton . . . and enough for any emergencies as well. After all there were always emergencies. Above all they must make for Newton where (with a little bit of luck) they might be able to wheel and deal and trade what they had to trade for that solar converter and even some of the solar cells for which Newton was so famous. If they could bring a converter back to Solis they would win new respect . . . new stores . . . money and fame. However, Newton was a long way off. First they must bury Bailey. And then they must . . . they *must* . . . get to Gramth.

People sighed and nodded. The parley was about to close when a voice was raised – old Shell. He was pointing at Timon and Eden.

'And what about them?' he was asking. 'What about those ones, what crept in just after our Ferdy was done in? I reckon they stand for bad luck . . . strangers breaking in on us at a strange time.'

Yves hesitated, frowning at Shell.

'But don't forget they stepped in and saved us back there!' he said. 'And what a show! I've never seen anything like it. Well . . . have you?' Shell was silent. Yves went on. 'Just think! We were all struck down a bit, weren't we? I think that crowd was going to sling us out. And then the smaller one –' he nodded in Eden's direction '– his act was amazing.'

'You say he saved us,' said Shell. 'But think about what he did? That magic of his – it wasn't natural magic, was it? I'm not saying we should punish them in any way – but we should think twice about letting them travel on with us.'

The whole Fantasia began to argue with itself, and only fell silent when Yves shouted.

'They *saved* us back there,' he repeated. 'What sort of a Fantasia would we be if we turned away from the wonders?'

'Yves is right!' cried Maddie. 'We've lost –' she hesitated, swallowing '– we've lost two treasures. We need something to balance things out, and that boy is amazing.'

Garland leaped to her feet.

'How can we trust strangers? How do we know they didn't run with the Road Rats? How do we know where they came from? We've never taken on strangers before. Outside of Solis, how can we trust anyone?'

Maddie looked at her with a sort of annoyed astonishment. The Fantasia began to chatter again, all staring at the two boys, some frowning, others smiling, some suspecting them, others willing to take them in. 'Listen to *her*,' cried Shell, pointing at Garland. 'She's a Maddigan, isn't she?'

'Ask *them*,' said Tane the clown, jerking his thumb back over his shoulder in the general direction of the boys. 'Do they *want* to come with us? Let them have their say.' And everyone turned to stare towards Timon and Eden. Timon cleared his throat.

'We're not Road Rats,' he said. 'We're just wanderers. We'll wander off, if there's no room for us here . . .' (he hesitated and looked at Eden and then over at Goneril holding the baby Jewel) '. . . though we'd like to stay.'

Goneril hoisted the little Jewel high in the air.

'Road Rats!' she screamed. 'Whenever did Road Rats weigh themselves down with babies? Road Rats have too much sense to waste their time changing nappies. I'm the one who gets stuck with all that stuff.'

'Let's stick with the old ways. Let's take a vote,' said Yves. 'And then let's move on. Those in favour – right! Those against – left!'

The Fantasia began with shuffle and flow . . . some going left, some going right.

'Garland!' said Maddie, watching Garland make for the left-hand group. 'Garland! What's wrong with you?'

'I don't trust them,' said Garland. 'I can't.'

Lilith went right, looking up at Timon as she moved – staring with admiration, Garland thought. Well, Lilith was only a little squirt. Of course she would be impressed by someone tall with golden hair and blue eyes like the hero in some old fairy tale.

Boomer sidled up to Garland's side.

'You're right,' he muttered. 'We shouldn't trust them.'

Yves and Bannister counted the heads.

'Fifty-fifty!' Yves said at last.

'Not quite!' said Maddie. 'I haven't voted . . . and I am going to vote the way Ferdy would have voted. When did we ever shut a great act out of our show? I don't care if it's talent or trickery . . . that boy's great. I want him, OK? I want him to become part of Maddigan's Fantasia.'

And saying this Maddie moved right.

'OK! You're in!' Yves said, holding out both hands towards the boys. 'Come on in and make yourselves part of us.'

'We're really grateful,' said Timon, nudging Eden forward. 'I don't blame you for being careful about strangers, but we'll be as useful as we can. We'll be true members of your circus.'

'We're not just a circus,' shouted Garland. 'We're a Fantasia.'

'That's right,' said Boomer. 'We're more than a circus.'

Timon looked towards Boomer and Garland.

'Eden and Jewel and me – we're nothing but wanderers . . . and wanderers in a strange country,' he said. 'We'll be glad of the company and we'll be glad of the safety. Because it's a rough world out there, isn't it? But I promise you wonders – I mean that's something we *can* do. Isn't a Fantasia a true home for wonders?'

'Your mum just wants to be the boss of everything,' said Lilith, frowning at Garland.

'She's allowed to be boss. She's a Maddigan! And this is Maddigan's Fantasia. OK?' Garland replied.

'And now that's worked through, we've got to be on our way,' said Yves. 'In and up and forward. And quickly.'

6

The Gorge

Almost at once the land began to swivel and buck. Hills hunched up higher on either side of them.

'This way – I think,' called Bannister, riding his bay horse and guiding Maddie's van, which bumped along at the head of the caravan, winding along the vague road. Light shone over his shoulder onto the map he held stretched out in front of him, then reflected back onto his frowning face. Garland thought she could almost see roads and place names marked in shadow on his skin. At last he looked up, and signalled back along the line towards Goneril's wagon at the rear, waving them all onwards with the map as it were a flag of battle. Garland, riding Samala, trotted forward anxious to be in the front of the procession. After all Maddigan's Fantasia should be led by a true Maddigan.

'I remember this part of the road,' Yves was saying. 'Well, I think I do. We're on track. We wind between the hills and come to the Thelwell Gorge in a mile or two. And there's that settlement at the other end of the gorge. We'll be able to put on a performance and earn ourselves fresh milk and eggs. Bacon too. They run a few pigs.'

'Eggs and bacon!' said Nye, rubbing his stomach, and pulling a face so that those around him laughed.

A kilometre and a half later, the hills stretched themselves even higher. Sharp rocks broke through the skin of the land as if something from deep in the dark heart of the world were gnawing its way into the light of day. The highest peaks had a little snow on them. The gorge grinned wolfishly out at them as they drove bravely towards it. The track tilted down. The rocks tilted up, and in its struggling but determined way the Fantasia tilted itself downwards too, first one van and then another. The gorge had its difficulties, but the Fantasia was glad to be in a familiar place, glad to feel sure of itself once more.

'Careful! Careful!' shouted Yves for, though downhill was much easier than uphill in some ways, downhill had dangers of its own kind particularly when there was ice on some corners. Garland dismounted and let Lattin lead Samala to the line of horses that straggled after the first three vans. Then she scrambled into her own van and sat beside Maddie, who was driving, inching along at the head of the line.

Garland remembered the gorge well, and felt all the familiar Fantasia relief at being in a place she could be sure of. But as they went down between the rocks she looked up and briefly glimpsed the two men on their black horses riding ahead of them along the top of the gorge. And, though she was still distrustful of the boys, she distrusted those men even more. One of them, glimpsing her upturned face perhaps, lifted his hand waving down at them. Garland did not wave back. She knew he was not being friendly.

She turned her head and found she could make out Eden and Timon, side by side, standing on the running board of Goneril's great van, and talking up to Tane who walked beside them . . . but, as she watched them, Tane left the boys, striding away between the stony flanks of the gorge and the moving line of the Fantasia as well as he could, making his way towards Maddie's van at the head of the procession. 'Hey! Kiora!' he shouted through the open window as they moved forward, inch by cautious inch, Garland leaning out through the passenger's window and Yves – *Yves* – sitting between them. Suddenly Garland could not bear to ride in that van with him.

'Mum, I'm going to walk a bit,' she said. Secretly, almost without knowing it herself, she wanted to talk to Timon and Eden.

'Be careful then. Don't get under the wheels,' was all Maddie had to say. 'Remember it gets narrower later on.'

It wasn't as easy to find walking room as Garland had hoped it would be. Maddie was right. The gully had been narrowing for some time. But then the track thrust out an elbow, and Garland edged into the elbow space, waiting in its ferny shadows until Timon and Eden, now walking and edging too, came alongside her. They looked at Garland cautiously.

'Don't worry,' she said. 'I don't want to fight.'

'Neither do we!' said Timon.

'Does it go on for long like this?' asked Eden, staring apprehensively at the wild sides of the gully.

'Not for long,' Garland said. 'You can see we're almost at the bottom. From now on it's more or less straight ahead. Once, years ago, there was a road that ran right along the bottom of the gully, and sometimes we can still find bits of it. And because we're driving vans it's much easier going this way than going over the hills.'

Both Timon and Eden looked down at the moss and leaf mould, then up at the hilltops which, from here, looked dark against the skyline.

'We have to pay a toll at the other end of the gully,' Garland went on. 'There's a tribe there. We usually pay with a little performance . . . but the last couple of times we've been through here they've asked for something they can sell in Gramth, which is the town we're mainly making for, or for pieces of silver which they can spend. We do sometimes get paid in silver or gold – or horses. So we sometimes have money or an extra horse or two we can barter, and they let us through. And now it's my turn to ask you something. Are you being followed?' She saw their faces grow suddenly sharp and serious. 'You are, aren't you? You're being followed by those two men – the ones that were asking about you back there. There's things you haven't told us.'

Eden looked sideways at Timon. Timon stared straight ahead.

'Yes,' Timon said at last, speaking rather unwillingly. 'We do have enemies – two enemies – who are following us . . . the Nennog's messengers. Ozul and Maska! Have you seen them?'

'A while back,' Garland said, pointing upwards. 'When the top of the gully was a bit more open I looked up and saw them riding along up there. They were keeping watch on us. And they don't have vans. Riding that way they'll get to the head of the gully a long way ahead of us in spite of the hills.'

'I know you don't believe us,' said Timon, 'but what we told you was true . . . we come from another time – a future time – and we came here to get away from my uncle the Nennog. And he wants us back as quickly as possible. Because everything we do here alters the future. A little thing changed here could alter whole histories out ahead of us. We've told you that. And if we'd got our time shift exactly right in the first place . . . if we'd saved your father . . . which is what we meant to do . . . well, things would probably have changed in our own time. I can't explain it all because I don't understand it myself, but we're fairly sure the Nennog would have lost power. He might have even stopped existing. But you need computers and screens and time-jump units to explain it properly . . .'

'Be simple! Be simple!' Eden interrupted his brother. 'Ozul and Maska are our enemies, and if they take us back I think the

Nennog will kill us. He killed our parents. And Ozul and Maska might kill us for him.'

'Why are you so important?' asked Garland, who found herself believing this fairy tale of theirs.

'Because when we came we brought something with us,' Eden said. 'We didn't steal it. It was ours in the first place, though we don't quite know what it is. We only know . . .'

'Eden!' said Timon warningly. He looked apologetically at Garland, and opened his mouth to say more. But before he could explain or apologize or say whatever it was he was planning to say, the sound of angry voices came back to them from the head of the Fantasia procession. There was something so urgent about those voices that Garland forgot the boys and their strange tale along with the mystery of what they had stolen.

She ran towards the argument, sliding and edging, jogged towards the head of the procession, aware that the two boys were sliding and edging close behind her. She came alongside her own van, saw Maddie and Yves standing and gesturing, looked on beyond them and saw they had almost reached the mouth of the gorge. There it was, leaping up and spreading its arms of rock wide, making a dark 'V' against the cloudless sky beyond. But the lower cleft of the 'V' was closed in. The way ahead was blocked with rocks and branches and this blockage was not an accidental one.

A crowd of people stood there, confronting the Fantasia and among them, blinking and grinning, were the two men she had glimpsed only an hour earlier: Ozul and Maska.

And there in the very centre of the group was someone Garland remembered from other journeys. A giant figure was confronting them, towering above everyone else . . . partly because of the rocks that seemed to be rising up under her, hoisting her towards the sky, and partly because she really was so very tall. Ida! Great Ida! The chieftainess of the gorge tribe. She was shouting at Yves and Maddie in her curious voice . . . deep and echoing, as if the gorge itself were speaking through her.

'Give them to us! Give them back to their father!'

Garland heard twin voices, almost in chorus, speaking softly behind her.

'Oh no!' they whispered briefly, and then she heard their footsteps. Garland did not turn to look behind her. She knew the boys were sneaking away, and that merely looking back at them might betray them.

'We haven't known them long,' Maddie was saying. 'But we've taken them into the Fantasia. We have to be true to our own.'

'Maddie,' said Yves in a low voice. 'We've only had them with us about a day. We don't know anything about them . . . and their families do have rights . . .'

'Well, where *is* their mother?' asked Maddie. 'Where's their father? Because you can't tell me those two men out there are anybody's fathers . . .'

'They belong to us,' Garland called, interrupting Maddie, and saw Yves's shoulders stiffen, while Maddie turned to look back over her shoulder in astonishment. 'I know,' Garland cried again. 'I know I didn't want them . . . but we *did* take them on, didn't we? You voted them in, and so now we've got to be true to them.'

'Listen,' Maddie said, shouting back to Ida now, 'we have to talk this over. We have to parley. That's our custom. And if we decide – if we decide not to hand the boys over we'll just go back again . . . take the long path over the hills.'

'No going back!' said Ida, pointing upwards with a curiously triumphant gesture. Maddie, Yves, Garland – perhaps the whole Fantasia – looked up and saw with horror, there among the trees and ferns that lined the walls of the gorge, some of Ida's men, standing beside rocks and boulders, levers in their hands. As the Fantasia looked upwards, some of those men suddenly sprang into action, leaning and straining, and among the ferns a great mossy boulder shifted unwillingly, then jumped away, crashing down, breaking branches and smashing small trees, as it rolled towards them.

'Watch out!' Maddie screamed, though there was nothing the Fantasia could do to protect itself. But the boulder missed them, shattering itself on other stones on the bottom of the gorge. Sharp fragments sprang into the air, chinking and pattering sharply against the windscreen of Maddie's van.

'Talk in! Talk out! Talk up and down or left and right!' yelled Ida. Her huge song echoed out over the Fantasia vans and horses, seeming to vanish into the gorge behind them, before it came booming back again, swollen with its own echoes. 'But don't talk long! And then, after all your talk, do what we're telling you to do. We've been paid to get those boys back to their family, and when we've been paid to do something we do it. So give us those boys, and you'll pass on by safely.'

There was a rippling movement as the Fantasia people scrambled down from their vans, trampling the ferns and mosses as they crammed themselves into that narrow space on one side of the gorge.

It was a parley of a sort, but not an ordered one. Everyone began shouting at once. Listening to the voices as well as she could Garland could tell that some people were now keen to pass the boys over. Others shouted that Maddie was right. The Fantasia had to be true to its own. Garland found that, since the morning, her own ideas were changing. *Blast!* she thought. *Can't I even rely on myself any more?* She looked up at those men standing by the stones high on the side of the gorge, and imagined more rocks crashing down on them. Yet she certainly did not want to hand Timon and Eden over to Ozul and Maska. Where were the boys anyway? They had disappeared. Well, *of course* they had disappeared. She had heard them go. And if she had been the one Ozul and Maska had been demanding she would have disappeared too.

Garland suddenly saw her bow and quiver hanging on the side of the van. Nobody noticed as she unhooked it. The argument was raging on and on, Fantasia people arguing with other Fantasia people. ('Fantasia people are true to each other,' Maddie was declaring yet again.) Nobody noticed as – one! two! three! Garland stepped backwards . . . nobody except Maddie that is.

'Garland!' she shouted. 'Garland! Don't you do a runner!' But there was so much distraction it was easy for Garland to pretend that she had not heard her mother. Sliding around the back of the wagon she looked up into the forest on the opposite side of the gorge. Where were Timon and Eden? Where *were* they? They must be hiding up there somewhere. It might be hard to see Eden, that bush-coloured stick boy, but Timon's golden hair should flare out like a soft flame. His blue eyes might even light up some shadowy hiding place. If he were hiding up there, not wanting to be found, he might have to close his eyes. But even if he screwed his eyes tight and clapped his hands across them, she would still find him. Sliding into the bush herself, Garland began climbing, leaving the Fantasia below her.

She climbed upwards on a series of rough wide steps under the tangle of trees and ferns clinging onto the gully wall. Scrambling up from one step to another certainly was hard work, but there were resting places in between. Garland paused, panting a little and listening hard.

'Timon?' she said aloud. 'Eden?' She was sure that there would be too much noise down below for anyone to hear her speak. The boys *must* have gone this way. They *must* be close at hand. 'Where are you?'

She heard a movement and turned gratefully towards it. But the figures that now came sliding out of the bush, closing in on her . . . reaching out for her, were not the figures of the boys. Suddenly Ozul and Maska were looming over her. Only a few minutes ago they had been standing down below, a step or two behind the giantess Ida . . . but then, only a few minutes ago, she too had been standing down there, half-hidden by Maddie and Yves.

No time to turn and slide away. No escape.

'Where are they?' asked Ozul.

'I don't know,' cried Garland. The sounds of argument drifted up from below. 'I'm looking for them too. They . . . they just disappeared.'

'Where are they?' Ozul repeated.

Maska spoke. 'Destroy her!' he said. He had a curious voice. The words were clear yet sounded as if they were being cranked out of some kind of machine that almost needed oiling. 'Destroy her! Then throw her out down there among them. That will send a message.'

He meant it.

And then suddenly everything erupted. Stones came flying out of the green curtains that hung around them. One struck Maska with a curious clanging sound. Ozul whirled, and, as he did so, yet another stone flew in at them, striking him full in the face. The very ground seemed to tilt. 'Run!' That was Timon's voice. 'Don't just *stand* there!' But Garland was already running – leaping away rather than running – diving in a frantic, stumbling dive, into that greenness behind her with no idea of where her dive might be taking her. All that mattered was getting away. Twigs tore at her. She could not tell if they were pulling her into hiding or pushing her away.

'Get them!' she could hear Maska shouting. 'Get them!' But now Garland had the advantage, being so much smaller. Shooting from one gap to another, she scrambled across those ferns, and under those clawing branches, in between trees and out into a small clearing. Turning, somehow jogging backwards, she slipped an arrow into her bow, and as she did this Timon's voice suddenly came from somewhere ahead of her and a little above her. 'Forget it!' he was yelling.

But her arrow was already fitted. She drew it back. Maska showed himself briefly, beating branches away from his face. Garland fired . . . sure she would hit him. But to her amazement he caught the arrow in mid-air as easily as if it were nothing more than a thrown stick, though catching the arrow meant that he released the branches he had been holding back. They swung in on him, pushing him back. And then a hand seized Garland, tugging her into hiding. 'Up here!' hissed a voice, and she was hauled up onto the next step a bare second before Maska burst into the clearing once more, charging across it like some wild animal. Ozul followed him. They ran straight ahead without looking upwards. Garland's foot was waving mere centimetres above their heads.

'They'll be back . . . back in a second,' hissed Timon in her right ear, as he hauled her up still further.

'Put your hand on this tree,' hissed Eden on her left. 'Great shot!' he added, but Timon was already clapping her hands against the trunk of a tree, pressing them against the bark with his own. In the distance Garland could hear the sound of a drum . . . Boomer's drum. She guessed that down below the Fantasia probably was buying time for its parley by putting on an act of some kind . . . juggling or, perhaps, the talented dogs. It was not the first time the Fantasia had bought time with their skills.

Timon was still pressing her hands against the tree bark.

Suddenly, everything changed. In half a breath Garland had become something different from anything she had ever been before. The drumming . . . the shouting did not entirely vanish but it became unimportant . . . a nothing . . . a tumbling sound being blown along by a wind. She suddenly felt she had lived with forest sounds for years (the sound of birdsong, the sound of wind and storm and rain on leaves) and, just as all these sounds had come and gone, that drumming would go too. Something more vital than a mere drumbeat was moving through her. She was becoming alive in a different way . . . a strange way . . . an ancient way. She had turned into something else. All the same she could still feel something of her old self, alive and watching . . . a thread of that usual self plaited with memories of being a fantastic girl living with the Fantasia. However, though she could remember the Fantasia so clearly, it was like an odd little dream off to one side. All that really mattered was the flow . . . the flow . . .

In that thread-like way she was aware of something beyond the flow, a clash and a shouting, and then a different sort of shouting further down the gully, and that thread of old understanding told her that somehow Yves and some of the Fantasia men had left Maddie and Goneril to distract Ida with some Fantasia display and had managed to slide up the slope just as she had done. They were struggling to disarm those men with the levers before they managed to bring any rocks crashing down onto the road below. And they might succeed, because the men with levers had probably been distracted, too, distracted by the jugglers, perhaps, or by the acrobats or the dancing dogs, only to find themselves part of Bannister's strong-man act as Yves, Bannister and other men looped in on them.

Still, none of this really affected Garland, mysteriously hidden, at rest yet working. All that mattered was stretching up towards the sun and down into the ground. All that mattered was the flow upwards and outwards into her invisible leaves. She had become part of the tree.

Down below Maddie was exclaiming, 'Garland! Where is Garland?'

'Well, we won that one,' cried Yves, dropping down beside her, flourishing one of the levers as if it were a wand. 'Let's say we've *negotiated*. They'll let us through now. You bet they will.'

'Garland!' Maddie was still crying. 'She climbed up into the bush, and those – those men followed her.'

'She must know where the boys went,' said Bannister. 'She must have been following them.'

Up in the side of the gully the ordinary-looking bark of an ordinary tree, a young totora, darkened then blurred. Eden suddenly dissolved out into the outside world. At first he looked like a ghost, colourless and transparent . . . then the yellowish brown of his jacket, the green of his eyes, slowly oozed back into him. Colour made him solid and real once more, but he looked so exhausted it seemed as if he might faint. He breathed deeply, closed his eyes and put his hand on the totora trunk. Timon dissolved out beside him.

'Where are they?' said Timon. He could hear the sound of someone scrambling up through the ferns below. 'What's that?'

'It's the Fantasia,' said Eden, panting. 'They're looking for us – well, for *her*, mainly. Maska and Ozul will keep away now that there are so many people around. We're saved. I think!' He looked at the tree. 'Where is she?'

'Garland?' asked Timon suddenly alarmed.

'I think I've lost her,' said Eden. 'I can't . . . I can't.'

'You must!' cried Timon. 'Bring her back now – *now* – because soon she'll be part of the tree – part of the tree forever.'

'You know what it's like!' Eden cried back. 'I do something and I use myself up . . . I need to grow back into my strength. You know that.'

'Garland!' Maddie was calling further down the slope. 'Garland. Where are you? It's all right. They're letting us through. Garland!'

Garland was feeling the tree's flow going through and through her. It was a huge pleasure. No! It was something more than pleasure . . . something *beyond* pleasure. But with that thread of her old self she was also hearing a voice . . . a necessary voice . . . calling her name over and over again. 'Garland! Garland! Garland!'

That thread of old self suddenly strengthened . . . that call out there was a call that must always be answered. A picture formed in her mind of her lips moving; an echo suddenly filled her . . . an echo of her own voice. 'Here I am!' it was saying. And now she felt . . . weak but strengthening . . . a necessary pull. Her mother was calling her. Step out! She must step out. And she felt herself stepping forward, stepping out of a dream.

Then, dream or not, she was outside – propping herself against the tree with Timon and Eden grabbing her by her arms and hoisting her onto her feet . . . and Boomer breaking in on them through other trees, seeing them and turning to call back into the gorge below. 'They're here!' he was shouting. 'This way! Here they are!' Then Maddie herself came scrambling up, panting a bit and bursting in on them, looking at first frantic, then relieved and then almost at once angry with them because they had worried her so much.

'It's dangerous,' she shouted. 'We live a dangerous life. It's all around us. Don't you dare make it more dangerous than it needs to be. Disappearing at a time like this. Never do it again.'

'We thought you might – you know – exchange us,' Eden began, trying to explain. 'And she followed us . . .'

'. . . she came to help us,' said Timon.

Maddie's anger seemed to drain out of her. She looked suddenly limp and hugely tired, even though it was only midday.

'I suppose I can't blame you,' she said in a weary voice. 'Life is so mixed-up at present. And as for Garland, she's a born runaway. She'd grab any chance. But, thanks to Yves, the ambush was undone. I talked, while he and all the men worked their way up to where the stones were balanced and . . . anyway it's over. And you boys – you have nothing to fear. Not everyone is happy about having you join us – some of us are very cautious about letting strangers into the Fantasia. But just wait. Work yourself in and in, say, and in a week or two longer even the cautious ones won't pass you over to enemies. You'll be just a necessary part of us. And who knows? We might even get an easier time over the next few days.'

Somewhere down below the giantess Ida was gesturing and shouting. The logs that had blocked the gorge were being pulled away.

'We can't pay them anything, but once we get through the gorge we've promised to forgive them and put on a performance,' Maddie said, still looking at Timon and Eden 'You see, we do carry treasure with us – something that everyone longs for. We've got entertainment to offer – transformation – wonder. And with a bit of luck we make people laugh. Laughing is so wonderful. Laughter and wonder – that's what lies at the heart of the Fantasia. And you're part of us now – even your little sister is part of us. So trust us! No more running away. All together! Right?'

'Right!' said Timon.

Maddie held out her hand and Eden took it . . . then Timon clasped both their hands around with his.

'We've been lucky to meet you,' he said. 'We needed good luck and we found it. Maddigan's Fantasia is our total, absolute good luck.'

'So far,' said Eden, and Garland thought there was a strange echo of wind-blown trees in his leafy voice.

7
The Other Diary

Dear Ferdy, you would have been so proud of us. We came through the gorge . . . all of us safe . . . and then we forgave them and put on a show for them, because, as Maddie said, we'll probably have to come back through the gorge one of these days, and it is better to have friends here rather than enemies. Tane really flirted with Ida, and you could tell she enjoyed that. I mean in the beginning she looked a bit suspicious, but then she loosened up and laughed and clapped, just like a kid. As for me I walked the tightrope. I did it so well you'd have been really proud of me. It really is my main trick, and while I'm doing it, I can almost forget the rope is there. Somehow I believe I have power over the empty air. I mean, space is still there. Space is beneath me waiting for me to fall into its jaws, but I just dance over it. And I did my trapeze somersaults and so on. But Eden – he slept on and on in Goneril's van. He was just worn out by putting me into that tree and then drawing me out again and he just had to sleep. I looked in on him and saw that he was frowning in his sleep as if he was being worried by some pack of wild, savaging dreams.

'**I**t wears him out . . . being that true magician,' Timon (who was sitting beside his brother watching him just a little anxiously) told Garland. 'But he should be sharp enough again tomorrow.'

As he said this Garland knew he was staring at her rather than Eden, and for some reason his blue gaze was making her feel shy. Being a Fantasia girl born and bred, she was not used to feeling shy, and she did not quite know how to manage this unexpected feeling.

'Where have they gone – the ones that were after you?' she asked a little absent-mindedly. She was staring out through the van window above Eden's head, and watching her mother, standing beside Yves and actually laughing with him. *How can she?* Garland was thinking. *How can she laugh? How can she stand there beside him, pointing things out to him as if he were her partner?* For some reason this angry feeling was rather more comfortable than the shyness with Timon. She was more used to it by now.

'They'll be back,' said Timon gloomily. 'The Nennog is driving them. They won't give up easily. They won't be allowed to.' He touched her shoulder. 'I've decided to show you something. Something that will prove some of the things we've been telling you.'

'Just as well,' said Garland, still concentrating on Maddie and Yves. 'Though I half-believe it because of – because Eden made me – well, he made me part of that tree in some way, didn't he? Anyone who felt that – that flow, just has to do a bit of half-believing. But how did he do it – make me part of a tree?'

'It's his skill,' said Timon. 'Dissolving barriers. He's what we call a boundaryman. He connects across barriers, like the barriers between men and trees, and sometimes he can carry other people with him. But look here – look what I'm showing you.'

Garland looked, a little impatiently, and found Timon was showing her an ancient book, holding it carefully as if it were a rare treasure. *It's not so great*, Garland thought. *I've got a better book than that.* Then suddenly it seemed familiar. How could she be recognizing something she had never seen before?

Timon nodded, and then, very gently, opened the book. Garland found herself peering down at faint, faded writing. But those written letters were not holding still. As she watched they swam like fish, briefly spelt out messages too faint and twisted for her to read, then shifted again. Garland frowned . . . screwed up her face . . . then she suddenly bent towards the open page, startled and more than startled – terrified. For that writing was her own writing. The book Timon was holding out towards her was her diary – her actual, own diary, grown faint and old, its blue cover faded to a faint greyish mauve, but her own diary for all that.

'Give it to me!' cried Garland, snatching at it, only to find with horror that the edges of the brittle pages began turning into dust as she grasped them. 'Where did you get it?'

'Careful! Careful! You'll crumble it away,' hissed Timon. 'It's old . . . old . . .' Very gently, he passed it over to her. 'It was in our library, in what they call "the archives" – old books and letters and things that no one really reads any more. But Eden found it and – well, we stole it out of the library.'

Garland began slowly turning the pages, gaping over them only to find that, a few pages further on, the writing crowded up and came to an end. *We will never get home. We will never get back to Solis. Maddigan's Fantasia has become a dream – just another dream left over after the Remaking.*

She looked up at Timon, horrified. Hastily, but still very gently, he took the book back from her.

'Don't worry. Not yet,' he told her quickly. 'Whatever's written there is just one possible future. Nothing is set. Eden and I have come out of the future into your time and that's changed the balance of things. Nothing in that book holds still now. It shifts all the time. What you wrote back then – I mean what you're going to write when the time comes –' he broke off, looking confused by his own words. 'Eden and me – we're altering things somehow by being here, but I can't understand just how it is working out. Last night the writing went on to the end of the book.' He opened it, turning the pages delicately. 'Look!'

And, looking back, Garland saw that the page which only a moment ago had been half empty, was now crammed with words, and had notes written down the margins. It was transformed.

'Sorry!' she said to Timon, and heard her voice was shaking as she spoke. 'Sorry! I have to go. I just have to – I don't know – *think* about it all.' And then she jumped up and ran off as if wolves were after her.

When, weeks later, Garland tried to recall where she had run to she found she could not remember clearly. She knew that later, riding Samala alongside the Fantasia caravan, she had watched the forest stretch its green knuckles upwards, softly punching towards patches of blue sky, and found she was some-how watching them through pages of that mysterious diary. Even later, when they camped for the evening, words in her own writing still crawled and vanished as she helped Tane and Nye make earth ovens in which to cook potato and kumera. She was aware of Timon and Eden, off to one side and peering over at her cautiously, but she looked away from them, chattering with Boomer and arguing with Lilith just as she usually did. And all the time the world quivered as the words rolled and flowed telling possible stories – stories that could go in every direction.

Early next morning, in the back of her own wagon, Garland slid her familiar diary from its hiding place yet again, shivering as she touched its cover. She squeezed it, stroked it, then opened it and saw, in the uncertain early light, that its cover was still blue, that its pages were not crumbling at the edges, that her own writing was holding still. It was just as it had been the day before last, and the words on the last page were the words she had written only yesterday.

All around her she could hear around her the familiar sounds of the Fantasia being pulled to bits, packed in on itself and folded away. She could hear Maddie calling her impatiently. 'Garland! Come on! We need a hand.' Those ordinary sounds, even the sharpness in Maddie's voice, seemed like treasures, and she swung herself out of bed, stretching her arms wide as if she was embracing that world just outside the van door, loving the *usual* sound of it all.

What she could not see or hear was that far up, high on the top of the gorge once more, Ozul and Maska were looking down on the Fantasia, and that Ozul was licking his lips.

8

Getting into Gramth

They left the gorge and its green bush, mosses and ferns behind them, burst out onto a scrubby plain, and began to crawl along a rutted road that they did not have to question. Bannister frowned over the maps, looking sideways at some book he was longing to read, but for the present the road was clear and running in the right direction. The wheels might bump but, though of course the vans had to travel carefully, they rolled doggedly on and by midday they could see a long smudged arm of smoke, waving up into the blue, beckoning them forward. Gramth! Gramth was in sight! Gramth a town big enough to trade in. They would be able to set up their biggest tent on the outskirts of this town and do a full performance. Garland felt that she would be able to settle down into real life again.

'I never really *enjoy* Gramth,' she said to Maddie, 'but, right now, I'm glad to see it.'

'We need stores. More stores!' Yves was declaring somewhere off on the left. He was never far away these days. 'Food and more fuel! And we might get them now we're out of the sticks and edging out of winter too.'

'We need more stores,' Lilith agreed, bobbing like a performing dog at her father's elbow, but looking sternly over at Garland just in case Garland started giving orders too. Lilith was only a little girl of course – ten last birthday – but she seemed to be suggesting that she was the Fantasia's true princess. But Lilith was not a Maddigan. There was no way that Yves could be allowed to take possession of the Fantasia – no way that Lilith could take over the place that had always been Garland's.

'How are you holding out?' Yves was asking Maddie. 'You don't have to try to do everything. I mean there isn't one person here who wouldn't understand if you took a bit of time off.'

Garland stared at him suspiciously. She had heard Maddie crying in the night, but during the day she was busy every moment of the day, as always. Garland wanted Maddie to rest and remember Ferdy, but she did not want her resting because Yves suggested it. After all, if Maddie was resting Yves would be able to move in and take over and soon the circus would be called Yves's Fantasia. Ferdy would be totally forgotten and all Maddigans – Maddigans like herself – would be doing what Yves told them to do.

'Oh no!' Maddie replied. 'I'm not just being brave, either. Somehow flogging myself along makes life easier to bear. I finish one thing and straight away there's something else waiting there in line, needing immediate attention . . . now, now *now!* It's better to be up and doing than lying in my van weeping and snuffling.' And as she said this, she did begin to weep a little. 'Come on. Let's get going,' she added quickly, 'or I'll begin snuffling now.'

Though Garland wanted that place on the front van to be hers and hers alone, she found that, on that particular morning, she did not want to sit beside Maddie. She did not even want to ride Samala any more. Now that her thoughts had settled down she simply wanted to walk with Timon and Eden and to ask them all over again about their claim to come from the future. Of course their story of a mysterious 'possible' Solis and a wicked ruler called 'the Nennog' were silly – they just *had* to be silly. All the same when she thought of what they had told her she found she was frightened, and being frightened always infuriated her.

If only she could forget their strangeness. If only she could work her way into feeling Timon and Eden were just ordinary Fantasia boys for, after all, they were good company. She liked Timon's ruffled fair hair and the blue flash of his eyes as he looked at her. Not only that, he was the right age for a boyfriend – older than Boomer who right now was still skirmishing around, riding in and out of the tussocks on his motorized bike. As she walked over to Timon and Eden, still watching Boomer shouting and waving and trying harder than ever to get her attention with some irritation, curious mixed-up, this-way-that-way feelings raced around in her head like badly trained mice. She was longing for Timon and Eden to be nothing but ordinary, and yet she kept on wondering if they might – they just might – be planning to make some great change in her own – in Garland's – time. Was she hoping they would? As she began trying to untangle these thoughts Boomer wove backwards and forwards, shouting and hallooing, now just behind them, now just ahead, darting into their conversations with cries and exclamations of his own. There was nothing important she could ask Timon and Eden without being interrupted.

'Hey! There are two men riding after us,' he reported, suddenly skidding to a stop beside them. '*Those* two men!' He looked at Timon and then at Eden. 'You know them, don't you? Don't you? Who are they?'

'Go and beat on your drum,' Garland told him. 'We're nearly there. We'll need the usual oompah pah!' She turned to Timon. 'We always let people know we're coming,' she said.

'We're nearly there,' yelled Lilith like a busy echo. 'I'm going to put on my Fantasia dress. I'm going to be princess of the circus.' And she raced away.

Though the Fantasia was on the road, somehow it was Gramth which seemed to be travelling, advancing towards them in slow, heavy steps.

'It looks . . . it looks *guarded*,' said Eden, sounding hesitant.

'What are those long lines of people waiting for?' asked Timon, when they were close enough to make out the queues of people snaking out from the city gates.

'They're farmers and traders wanting to get into the markets – wanting to buy and sell, wheel and deal,' said Garland, pleased to find that she knew more than Timon did. 'There's usually a lot going on around the edges of town, but you can make more money if you work your way into the heart of it, which is what we have to do. Because people can't just come and go. Gramth tries to look after itself. Everyone has to pass the guards and sentries, and fill in all the right forms. But I think Maddie's done all that form-filling for us.'

'Why?' asked Eden. 'Why are they so careful?'

'Hey, think about it,' Garland replied. 'It's a dangerous world, right? Probably dangerous here in a different way from the way it's dangerous in your time – but still dangerous. And Gramth has grown strong through being careful, so I suppose it's become a sort of habit. Look, Yves is grabbing Boomer. The band's going to lead us in.'

They rolled on confidently to the outskirts of the city, their band marching in front of them playing the Fantasia's triumphant music. Ozul and Maska rode not far behind them, like careful wolves following a herd, hoping for the chance to scavenge some slow prey from the herd edges. The Fantasia clustered at the main gate, van after van, with riders spreading out around them. A whole tribe of officials came hurrying towards them. Swerving sideways as they approached the town gates, Ozul and Maska hesitated, then, nodding to each other, chose what looked to them like the shortest queue. Almost immediately other straggling people closed in behind them.

Columns of smoke were rising from behind the city walls and a great mixture of smells, swelling up and out in an invisible cloud, came softly over them to sink around the waiting people. Garland sniffed sawdust, hot metal and, above anything else, food. Boomer, drum and all, came prancing down from the head of the Fantasia queue.

'Here we are! Here we are!' he was shouting.

'How long will we have to wait?' asked Eden a little wearily. It was his turn to put on the baby sling and carry Jewel but she kept slipping from side to side, grizzling and complaining. Now he hoisted her straight again, and patted her back just to let her know she was being looked after.

'I'll take her,' offered Timon, but Eden knew that things had to be fair.

'No, it's my turn,' he said. 'She's probably a bit hungry.'

'It's awful waiting,' piped Lilith, 'but I'll entertain her.'

Garland groaned aloud, but Lilith took no notice of Garland. She began to dance and sing, kicking her legs, beaming at Jewel and holding her skirts out on either side.

'There's a rainbow round the corner
With room for you and me . . .'

Her voice wavered and she lost the tune for a moment (Garland often imagined Lilith as being tangled up in lost lines of dying songs). Her kicking sank down into a shuffle. But then she remembered the tune and the words once more.

'Where all my cares are bluebirds
That fly across the sea . . .'

A young man suddenly burst out of nowhere and began running alongside the queue, shouting as he ran.

'No more oil slaves! No more oil slaves!'

He shoved Lilith roughly to one side as he ran by, but already Gramth officers were closing in on him, flourishing the long metal poles they called their rods of office. One of the officers reached out, touching the young man's shoulder with the rod. 'No more . . .' he was crying yet again. But there was a curious sound . . . half-zing, half-crackle. The man's words melted into one another, becoming a scream, while his running turned into a shapeless leap. He stumbled; he fell. Officials closed around him.

'Hey! Awesome!' said Boomer in a quavering voice.

'Think so?' said Timon. He watched two officers hoist the young man onto their shoulders and carry him away, then looked anxiously to the head of the queue. 'Something's wrong,' he said as he watched officials in grey uniforms studying the papers Yves and Maddie were passing towards them.

'No. It's always like this,' said Garland, then thought that perhaps it *was* different this time, because it was Yves, not Ferdy, wheeling and dealing at Maddie's side.

But Maddie was turning and gesturing back along the Fantasia line in her commanding way. Boomer shot off, drum and all, anxious to be part of the band again, and the Fantasia leaped to life. The grey officials passed the papers back to Yves, Garland noticed with annoyance. Then chief guard waved and the great gates opened. To the sound of its own music, the Fantasia marched though down the main street of Gramth making for the big square in the middle of town.

Looking around as they drove through the main gate, Garland suddenly glimpsed Ozul and Maska caught up in the next queue along, trapped by the people in front of them and the people behind. *Surely Ozul and Maska would never let themselves be captured by a mere queue*, thought Garland. Then she smiled. Even if they tried forcing their way to the front the officials, lined up by the main gates, all armed with their rods, would not let them through until they had all the proper documents, stamped and signed. Perhaps Ozul and Maska might be caged in after all. She could see the Aide, the senior Gramth official representing the Mayor, climbing up into the front of the van beside Yves and Maddie. The Mayor of Gramth, who was like a small-time king (though he was never called a king) lived in the centre of the city, and almost never came out of his office of brick and stone. *Of course*, thought Garland, *he might . . . he just might . . . come out for the Fantasia performance tonight for, though he was a strong and serious man, he loved clowns.* The last time they had been here he had actually laughed while they joked and tumbled.

The Fantasia swung on, following their band, not so much marching as dancing down the main street and making for the city centre. People clustered along the edge of the street and the Aide waved to the crowd as if he, not Yves, were the true ringmaster. However no one cheered him or waved back to him. But that was not the Fantasia's business. They were on their way again, being themselves, half-performing already, band playing, acrobats cartwheeling, horses arching their necks as if they were proud to belong to the Fantasia.

Eden decided to join in like a true Fantasia man. He passed Jewel over to Timon, then clapped his hands. A bright ball suddenly appeared, sparkling and pulsating between his fingers. He bowed left and right then tossed the ball into the air. It burst into shooting stars of coloured light. People threw out their own arms, shouting with pleasure. Lilith shouted too, but for a different reason.

'Shops!' she cried in delight. 'Real shops.'

Garland looked around her with unwilling wonder. Though she was older than Lilith, she couldn't help being enchanted by those shining windows, glimpsed every now and then in between the heads of the jostling crowd. Once the whole world had been a little like this. Perhaps it had *all* been like this, panes of glass giving off a soft beckoning glitter. Once there had been town after town, tied like knots into the net of roads that had held the land captive, and every town had been filled with shops. But that was back then. This was now. They were the Fantasia, marching into Gramth. The reluctant crowd began cheering and waving, faces were suddenly smiling and Garland waved back, smiling too. Tane the clown put on his red nose, and somersaulted and cartwheeled, spinning in and out of the crowd. Shell even let his parrots fly free and they circled above him, then flew back to perch along his outstretched arms as if they were finding places in a friendly tree.

But up on the front of the first van Garland could see Maddie and Yves were looking suddenly dismayed, while the Aide, who was now sitting in Garland's usual seat frowned and folded his lips in a determined way.

'It's wonderful!' Eden was crying, enchanted. 'Wonderful!'

'Yes, but I think something's wrong,' Garland said, staring over at her van. The Aide was shrugging his shoulders.

They had reached main square. The Fantasia, which had marched as one unit, split and spread out into many. They rushed to unfold their canvas, drive in the pegs and raise the poles. The Aide was now watching with satisfaction, Garland thought, but Maddie was frowning as she climbed down from the van. As soon as she could Garland raced over to her mother's side.

'Mum!' she cried. 'Mum! What's wrong?'

'Gramth always feels funny,' Maddie said, 'but it feels really strange this time. It feels – well, it feels somehow stormy . . . dangerous even. But that's not our business. The thing is they're saying . . .' Maddie stopped, looking curiously unsure of herself.

'They've run out of fuel,' squeaked Lilith. Only a moment

ago she had been walking with Garland and Boomer, but she must have raced over to the van, getting there first, and asking Yves the same question. 'The factory that works on the oil has broken down. They say we might have to stay here all winter. I don't mind. They've got hundreds of shops.'

'Yes . . . well,' said Maddie, 'that just won't do. Somehow we've got to keep going. We've got to leave tomorrow . . . or the next day at the latest.'

The Aide jumped down and stood beside her, ignoring Lilith and Garland.

'I'm not sure that that will be possible,' he said, smiling. 'There's a long wait for an exit visa these days. You don't want to try fighting your way out do you?'

Maddie turned, narrowing her eyes, and he looked away from her rather quickly.

'Why not stay on here for a little?' he suggested. 'We would have a use for you for a while. Bread and circuses, you know.'

'Are you telling us we're prisoners?' cried Maddie.

'Prisoners? Of course not,' said the Aide. 'You're our *guests*. And we need – we do need –' he looked around, making his voice suddenly pathetic '– guests like you. We work so hard and we long for a little colour in our struggling lives.'

'One performance!' said Maddie. 'Two at the most! We must press on. That's what we do.'

'There are no "musts" since the Remaking,' the Aide said, sounding rather cold once more. 'There are only possibilities and impossibilities. And it may just be impossible for you to leave for a while. But aren't you happy to be needed?'

'We're not happy to be trapped,' put in Yves.

For the time being the show had to go on. The big tent was rising higher, the band stopped playing. Boomer came wandering towards them, his drum in front of him. Sometimes, when he wore his drum, that drum seemed more powerful than

Boomer himself, and he looked rather like a little motor attached to it. Lilith, meanwhile, entranced by the town square and the glimpses of shops and stalls, edged away staring outward while the rest of the Fantasia stared in. Boomer, shrugging off his drum, watched her.

'I'm going to look around,' he said. 'I'll be back in a bit.' But Garland was not listening to Boomer. Without his drum he was nothing but a boy – and a boy who was nearly a year younger than she was.

'Kill them!' said Maska in his grating voice. It seemed to be something he said very easily.

'No,' said Ozul. 'Not now.' He nodded towards the distant gate. 'There are guards there . . . quite a lot of them. They would be too much for me – possibly even for you. No! You'd find those rods they are carrying very *unsettling*, wouldn't you? We have to take things carefully here.'

The men in front of them moved on, and suddenly Ozul and Maska were confronted by two officials.

'You have been here before?' asked one of them . . . the one sitting at the little box desk, with papers fanned out in front of him.

'No,' said Ozul quickly. He must be the one to speak here. He was the one who could make his voice quiet and humble, which was something Maska just could not do. 'We are strangers. But we had heard that your town is a place where travellers can rest.'

'Do you want to trade?' asked the standing man. 'And if you want to trade, what have you brought with you that is worth trading?'

'We don't want anyone coming into our town and spying out our systems,' said the sitting man, looking them up and down with puzzlement and suspicion. 'We have to protect our citizens you understand. That is our duty.'

'It's what we're paid for,' added the man who stood beside him.

'Letting us in could be to the benefit of your town in – in various ways,' said Ozul. 'You mentioned being paid . . .'

He drew a large green bag from his belt and shook it a little. It jingled, and the expressions of the two officials immediately changed, becoming (perhaps) a little easier.

'But you have no passports,' the standing man said. Maska made an impatient movement and Ozul quickly laid a hand on his sleeve. His other hand, the one holding that jingling bag, fell down to his side again.

'We hope to acquire passports,' he said. 'We believe it would be to our benefit – and yours.'

'I do hope you're not trying to bribe us,' said the sitting man in a particularly good-natured voice, and Ozul hesitated.

'Of course not,' he said. 'I wouldn't suggest such a thing, except by way of a – a joke between understanding friends.'

The sitting man smiled, but the standing one straightened himself and pointed.

'Every man in Gramth has a great sense of humour,' he said, frowning. 'We all like to laugh. It is one of the rules. So over there!' He shook his pointing finger. 'There is a booth over there where you can exchange a joke or two and get passports. It will cost you a little, mind you, but it will mean you have the right to come into our town any day or night over the next year.'

Maska and Ozul turned out of the queue and made for the shorter queue outside the booth that had been pointed out to them. They did not know that someone was watching them. Boomer, lighter and freer now that he was without his drum, was staring them with interest, knowing that these two men were certainly not friends of the Fantasia. And whatever arguments Boomer might be having with Garland and her new friends, those new friends *had* been chosen by the Fantasia, and Fantasia people must always stand by one another.

Ozul and Maska took their places in the shorter queue, standing back from the people directly in front of them. As Boomer watched, Ozul reached into his bag and brought out something that looked to Boomer like a power book. Boomer's expression changed. Power books seemed to him like rare and magical devices, left over from the days before the Destruction. They were treasures and he longed to have one. Ozul said something to Maska, then flicked the power book open. There was no way of knowing what Ozul might be looking at, but Boomer could see a green light flooding out from the little screen, colouring Ozul's face, so that it suddenly looked as if a strange, unwholesome moss were growing across it. Boomer edged close. Ozul's lips were not moving, but all the same a strange half-whispering voice was making itself heard. 'I await your report. Do not keep me waiting. Or I will have you deleted.'

9

Meeting a Rebel

'It's a town, a real town,' Garland was telling Timon and Eden, at the exact moment that Boomer was out and about, studying Ozul and Maska. She did not love Gramth, but just then she was feeling rather proud of it. 'There aren't as many real towns as there used to be. You *know*! The Destruction came, back a bit, and then the Chaos. The bombs fell and all that. Buildings just toppled over! Whole cities sank into the ground or turned to dust. It must be part of your history too. Well, isn't it?' She did not wait for them to answer, but hurried on. 'And then slowly the Remaking began. But we've never caught up with what we used to be. We're still being remade I suppose.'

'Yes,' said Timon, shifting Jewel just a little. Goneril was having to do some Fantasia work so Timon had the baby slung across him. 'And in our history we still call your time the Remaking, because things started to get going again. Hey! You were the ones. You remade us.'

Garland felt suddenly proud of her time, but at that moment Yves walked by, trying to talk to some man, bright in a powerful uniform. Yves frowned as he listened to what the man had to say, but he was also distracted, because Lilith was pulling at his arm, and pointing towards the shops. Her looped plaits, tied with ribbons, looked like butterflies perching on her ears. Yves seemed not to know quite what to do next. Then he glanced over her head and saw Garland and Timon watching him. His face cleared. He said something to the man at his elbow and then came rapidly towards them.

'Just keep an eye on this one will you?' he said. 'I don't want her losing herself, and I haven't time to watch over her myself.'

'Lollies,' said Lilith. 'Give me money. I want lollies.'

'As long as they don't stray out of this sector,' said the man beside Yves rather quickly. 'It wouldn't be safe for them.'

'Look! Just keep an eye on her,' Yves told Garland, and turned away quickly.

'Surely we can come to some arrangement,' he was saying as he walked off, keeping pace with his companion.

'I think that was the Mayor,' said Garland. 'He doesn't show himself very often. I hope Yves doesn't give in to him.'

'Can we go to the shops now?' asked Lilith.

There was nothing for it. Garland would have to look through shop windows with Lilith, but she did not really mind, for secretly she wanted to look at the shops too. Lilith-care would give her a good excuse.

They wandered into a narrow street, Lilith prancing a little in front of them, Garland and Timon vaguely following. The windows closed in on them like glassy walls. 'I don't think there's any place (except for Newton and Solis) that has so much glass in it,' Garland said. 'Oh look at that! Books!'

'Better not let Bannister come down this street,' said Timon. 'We'd never get him out again.'

'Where are the lollies?' called Lilith, looking back over her shoulder.

Suddenly there was a cry of alarm and the sound of a scuffle behind them. Garland and Timon swung round only to see Eden struggling with a tall girl, who had seized him by the throat.

'Shut up! Shut Up! Don't scream!' she was pleading with him. 'I just want to talk to you.'

Timon pulled Jewel out of the sling and thrust her into Garland's arms. Then he leaped forward, grabbing one of the girl's arms and wrenching it up behind her back.

'Ow!' she screamed. 'Enemy!' and turned to look up at him through glasses with twisted silvery rims.

Garland could see that the girl was not alone. There was a younger boy following her and in a curious way he was rather like Eden – a stick boy but a town boy too. The girl began talking very rapidly, looking right and left as if she were terrified of some sort of intrusion.

'Listen! Just listen! My name's Chena, right? And that boy there's my brother Tarq. And he's eleven next week. You know what *that* means.'

'We don't know,' said Garland. 'We don't live here.'

'No, I know. That's why I grabbed you. You're circus people, aren't you? We want to join the circus.'

Garland sighed. It was not the first time she had had children come up to her, longing to join the circus. A circus always looked such fun. Well, the Fantasia certainly tried hard to make it look like fun. They tried to hide the worry, the endless work, the hard times and make their work seem like a great whirling game that they were playing with a difficult world.

'What can you do?' she asked Chena. 'Can you juggle? Can you clown?'

'Of course not,' cried the girl. 'We just want to escape. He's eleven next week and he doesn't have an exemption and they'll put him to work in the mines (if they catch him, that is). He'll have to work and work underground pumping oil and crushing coal into fuel for people like you. It's what happens here if you don't have powerful parents. Take him! Hide him. Please!'

And then, before either Garland or the boys could answer, she seemed to hear something.

'Wait!' she hissed. 'Don't go. Promise! Just look in the windows.' And she spun around, grabbed her brother and pulled him into a narrow alley between two glassy shops. Just in time as two guards came marching around the corner. They stopped at the sight of the Fantasia children, muttering to one another. But then they smiled slightly, walked on by and disappeared around a corner.

'Have they gone?' the girl asked, peering from the shadowy slot in which she and her brother were hiding. 'I can't really come out. I shouldn't be here. I'm in the wrong sector.'

'How come you aren't in these mines yourself?' asked Timon. 'You're older than he is.'

'Is it because you're a girl?' asked Garland.

'No,' Chena answered scornfully. 'But I've been in hiding with the rebels. We want to get rid of the slavery that's taken us over. We want everyone to have good chances . . . not just the powerful ones. And that's just the beginning, because there are a lot of things wrong with the world. But we're going to change everything. When we're organized, that is.'

'Yeah! Right!' said Timon rather sceptically. 'I mean – the people here don't seem to be complaining much.'

'A lot of them don't quite know what's happened to their children. I mean they know they're working in the mines, and they're starting to be angry about that. But they don't know just how they're being treated My friends and me – we're going to show them what's wrong and give them the – the *power* to fight against it,' the girl said, thumping her clenched right fist into her left palm, then thrusting it up over her head. 'Anyhow get Tarq out of here to – to some safe place. Let him join your circus and move on with you lot.'

'I don't know when we'll be able to go,' Garland said. 'They say there isn't enough oil for us to move on.'

'Well, they're lying,' Chena said, 'and I can prove it. Look, we've got to go. We've got to hide. But do you know the southern wall? Between Sector Three and Four?'

Garland tried to remember her other visits to Gramth.

'I think so,' she said a little doubtfully. She waved her hand in what she thought might be the right direction. Chena nodded.

'More or less,' she said. 'Anyhow there are signs that point the way. Meet us there in about half an hour. I'll – I'll sort of disguise Tarq a bit, and if you promise to take him, I'll show you where the oil is. Plenty of oil!'

And then she grabbed her brother's arm and they shot away down the narrow lane between the shops, while Timon, Eden and Garland stared after them, mouths open.

'Do you believe any of that?' asked Garland.

'I sort of do,' said Eden, taking Jewel back from Garland and patting her back. 'I can't help thinking this is the sort of town where the children of poor families might be somehow *used*. And as we came in there was that odd angry feeling in the people around us, wasn't there? Something's wrong here.'

'We should get back to the others,' Garland said, interrupting him. 'Quickly! We should get Yves and Bannister . . . Bannister's our strong man and . . .'

'And where are you off to?' asked a strange voice . . . a sudden gruff voice that sounded as if it belonged to someone in charge. And there beside them was a huge man in a grey uniform scribbled with golden braid. 'What are you doing in this sector? And what are your names and ages?'

He did not look like a man who would believe they belonged to the Fantasia. He did not look as if he would believe in the Fantasia itself unless he was forced to watch it perform.

'We were wondering about – about that fire over there,' Eden said quickly, pointing and then waving his right hand in rather a strange way. And sure enough, there at the end of the street flames were suddenly leaping up and a great cloud of smoke came billowing towards them. The guard stared. Then he grabbed at a whistle that hung around his neck, blowing on it fiercely as he raced away from them, vanishing into the smoke.

'Rebels!' they heard him shouting.

'Nice one!' Timon said to Eden. 'Grab Lilith and let's be off.'

Lilith! They looked around blankly. They looked around desperately. But there was no sign of her. Lilith had completely disappeared.

At the end of a long open counter with brown petticoats dangling down in front of it, Ozul and Maska were poised uneasily in front of the booth and being asked, yet again, to fill out forms . . . yellow ones this time.

'Names of course,' said the woman, seeing them hesitate. 'Names are what matters. Oh, and addresses too. And ages. And occupations.'

'Occupations!' exclaimed Maska, making the simple word sound ominous. 'How do you spell "assassin" in this part of the world?'

'Have you any identification?' asked the woman, her voice sharpening. 'Something to show you aren't vagrants.'

'We have money!' said Maska in his curious metallic voice, and, saying this, he laid a green bag similar to Ozul's bag on the edge of the little counter.

'It's true that money reassures us,' the woman said. 'Money is reliable!' Watched by both Ozul and Maska she picked up Maska's bag and emptied coins out of it. 'Goodness, what are these? I never saw this currency before.'

She slid all the coins carefully back into the bag, except for a last one which she held up to the light, turning it this way and that, studying the gleam on its surface.

Maska and Ozul both stared up at the coin as well. 'You can see it's gold,' said Ozul. Neither he nor Maska nor the woman, all intent on that single coin, noticed a hand creeping up over the counter and closing upon the other green bag which Ozul had carelessly laid there.

'It certainly looks like gold,' agreed the woman, but then she rang a bell. A man who had been watching them – one of the Gramth Aides, no less – moved towards them.

As he strolled up to the booth, Ozul let out a cry of fury.

'Gone!' he cried. 'Where is it? It was here – here beside me. And now it's gone.'

The anger of his cries echoed back from the town walls. Not only the Aide but two guards came running towards them.

'Leave us alone!' Maska shouted at them in that strange metallic voice which echoed even more strangely than Ozul's.

'Quiet. Quiet.' Ozul hissed. 'Now is not the time. Quiet.'

'Step out of the queue,' the Aide was saying. 'Other people are waiting.'

'Someone has stolen my bag,' Ozul explained. 'You!' he said, fixing his small eyes accusingly upon the woman. Then he spun around to glare at the people behind him, all of whom shrank back a step or so, looking bewildered at first and then indignant or alarmed. 'Or one of you!' Ozul cried. Some of people began protesting noisily, and one of the guards said that he had been watching them, and was sure that there had always been space between Ozul and Maska and the family directly behind them.

'We wouldn't get too close to those two freaks,' said the father of the family. 'Well – who would?'

Meanwhile, Boomer wriggled, unnoticed, from under the drapery of the long counter. He crouched for a moment among a group further down the queue, pretending to pick up something from the ground, then stood with his back turned firmly to the angry voices. At last, hooking the green bag onto his belt, he strolled slowly – casually – down the counter and into the crowd.

Garland, Timon and Eden had hurried up one street and down another.

'Lilith!' they had called desperately. 'Lilith!' knowing all the time that calling was useless. They could see that Lilith was not in the streets ahead of them. There were men and women strolling along or peering into windows, but there wasn't a child in sight.

'Lilith! Lilith!' The Gramth people stared at them as if they were curiosities of some kind. And of course they dared not shout too loudly. Guards might be listening in. Then all three of them came to a standstill, almost as if someone inside their heads had shouted 'Halt!' They were staring into one particular shop window. A sweet shop.

'Lollies!' said Timon. 'It's worth a try. Keep watch and I'll ask. She'd be noticed. There aren't that many kids on the streets here and . . .' He vanished into the shop.

'. . . and anyone would notice Lilith,' added Eden. 'I mean if they didn't notice her she'd *make* them notice her, wouldn't she?'

'I was supposed to look after her,' Garland mumbled. 'Yves will kill me.'

Timon came out of the shop once more. He looked worried.

'It sounds as if she did go in there and did buy her lollies,' he told them. 'But . . .'

'What's wrong?' cried Garland, for she could see by his face that something was certainly wrong.

'They say she was picked up by the exemption police,' Timon replied. 'You know! Those guys that tried to take us in.'

They stood there staring even more wildly at one another.

'Look! Let's take Jewel back to Goneril and then we can . . .' Eden began. Garland interrupted him.

'Wake up! We just haven't time,' she said. 'If we get in touch with that girl . . . that Chena and her brother, she might be able to tell us where Lilith is. What did she say? South wall of Sector Three and Four. In half an hour, she said, didn't she? We'd better go straight away.'

'Give me Jewel . . .' Eden began again, and Timon interrupted him.

'No way, Eden. We're not losing each other in this town. It's a real pain, carrying a baby, but I've got the sling to carry her in. When we get back to the Fantasia I'll rig up some sort of sling for you too. Then when Goneril's busy we can take turns. And Garland's right. Let's go to this southern wall as quickly as we can. Garland – you know the way.'

'More or less,' Garland said, trying not to sound too doubtful.

Then she set off with the boys at her heels, weaving her way through busy streets, trying to stay alert and to watch out for exemption guards, trying not to be distracted by glassy shop windows and trying above all to remember just how the jigsaw of Gramth worked. South! But were they really going south? When you have turned around and around a few times in a strange place it is hard to be sure of directions.

And then she felt it once more – that dizzy quivering as if a note of strange music, being played in her ear, and going through her like a silver sword. Garland also felt herself beginning to tremble a little. By now she knew what these strange feelings meant. She was going to see the silver girl. So she stopped and stood stubbornly still, staring around her, and there – *there* – beyond a crowd of jostling people, the silver girl was taking form as strange and vague as ever, not quite real, yet utterly inescapable. There was the silver girl, pointing, as she always did, at something she wanted Garland to see. Garland obediently looked in the direction in which that arrow of a finger was aiming itself, and saw a corner.

'This way!' she said, perfectly sure of herself at last. As they approached the corner the silver girl's waving changed into something else. She was still pointing with one hand and yet holding up the other. *That is the way*, she was saying. *But be careful!*

'Wait!' said Garland.

'What? Why?' asked Timon and Eden on top of one another.

'We have to be careful,' said Garland, slowing down yet still sidling to the corner. It was somehow chilling to think she might have to walk right through the silver girl, but like a well-behaved ghost the girl began to fade as Garland walked sternly towards her, then disappeared. No more silver! No more ghost!

It was just as well she had been warned. When they looked, very carefully, around the corner they saw two guards with guns and power rods, patrolling a wall. 'Sector Four' said a sign on the wall behind them.

'How did you know?' Timon asked, staring at her curiously.

'Lucky guess!' said Garland. 'But Chena wouldn't bring Tarq anywhere near those guards, would she?'

Somewhere perhaps a street away a bell rang and one of the guards straightened, put his rod of office across his shoulder and marched away in the shadow of the wall, and out of sight.

'They might have got her already,' said Eden. 'What do we do?'

The bell must have been a summons of some kind. The second guard was now marching after the first, and the children were able to see they had been guarding a space set around with posts and chains . . . and beyond this space, set into the wall, was the outline of something like a door – a door with a grille.

It reminded Garland of something she had seen in Solis – that city of unexpected wonders.

'Hey!' she said. 'I think – I think it's one of those . . . those little rooms that go up and down. An – an elevator! A lift! They were guarding the door of a lift!'

Still tingling and quivering Garland immediately walked towards that enclosed space, and the outlined door behind it.

'How did you know where to look?' asked Eden.

'Hey!' Garland said, hearing a little triumph echoing in her voice, 'you've got your sort of mysteriousness but I've got my own mysteriousness too. I'm sure – I'm pretty sure – that Lilith might have been taken down in this elevator. Don't ask me how I know. But I feel sure I do know. Let's go. Quickly!'

Eden groaned. 'What's wrong?' Garland asked.

'He gets funny going underground, or being shut in,' said Timon. 'Some people do. It's called claustrophobia. But I'll come with you. We'll check it out.'

'I'll hide up here,' Eden said, with a sigh. 'Give me Jewel and give me that sling. I'll carry her.'

'No one needs to come with me,' Garland said, though she was pleased when Timon passed Jewel back to Eden, unhooked himself from the sling and gave that to Eden too. Then he moved up beside her. They stood side by side, pretending to look around Gramth, waiting for the right moment – that moment when no one was watching or passing by.

'Now you wait for us. Hide! And watch out for those guards. We won't be long,' Garland said to Eden, but he shook his head.

'You don't know whether you'll be long or not,' he replied. She could hear a trace of desolation in his voice, probably because his older brother was about to vanish down in a lift that, for all they knew, might go down into the very heart of the world.

'We'll find Lilith – if she's there, that is,' said Timon, doing his best to reassure Eden. 'And anyway – you're the one that can come and go. Mostly I just skid along after you . . . waiting, waiting. Your turn to wait for me.' None of this seemed to comfort Eden in any way.

Garland pressed the button beside the door and the door slid sideways.

'Right! It *is* a lift!' she cried softly and triumphantly.

'Now!' said Garland, stepping into the lift and studying the buttons and levers on the control board. 'Look! This button has an arrow pointing down. Do you think . . .'

'Give it a go,' said Timon. 'After all, it can't go up unless it's able to fly in some way. There's nowhere for it to go up to.'

'I think this closes the doors,' said Garland, pressing a green button, and was gratified when the doors closed obediently, shutting out Jewel and Eden who had been staring in at them a little vaguely, as if the space inside the lift were full of dreams that only he could see.

10
Dark Happenings

Down! Down! Down!

'It goes on forever,' said Garland impatiently.

As she spoke the lift jolted to a stop. Garland turned, wondering how she was going to find the right button there in the gloom, but the door hissed at her then opened under its own steam.

'Barrels!' exclaimed Timon, and he was right. Barrel upon barrel upon barrel. 'Rails,' he added a moment later. Garland thought she could hear in his voice that he was frowning in the dark. 'Too small for train rails,' he continued; and then a moment later said, 'Cart rails of some sort!'

'It's a sort of crossroads place,' Garland added, half whispering.

They were standing in a passage. To their right a row of lamps wound away into the darkness, weak light sifting into the air around them. They could make out other tunnels, branching off from the main tunnel, and gaping at them greedily with wide black mouths.

'There's something coming,' said Garland, laying a hand on Timon's arm, and they both shuffled an uncertain dance into the shadows just before a cart, empty perhaps, or filled with something impossible to recognize, came rattling down the tracks towards them. The rattle became an embracing roar, as the sound swept around them . . . over them . . . and then moved away, growing softer with distance.

'Let's follow it,' Garland said. 'It must be going somewhere.'

'And I think there's stronger light in that direction,' Timon agreed. 'So let's make for the light. If Lilith *did* come down here that's probably what *she* did. Mind you, it's hard to believe she did come down here. This isn't a Lilith kind of place. No lollies!'

'She did,' Garland replied, trusting that silver girl. 'I'm sure she did. Maybe she was *brought* here.'

As she said this they heard – they actually heard – in the dark distance a protesting voice – Lilith's voice. It was almost as if she was shouting to them through the night of the tunnels.

'I'm not one of you. I'm part of Maddigan's Fantasia,' she was screaming.

'See? There she is,' said Garland a little smugly. 'Come on.'

It was not hard to find a way once you were used to the twilight. The line of lights reflected on the rails, and those rails, gleaming a little in the semi-darkness, seemed determined to lead them on.

'How much further?' whispered Garland, and was sorry she had asked. Her whisper, soft though it was, immediately echoed in a peculiar way, becoming a whole chorus of whispers racing ahead of them only to dive back in on them from every direction. Then, almost as if she had heard that echoing whisper, they heard Lilith begin screaming again, but much closer this time, and much more distinctly.

'Ask my dad! Ask Maddie! Ask anyone!'

This time the chorus of echoes shrieked around them, and, as it did so, they edged out into a huge cavern, its floor scribbled with rails, all twisting across one another like eels tipped out of a basket. Looming up behind the scribble, they made out an indistinct castle of square storage tanks, one on top of another, with shadowy figures moving backwards and forwards in front of it.

'Please!' screamed Lilith really close at hand now, and then a wild wailing filled the air.

'Lilith!' muttered Garland. 'I'd know that grizzling anywhere. This way.'

'This place . . .' said Timon, hesitating and looking around, 'it's a mine of some kind. Isn't it? But what are they mining down here? It looks like oil doesn't it? What's that sound?'

As he said this, a great many small blurred figures came stumbling towards them out of a tunnel to the right. It was almost as if they were being surrounded by a colony of mining trolls. But the trolls took shape as they came towards the centre of the cavern, and became a group of children, panting and straining, pulling a loaded cart along its rails. To their horror Garland and Timon could clearly see that each child was linked to the next by a large dragging chain. Looming behind them marched the obscure figures of two guards, one looking towards Garland and Timon without seeming to see them, while the other struggled with a small but furious figure – Lilith – arms and legs shooting out in all directions.

'What can we do?' Garland breathed.

'Just watch for a moment,' Timon breathed back. 'We'll try to get the hang of what's happening.'

As he spoke one of the guards said something to the other. They both laughed. Then, picking up one of the lamps, the first guard came walking straight towards them. Garland caught her breath, certain they had been seen, but the man turned off into a small passage she had not noticed until now. And as he swung into this passage, Garland noticed something else . . . heard something too. He had a big ring of keys jangling at his belt. Immediately she glanced over at the children and believed she could make out the padlocks that kept those chains fastened around them. 'Keys!' she said to Timon.

But there in the dark he was standing up, staring at the remaining guard, freezing if it seemed the guard might turn to look in their direction. Garland stood too. Gently! Gently! There must not be the slightest sound.

'I'm a Fantasia girl,' Lilith was howling. 'You'll get into trouble for this.'

However, she was sounding less sure of herself – more frightened. Garland thought she might even be crying. And then Garland was following Timon – at least she thought she was. He was making for the faint glow of lamplight edging into that small passage and Garland picked her way after him, carefully feeling for any loose stones before she put her foot down.

Suddenly the walls seemed to peel back and, abruptly, she found herself in a rocky chamber, moss growing on its uneven walls. And there was the guard, standing still, leaning back a little, and peeing against the wall in a relaxed fashion. And there was Timon, arm raised, a rock in his hand. It was hard not to shout out and warn the guard, but even if she had been silly enough to do this, Garland would have been too late. Timon banged the rock down, and the guard staggered a step or two and then tumbled sideways. Timon leaped in, tugging first at the bunch of keys hanging at his belt, and then at the thin rope that hung beside them.

'Help me,' he ordered Garland urgently. 'Have you got a handkerchief or anything? A big one?'

Garland patted her pockets.

'Nothing big. But he's got a sort of scarf around his neck,' she said, falling on her knees beside the fallen man, and struggling with the knot of the scarf. She knew just what Timon had in mind, and so, as Timon tied the man's hands and feet together, she pushed moss into his mouth and then tied the scarf tightly around it, safely gagging him.

'Bound and gagged,' said Timon, holding up the keys. 'Hey! We're quite team aren't we?'

'Quickly!' Garland said softly. 'No mucking about.'

And, side by side, they slid back down the passage, trying not to rattle the keys, and leaving the gagged guard beginning to wake and twist on the stones behind them.

Back in the main cavern again from somewhere along the gleaming line of the rail there was the sound of metal falling.

The guard who was standing over Lilith turned his head.

'Trouble!' he said. 'They will do it.' There was a further rattling and collapsing. The guard looked down at Lilith.

'Well,' he said. 'Wait for me. Not that you have any choice.' And he left her lying there, kicking her chained feet against the wall.

'You wait!' she was shouting. 'You just wait. I'll *get you.*' She shouted it over and over again although there was no way in which she could break free from the chains.

Then suddenly there was a soft thud beside her – a whisper in the air. Garland was kneeling on one side of her, Timon was standing on the other. Garland had a finger across her lips. *Shhh!*

Lilith stared as if she could scarcely believe what she was seeing.

'It is us,' muttered Garland, though Lilith could easily see who it was. Then she held the keys up and rattled them very softly.

'Pigs!' shouted a distant voice. 'Mongrels!'

'Can't be Lilith this time,' said Timon.

'It's that girl Chena . . . the one we were supposed to meet by the wall,' Garland said despairingly. 'They must have caught her . . . and her brother.'

'Beastly servants of oppression,' the faraway Chena was yelling.

There in the shadows Garland took a breath. No use trying

to fit keys into a padlock if your hand kept shaking.

'The people will rise up,' Chena was screaming in the distance. The guards were roaring back.

'The people will do as they're told,' one of them yelled.

'This is the right key,' said Garland. She turned it. There was a faint click. The chains fell away and Lilith leapt to her feet.

'Hey! This way,' Garland said, grabbing her and spinning her around. 'Look! Along here. Follow Timon.'

They set off in single file. Along that tunnel on their left they heard a voice cry out in pain. Chena was screaming, and suddenly Timon came to a standstill.

'Give me those keys,' he said to Garland. 'Listen.' They could hear voices, faint but despairing.

'I just can't – can't walk away and leave those kids here.'

'But we can't save them all,' Garland argued. 'We could get trapped down here ourselves. And then the Fantasia would have to stay in Gramth forever (because they wouldn't move on without us) and the converter would never get back to Solis and – I don't know – the Remaking would probably unmake itself.' It seemed to Garland as she said all this that the whole future of the world was depending on her. 'Isn't that more important? I mean we could come back and save them later.'

'You go on,' said Timon. 'Take Lilith with you and get up to the surface. Get to Newton. Bargain for the converter and then . . .'

'I'm not leaving you down here,' Garland argued obstinately. She listened to those faint cries and knew exactly what Timon was feeling. The desolation of the chained children was something they could not walk away from. 'Oh all right,' she said, 'let's go back.'

'No way!' moaned Lilith. 'Don't leave me.'

'We won't be long,' Timon said, though he could not possibly be sure of this. 'We'll be back for you soon. But just keep your great big mouth shut tight, or they'll quickly find out where you are.'

'Don't you dare sing,' Garland said, making a joke which Lilith did not enjoy.

And then, like blacker shadows in a world of shadow, Timon and Garland were gone, leaving Lilith waiting alone in the dark, teeth clenched, lips folded hard against each other, trying not to whimper.

There was certainly no chance that she might sing, even to raise her own spirits.

'Along here – I think,' Timon whispered. 'It's a bit hard to be sure. Listen?'

But he was right. An odd, rhythmic thudding trembled in the rocks below them, coming up through the soles of their boots and tingling in their feet. The tunnel Timon had chosen was leading to yet another of those lighted caves. The rocky roof, curving over their head was rough and low. Very few adults could have stood upright. Even Timon had to stoop a little, and Garland put one hand up to the rocks above anxious not to bang her head. They crept to the edge of that circle of light and found themselves looking in at more children, blackened and weary, linked to one another by long chains, bent over with the weight of the pickaxes with which they chipped at the walls around them. There was Tarq, and there, standing as tall as possible, was Chena.

Garland watched her throw back her shoulders, stretch herself and then lean back obstinately against the rocky wall.

'I'm not going to work for them! I'm not!' she cried to Tarq, who was hitting rather feebly at rocks which leapt mockingly away from his pickaxe rather than actually breaking.

'They'll beat you,' Garland heard him say.

'They can *kill* me,' she cried defiantly. 'I'm not working for them.'

'They might beat *me*,' said Tarq fearfully, and even in the shadows Garland could see Chena's expression change. And now Garland found herself moving forward beside Timon, hissing like a shadow given its own shadowy voice.

'It's us!' she heard herself saying. '*Shhhh!* It's us. Look, we've got the keys.'

'You!' Chena hissed back. 'How did you get here? Did they catch you too?'

But Timon was already bending over the locks, squinting downwards and struggling yet again to find the right key. Not the first one . . . not the second . . . not the third. Garland could hear the keys tinkling against one another and Timon breathing hard as he concentrated.

Suddenly someone shouted out behind them. The words came rolling and echoing out of nowhere.

'Man down! Man down!'

'They've found the guard,' Timon muttered, and as he said this the key he was trying out turned smoothly, the lock snapped open and the chains fell away from Chena.

'Get out!' Chena said. 'They'll get you next.'

But Timon, having found the right key was already unlocking Tarq's chains.

'Man down!' howled the voice out in the dark.

'Here!' said Chena. 'You take Tarq and run for it. Give me the keys and I'll try and free the others.'

And she snatched the ring of keys from Timon just as a group of guards in their blue uniforms, flourishing clubs and torches came into sight on the far side of the circle of light.

Garland ran towards the mouth of the tunnel. She hadn't asked for this, but all the same she knew it was her turn to be heroic. Those guards just had to be distracted and led away.

She danced and waved her arms.

'Hey! Over here! You stupid or something?'

'Good luck,' Timon whispered to Chena. Then pulling Tarq behind him, Timon joined Garland and they made off down the tunnel, hearing the guards coming after them, feeling the pounding of their feet beating down on the rocks as they scrambled over them.

'Faster!' panted Timon.

'Closer!' muttered Garland. 'They're closer.' For the scrambling footsteps were indeed catching up on them.

'Timon!' cried Garland desperately. 'Do something magical.'

'I can't,' said Timon. 'I'm nothing more than a trickster. Eden's the magician.'

As he said this they burst back into that wide stone hall, scribbled with shining cart rails, only to find two guards running at them from the other side, while a third followed them dragging a furious Lilith along with him.

'Are you sure you can't do magic?' Garland asked. 'We need it.'

'No way!' Timon replied.

And yet at that moment – a remarkable moment among remarkable moments – a ring of fire sprang up around the guard who was wrestling with Lilith. He dropped her and sprang away from her as if she, too, had suddenly become red-hot, while Lilith rolled over, staring around her as she rolled. Then, leaping to her feet, she pelted right through the flame towards Garland and Timon.

'What's happening?' Garland cried.

'Eden! It's got to be Eden,' Timon cried back. 'He must have followed us after all.'

The guards, shrinking back from the fire, now wheeled to face them, took a few threatening steps then hesitated.

'Leave us alone,' Timon cried warningly 'Or you'll be burned meat.' The guards stepped back, glancing rather wildly at one another and, as they did so, from beyond the flames, there came the echoing rumble of an approaching cart.

'You children,' Timon cried, gesturing to Tarq on one side of him, and then to Lilith on the other. 'Those flames won't hurt you. Run quickly – you'll be all right.'

'Quickly,' yelled Garland grabbing Tarq's upper arm. 'Do what he says.'

'Come on,' Lilith called imperiously to the others. 'Watch me!'

'She ran forward with Timon and Garland pulling Tarq close beside her just as a cart suddenly shot along the rails scattering the cluster of guards on one side of the fire and sending them sprawling. It was steered by Eden.

'Pile in! Pile in!' screamed Garland. For by now the guards, rapidly recovering from their amazement and initial fear, were picking themselves up and closing in on the cart, while the guards on the other side of the cave, overcoming their fear of fire, began running through Eden's flames themselves.

But the cart was already picking up speed.

'All right!' yelled the tallest guard in a savage voice. 'Let's see how far you get in the dark . . .'

And he swung down on a lever just at the mouth of the tunnel.

The lights along the tunnel faded and then went out altogether.

11

A Scaly Hand

In the shadow of a locked doorway Boomer crouched over the bag he had stolen from Ozul and Maska. He counted the coins out triumphantly.

'Rich!' he mumbled, scarcely able to believe in the small piles of silver coins and the even smaller pile of gold ones. He shook the bag and – small and black – a powerbook tumbled out to lie at his feet like a message folded in on itself.

Curiously Boomer picked it up and turned it over and over. After a moment his fingers touched a catch in the side and he clicked it open. It opened like a book, then the right-hand page lifted itself and somehow unfolded then unfolded yet again. Boomer found himself staring into a screen . . . and a strange screen too, for though it had a shape it seemed to have no surface. He was staring into space . . . a deep endless, seething space. Boomer blinked, and then very hesitantly put out his left hand towards it. But suddenly the space began to spin and glow. It glowed green, and a terrible voice spoke to him out of that greenness.

'Do you have them?'

Boomer was silent.

'Do you have them?' the voice repeated. 'Speak now!'

'I – I don't – I don't know . . .' stammered Boomer.

'Who is that?' asked the voice. Then, incredibly and horribly, a scaly hand thrust out through the green glow and snatched for Boomer's throat. Boomer dropped the power book and fled as if the book might put out horrible legs, (just as it had put out that horrible hand) so that it could leap after him and run him down.

'Go!' Eden was panting and the cart started speeding now . . . faster and faster along the dark rails. 'Hey! Watch out for Jewel. She's on the floor. Don't step on her.'

Timon scooped up the grizzling baby.

'I've got her. But be careful! Don't kill yourself!' he cried to Eden, and as he spoke the rails ahead of them sloped down a little, and Eden relaxed, slumping against the side of the cart.

'Here! We're coming up to the lift. Isn't that the lift door?' Garland yelled. 'Yes, there it is. Can you stop the cart, Eden?'

Eden turned, blinked, closed his eyes. Even in the twilight Garland could see the effort it was costing him. Yet the cart slowed obediently and stopped right beside the lift that had carried them down to this fearsome level – was it only twenty minutes earlier? Was it days ago? Time had stopped making any sense at all.

'Follow me!' screamed Lilith. 'I'll go first and show you the way!' and she swarmed into the lift.

'Light's coming up behind us,' Garland gasped. 'Not Eden's light. Another one. Quickly. Get it going.'

'I can't quite work it out,' said Timon, and as he said this two guards, torches and all, came charging towards them.

'I – I can't help you,' gasped Eden. 'I've used myself up. He flopped against the side of the lift as the guards came up to the open door.

They're going to get us after all, thought Garland.

'Power to the people,' yelled a voice, and Chena, together with a group of wild children armed with spades and forks, burst in on them out of the shadows. The battle was short and furious. Within a few minutes the guards had retreated, but not into silence. Somewhere beyond the space in front of the lift there came shrieks of fury, cries of dismay.

'It's started! It's really started!' Chena shouted. 'We're rising up, and this time the people out there are with us. Power to the people. Go on. On. Take Tarq. I'll follow you.

In yet another queue Ozul and Maska came at last to a desk and presented their forms yet again, only to be told they had filled them out wrongly and must go back and complete them for a third time. And now Maska drew himself up, snorting with fury. His teeth, grating against one another, sounded as if some mad machine was working inside his mouth.

'No!' Ozul hissed at him. 'No. Not yet. The time will come. The time will come I promise you. You will be able to do what you were made to do. You will get your satisfaction. But not yet.'

Maska was not to be subdued. His snarling grew more and more ferocious, making a sound no sentry could ignore. Guards left the gates and began moving cautiously but firmly towards them.

'Kill them all,' Maska was muttering through his teeth. 'Strike them out. Unmake them! We don't have to take notice of these weak toys. Delete them!'

'No! No! But the time will come,' whispered Ozul, watching the guards closing in around them. He sounded desperate. 'But not now! Maska, I stand for the Nennog so this is an order from the Nennog!'

A strange shuddering relaxation ran through Maska almost as if he might be about to fall into trembling pieces.

In the heart of Gramth the Fantasia was preparing for its evening performance, but Yves was not concentrating. Desperate about Lilith, he paced around, peering past the tents and vans at the shops around the square. Suddenly he heard a small voice calling. 'Daddy, Daddy!'

There, like a little scurrying nymph, he saw her scrambling towards the magic circle of the Fantasia. And she did not come alone, for almost immediately other children – a whole crowd of strange children, smudged and filthy – came tumbling behind her, and then, behind everyone else, almost as if they were herding them on, came Garland then Timon supporting Eden. There were sudden cries from around him . . . from other parents, perhaps, suddenly seeing once more children they had believed were lost. Garland pelted towards Maddie, shouting and pointing. 'Fuel! There is fuel stored under the town. I saw the tanks.'

'Tanks? Well, they may have been empty,' said Yves, but all the same he and Maddie turned and looked sternly towards the Aide.

'Dad! I rescued all the kids who were made to work in the mine!' Lilith was yelling. Yves snatched her up, holding her out in front of him and looking at her as if she were a beautiful picture, before he began hugging her.

Maddie grabbed Garland. 'Where have you been!' she cried. 'How did you get so dirty? Why do you always run away?' And then began hugging her too.

'We found oil! Lots of oil!' Lilith screamed. 'Barrels and barrels and barrels of it.'

Maddie straightened. Then she turned and looked at the Aide once more.

'We didn't ask for much,' she said coldly.

'It *is* ours, after all,' said the Aide, though he sounded less certain than he had sounded only a few minutes earlier. There was a murmur in the air – a murmur that did not belong to the Fantasia. 'Ours to sell at the price we choose,' he said, looking around rather wildly. 'Without argument.'

'Over the years we've been good customers,' said Maddie. 'All right! I want to see the big man – I want to see the Mayor himself.'

The Aide suddenly hesitated.

'No need,' he said quickly. 'We'll sell you what you need. But it isn't quite so easy to come by these days. Difficult times.'

'All times are difficult,' Maddie replied. 'What's been going on here? Who are these children? And what's that sound?'

It was the sound of voices . . . rising and falling . . . rising and falling.

'Our children are our business, not yours,' the Aide said.

The crowd that had been watching the Fantasia set itself up suddenly began stamping and shouting. It was as if a message were running from person to person . . . some message that excited and infuriated everyone who heard it

'Just–ice! JUST–ice! Fair! Fair! Fair! Down – down – down with the Mayor, Mayor, Mayor!'

And now the Aide was suddenly anxious to please them. But though it had been Maddie who had pinned him down, unfairly he was giving his deepest respect to Yves.

The stamping and shouting grew even louder. There was Chena, marching towards them with a crowd of children skirmishing around her and an even bigger crowd of adults behind. 'Power to the people!' she was yelling.

'Power to the people!' echoed the huge chorus behind her.

The Aide looked right and left.

'I must go,' he said in a curiously polite voice. He wheeled sharply, walked a few steps, looked over his shoulder, and then began to run.

'What's happening?' asked Maddie.

'I don't think they'll want a show tonight,' said Garland. 'I think they're putting on a show for us. But I think we'll get a bit of fuel. Probably as much as we ask for.'

'That's right,' said Timon next to her, 'I think that Gramth is going to sell you that fuel all right.'

'Or we might get fuel just *given* to us as a sort of reward,' said Garland hopefully.

'Could be,' agreed Timon. 'Either way we'll be able to hit the road again. And you are people who like to be on the move, aren't you?' he added a little mockingly.

'You want to get on too, don't you?' Garland replied, mocking in reply. Suddenly they were looking into one another's eyes and laughing.

Something stirred beside her, and Garland turned to find Boomer edging up to her . . . but this was an unexpectedly subdued Boomer . . . quiet and still when it seemed as if the whole Fantasia should be dancing and rejoicing. After all they had won out again. But Garland realized something had frightened Boomer and was still frightening him.

'Hello you!' she said, speaking sideways. 'What's wrong with you?'

'Them!' hissed Boomer, nodding over at Timon and Eden. He looked past Garland and spoke to Timon.

'He's after you.' He held out the bag he had stolen from Ozul.

'Who's after them?' Garland asked, mystified, but both Boomer and Timon ignored her. Timon seized the bag, looked sharply at Boomer then opened the bag and peered down into it. He seemed to freeze, still staring into the bag as if it held some horror like a human head. Then he reached into it and drew out something Garland did not recognize . . . a strange little screen tilted up out of an oblong black box. As Timon held it, looking as if he was not quite sure what to do with it, the screen suddenly lit up. It was turned away from her and she could not see anything it might have to show, but a green light was beating up out of it, dyeing Timon's face green as well. For one weird moment he looked like some other sort of creature altogether. For that moment he looked terrifying. But then he snapped the screen down and flipped a lid over it, and became himself once more.

'What is it?' Garland asked, but Timon did not answer. He simply let the box, with the screen inside it, along with whatever terrible images it might have shown him, drop back into the bag as quickly as if it had suddenly started to burn him.

'I stole that bag from those two men,' said Boomer. 'There was money in it and there was that little screen as well.' He fell silent and looked at Timon, licking his dry lips. 'A monster looked out at me,' Boomer blurted out at last. 'It wanted you, and it found me. It put out a claw.'

'Yes! The Nennog!' said Timon, looking over Boomer's head and meeting Garland's eyes. 'I told you about him. He's been sending a sort of ghost of himself back through time to tell Maska and Ozul what to do next. And to haunt me, I suppose.' He looked at Boomer. 'But don't worry. It's just a ghost! Green mist on a screen! He can't really come after us. His mind is strong . . . it can twist part of itself backwards through time . . . but his body is too weak to come with it. He can't be here in the way that Eden and I are here. No way! It's his men we've got to watch out for.'

Meanwhile, out at the head of the final queue, watched by suspicious guards, Ozul and Maska were passing over their new passports and entry paper. 'Right!' said the official. 'Very good! Just fill out this form.'

There was a pause as Ozul studied the man's face.

'Enough!' he said, struggling to control his anger. 'We've changed our minds. We don't want to go into your wretched town. We will wait outside.'

'Renouncing fellowship?' said the official. 'Very well if you are sure that is what you want to do. Now, if you'll just fill out this deed of renunciation . . . and then go over to queue eleven. That's the one over *there*. If you hurry there will only be a few people ahead of you.'

12

ʃInto the ʃwampland

Dear Ferdy, when terrible things turn out well we call them adventures. Back there in Gramth we had a great adventure. The thing is someone like Chena made a difference to what was going on around her. And the Fantasia people made a difference too. I don't know how Gramth will turn out . . . but it will never be the same again. When we come back again Chena might even be the Mayor. At any rate we have our fuel and that is what matters.

Anyhow since then we've been struggling for days through mists . . . just endless mists. Water everywhere and none of it fit to drink. I did warn Timon, but I don't think he believed me until we actually arrived in the swamp.

'Swamps next,' Garland had told Timon three days after leaving Gramth. She was suddenly sure of the road ahead and world around it. Great to be in a part of the country where things had held still since last time they had been there. 'Quite soon,' she added. And, sure enough, they came over a faint rise in the land, and there in front of them the river's banks somehow dissolved so that the water bled out over the land, conjuring up a kingdom of wild bogs, of soft, sullen pools lashed with dark green water grasses, and of reeds, reeds, reeds. The Fantasia people looked out over a strange greenish-brownish landscape, stabbed through and through by sudden daggers of light.

'We have to go around the swamps,' Garland told Timon and Eden, waving her hands as if she were conducting music. 'See how the land rears up over there . . . that's the mountains putting out a hand to help us . . . well, not so much to help us, but to sort of welcome us. So now we swing off towards that first hill –' Garland swung her hands again, illustrating how they must go '– and there at the bottom of the hill is the land of the Witch-Finder.'

'Witch-Finder,' said Eden uneasily. 'Sounds dangerous!' Garland couldn't help boasting. 'Our life *is* dangerous,' she said. 'No way out of it. But they're always pleased to see us over there. It's a place we can rely on. Look . . . we're making the turn.'

And Maddie's van, leading the Fantasia on its inching progress, slowly swung to the left in a half-turn as it began its long, slow trek around the edge of swamp towards the small hills and the kingdom of the Witch-Finder. On and on! On and on!

'On and on forever,' groaned Boomer. His drum was packed away at the end of Goneril's van but he pretended he was wearing it and beat the empty air. His green eyes flashed as he blinked in time to his own rhythm. 'Boom! Boom! Boom!' he chanted. 'Boom! Boom! Boom!'

As Boomer beat the empty air Garland felt as if a single chord of music had begun to vibrate, not simply in her ear but right through her. She looked left, looked right, looked back ahead, and there, sure enough, was the silver girl floating and gesturing. Her lips seemed to be moving, but Garland couldn't make out what she was trying to say.

'What is it?' Timon asked, looking at her face, then staring himself, trying to see what Garland was seeing.

'I think I got a sort of warning,' Garland said vaguely. She did not want to tell anyone about the silver girl, particularly when there was never any silver girl for anyone else to see. And it was not as if her strange vision ever lasted for long. Already that sifting shape was beginning to fade . . . to blur back into the empty air.

As if nothing had happened Garland told Timon, ignoring Boomer, 'Their town has no name. At least it didn't last time we came by. They say the Witch-Finder eats names. We just call it the Community. Look! They've seen us even though we're such a long way off. They're coming to meet us.'

And indeed a mob of people, the children in front, waving their arms and cheering, came running towards them. Within a few minutes they were surrounded by the children and then their parents, holding out apples left over from the autumn's crop, or stretching out their hands so that they could brush fingers with Fantasia clowns and acrobats.

They marched in through the gate with the ancient sign over it.

Tane read aloud with a mixture of pride and uncertainty. 'Here is the place of the . . .' He fell silent.

'Go on! Say it!' shouted Goneril. 'Don't be a wimp! Witch-Finder! That's what it says over the gate. Here is the place of the Witch-Finder.'

Tane made a gesture as if Goneril's words were troublesome flies and he had to beat them away.

'What's that place up on the hill?' asked Eden. 'Some sort of lookout post?'

'That place?' cried a girl in the crowd, looking him over with admiration. Garland found she remembered that girl from last year. Her name was Sara. 'That's the tower, that is, and the tower's full of ghosts,' Sara said with a curious note of triumph in her voice. 'That tower shines out at night. We're a special place – because the Witch-Finder lives there, these days, keeping the ghosts from coming in at us and eating our souls.'

'There's one with snapping jaws,' cried the boy beside Sara, holding up his hands, cupping them a little, then clapping them together, turning them into a greedy mouth, lunging and biting the air. 'Snapping jaws . . .'

'And claws . . .' added another boy, and suddenly all the children close enough to hear these stories began imitating a curious swaying walk, holding their hands high and hooking their fingers forward as they did so.

'Do *you* believe in ghosts?' Timon asked Garland. 'I don't. Well, we don't. Not in my time.'

'That's because you *are* ghosts,' Garland said quickly. 'Ghosts probably don't believe in other ghosts.'

Timon laughed as if he might be agreeing with her.

'Anyhow, we have worse things to worry about,' said Eden a little gloomily as if the joking was somehow turning serious, and Garland immediately felt herself turn serious too.

'I half-believe in ghosts,' she said. 'Every now and then I think I see one.' Suddenly she felt she could, after all, tell Timon about her impossible silver ghost, partly because he was wanting her to believe something impossible about himself, and partly because she suddenly wanted to hear how her haunting would sound, turned into words and let loose in the outside air. 'Sometimes I see a sort of silver ghost-girl . . . and she's always pointing something important out to me. It's funny, because she's really weird, and yet I'm not frightened of her . . . well, not exactly frightened. I don't know how to tell about the feeling she gives me. Anyhow you must altogether believe in ghosts too, because what about that Nennog of yours . . . the one Boomer saw?'

But Timon was shaking his head. 'Boomer saw the Nennog through science, not a haunting,' he declared. 'That's even worse, if anything.'

'But maybe science and ghosts are part of the same thing,' suggested Garland obstinately. She wanted to go on arguing about this, watching the way Timon's fair hair was tumbling onto his forehead, catching the light and shining with hidden gold, but Maddie's van had reached the edge of the settlement. Yves (with Lilith beside him) was already leaning sideways out of the window . . . waving . . . shouting . . . pointing.

The Community was a town of shacks and cabins built on green blisters of dry land, linked by curving bridges, with swamp mists rolling like constant unwelcome visitors down its narrow streets. The Fantasia frisked and danced over the first bridge, across the first island, over a second bridge and into a main street. The swamp deepened at that point, and water took over – spreading itself out into a little lake fringed with reeds.

On the edge of that lake a strange shape, a cumbersome see-saw of a thing, was squatting, stretching one of its arms out over the water. Garland had seen it before and it always filled her with suspicion and anxiety. There it sat, that one end hoisted high in the air, the other resting on a beach of slimy stones. The high end ended in a chair . . . a rather grand chair with armrests and what looked like a footplate with great iron boots welded onto it. It was hung around with silver chains and, for all its empty grandeur, looked particularly threatening there, squatting above the mists, but reflected darkly in the dark water below.

'What on earth's *that*?' asked Eden, staring over at this strange machine with a troubled expression.

'It's for dunking witches,' Garland said. 'They're worried about witches here in the Community. That's why they have a Witch-Finder.'

'Set up! Come on! Quickly! Set up!' Yves was shouting. Then he swung down from Maddie's van, and began walking the length of the Fantasia wagon train, still waving and yelling instructions. Lilith scrambled down too, and followed him, pointing and shouting like a squeaking echo. Garland saw her chance to have Maddie to herself for a few minutes. Tearing herself away from the boys, she swung herself up into the cab of the van only to find Maddie was preparing to clamber out. And before she had a chance to say anything much, Yves was back, looking in at the window on her side of the van, but talking past her.

'We'll do the rise-of-Solis act here,' Yves was declaring. 'There's good flat ground, and now we've got fuel for the lamps. We'll be able to make that bookshop part of the act really glow.'

'Mum,' said Garland. 'He's calling it a bookshop, but that act – well, it's about a magical library, isn't it . . . all that juggling with books that appear and disappear? It stands for dancing with wisdom. You told me it was old Gabrielle's fancy back in the beginning.'

'Yves knows all that. Right now he's only joking a little,' Maddie said. 'Come on! We need a bit of light-heartedness. The last few days have been just so difficult.'

'But he's taking over!' Garland cried, looking straight at Maddie, but pointing secretly at Yves. 'He's acting as if the Fantasia was *his* and it's ours . . . it's Maddigan's Fantasia. And he's taking you over, too.'

'Look, darling girl! I just haven't time . . .' Maddie began with something of a deep impatient sigh in her voice. 'Darling Garland – (that's "darling" twice over – I hope you noticed – I know we need to find the time to talk, but right now there's just too much to *do*. Look around you. We've just arrived in the Community. We've got to get organized – set up! It's what

Ferdy would have wanted. Just remind yourself about what you know already.' As she spoke she was moving from side to side a little, looking and listening past Garland. Her expression changed. 'Listen to that. What's happening?'

It was hard to describe what was happening. It is usually shouting that makes people look around and wonder. Silence should be safe and peaceful. But this was a twisting silence, a dangerous one. The crowd, which had been cheerfully jostling and cheering only a moment ago, had grown suddenly still. The faces around them were poised and watchful. 'I don't know,' said Maddie a little wildly. 'We've never had a journey like this before. Every town seems to be having some sort of mad trouble. What's happening to the world?' Garland turned away from Maddie and looked out from the van. People were bowing their heads a little as if they were surrendering, and making way. A single shape, a woman, was working her way through the crowd, walking towards the Fantasia . . . towards Yves who was now advancing, rather quickly, to meet this newcomer. Maddie groaned softly, then slid down and marched around the front of the van. As Garland peered out of the window Eden suddenly rose up beside her, standing on the van's running board.

'Who is *she*?' he asked, rather apprehensively.

'The Witch-Finder,' Garland answered, watching Maddie and the Witch-Finder meeting and greeting. 'In a funny way she's like the boss of the Community and she's always suspicious of us, most likely because the people here love us. We make them laugh, which brings on a bit of Witch-Finder jealousy. See that stick she is waving? That's her wand.'

The Witch-Finder was dressed in layers of crimson and gold. Her shirts and skirts swirled around her as if worked on by a wind that nobody else could feel. Those skirts were clean and shining and yet they gave her a curious, ragged look, while the long, lumpy rod she was holding in one hand (she was waving it almost like a sword) resembled a piece of polished driftwood, forked at the top like a diviner's rod, with a swollen knot just below the point where the arms of the rod divided, springing up and out as if the rod was warning the world of danger. The Witch-Finder's long fingers were hooked around that rod like claws, while in her other hand she carried a whip which she cracked as if she were herding the wind ahead of her.

'People here are a bit scared of her wand,' Garland told Eden, looking at it rather uneasily herself. A curious buzzing sound began to echo around the town. First one and then another disturbing shadow flitted out of one street only to slide into another, not so much parting the visiting swamp mists as skidding across them.

'What's that?' Eden cried. 'What are those – those things?'

The woman cracked her whip again and suddenly they seemed to be surrounded by insubstantial yet somehow ominous figures flying around them and then dissolving out of the mist once more.

'What are they?' Garland cried.

A new voice cut in on them.

'The Witch-Finder calls them "will-o'-the-wisps", but outsiders like you call them "spirits".'

Garland turned. She found she recognized, yet again, the girl who was speaking to them.

'Hello, Sara!' she said, pleased to see this friend. On other visits they had liked each other. Perhaps that was why Sara had come edging up to her. But Lilith was pushing in and interrupting in her bossy fashion.

'Are they ghosts . . . those shadowy things?'

'Sort of ghosts!' Sara began, frowning doubtfully, but the Witch-Finder was really holding forth by now, and when the

Witch-Finder talked even the gossipy Fantasia fell into careful, listening silence.

'What's she saying?' asked Eden.

'I can't understand it all,' Garland replied, 'but I think she's saying we – the Fantasia that is – are bringing something evil into their town. She says she can – I think she's telling Yves and Maddie that she can sense evil . . . that she can detect it with her wand.'

'Does she always do that?' asked Eden, turning his head away from her as if she might not notice him if he didn't look at her directly.

'No way! This is the first time!' Garland replied, feeling Eden's uneasiness in her own head, just as if it were catching. 'The first time like this, anyway.'

Now the Witch-Finder lifted the forked ends of her stick into the air. Holding it out in front of her as if she were indeed going to divine something – either water or wickedness – she touched Maddie then smiled and nodded. She moved on and touched Yves, looking at him seriously, before moving on to touch people and things as she moved by, using her wand to finger those members of the Fantasia who stood close to her. She also touched the ropes . . . touched Tane's trumpet in its black case.

Suddenly the stick began to twitch. The Witch-Finder held it higher, pointing it towards Garland. It grew even more agitated, and Garland suddenly felt terrified as if she might, after all, be guilty of some wickedness she did not know about. For, after all, these days she had her private ghost. What would a Witch-Finder make of that? But suddenly the Witch-Finder was pointing her stick towards Eden and suddenly the stick was leaping away from her, flying through the air to lie on the ground, twisting as if it were in huge pain before turning back into an ordinary stick once more. Eden jumped down from the van's running board and made for Timon, who flung an arm around him. They drew together while the Witch-Finder stared at them. She seemed frightened, and somehow the Witch-Finder's fear was even more frightening to other people than her writhing wand had been. Then she began to shout and point, and, though Garland could not quite understand what she was saying, she was sure that the Witch-Finder was ordering the Fantasia to move on immediately. Maddie watched with some confusion, turning and talking rapidly to Yves, glancing across at the boys as she did so. Yves began frowning and shaking his head. And suddenly Timon leaned forward as if he were part of the secret conversation. 'Don't give in. Stay here!' he was telling Maddie in a low voice. 'Don't move on!'

'Right! I don't see why we should be dictated to,' Yves was saying. 'Look at all the people around us. We need to *give* a show. They need to *see* a show. We've got what they want . . . what they need. What's wrong with that?'

Timon nodded.

'What's wrong with that?' Garland heard him say, like a slow, low echo, underlining Yves's question.

'What does it matter to you?' Garland called, tumbling out of the van as Timon straightened up once more. He frowned as if he wasn't too sure of himself, then slowly walked across to her, sighing and shrugging. 'I don't know,' he said. 'It was just that I – for a moment there your Witch-Finder reminded me of the Nennog in some way. It's as if she had some sort of darkness in her head, and when they have that darkness – when they lose the light – people stop seeing clearly. I think you have to stand up to them in some way.'

Eden had joined them. 'Our parents . . .' he put in, 'they saw the light. I mean they kept on seeing it. They utterly absolutely refused to give in to the darkness.'

'Your parents!' said Garland, and felt once more that stab of grief that she was getting used to by now. 'Won't they be worrying about you? Won't they wonder where you are?'

'They're dead,' Timon replied. 'I told you. Remember? Murdered I think. That's how the Nennog became our guardian. Mind you, I think he wanted Eden more than he wanted me, because of Eden's power, but he grabbed us both.'

'They were scientists – physicists, ' Eden said. 'They studied time. String theory! They were the ones that worked out a way of expanding the time pulses so that people could ride a pulse in the way we did.'

Garland did not have any idea what they were talking about, but she decided it would be better not to ask them to explain, for any explanation might only confuse her even more.

'But you've escaped,' she said. 'Not that it's totally safe here . . . the world's still dangerous . . . but . . .'

Timon sighed, shaking his head as if he had a fly in his ear.

'We haven't *absolutely* escaped!' he cried in a soft impatient voice. 'There's no *total* safety. And it's not just us the Nennog wants. Remember? It's something he calls the Talisman. He knows we've got it. *We* know we've got it. We've inherited it, but the weird thing is . . .'

'. . . the weird thing is we don't really know what it is,' said Eden. 'Our parents knew, but they never let on. They'd just look at each other and smile and call it the Talisman. "The Talisman will bring us luck" they'd say. We used to ask them what the Talisman was. "All in good time" they'd say.'

'But the good time never came,' murmured Timon. 'Not for them, anyway.'

'The Talisman! It sounds like – I don't know – a magic lamp,' said Garland. 'Or like that medallion you wear,' she added, looking at Eden. 'Maybe that's the Talisman and maybe your magic power comes from that.'

The two boys looked at each other.

'His power doesn't actually come from that,' said Timon, 'It's something from deep inside him. But we do think that medallion might be the Talisman. We do think our parents might have melted powers into it in some way. And Eden wears it, because he's got the power to protect it. Anyhow we'd do anything to keep it away from the Nennog.'

They had been standing there, guessing and gossiping, almost forgetting the dark looks of the Witch-Finder but suddenly she was striding across the circle of vans more like a wizard than a witch. Garland realized, as she watched, that she had always imagined a witch slinking in the full light of day, but the Witch-Finder swirled and blazed in her coloured skirts as she held out her wand once more – not at Eden this time, but at old Goneril. Once again the rod twitched madly. Then the Witch-Finder spun around and pointed it at Eden again, and once more it writhed.

'Demons!' she shouted. 'A witch and her demon familiar.' And, as she shouted this, there was a sudden flood of angry, hot light. A nearby barn had burst into flame. 'Demons!' shrieked the Witch-Finder again. 'I recognize them! I can feel them! I *know* them!'

There was confusion as people, including the Fantasia crew, ran to put out the fire. But a few Community women closed in on Goneril, sitting there with little Jewel on her lap – some accusing, some apologetic – while others grabbed Eden, and yet more stepped forward to keep other Fantasia people at bay. One of the women drew a knife.

'Stop!' cried Timon, ignoring it, though it looked extremely pointed and sharp. 'Don't touch him! Let him go!' But Yves, coming up behind him, seized his arm.

'We won't desert them,' said Maddie, closing in on Timon's other side. 'But we'll just take it easy for a few hours. We don't mind an argument, but we don't want a battle. Look! Goneril knows what to do. You know what a scolding old thing she can be, but right now she's going gently. Just look how calm she is and try to copy her. Be calm too.'

The Witch-Finder had now closed in on Eden, staring down into his face. Suddenly her hands shot out and clasped him around the back of the neck.

'The medallion!' cried Timon. 'She's taking the medallion!'

'I promise you,' Maddie muttered in his ear. 'We'll get it back. But if you fight now – if we fight now – we could all come to harm. And look at those people watching us. None of them are in a playful mood and our animals are out there – our jugglers and performers . . . we need to get them closed in and safe once more. Then we'll get Eden and Goneril back again. Promise!'

The little Jewel, now in the arms of an acrobat called Amy, began to cry, and Amy ran towards them.

'They say they're going to duck Goneril and Eden!' she cried. 'The Witch-Finder and her friends say she is a witch, and tomorrow morning they are going to lock her into that ducking stool by the swamp and duck her. They say it will wash the witchery out of her.'

'To the jail! To the jail!' a chorus of voices began to cry. 'We find them! We find them! We bind them! We bind them!'

And then, amid all the confusion a strange thing happened. There was a sudden soft explosion of another sort of light . . . not the light of the torches or the burning barn . . . but something coloured blue and green and gold. Up on the top of the hill the windows of that dark tower had burst into light. Looking up Garland saw vague shapes swimming backwards and forwards behind the coloured glass . . . saw shadow-shapes, mouths opening and closing and heard music floating down towards them – not complete tunes but scraps of songs and melodies that seemed tumble softly towards the crowd below like autumn leaves drifting from a tree.

The Fantasia people stared up in puzzlement and perhaps apprehension, but the people of the Community, those who were not fighting the fire, were suddenly beaten into a sort of surrender. They bowed their heads, turned their faces away and scuttled away from the Fantasia as if anxious not to be seen in dangerous company.

'The Witch-Finder is jealous of us,' said Maddie with a sigh. 'She's always been jealous of Goneril, and it goes a long way back because they knew one another slightly when they were girls – back when old Gabrielle led the Fantasia. And this time I think she's jealous of Eden's magic as well, and she's getting her own back at us by picking on Goneril.'

'But, Mum,' Garland said, 'that barn did burst into flame . . . and then that tower lit up. She's not only a witch-finder . . . she's a sort of witch herself.'

'I don't know,' said Maddie. 'Who knows who's hiding what and where? We'll give it all time to quieten down overnight. And in the morning . . . in the daylight . . . we'll begin our arguments again, and we'll buy them back. We won't desert them. You know that.'

It seemed impossible to sleep. Lying in her bunk, Garland tossed and turned then lay almost but not quite dozing. What a strange world it was, this world putting itself together after the Chaos. But perhaps it had always been like this. Perhaps there were always some people who longed to be in charge of everyone else. Gramth and its Mayor . . . and now the Community with its Witch-Finder. And perhaps small towns in an uncertain land were always frightened of the dangerous world around them. Perhaps having someone fierce in charge of them also made them feel they were being protected. Garland shook her head restlessly. She heard the wind sigh around the van and heard Maddie sigh in echo, weeping a little in the private silence of the night. But then Maddie's sighing became a steady breathing. She was asleep. Garland, however, could not sleep no matter how hard she tried. Thoughts about the wild world out there seemed to be haunting her and the night seemed to stretch out into several nights before finally she found she could see early morning staining the inner roof of the van. No possible sleep . . . not now! Garland decided to wake up properly . . . to slide silently out of her bunk, just as silently into her clothes and then (even more silently) into the outside world.

'Where are you going?' came Maddie's voice, unexpectedly. She had not been as deeply asleep as Garland had thought she was.

'Nowhere,' Garland answered. 'But I can't sleep . . . and I thought I'd get up and do a bit of work . . . rub the horses down . . . talk to Samala. I haven't been riding her much lately.'

'Keep your head down,' said Maddie. 'And Garland. No running away. I forbid it. I'll be up myself in a moment. It mightn't look like it, but I'm working already, lying here and thinking things through.'

13

Waking Sleeping Beauty

It was going to be a fine day. The sky was mostly clear – though huge streaks of cloud, lying low over the hills fiercely slashed the east with scarlet and gold. It was as if the Witch-Finder herself was somehow flying across that morning sky and setting the world alight. Garland looked around the tents and wagons of the Fantasia, and suddenly loved it all over again, for these vans and tents and even the spaces between them made up a home-town for her – a true place. She somehow felt all the Maddigans who had gone before her – Maddigans she had never met but who were still part of her even including old Gabrielle who had started the Fantasia and then disappeared so mysteriously – all moving around her, smiling, putting their hands on her shoulders and pushing her forwards. *Get going!* they seemed to be telling her.

Over in the Community she could see a few Community people stirring and beginning to go about their day-to-day lives. And there – over there – beginning to climb through the scrub that patched the lower slopes of the hill, clambering towards the tower at the top, she suddenly made out two scrambling beetles – two figures that would be largely invisible from the Community. She immediately knew who they were, even though they were too far away for her to see them properly.

Timon! Timon and (she wrinkled her face incredulously) –
Boomer! Boomer? And they were carrying something. What
was it they were carrying? Garland stared, concentrating, but
she could not work it out. However there was one thing she
knew – knew instantly. She, Garland, a true Maddigan, must
not be left out of any adventure. Climbing up the hill towards
the tower could not possibly count as running away. It was just –
just a bit of exploring.

Slipping behind Goneril's empty wagon, and then Tane's
tent, angling herself away from the Community and from the
Fantasia as well, Garland leapt through morning grasses, growing tall and tangled around the base of the hill, and then began
scrambling after the two boys, feet pushing, hands grabbing at
the tussock and the branches of scrubby trees on the sharp
slopes above her. Unencumbered as she was, she soon found
herself catching up with them, and was able to make out what
they were carrying. Stilts – Byrna's stilts. And no one would
carry stilts like those up a hill unless they were planning to use
them.

'Hey!' she called in a soft, panting voice. 'Wait . . . wait for . . .
wait for me! What . . . what are you doing?'

The boys swung around, and the stilts swung with them,
striking wildly through the air. Garland leapt back and ducked
down, even though she was in no real danger.

'What are you doing?' she repeated, gathering her courage
(and her breath) once more, and drawing alongside them.

'We're going to break into that tower,' Timon said. 'We're
going to find out what's going on in there. Well, I have to. I have
to rescue Eden. A brother can't see another brother locked into
a ducking stool and sloshed down into a swamp can he?'

'It was *my* idea,' said Boomer quickly. 'I mean, the stilts were
my idea.'

'I'll help you,' offered Garland. 'Three's the right number

for an adventure, isn't it? There's three in all the old stories.'

'Okay! Come on then! You can hold back branches and things,' said Timon, breathing hard. 'It's difficult to – you know – *manoeuvre* when you're carrying stilts.'

Together they swarmed up the last third of the hill, and suddenly there was the tower, so much bigger than it had looked from down below . . . so powerful . . . so invulnerable. Garland, Timon and Boomer stood like frozen people, staring up towards the top of the tower, then staring at each other, too out of breath to say a word. Then, still wordlessly, they leaned the stilts against the tower wall, and began to walk around the tower, looking at the stone surfaces, looking up towards the uneven summit, and testing every window of dark glass along with the two doors, both of which were closed so tightly they seemed to be sealed shut. There were streaks of light frost on the ground and on those walls, but as Garland ducked under the branches of an apple tree that grew close to the tower she saw plump spring buds waiting to break out on its bare branches. The seasons were changing places as they danced their ancient dance.

At last they came back to the place where the stilts still leaned patiently against the wall. 'Just as well we left the stilts here,' Garland said, 'or we might have walked round and round this tower for an hour without remembering where we started from.'

'Locked. All locked,' said Boomer gloomily, 'except . . .' and he pointed upward. Following his gaze Garland saw for the first time that one of the narrow slot-like windows high in the wall was tilted open – just a little bit open.

'That's why we need the stilts,' Timon said. 'I mean, I didn't know what we'd find when we got up here, but I thought it was best to be prepared, just in case there was only the one way in.'

'But Goneril and Eden aren't in there!' cried Garland.

'No.' Timon agreed. He stood there, touched by early sun-light, looking almost like the sort of fairy-tale prince a princess in a story might marry. 'But I think the answers to all the Witch-Finder riddles are in this tower. And if we can answer those riddles we might get power over her. And if we have power over her we'll get Eden and Goneril back again. Now the thing is – can we get through that window without waking her up?'

'If you could stand on the stilts I could stand on your shoulders,' Garland suggested.

'I was going to do that,' said Boomer a little indignantly.

'But I'm taller,' said Garland. 'And I can walk the tight-rope. And sometimes I've stood on Byrna's shoulders when he was stilt-walking. I can balance. I'll stand on Timon's shoulders and somehow he'll get up onto the stilts.'

'It might work,' said Timon. 'If we can hoist Garland up onto my shoulders she could put one hand against the wall to steady herself, and then I could try to get up onto the stilts. It won't be easy.' He looked at Boomer. 'If you could turn yourself into a sort of box, and I used you as a step . . . I mean I wouldn't stand on you for long.'

'Let's try,' said Garland.

Timon dropped down onto his knees, stretching his arms up to ear level. Garland took his hands, put her foot into the small of his back, hoisted herself high, then stepped up onto his shoulders with an ease that surprised her. Timon stood up, straightening very slowly, wobbling a little then growing steady enough for Garland to balance without any trouble while Boomer passed Timon the stilts. Then, rather heroically, Boomer dropped down onto all fours so that Timon could step briefly onto his arching back. Boomer grunted but held firm, as Timon, hooking up one of his long legs in a way that would have done credit to any Fantasia acrobat, placed a foot on the foothold of the first stilt.

'This is the hard bit,' he said, hoisting himself upward. He swayed; he wobbled; he took an accidental giant stride forward and nearly tumbled: he leaned back a little and it was Garland's turn to sway and gasp, bending to grab handfuls of Timon's golden hair. Somewhere Boomer groaned. And then suddenly Garland found Timon was actually standing tall on the stilts and she was standing, even taller, on his shoulders, while Boomer was rolling on the ground far below her. The open window was right beside her. Just for a moment Timon swayed backwards and forwards and she thought he was really going to topple this time, and then, of course, she would have to topple too. She imagined herself smashing down on the stony ground below them, and (up there on Timon's shoulders) half-crouched, preparing to turn her toppling into a jump. But then Timon's shoulders seemed to strengthen under her curving feet once more, and even broaden out.

'I'm going to swing around a little,' he said warningly, sounding somehow far, far below her. 'I'm going to try lifting the right stilt. Ready?'

Reaching back, Garland grabbed hold of the windowsill.

'Ready!' she said, and felt Timon swing for one dangerous moment.' But now she was facing the window and could hook one arm up over the sill, and reach in to touch the catch which was unexpectedly simple. Releasing the window and swinging it wide, she strained upwards, standing on tiptoe and then she was hauling herself up . . . up and over . . . so that the sill was at waist level. Bending forward, grunting, struggling, and using that sill as a sort of pivot Garland found herself thinking for the first time, 'I hope the Witch-Finder isn't sleeping in *this* room. I hope this isn't her bedroom.' Then she pitched forward and the floor came up to meet her before she was ready for it. She hit it shoulder first, slid sideways, scraping her ear, and for a few seconds all she could think of was how very much her shoulder and her ear were hurting.

The room was empty. Garland lay there, getting her breath again, looking sideways at a small closed door and hoping all over again – 'I hope it isn't locked.' She sat up, took a moment to rub her bruises, scrubbing at them as if pain was something that could be wiped away, then scrambled to her feet. At last she was able to look briefly out of the window, waving triumphantly to Timon and Boomer standing below her looking up anxiously. She could see them both grinning with relief as they waved back. Turning, she made for the small door on the other side of the round room. It opened easily.

Garland now found herself confronted by a narrow winding stair. She followed it down, walking as silently as she could, quite determined, yet also frightened that she might encounter, around one of those echoing curves, the Witch-Finder herself, perhaps, climbing towards her, claws raised. But the stair was empty. Two twists downwards and she found herself a room which seemed to be a space entirely used to store old toys or machines that nobody wanted any more. But there was no time to look at anything in any detail. Softly, softly, half-holding her breath, she crossed the room only to find it opened onto another small landing, to the top of another stair. Down . . . down. She must surely be at ground level now, she thought, and the door over there – that must be the door that would open to the hillside. There was a key hanging on a nail beside it. Garland took it down, slid it into the keyhole, seized it with both hands and turned it. She had imagined it would be stiff and unwilling to unlock the door, but it turned easily. The door swung open as if it were glad to be opening on an outside world.

Within a moment Timon and Boomer were crowding inside with her. The tower around them felt as if it were waiting to hear them speak, but they looked at each other in questioning silence. Garland, putting her finger across her lips, pointed up the stair behind her. Then, Garland first, Timon next and Boomer last of all, they climbed back up the lower stairs, and into that room of toys.

It was like being in a small museum, shelves filled with dolls and puppets, some bigger than life-size, teddy bears, bowling balls, yellowing photographs of places and people that might not exist any more – stiff people caught on cards that curled with age bowing the pictured people over. Standing on the floor, taking up a lot of room, were ancient pinball machines, pots that must once have held big plants or trees, and there, against one wall, a long box that looked like a coffin, with a veiled figure lying inside it.

'A Sleeping Beauty,' whispered Boomer, but Garland thought it might not be a beauty. She did not altogether want to see the face under that veil.

'Look!' exclaimed Timon softly, and both Garland and Boomer looked, in spite of themselves.

'What are they?' asked Garland, staring down at the great tray of objects that had caught Timon's attention.

'Fire crackers?' whispered Boomer.

'I don't know,' Timon said. 'They're before my time . . . before yours too probably. But I think they're weapons of some kind . . . what they used to call detonators. And I'm pretty sure that that thing under the tray – that – that's a flame thrower. And . . .' his voice suddenly changed. 'Hey! Look! Here it is!'

He was holding the Witch-Finder's wand. 'Look!' He tilted it towards Garland. The big knot at the base of the cleft was a dial. Timon touched the glass and the stick twitched wildly. 'If I just . . .' said Timon, running his fingers along the shaft.

Suddenly there was something like a loud pop. The ceiling above them lit up. A series of colours passed across it and then a series of shadows, strange and yet somehow familiar, rose up from among the couches, the pinball machines and the free-standing shelves of toys.

'Will-o'-the-wisps!' cried Boomer, too startled to bother about silence.

He was right. The room suddenly seemed crowded with will-o'-the-wisps. They were more than shadows. They had shape and form. They had glowing eyes. For all that they were not much more than ominous toys.

'Don't be frightened,' Timon told Boomer quickly. 'They're not real.' And saying this he boldly turned his back on them.

This was a mistake. Immediately one of the will-o'-the-wisps leaped at him. It was real . . . real enough to have claws with which it tore at Timon. Garland swung at it, knocking it across the room, but the other figures were now closing in on them.

'Get away!' yelled Boomer. 'Get away!' and he snatched something off the shelf next to him and flourished it at the approaching will-o'-the-wisps with all the force he could. They seemed to waver for a little but then advanced again.

'Get away!' yelled Garland and Boomer struck out with the only weapon he had – the object he had snatched from the shelf beside him. It suddenly lashed out with a long black tongue. Boomer flung his arm up and down again.

CRACK!

Garland and Timon leaped at the sound, then looked at Boomer incredulously. But he was looking at his own right hand with even more astonishment. He had snatched up the Witch-Finder's whip.

CRACK!

The will-o'-the-wisps stood still. Garland thought they were looking at Boomer with a kind of obedience, waiting for him to tell them what to do next.

And then there was another sudden movement – a terrifying one. Garland thought she might die of fright. The figure in the coffin sat up, the white veil falling away from its strange face. It raised its arms and held them high. It had claws not hands. Its carved face was the face of a demon. It swung itself sideways and stood up. Then, holding its claws high it advanced upon them. Boomer ducked down. Garland dodged, but the Sleeping Beauty, sleeping no longer, seized Timon and began to dance with him.

'That switch!' hissed Timon desperately as Garland snatched the rod from the floor where he had dropped it, and stared down at the dark wood. There below the dial, barely visible, she made out two buttons set into the shaft. She pressed one . . . and suddenly the whole room seemed to come alive. The great dolls, heads lolling as if their necks were broken, began an ungainly waltz. She pressed the other and the Sleeping Beauty flung its arms wide, releasing Timon who rolled away, then leaped to his feet and made for the top of staircase. But Garland now found that, by pressing the buttons, she could control that clawed dancer. She could make it turn left and right, make it spin and bow. She directed it towards the window. As it turned it swept the curtain aside.

'It's morning!' shouted Boomer, so taken aback by the sunshine that now burst in on them, that, once again, he forgot to whisper. And a moment later the sound of shattering glass filled the room. Due to some accidental movement of Garland's, the Sleeping Beauty had dived through the window. Running to stare down after it, appalled at what she had done, Garland found she could see it somersaulting down the slope over and over to the edge of the water where a whole group of people had gathered.

'Look! It's Goneril. They're going to duck Goneril,' said Timon. 'They've got her tied to the ducking stool. The Witch-Finder must be down there already. Eden too! Come on! At least we can prove that the Witch-Finder isn't magical. We can show them the wand is – well, some sort of radio-controlled thing.'

However Garland and Boomer were swinging the door wide.

Down at the water's edge Maddie was standing between the Witch-Finder and the ducking machine, arguing with the Witch-Finder, gesturing as if she were writing orders on the air in front of her.

Yves was standing at her shoulder, ready to move in, but Garland could tell he was only waiting to see if Maddie could talk the Witch-Finder into bringing Goneril down. If Maddie did not succeed he was prepared to lead Tane, Bannister and indeed the whole Fantasia into battle.

'All witches must be put to the test.' The Witch-Finder was crying furiously.

CRACK!

A few people started and looked around.

'She's not a witch . . . she's our Maddigan grandmother,' Maddie was crying back, glancing up at Goneril. 'She looks after our little children. She's got a kind heart.'

'Duck her!' yelled someone in the crowd.

'Oh no,' said Maddie. 'I'm in control of your horrible machine and she's not coming down until you promise me it's safe for her to come down.'

CRACK!

More heads turned, for how could the Witch-Finder be cracking her whip when she was standing there by the ducking machine, both hands empty.

'Look at the tower! Look at the tower!' someone began shouting, and all the Community people looked up, amazed to see the tower flashing with light and giving off sparks as if it were burning.

'Dunk her! Drown her!' shrieked the Witch-Finder, trying to get the crowd to look back at her, desperate to take charge once more.

By now most people had stopped listening to her.

Down the hillside came a terrible untidy procession of dark shapes. Will-o'-the-wisps, arms raised, came sliding towards the water. And in front of the black will-o'-the-wisps came the broken marionette, now headless, but still waving its wild claws, while Garland danced beside it, waving the wand. Press the top button and up went those snapping claws into the air. Press the bottom button and the arms fell to its sides. Push the top button to the right and the marionette danced right. Push it left and then up and it swung left, clacking its claws savagely. Timon and Boomer came last of all, like shepherds directing a wild herd towards the water.

'What have you done?' shrieked the Witch-Finder. 'You have released the will-o'-the-wisps.'

Boomer swung away from Timon, and came leaping past the will-o'-the-wisps towards the astonished crowd.

'It was all tricks!' he began shouting. 'That isn't a true wand. That thing with claws isn't a monster. It's just a puppet and we can make it dance. Look at it.' He turned. 'Make them dance!' he shouted to Garland. 'Make the will-o'-the-wisps behave themselves.'

CRACK! Timon stepped off to one side and cracked the whip. The will-o'-the-wisps stood still. One or two of them lolled a little. Garland held up the forked stick and the clawed creature danced obediently.

'And if you can make a monster walk with a wand like that one!' yelled Timon, panting and talking past Maddie and Yves to the Community people beyond. 'I think you could set fire to a barn from a distance.'

The marionette, still waving its claws, came up behind them. Garland turned and hit at it with the wand that she held. It crumpled sideways and lay there, twitching, looking ridiculous now rather than frightening.

The Community people looked at the twitching doll, lying in the tussock, snapping its claws at the empty air, then over at the lolling will-o'-the-wisps, then up at the tower, still trembling with its coloured lights, and then, rather more darkly, at the Witch-Finder.

CRACK! Suddenly the will-o'-the-wisps were on the move again. Timon seemed to be herding them towards the Witch-Finder herself.

'What are you doing?' she screamed.

'Giving you a taste of your own medicine,' cried Garland.

'Stop! Stop!' the Witch-Finder screamed as the will-o'-the-wisps began edging her towards the green grubby water of the swamp. Goneril looked down from high in the ducking stool as the Witch-Finder was edged into the water, through the cresses . . . deeper . . . deeper.

'Leave her!' shouted Goneril. 'She's just a silly old woman. Leave her alone!'

So Garland swung the rod she was carrying, striking out at the nearest will-o'-the-whisp. Its black head leapt off, looping through the air as if it had a life of its own and as if it knew exactly where it was going. It fell, rolling, among a group of Community people, all of whom shouted and shrank away from it, as if it might snarl and bite them, but the head merely rolled over until it struck a tussock where it lay, staring up with its wild red eyes. After a moment one of the men picked it up . . . a round head, red eyes blinking and fading, wires dangling down below it.

'It's just a robot,' Garland explained. 'They're all robots powered by a – a –'

'– generator!' shouted Boomer. 'Up in the tower!'

Timon helped the Witch-Finder to her feet once more. She stood beside him wordlessly, staring at Yves, at Maddie, at the whole Fantasia. At last she looked back at Garland, but still had nothing to say. Garland caught a glimpse of silver around her neck. She was wearing Eden's medallion.

'And now we want Eden back,' said Timon, shaking the Witch-Finder's arm. 'We don't mean you any harm. Just bring Eden back . . . the boy. The magical boy!'

'And bring Goneril down from that perch up there,' said Maddie, cutting in quickly.

Unexpectedly the Witch-Finder grinned at them. 'You think I can't make these fools turn on you?' she murmured. 'Their fear of me is so ingrained by now that doubting me will tear them apart. Look around. Even now – even with the evidence in front of them – they don't want to believe you.'

Timon took something from one of his pockets and showed it to her.

'See what I have here?' he asked her. 'A detonator. You burnt that old house yesterday, but we – we might burn your tower up there.'

Garland put out a finger. 'If I press this button here . . .' she said.

The Witch-Finder buried her face in her hands for a moment, but now she looked wildly up at Goneril. 'Bring her down!' she shouted. 'Now!' Then she signalled to one of the Community men who nodded twice, turned and vanished. And within five minutes Goneril was on solid ground once more and shortly afterwards Eden was back with them.

Lilith flung herself at him. 'I rescued you!' she cried dramatically. 'The Witch-Finder has been tricking everyone but I was too clever for her.'

'I knew you'd find a way,' Eden told her. 'I even slept well.' But, as he said this, he was looking over her head at his brother, at Garland and at Boomer.

'Good for you,' said Garland. 'We didn't.'

Timon put the whip into Eden's hand, then nodded in the direction of the Witch-Finder.

'How about a swap!' he muttered. 'Just suggest it.'

Eden nodded, turning to the Witch-Finder. But she was already holding out his medallion. Eden took it and carefully hung it around his own neck then handed her whip.

'What is it, though?' asked a voice. 'What's going on?' Garland turned to find the girl Sara standing there, looking puzzled. 'Why are things changing? What's happened?'

'Well, that tower wasn't haunted,' said Garland. 'The Witch-Finder made you think it was, because she found a way of filling it with strange dolls and toys that moved. I think they must be things left over from the days before the Destruction. And she found a way of moving them, a really old, ancient way. But they worked by a sort of – well, a sort of science I suppose. Nothing to do with hauntings or ghosts.'

'No ghosts?' asked Sara incredulously.

'No ghosts!' Garland repeated.

'Everyone set?' Yves was calling. 'Come on everyone. Let's get back onto the road.'

'Aye!' Garland heard a dozen voices reply, but she kept watching Sara, waiting for her to look free from hauntings – relieved – even happy.

As Sara stared up at the tower a strange, obstinate expression crept slowly across her face.

'You don't know!' she said. 'It *is* haunted. The Witch-Finder's just tricking you all over again.'

Garland felt her own face wrinkling with astonishment. 'Aren't you pleased?' she asked incredulously. 'Aren't you glad not to be haunted.'

'We *are* haunted!' Sara declared obstinately. 'We *are*!'

Garland opened her mouth to argue again, but a hand fell on her shoulder and a voice muttered in her ear.

'Forget it,' Timon was saying. 'OK, so she's scared of the ghosts, but they're what makes her town special. They frighten her but I don't think she wants to give them up.'

'All's well!' Maddie was shouting to the whole Fantasia through the window of her van, and Yves was echoing her.

'All's well, but back to work! On to the next place.'

Sara turned and stalked haughtily away.

Boomer, shooting around on his bike, tried waving to the people of the Community, but they turned their back on him, and as the Fantasia moved on, leaving the Community, they moved on in silence.

So strange, Ferdy, it is so strange. People sometimes just fall in love with dark ideas. Sara was frightened by ghosts but at the same time she wanted ghosts. Ghosts made her town seem special. Dark ideas grow and grow and somehow wrap themselves around people's thoughts. Somehow there has been something dark going on in every town we have travelled through. Is it just a sort of coincidence. Or is it the way people are ... not all people of course ... just a few. And perhaps the few dark ones somehow become powerful because of their darkness. Maybe you could tell me. I wish we could talk about it Anyhow we've got to press on ... press on to get that converter thing and get back to Solis. I always think of Solis as a bright city, so if Solis survives a thousand false witches will bite the dust.

Looking sideways through the van window up at that distant hill she could see the tower – still and dark now – and thought she could make out a figure standing at one of the windows – the very window she had tumbled through only a few hours earlier. But perhaps she was wrong about that. After all, it was a long way off by now. Perhaps she just had a picture of that window and that dark figure in her mind.

14

Fantasia Fever

I know you're there, Ferdy, reading what I am writing now. I know that nothing I write is certain. I've seen the words swim about the page like fish and Timon and Eden say that words alter if someone changes the past. If someone changed the past so that there were no wars, no plagues, none of that great Destruction, none of the Chaos, none of our Remaking, what I am writing now would somehow change. Mind you my idea is that the Fantasia would stay more or less the same. Bad times – good times, people would still laugh at the same things and be amazed at the same things. Because somehow something deep in the world stays true, doesn't it? Because one way and another the Fantasia still here and still going on.

And we're in South, which is called South because once it was south of a bigger place which isn't here any longer. We arrived here with stuff to trade and we thought people in South would want to trade too. But what they have to pass on is a sort of sickness. Get going quickly, said Yves, when he realized how serious it was, but by then some of us had the South plague . . . it must be very catching. Tane fell ill so quickly he must have breathed it in before we even arrived. And then there was the rain . . .

arland stopped writing and looked through the van window . . . through the rain and out into even more rain. Some drops bounced up from the mud, others sunk into it. She felt that Doom was grinning back at her . . . Doom, a dark and bony dancer, leaping and twisting between the Fantasia vans. They should move on. They *must* move on. At the same time Garland knew that moving on was as unwise as staying still. 'We should keep on the high ground until the rain is over,' Yves had said to Maddie. 'You know that.'

'Some of us think it's worse to stay on here,' Maddie had answered. 'Tane's not the only one who's caught whatever it is that's out there. That little one – Jewel – she's ill too, and Goneril will probably be next. Because she's taking care of the sick ones. She must be breathing in the bugs.'

'We stay here,' Yves had said obstinately, and Lilith, standing at his elbow had beamed up at him, proud of having a father who was in charge. 'They say Jewel's got great big red boils all over her,' said Lilith sounding horrified, but interested too. Though she was frightened of what was going on she was somehow caught up in the adventure of it.

'Well, it's not true,' Garland said sternly. 'The sick ones are just lying there terribly hot and feeling all dizzy. It's really awful for them. They might die.'

Remembering her own words, Garland frowned and sighed, and then, hearing a step out at the front of the van (a step too light to be Maddie's), she hastily pushed her diary out of sight just a moment before Lilith appeared. Without being invited, Lilith flopped down on Garland's own bunk bed, spreading herself out as if the bunk was really hers.

'Rain's boring,' she said.

'Is it getting any better?' asked Garland.

'No,' said Lilith. 'Wetter and wetter, not better and better.'

Then she laughed, looking over at Garland to make sure Garland was laughing too.

'Ha! Ha!' Garland said, sighing inside herself. She did not want to hurt Lilith's feelings . . . but she did not want to have Lilith sitting beside her watching her . . . spying on her, almost . . . and trying to talk or play with her. She picked up a nearby book and pretended to read.

'I can read,' said Lilith immediately. 'My father taught me.' Garland nodded. 'Did your father teach you?'

'My father *and* my mother,' Garland mumbled.

'It's funny,' Lilith went on, 'you having a mother but no father any more, and me having a father and no mother.' She was not asking a question, and yet, when she paused, Garland could tell Lilith was expecting some sort of answer. Garland remained silent. Being silent was like some sort of loyalty to Ferdy who seemed to have been so quickly left behind and forgotten. Silence was often all she had left to offer him.

And suddenly Garland felt she could not bear to lie there pretending to read while Lilith, who was so much younger and who just could not be expected to understand Garland's sadness, tried to match up Yves with Maddie. She leapt to her feet.

'Rain or not,' she said. 'I'm going out. I'm going to check on Goneril.'

As she pulled on her sheepskin coat (woolly side in, skinny side out) and jammed a sheepskin hat down over her ears. Lilith leapt up too, utterly determined that Garland should not leave her on her own. As Garland pushed her hair in under her hat, Lilith danced from one foot to the other, glad to think that something was happening, even if it was only a walk between one van and another.

Outside the rain was coming down . . . not fiercely but steadily. All around them the land drank until it could drink no more, after which it pushed the water out and away, forming great puddles, and thin streams which tangled together like silver strings – like the roads of the land.

'The weather's being mean to us, isn't it?' Lilith cried.

'Not just us,' Garland said, sighing. 'It's being mean to anyone who's out in it.'

And other people were out in it too.

The rain came down and the wind blew. Maska's horse suddenly struck a soft pocket of mud. Its legs sank deeply . . . it rolled its eyes and put it ears back. Ozul dismounted and sank into the mud himself.

'This time! This place!' he said bitterly. 'This wretched time! This horrible place! Why did it have to be here? Now?'

'We can't go back,' said Maska in his curious voice. 'The place is a horrible place, but it is the right place.'

'They must have gone this way,' Ozul persisted. 'Look! Wheel tracks . . . hoof marks! If we hadn't been held up in that wretched town . . . and taken the wrong road . . .'

'We can't go back,' repeated Maska. 'We can't go back without the Talisman, or the Nennog will delete us. At least rain is better than deletion.'

'Oh, no doubt about that,' agreed Ozul, and then spoke to Maska's horse. 'Up! Up!' And the horse did come up onto wet, slippery but solid ground once more. 'Onwards then!' ordered Ozul, mounting own his horse. And on they went, following, always following, the dissolving trail of Maddigan's Fantasia.

As they came towards Goneril's wagon, Eden loomed up in the doorway, and Lilith made a sound of pleasure. Company, she was obviously thinking, bored with Garland, though not totally ready to let her go. Garland looked towards Eden, knowing he was worried about his little sister in an ordinary brotherly way, yet it was hard to think of him as anyone's ordinary brother. He still looked like some sort of young tree given a human shape but without entirely giving up its gentle twiggy look. Lilith fluttered backwards and forwards in front of him like a butterfly, looking for a place to perch and open its wings.

A hand fell on Garland's shoulder. Both Lilith and Garland turned, squinting up through the rain to see Yves, coated and booted, standing behind them.

'No,' he said to Lilith. 'No going inside that wagon.' He looked at Garland. 'They're sick in there . . . Tane . . . the little one. Keep away, both of you.' He said *both* of you but it was Lilith he guided away. 'And your mother certainly doesn't want *you* going in there,' he told Garland, speaking back over his shoulder. And she doesn't want you running away either, so even if we aren't moving on in the usual way, just be patient. Stick around. You're keen on reading, so read some good book or other.'

Garland immediately decided to show Yves that she didn't have to do what he told her to.

Though she had not really intended to go into Goneril's wagon, merely to ask through the door about Jewel, she now put her foot on the wagon step, and swung herself up beside Eden.

'We're not to go in,' said Eden. 'They're all sick in there. Well, all except me and Boomer. We're helping Goneril . . . running errands, bringing water . . . all that sort of thing.'

'Who is it?' called Goneril from somewhere inside, and then the curtain across the door wavered and there she was, Goneril, balancing beside them, breathing deeply as if breathing was something she had just learned to do, and coatless but seeming to enjoy the feeling of rain blowing in at her.

'It's the same thing with both of them,' she said. 'And with old Shell now.' She looked down at Eden. 'Your little sister is very ill I'm afraid, and I can't do anything about it but keep her warm and make sure she drinks a lot. Once they had ways of curing all kinds of illness but most of those cures are lost in these times. We've nothing left but stories. Stories! You know, once upon a time, actually not too far from here now I come to think of it, there was a man called Pokka who had a theory of how to make everyone well. Pokka's Theory. It's in the stories. When I was a young thing travelling with the Fantasia, and Gabrielle Maddigan was in charge, I can remember voices, all up above my head, talking about Pokka's Theory. Well, we need Pokka right now . . . and not just his theory. We need his tonic. If ever he had one, that is. Now, off you go.'

And at that moment a bell rang. They were being called for a Fantasia parley. Everyone gathered quickly, jamming together within the circle of vans . . . clowns and acrobats, riders, jugglers stilt walkers, men, women and children all wearing coats and hats and boots. The rain patted them gently, bounced off or ran down them in little trickling streams to drip into the ground around their booted feet. Yves stood at the front of Maddie's van. Garland edged up beside him and heard him talking to Maddie in a low urgent voice.

'Every day we stay here,' he was saying 'is a day lost and not only a day lost. It's another day for the sick to infect the healthy. You saw what happened in the South. They were all dead.'

'What's happening?' asked Garland. She knew Yves was about to make something happen and she wanted to argue about it, whatever it was.

'Nothing,' Yves said. 'Well, I'll tell everyone really soon.'

Garland turned away impatiently and just for a moment, though the whole Fantasia was pressing in around her she felt she was on her own. And then as she turned she felt once more that strange vibration. Each time she felt it seemed she was feeling it for the first time. But by now she knew just what to look for.

So she did look . . . looked left . . . looked right, and (looking right) saw that wavering girl shining faintly through the drizzling rain . . . her own silver almost hidden by the silver of falling rain.

Garland glanced sideways. Eden was standing next to her, and staring blankly in exactly the same direction as she was, but he did not seem to be able to see anything unusual. Penrod came hurrying up towards the parley, and hurried right through that silver ghost without appearing to notice anything unusual. *But I see you. I know you*, thought Garland. *I've known you for ages – known you when you were weren't silver. But where? When? Why has everything gone so strange?*

The silver girl was holding up her hand. Garland leaned forward a little, staring. She was being shown something.

At that very moment, somewhere far beyond them, clouds must have parted and a beam of watery sunshine shone down through the fine rain. The girl was holding up a blue jar, trying to fix Garland's attention on it. The girl and the jar shone out with blue fire, wavered and then grew faint in the pale sunshine. Suddenly the jar looked like a blue star, held in the fingers of a silver spirit. And then a voice cut into her moment of vision.

'Now listen here,' Yves was saying, and they all listened. 'We've got a sickness riding with us,' he said. 'It's not the first time it's happened and it won't be the last. The question is, what do we do about it? I don't think there's time to stop and nurse the ones that are ill. And besides, those who are ill will only infect the rest of us. And besides *that*, we're going to need people to help shift the heavy vehicles, and you can't do that if you're beginning to feel all hot and faint. So those of us who are well must move on . . .' Garland let out a cry. She heard her own voice as if it belonged to someone else. 'No!' she was crying. 'That's not the Fantasia way. We've got to stick together.'

Some voices cried out, agreeing with her. Others backed Yves. Yves began shouting. Maddie shouted too.

'Look! Hey! Quiet there!' Yves held up his hands. 'Listen! It's not just us. Nothing's simple. We're running this errand for Solis, remember, which is like running an errand for – well, for what's left of civilization, and we count ourselves as being part of civilization, don't we? Suppose we stick together and we all die together – who's going to take the converter back to Solis? Do we run the risk of having every Maddigan fade into nothing? I wonder what old Gabrielle would have to say about that?'

Arguing voices crossed and clashed like battling swords. But now Maddie was leaping up beside Yves. 'Listen! Listen!' Maddie yelled. 'We can't deny the sense behind the things Yves is saying, but it doesn't have to be just one thing or the other. Some of us will move on and some will stay behind to support the sick and to move on more slowly when the chance comes. We'll arrange a catch-up point down the road. And we'll try to keep a bit of space between our two halves so the disease can't jump from the sick ones to the rest of us. That's practical, right?'

And that's what was decided – partly because it made sense, partly because it was Maddie speaking and, after all, Maddie was a Maddigan.

A little while later Bannister came over to Goneril's wagon with a book in his belt, and his hands filled with maps . . . and copies of maps. 'I think you know this part of the country pretty well,' he said to Goneril. 'Better than that lot over there,' and he nodded at the wagon next to them. 'They're beginners compared with you. Now – it's straightforward until you get to Greentown. After that . . . but anyhow we'll be in Greentown for a day or two. We'll be waiting for you. And I've copied these maps as well as I can so – just in case you need them,' he said.

'I'd like to stay on,' he added awkwardly, 'but they're going to need all the muscle they can get if they strike mud. And we'll mark the difficult places with flags so you can go round them if you follow us – I mean *when* you follow us.'

Maddie came charging across to Garland.

'Come on,' she said, 'you don't have to stay. You come with me.'

Garland took a breath. 'I'm not going,' she said. 'I'm staying here. You're doing what Yves tells you to do, but I'm staying with the deserted ones. Boomer's helping Goneril, and I can too. I'm the true-born Maddigan. You're only a married one.'

Maddie looked furious.

'Well, why do you do everything Yves says?' Garland cried quickly. 'Anyone can tell he's more interested in saving himself and Lilith than he is in saving the Fantasia.'

'None of this is fair, Garland. Yves listens to me. And right now, I haven't got time to argue,' said Maddie. 'Yves is a good man and I don't care what you say – he's keen on saving the Fantasia, too. Why wouldn't he be? He makes his living being a Fantasia man.'

'Old Gabrielle would never split the Fantasia in two.' Garland was almost weeping. 'She'd never desert Fantasia people just because they were sick.'

'We're not deserting them,' said Maddie. 'We're just putting the sick ones at a bit of a distance so that the rest of us don't catch the plague. And I *am* a true Maddigan too, even if I wasn't born one. Listen! Old Gabrielle once said, "The Fantasia must move on". So it must, and we must move with it. And we must earn our way . . . and we must entertain this battered old world. There's places out there that struggle to survive and we *help* them survive by bringing a bit of wonder and laughter into their lives. They need that wonder. They need to laugh. All this fuss you're making is because you think I don't miss your father. Well I do. Every moment when I stand still and look around me I miss him dreadfully. And every moment when I'm working (which is most moments) I feel him there, standing beside me, cheering me on. He was a Maddigan and he would *want* me to keep things going – so keeping those things going is my way of keeping part of him alive.' She looked left, looked right, turned and looked behind her. 'Garland! I just can't stand around arguing about this. Get into the van and we'll be off.'

'Boomer's staying. Timon and Eden are staying . . .' Garland said, suddenly torn. 'Tell them to come too.'

'The little one in Goneril's wagon is their sister,' Maddie said. 'They've got the right to stay. But you haven't.'

So the Fantasia splintered. Timon and Eden watched wagons trail off into the distance . . . and then, just as they were about to turn away, Timon grabbed Eden's arm.

'There!' he exclaimed. 'Look there!'

Someone had dissolved out of the last van . . . or perhaps had merely leapt through its back door. It was hard to say, but someone was certainly running back towards them.

'It's her,' said Eden. 'She's coming back to us. Why?'

'She must think it's the right thing to do,' Timon said. 'She's running fast. We'll be able to ask her soon.'

'She likes you,' said Eden, and there was a faint note of mischief in his voice.

'That's all right!' said Timon. 'She likes you too.'

'You know what I mean. She likes you and you like her,' said Eden nudging his brother in a way that made Timon grin in a silly shy fashion.

And ten minutes later, Garland, her red hair flaring out around her, her bow across her shoulder, a sheath of arrows at her belt, came cantering up to them, panting and triumphant.

'Maddie will be really angry with me,' she said. 'She'll be absolutely furious. And I would have gone with them – but back there a bit I had a vision. You aren't the only ones to live strange magical lives. I had a vision of – well, that's my secret. Anyhow I think it meant me to stay here and try to find something.'

The rain had stopped. The clouds were disappearing. However the mud remained. Eden sat at the front of Goneril's van, idly studying the maps which Goneril had tucked under a box on a ledge just inside the door, while beyond him Goneril bent over the restless Jewel, who was whimpering and struggling against the blankets. And on beyond in two other bunks lay Tane and old Shell, quite still, though their hoarse breathing made it sound as if they were working hard. At the very back of the van Goneril had made a bed on the floor for Nye, and Boomer was filling Nye's water bottle.

'You should sit outside,' Goneril told Eden sternly. 'You too, Boomer!' She straightened. 'Oh dear,' she said.

'What's wrong?' Eden asked, looking at her with a deepening alarm. 'Is Jewel worse?'

'No – she's no worse, but I don't feel so well myself,' Goneril said, sounding very tired. 'Only to be expected, but . . . anyhow you young ones get outside. Breathe in a bit of fresh air. Get as much of it as you can.'

Eden was the last to leave the van. He climbed down the steps, one of Bannister's maps folded in under his arm, then looked around for the others. Boomer, Timon and Garland had moved a short distance away, and were standing, staring out towards a distant rise. Something was moving on the bare flank, golden with tussock . . . a distant caterpillar was crawling across it.

'There they go,' said Timon. He nudged Garland. 'You should have gone with them. I mean – really you should have!'

'There was something about my vision,' said Garland. 'It seemed to be showing me something I should watch out for and I felt that this was the place I should start my watching from.'

'Well, *I've* got something to show you,' said Eden. His teeth were chattering a little as he spoke.

Timon looked at him in sudden alarm. 'You!' he said. 'You've got it too.'

'Yes,' said Eden. 'But I want to show you this, it's utterly, utterly important . . . I think.' His voice trailed away doubtfully.

'Well, go on! Tell us,' said Timon. 'Quickly!'

Eden took the map from under his arm and began unfolding it.

'Remember Goneril talking about something called Pokka's theory . . . some cure that could be found in this part of the country?' he asked.

'Yes,' said Garland. 'Have you found it written on that map, or something?'

Eden sighed and shivered again. He took a deep breath. The paper rattled in time with his shivering as he held the map out. 'I was looking at this map,' he said. 'See? Not very far from here there's a place called *Apothecary's Nidus.*' I don't know what a *Nidus* is but – Pokka's Theory – Apothecary! It sort of matches up, doesn't it? Echoes! And an apothecary is a sort of doctor – right?'

'Hold it still,' said Timon gently. He took the map from this brother's trembling fingers. 'Where are we now?'

Garland peered at the map. 'There, I suppose,' she said, pointing. 'There's a crossroads there and the river runs beside the road. But what's a Nidus?'

'I don't know,' said Eden again. 'I'll leave it to you to work out. But I have to sit down . . . I have to . . .'

Timon took his arm. 'Let's get you inside again,' he said, and he helped his brother back towards Goneril's van leaving

Garland staring at the map. She had never seen it before – maps were always the business of the mapmaster – but she had a curious feeling of recognizing something. It was as if somewhere, somehow, someone had already shown her this particular map and pointed out to her the Apothecary's Nidus. At the same time she knew she had never really seen it before.

Timon came back, frowning and screwing up his face.

'Not good!' he said. 'Nidus. I think it means something like a nest – a place of beginning.'

'You think you know everything,' said Boomer.

'Back in my own time . . . I mean on ahead in my own time . . . I read a lot of old books,' said Timon.

'No arguing,' said Garland. 'Let's go. Because an apothecary was a sort of doctor, right? And we need a cure. I don't mean we're going to find one, but now there's this name on the map and the vision I told you about. They might not mean anything. But then they might.'

'It looks as if there must have been a fire going when they drew this map,' Timon said. 'Or fires. Look. That's supposed to be smoke, isn't it? Smoke here. Smoke there!' He hesitated, twisting the map around. Then he pointed ahead. 'Over there!'

'There *is* smoke there,' said Boomer uncertainly. There was certainly a pale haze smudging part of the land on the other side of the road.

'That's not smoke. It's mist,' Garland. 'It dips down a bit over there so it might be boggy.'

'It's not boggy,' argued Boomer. 'There are rocks poking out everywhere.'

'It might be boggy between the rocks,' Garland argued back.

'No fires in sight anyway,' cried Timon. 'Let's go!'

So they leapt across the road, Timon bounding like some sort of golden-headed deer, while Boomer came stumping along at Garland's elbow. They jogged across an open patch of grass and weeds, and suddenly they came on an unexpectedly deep crease in the land. They dipped down into it and wound between the rocks, looking like ghosts to one another in that filmy air. And as Garland walked along she had an odd feeling. A curious warmth was coming in through the soles of her boots and creeping up her legs.

'This path seems sort of *hot* doesn't it?' she complained, lifting her feet higher than was quite usual. 'And doesn't it *smell* funny?'

'But you did say this was the way to go,' said Boomer. He was bending over and feeling the ground. He looked up, with an expression both incredulous and frightened.

'Hey, you're right,' he said. 'This ground *is* hot.' Then he yelled, 'Look! Over there. It *is* smoking. That mud there! It's – it's boiling.'

And as he said this there was a furious hissing and a huge wild sigh. A fountain of steam burst from the ground almost at their feet, and they raced away wildly.

'This way! This way! There's a track here!' Garland shouted . . . but a moment later, fountains of steam and hot water seemed to burst up around them again, smudging the path ahead and making it difficult to be sure of any direction. Boiling mud and water began to rise up between the rocks. Beating at the steam as if it were some kind of curtain she might push aside Garland was aware of Timon at her shoulder.

'Boomer? Boomer?' she called, jumping up onto a rock and standing, safe for the moment, above that dangerous tide.

Boomer's voice came back to her from somewhere in the steam.

'I'm here. Where are you?'

'Stop! Stop!' Garland cried even though she had stopped already. 'Where is he? He isn't with us. Hey, Boomer, can you hear me? Follow my voice.'

There was a silence.

'I can't,' said Boomer.

'Why not?' Garland called again. 'You can hear me, can't you?'

'I can see something you can't see,' he replied in a quavering voice.

At that moment a mocking breeze pushed in at them from nowhere. The steam around them bowed and curtseyed and shifted as if it were the curtain in a wild theatre. And there, the solitary actor on a savage stage, stood Boomer on an island in the middle of a small sea of boiling water and mud. The sulphurous smell in the air around them grew stronger and stronger.

'How are we going to get you over here?' asked Timon.

'I was wondering that,' Boomer replied.

Rags of steam were now blowing away and dissolving around them. The eruption such as it was seemed to be over. And now they could see that they were, each of them, marooned on rocks in a sea of simmering mud. And staring out across the mud Garland saw something else.

'Look!' she called, and even Boomer briefly forgot his danger as he stared in the direction in which she was pointing. There on a distant hillside they could see trees and among the trees the roof of house, And over there beyond the mud, just where the grasses took over again, she could make out the broken remains of a track, leading towards that distant hill.

'Yeah, right! But how do we get onto that track?' asked Boomer shrinking back as the mud bubbled and spat at him. Garland looked at Timon and saw that he, too, was looking unsure of himself.

'Is it often like this?' he asked.

'Not often, but there are places that are famous for being sort of volcanic,' Garland said. 'Listen! In your time do they still play pekapeka?'

'What?' Timon asked, wrinkling his forehead.

'Pekapeka!' You can't. It's too dangerous!' Boomer yelled.

'It's dangerous to stay where we are,' Garland said. 'We've got to try. And we've got to be very careful. It goes like this,' she told Timon. Then she leapt from the safety of her rock to another rough stony surface sticking out above the mud a little to her left. She leapt again to yet another rock and then to another. It wobbled madly. Garland couldn't help crying out in fear, flinging out her arms as she wobbled along with the rock below her. The mud steamed and seemed to lap up the rock trying to cover her shoes. But she got her balance again and leapt onwards, rock to rock, rock to rock until she reached the path. Turning, she saw Timon close behind her. Boomer hesitated.

'I don't want to,' he said.

'It's just a game,' Garland told him. 'Well, imagine it is. Imagine it's just a game.'

'I hate imagining,' whined Boomer. 'You know that.'

'But we have to check out Pokka's Theory,' Garland said. 'We have to save the sick ones back there. There's no one here to save us, so we have to save ourselves. Look! There's a good rock quite close to you. Turn around carefully though.'

Boomer took a deep breath turned, leapt and landed . . . then leapt and landed again. Suddenly he seemed to be almost enjoying his game of pekapeka. He flung his arms up . . . flung them wide.

'Ahhhhhhh!' he shouted, leaping a last leap and landing safely on the track beside them.

15
The Apothecary's Nidus

Wild bush advanced to meet them. They followed the track towards it, then pushed through leafy branches which bent obediently before them, then closed up after them.

'Perhaps that house is actually up in the trees,' said Garland, guessing as she scrambled. 'If *nidus* does mean *nest* that is. Nests are mostly in trees. Of course kingfishers nest in little tunnels in banks . . .'

She stopped.

'Go on!' said Boomer, pushing impatiently at her back. 'What is it? Let me see.' Garland moved on through the branches and Boomer followed. Then the three of them stood in a row, staring at what was in front of them . . . the house . . . the ruined house.

At last Timon slowly walked forward. 'Well, here it is. I suppose,' he said, sounding rather uncertain. 'At least it isn't up a tree.'

'There are a lot of ruined houses,' said Garland, afraid to hope that they had actually found what they were looking for, but Timon half-turned towards her, pointing out a faded notice hanging down across the porch. The words were largely undecipherable but if your head already had possible words in it, you could make out the word 'Nidus' cut into the crumbling wood.

'Come on,' said Timon. 'I mean we've got this far so let's go.' And they cautiously climbed the rotting front steps (shifting uneasily under their weight) and crossed the porch leaving footprints behind them. Garland pushed the front door and the whole door immediately tumbled inward.

'We'll have to be careful,' said Boomer. 'This whole place could fall in on us.'

'Clever of you to notice,' said Timon. 'Bright boy! Big brain.'

Trying to make themselves weigh as little as possible they edged, one by one, into the room beyond the door and stared around incredulously. The walls, still standing, were set with shelf upon shelf, and the shelves were crowded with bottles, jars, tins and crumbling boxes, all labelled. There was one shelf that had collapsed and underneath it lay a pile of books. Timon moved carefully to stare down at the tattered pages while Garland studied the tins and bottles and boxes.

'These books,' called Timon wonderingly. 'I think they had these – well, I think they had that green-covered one anyway – in the library back in Solis . . . the Solis of *my* time that is. It was in a glass case. No one was allowed to touch it. It was rare and precious.'

'Someone wise must have lived here,' Boomer said, staring at the decaying books spread across the floor.

'Yes! The apothecary,' said Garland, her eyes running along the shelves searching, searching for that blue bottle that had shone like a star in the silver girl's hand. 'But he's gone.'

'I don't think so!' said Timon in a peculiar voice. 'Actually he's still here.'

There was something about the way he spoke that made Garland pause and forget her search. She turned back towards Timon trying to see what he was seeing.

It was not hard. He was staring at a cot pushed against the

wall and there lying on it, spread out, at ease with the world, was a human skeleton.

'He won't be able to actually *tell* us,' whispered Boomer. 'Unless . . . hey! What's he pointing at?'

It did seem that the finger bones were pointing from the yellow sheet on which they lay towards a little door across the room from them.

'Let's try,' said Timon. 'After all we've got to begin somewhere. What exactly are we looking for?'

'I don't exactly know,' confessed Garland, crossing the floor gingerly.

'Oh great!' said Timon, following her.

'Something blue!' said Garland.

'Oh great!' said Boomer like Timon's echo.

They pushed the little door open and crowded very carefully into the room beyond . . . a room lined with shelves . . . lined with shelves crowded with jars, small corked pottery containers and hundreds of bottles. They stood there, huddled together like eerie watchers waiting for some ghostly Fantasia performance to begin.

'We'll start looking,' said Timon. 'It won't take long . . . only about year if we work quickly.'

But Garland ignored him. Something was shining out at her like a single, unwinking eye set among those jars and bottles. There was a crack into the wall behind one bottle and a thin dagger of light was thrusting through and shining into the room through glass – bright blue glass.

'There it is!' she cried in wonder and triumph. 'That's the medicine we must take. I know it is.'

She almost bounded across the floor and immediately the whole room began shaking.

'Easy! Easy!' yelled Timon as Garland snatched up the blue jar.

'But how do you know?' asked Boomer, looking at the dilap-idated shelves and the jars and bottles elbowing each other across them. 'How do you know which one is the right one?'

'I keep telling you,' said Garland. 'I was shown it. I was shown it in a –' She broke off; she could not tell Boomer about the silver girl. '– in that sort of dream I had.'

'What's it got in it?' asked Boomer, and Garland looked down at it, frowning.

'There's a label on the jar,' she said. 'It's hard to read, but I'll ask Goneril. She can read old writing and she'll have some idea about what to do. Come on. Come quickly! Let's pekapeka our way home! This is the cure.'

'What will I do?' Goneril was thinking. 'What happens if I get ill too?' Her head was spinning a little. She laid a cool cloth on the perspiring forehead of little Jewel. 'Don't cry,' she said wearily and uselessly. 'No more crying. I'm getting too old for crying. Too old for any of this.'

And then, suddenly, just as she was thinking about how old and weak she was . . . just as she was sure that she could not keep going . . . the door of the wagon burst open. Suddenly they were bearing down on her . . . looming over her . . . those two strange men. Those enemies who had been trailing after the Fantasia, following Timon and Eden.

'Get out!' she screamed, but she already knew they would take no notice of her.

'Do as we ask you, if you want to live,' said Maska in his grating voice, but Ozul held up his hand. He moved forward a few steps, leaving Maska guarding the doorway.

'We don't want trouble,' he said, sounding kind and rea-sonable, holding out his hands palm upward. 'We just want what is rightfully ours. Our – our wards. The children. Our dear children.' But in spite of his affectionate words spoken in that reasonable voice Goneril's expression did not change. He was an enemy and she knew it. 'We want *her*,' Ozul said, pointing at Jewel. 'And *him*,' he added, looking down at Eden. Then he bent over Eden and lifted the silver medallion from Eden's sweating chest. 'And *that*!' he said.

Eden stared back at Ozul. Then he closed his eyes.

The van began to tremble a little. Then it began to shake. The kitchen shelves began to rattle. It began to rock wildly, and everything it held began to tumble. Pillows fell to the floor, a narrow cupboard burst open and plates and cups . . . knives and forks . . . shot out as if they were anxious to escape from their shelves and boxes. Goneril toppled sideways into an empty bunk. Ozul dropped the silver medallion, holding out his hands sideways and trying desperately to keep his balance.

'What's happening?' cried Goneril. 'Oh lord! What's happening?'

The wagon rocked even more violently. Jewel started to scream. Goneril reached over to Jewel's bunk and pulled Jewel over beside her, struggling to wrap her in quilts, trying hard, even in that incoherent moment, to keep her safe . . . safe from the tumult. And particularly safe from Maska – Maska who, for some reason, seemed ominous and more than ominous . . . who seemed inhuman. For all that, the sudden rocking of the van took him by surprise, and both Maska and Ozul crashed, first to one side and then to another. Somewhere at the back of the van old Shell moaned and Tane woke up out of his fever-dream, shouting wildly. And then, slowly, as if it were giving a dignified if noisy curtsey, the whole van toppled sideways too. Maska staggered, then sprawled against the driver's seat. The van hesitated, rocked back up again, straightening though tottering, and then fell once more, but this time with a feeling of final surrender. Maska and Ozul were rolled backwards, breaking through the narrow door behind them.

Though badly splintered, though suffering the impact of Maska smashing through it, the door slammed shut. As Goneril – head spinning – looked up, she saw the key turn in the lock.

'Those men,' she gasped, looking at Eden. 'That door won't keep them out. Not now!'

'They might hesitate,' said Eden, panting like a dog, sweat seeping from his forehead, past his eyes and running down past his nose. 'They might wait to see what happens next. And while they're thinking for a moment the others might come racing back to rescue us.'

But Goneril looked over at Tane and old Shell, rolled out of their covers. 'I'll . . . I'll be back in a minute,' she promised them. 'I'm not leaving you. But you know what wretches babies are!' Someone kicked at the locked door. Someone began to struggle through the hole in it, ignoring the splinters around the hole. Shivering, Goneril snatched Jewel out of her cocoon of quilts and made for the door at the back of the van . . . the one near Shell's feet. 'Babies! More trouble – more trouble than they're worth!' she was shouting. But, as she shouted and struggled on, a hand fell on her. She looked up into Ozul's face.

'I mean you no harm,' Ozul said, smiling falsely while Maska stood behind her. 'Just give me the child. She is ours, not yours.' Goneril freed a trembling hand, and lifted it to deliver a vague, wild blow, but Maska moved in on her, seizing her collar and hoisting her up. Goneril held Jewel tightly and Maska held them both, dangling like dolls, kicking, swinging from side to side, Jewel screaming and Goneril croaking. Ozul pushed forward to peer down at Eden, shivering and exhausted. Around Eden's neck the chain of the medallion blinked briefly at Ozul.

'I think you are ours!' said Ozul. 'You and that Talisman you wear. I was set to find you, and I have.'

'Gloat later,' grunted Maska. 'Set up the device, and report back to the Master. We will soon be at his side once more.' He dropped Goneril, and stepped over her, leaving her lying on the ground with Jewel still in her arms. 'Don't move,' he told her, 'or it will be the worse for the child. And stop her crying or I will stop her myself.'

From the pack on his back Ozul was extracting a series of rods and little units which he fitted together rather like a child assembling a familiar toy. Once connected, the rods began to blink and tweet with a rich blue light and the same note sounding rapidly over and over again. Maska, meanwhile, had taken another power book from his pocket. He touched a button and it opened, stretched, and became twice its original size. He passed it to Ozul. The familiar greenish glow welled out of it, staining his face and chest with an unwholesome light. 'Home!' Ozul said. 'We're coming home. We have the Talisman. And we have the little child and the younger boy . . . the magician.'

A voice came struggling through.

'You don't have Timon?'

Ozul hesitated.

'Lord, do we need him?' he asked. 'He has no powers.'

The light changed . . . became more livid. The strange voice came hissing and yowling out at him.

'I will tell you who is important. It is not for you to try telling me. Timon is the most important and it is I who say so.' There was the sound of hands clapping a slow clap. 'Do not bother me again until you have all three,' said the voice.

Ozul kneeled for a moment as if something serious had interrupted him. Slowly he turned his head, looking up at Maska. 'The Nennog – the noble Nennog – wants the bigger boy too,' said Ozul. 'He says he must have the bigger boy . . . he must have all three.' He peered into the green glow once more as the spitting snarling voice began again. And, listening,

Ozul's expression began to change. A curious look of resignation mixed with fury began to show itself, while the snarling voice kept on and on and on . . .

'I hear voices,' said Maska suddenly. 'They are coming back. Sign off. Sign off.'

'Majesty,' Ozul said, bowing into the greenish glow. 'We go to get the boy. We will bring him back to you. We go.' And he closed the power book, tapped it so that it shrank back to pocket size.

Goneril watched him with a sort of limp despair as he began to disconnect his rods.

'Hurry! They are close,' said Maska. 'I will go and welcome them.'

'Don't kill them,' said Ozul. 'Well, not Timon. The Nennog wants him. But you may kill the other two with pleasure.'

They had closed the Nidus door behind them leaving the apothecary alone once more. They had come down through the bush and along the track. Once again they approached that seething stream of mud and boiling water, staring at it with apprehension.

'Home soon!' said Garland, preparing to jump from rock to rock once more. *Be tough!* she told herself. *Maddigans are famous for their toughness.*

'Don't let that medicine steam up,' said Boomer, watching her anxiously. 'It might not work if it gets hot. Well, it might not work anyway.'

'I was *shown* it,' Garland said obstinately.

Once again they began their dangerous progress from rock to rock, feeling the heat beat up against them fiercely, determined to overwhelm them. Garland imagined she could feel it building up under the ground gathering its powers and preparing to spring up around them.

'Pekapeka this way! Pekapeka that way!' she sang, determined to keep up her courage, hopping and leaping, screaming a little as a rock shook under her, but successfully bouncing on to the next.

When they talked about it later they found that none of them could say exactly when Maska appeared, but suddenly he was there, waiting for them on the other side, a black demon shrouded in steam.

'Back!' screamed Garland. 'Back!' but Timon, veiled with steam himself, turned perilously on his rock and faced her.

'Who do you think he wants most?' he asked her.

'You!' said Garland. She suddenly realized that Timon was sharing a plan with her, and she turned on her own stone. 'Hey, Boomer! Ready to catch?'

Boomer stared at her desperately.

'Right!' he said.

'And when you catch it, head over there,' pointing to a safe landing spot well away from Maska. And she threw the precious bottle across to Boomer. He grabbed for it desperately, skidded a little on his stone, yelled with alarm, the bottle sliding between his fingers as if it were trying to escape from him. But then he held it safely.

'Wait for your chance,' yelled Timon and set off again, straight towards Maska – pekapeka, pekapeka – bounding from rock to rock, taking risks with small steaming stones, jumping dangerously on slanting rocks. Garland followed him, and Maska stalked along the edge of the boiling river, keeping his gaze fastened remorselessly on Timon. As they moved away from him Boomer played his own game in the opposite direction. The mist swirled around him as if it were anxious to hold him in, but by now Boomer knew how to play this game. One last desperate lunge and he stood on solid ground.

'Run!' yelled Garland. 'Run! Get help!' Boomer ran, but

Maska ignored him, staring through the steam at Timon.

Garland and Timon leapt too. 'Where are we going?' asked Garland.

'To the land of lucky chances,' Timon said. Sickly trees closed around them. 'Isn't this the place where we came across?'

'It was about here,' Garland answered. 'Yes. It was here.'

'Stop then,' said Timon.

And they stopped standing stiffly on their various rocks, turning to face Maska who looked at them, then did his own pekapeka, stepping onto one huge rock then onto another.

'At last,' he said. Garland stared up at a face that seemed to be skin and bone like any face and yet was somehow unreal – somehow a mere mask of reality. 'At last! And – soon – goodbye to this horrible stinking land. What *is* that smell?'

'The land is rising up to meet you,' Timon said.

And, as he said this, the land exploded under Maska's feet.

'Pekapeka!' Timon screamed to Garland, but she was already jumping for another rock, holding her hands over her head and feeling little explosions of pain as drops of boiling mud and water rained down on her. Maska, however, was overwhelmed by a geyser of steam and water and mud. Garland and Timon reached the bank at almost the same time. 'Run!' yelled Timon. Garland ran, but feeling suddenly sure she was not being followed could not resist turning as she ran, and looking over her shoulder saw Maska jerking convulsively. Sparks flew from his joints so that he looked like some huge firework exploding on the banks of the steaming river.

'Don't look!' said Timon, though he had already looked himself. And they ran on side by side towards Goneril's van.

Only a few minutes earlier Boomer had run towards the van too only to stop in dismay as he saw it lying on its side. He paused to catch his breath, trying to work out what had happened, then pelted on towards it even more desperately than ever. With something approaching despair he saw bodies lying on the ground . . . Jewel, Goneril, Tane Shell.

'Goneril?' he shouted dropping on his knees beside her. 'I've got the cure. Goneril?'

Goneril stirred . . . opened her eyes . . . Boomer felt himself smiling with relief.

'I've got it,' he repeated. 'It might be all right.'

'Run!' said Goneril, like a curious creaking echo of Garland.

'What?' asked Boomer. 'I did run. I'm here to save you.'

Goneril shook her head feebly. 'Run!' she said again.

'Too late,' said a voice behind him. Boomer swung around only to find that Ozul, holding a limp Eden in his arms, was standing over him.

'I think you're too late for them,' he said. 'But I'll take your cure. Just to be on the safe side. After all it seems to be catching, and I don't want to be disadvantaged by any illness.' He paused. 'Where is the big brother? Where is Timon?'

'He's on his way,' Boomer said rather vaguely, looking back over his shoulder. Ozul made a movement towards him, but he dodged away. Ozul sighed and put Eden on the ground.

'Give me the cure,' he said. 'Give it to me now.'

There was a shout from the distance. Boomer did not have to turn to know that Garland and Timon had caught up with him . . . that they could see the difficulty he was in. 'Every minute saved means something,' he thought, dancing just beyond Ozul's grabbing hand, and longing for his bike with its little motor. On that bike Boomer felt he could dodge the world's worst villains, past, present or future. As he did his wild dance he saw Eden turn over and then, supported by his thin arms, struggle upwards. He didn't have the strength, it seemed, to sit up properly, but propped himself up rather uncertainly, blinking vaguely. Garland and Timon came jogging up, panting and desperate.

'You must do what I tell you or it will be the worse for your brother,' Ozul now said, ignoring both Garland and Boomer and looking only at Timon. 'I was instructed to bring you back with your brother and sister. You are to come back to your own time and receive your punishment.'

Garland could hardly believe it. They had been so clever, they had struggled so hard and then just as they were bringing back the apothecary's potion to save others their victory had been snatched away.

'You have a cure? Give it to me!' Ozul repeated turning back towards Boomer. Boomer hesitated and then, feeling perhaps that there was no choice, tossed the blue bottle towards Ozul. The bottle curved upwards and Ozul held out his hand expecting the bottle to fall into it.

But in the middle of its flight the bottle stopped – stopped in mid air and hung there. Ozul dived to catch it but missed. Behind him Eden fell backwards, worn out by a last bit of magic. And Garland, quicker than Ozul, threw herself forward and snatched the bottle just before it struck the ground, grazing her knuckles as she did so.

And then, out of the blue, there was a small sharp explosion. Ozul swung around convulsively, stumbled and fell to his knees. From where the stream curved out of the trees, half a dozen figures rose . . . armed and ready. Garland could hardly believe it when she saw that the tallest among the men was Yves.

'Leave those kids alone!' Yves was shouting. 'They're Fantasia people. They belong to us.'

Ozul picked himself up clasping the back of his shoulder with one hand. He turned, looked back towards the toppled van, and then at the advancing men. And then he ran madly for his horse, swung himself into its saddle, and set off without waiting to find out what had happened to Maska. Maska's grazing horse lifted its head, staring as if it was not quite sure what to do next. Then it made up its mind and galloped off after Ozul.

'Don't fire again!' Garland heard Yves saying. 'They've turned tail. Goneril! What have they done to you?'

'Yves came back for us,' said Timon. 'He must have changed his mind.' But all Garland could think of was carrying that blue jar to the wrecked wagon, for she felt sure that the apothecary's jar she held contained an apothecary's cure, and that she was about to save Goneril and little Jewel along with Eden, Goneril, Tane and Shell – and perhaps others as well.

'We got over the rise there,' said Yves, looking just a little sourly at Garland, 'and suddenly your mother realized you were gone.'

'It would have been really hard on us if you hadn't come back,' agreed Garland. 'Thanks!' She looked at Goneril, as the van, back on its wheels once more, but damaged and totally disordered, lumbered along following the track left by other vans. In another hour they would be part of the Fantasia once more, contained and safe from the dangers of the wild world around them.

'How are you?' she asked.

'I've been better,' said Goneril. She sounded a little weak, perhaps, yet the old tough Goneril was back in power. 'An hour ago I was a lot worse,' she added, winking at Garland. Then she looked over to where Jewel and Eden slept peacefully side by side. 'It changed everything – that medicine of yours.'

'Garland says she saw it in a vision,' said Timon, and looked at her in a puzzled way. 'How?'

'Because she's a Maddigan,' said Goneril. 'From old Gabrielle on, Maddigans have been able to bring magic out of themselves. They're fantastic. That's why we call the circus they invented Maddigan's Fantasia.' Garland smiled, nodding as she yawned. It was almost true. Of course, deep down, she knew there was more to it that that. Right at that moment all she wanted to do was go to sleep but she had something to do first.

Dear Ferdy, it's been such a hard confusing day, but I think it has ended well, because we found the medicine and already Goneril, Eden, Jewel and the others too are feeling better. So we are moving on . . . moving on again, together. And I'll tell you all about it tomorrow . . . but all I want to do now is to sleep.

16

Greentown

Dear Ferdy, We're on our way and the land unfolds around us. And we're into spring by now . . . new leaves on the fruit trees and nesting birds in some of them. You probably remember it all just as well as I do. We have been this way before, making our way to Newton. Isn't it great to recognize certain signs and to know that, in spite of all that has happened, we are on the right road. Well, more or less the right road. We are going in the right direction anyway. Bannister sits with the maps spread over his knee, but every now and then he looks sideways at his book. He wants to read – but not maps. He wants to get into his book and to find out what happens next. But books are part of the Maddigan tradition too. At least all the stories about Gabrielle tell us that she loved books and carried them around with her in the same way that Bannister does.

So here we are, going up and over a lot of little hills and swinging and singing round the big ones, and swaying out even more widely around all those places ruined by the Chaos – those places where poison still lurks and the plants and the birds grow all strangely shaped and you told me we would grow strangely too if we drank the water or camped there.

And we're still being followed. Ozul and Maska are trailing after us, though I wouldn't think things would be working too well for Maska after our last adventure. Sometimes it seems as if we are finding our way through one of Bannister's adventure books . . . off one page and on to another. We've been travelling for a while now and we are getting short of food again. Maddie and Yves are arguing about what town to go to next . . . but Maddie has won. Hooray. Yves wants to go to Greentown, but . . .

There was a sudden sound of voices . . . voices raised, excited about something and, Garland thought, rather dismayed. She scrambled up and peered through the window.

They had reached Kapai, the little town by the river which Maddie had wanted them to visit. 'It's a friendly place,' she had said to Yves. 'We'll get a few stores there and then go on to Greentown. It's only about two or three miles out of our way, and having a circus turn up really *means* something to a place like Kapai. I remember the last time we were there . . . it was so exciting for them that we gave one of our most amazing performances.'

Garland remembered Kapai's pleasure too, and she was glad to think that they might go back there. And she was glad to think that Maddie was prepared to argue with Yves and get her own way. But as they trundled towards Kapai she began to feel uneasy and then something stronger – distress. No one came running to meet them . . . indeed there was no sign of anyone moving in the town. As they moved even closer they could see houses looking as if no one had lived in them for a long time, doors swinging open, weeds growing tall or sprawling around the steps. Yves ran out in front of Maddie's van signalling that the Fantasia should stop, and one by one the vans jolted to yet another standstill. Fantasia people clustered on the fringe of the town staring into it doubtfully.

'What's happened?' Garland cried. 'Where is everyone?'

'That's a good question,' Yves replied. 'Hey! Hello! Is anybody there?' he shouted. Faint echoes answered him from vacant doorways along the small main street.

'Well,' said Maddie blankly. 'There's nothing for it but to swing back to Greentown. They'll probably be able to tell us what's happened here.'

Yves nodded, trying not to look as if he had told her so.

'It was a really nice place,' Garland said sadly. 'It looks so ghostly now. Luisa's house was down there. That was her apple tree.' She turned to Boomer. 'Remember? You fell out of it.'

Boomer looked embarrassed. 'I sort of remember her,' he mumbled. 'I remember trying to fly from branch to branch.'

This was not the first time they had found some community had simply vanished away. The Fantasia danced its strange way backwards and forwards across a countryside that shifted and changed as if touched by the wand of a dark magician.

So, once again, they climbed into their vans or onto their horses and turned back the way they had come.

It was late afternoon by the time Greentown came into sight – a walled town with flags flying at its gates, and wind generators on the hill behind it.

'Good timing,' said Yves. 'We'll be able to turn on a show this evening no trouble at all.'

'Strike up the band,' suggested Maddie. 'Let's announce ourselves.'

Out beyond the town walls, the band struck up and, in answer to the music, the Greentown gates opened and people streamed out to meet them . . . laughing, shouting and welcoming them in.

Other people were noting their arrival too.

'There they are,' said Ozul. There was relief in his voice. 'I thought we had lost them.'

'We would have found them again,' Maska said gratingly. 'But perhaps it would be better if we were to wait near the back gate of the town. They might not see us so easily. They have proved unexpectedly difficult. And anyway in our line of business surprise is always an asset.'

By now there was something rather battered about Ozul and Maska, and it was not simply that they were now riding mules rather than the dashing black horses they had first ridden. Winding away from the front gates, retreating from the Fantasia band and the cheerful welcome, they moved in a disconsolate way . . . less sure of themselves than they had been in the beginning. And when at last they came to the back gates which were locked and barred they stopped short. For there, piled in great heaps, was the rubbish of the town . . . compost heaps of decaying food scraps, bones protruding from some of the piles . . . pieces of twisted metal, wooden off-cuts, tins rusting into ginger-brown flakes, while bottles . . . jars . . . tins . . . any objects which could be reused, were stacked on long shelves outside the walls.

Meanwhile beyond the back gates and those rubbish heaps, safe in the busy heart of the town, Garland was staring in amazement at people dressed in beautiful, colourful clothes and the markets set up around the circular space that embraced the Fantasia, every counter, it seemed, glittering with wonderful and entertaining things. Lilith squeaked with pleasure at the sight of so many bright possibilities.

The crowd around them was certainly welcoming. People clapped and cheered and then through the crowd came a small procession of about ten people offering a welcome that was somehow ceremonial. Garland suddenly found herself remembering the women who led this group.

'Those two in the front of everyone else are sisters,' she told Timon and Eden. 'They run Greentown. That first one – the one in blue – is Mayo and the one in yellow is Greeta.'

'They do look pleased with themselves,' said Timon.

'They are! They're really bossy,' Garland agreed. 'But I suppose if you're the boss of everything you can't help showing it. And they're – I suppose they're good-hearted. They're really generous.'

Later that evening, when the Fantasia had set itself up for a full performance, the sisters certainly showed their bossiness, but they showed their generosity too. They swept into the performance, taking their seats side by side in the grand red velvet chairs that had been prepared for them while servants set out a little table in front of them and loaded it with bowls of fruit and little cakes and bottles of wine. A tall man called Brewer stood behind their chairs. He rather puzzled Garland. Sometimes he seemed like a big brother taking care of them. Sometimes he seemed like a butler.

'Bring us drinks, Brewer,' Greeta cried aloud, ordering him about in a careless airy voice.

'Very good, madam,' Brewer said promptly.

'He's a treasure,' Garland heard Greeta telling Maddie. 'A bit of a know-all, but hard working.'

'This is going to go well,' Maddie told Yves a little later, with a great sigh of relief. 'It always helps when people really want to be entertained, because they come halfway to meet you. Look at those people out there. I don't think I've ever seen such a cheerful audience before. It's almost as if they want to entertain us back.'

'They do,' replied Yves. 'We've been invited to a feast afterwards. That doesn't happen often. I must say I'm really looking forward to a bit of fun, after the last few weeks. Who knows? We might even get to dance.'

'I'm not sure I feel altogether like dancing,' Maddie said. 'And what would Garland think of me?'

'Ferdy would tell you to dance,' Yves said. 'Firstly because he loved dancing himself and secondly because he'd want you to be moving back towards some sort of happiness again. You know he would. And before you say it seems as if everyone is already forgetting Ferdy, let me tell you what he would say. He would say dancing was the best way of remembering him. Dancing and putting on a good show for Greentown.'

And indeed it did seem as if the evening would go like a dream. The first acts went wonderfully well; people cheered, gasped at the trapeze acts, cheered Garland's tightrope walking and laughed at the clowns. There was only one hesitation and that was when the band came on, Boomer booming away in high spirits. The two sisters rose as one sister, making sideways gestures with their hands, and shaking their heads. No band! No music. And especially no drum. Brewer stepped forward in a commanding fashion and the drum was firmly taken away from Boomer in his first moment of hesitation. There he stood, his sticks poised in the air, while Brewer whisked the drum harness down over his arms.

'You can have it back when you go, sir,' he said and then carried the drum away with him and set it down beside the twin chairs, just in case Boomer might be tempted to do a little private drumming. There was nothing Boomer could do except to slide backwards, defeated and grumbling, and stand beside Garland.

'It's not fair,' he muttered sideways to Garland. 'I'm a good drummer. Why pick on me?' But Garland was not listening. Suddenly she was sure she had seen her Kapai friend Luisa standing behind the twin chairs. They looked across at one another. There was no doubt about it. Even though the girl was half-veiled it certainly *was* Luisa. She was dressed in filmy golden clothes like the other girl servants and held a long graceful pitcher. Whenever she saw some Fantasia person with an empty glass it seemed to be her job to fill the glass again. She was doing her job well, too, nodding and smiling, but she did not seem to recognize Garland. Standing there, off to one side of the performance ring, Garland waved at her but, though she was sure Luisa must have seen her waving, there was not the slightest response, not even a smile. Garland waved again – but then Boomer tugged at her arm impatiently and she had to hurry to take her place in the final act, to spin on the tightrope with the whole Fantasia dancing, juggling, stilt walking and lifting weights below her. The performance had come to an end. The audience was cheering them hugely. Mayo stood up, a massive figure in her blue robes.

'Wonderful! Just wonderful! Many thanks!' she cried. 'And now for the feast.' Greeta stood up, inclining her head and clapping too. Immediately servants glided out holding trays of food and wine . . . more delicious food than the Fantasia had tasted for a long, long time. As they ate and drank they mixed with the Greentown audience, laughing and light-hearted. Even Garland felt a sudden relaxation . . . a great ease. Just for a while she was able to – not forget Ferdy's death – but to put it a little to one side and to think that happiness might be possible again. She moved confidently over to Luisa's side.

'Hi there! Remember me?' she said.

'Hey! Luisa!' Boomer echoed.

Luisa looked at them. Her expression was somehow peculiar. She was still smiling, and yet there was nothing behind the smile – no happiness, no true friendliness – just a strange space. The corners of her mouth had twitched up, which meant she was officially smiling, but somehow (seen close up) that smile of Luisa's did not mean anything. It was there, but there was nothing real about it.

'Remember me? Garland?'

'Garland,' repeated Luisa, but not as if the name meant the slightest thing to her.

'We knew one another when you were living in Kapai,' Garland persisted.

'Kapai,' Luisa repeated, and something in that blank voice sent a small chill through Garland.

But the feast was going on all around her. The Fantasia people were all able to forget how hard life had been for them, how hard it might be again tomorrow. This was one of those rare occasions when they could toss their struggles to one side and could dance and joke and spin, just enjoying the pleasure the moment was offering them.

Boomer, on the other hand, looked grumpier and grumpier. His fair hair seemed to stick up in spikes of fury. He hated seeing his drum there by the twin chairs, not exactly deserted, not exactly out of his reach, but in a place where he could not claim it. And those sisters, those two grand women, had not enjoyed the band, or his own beating on the drum. More food was carried in to the sound of music – music of a sort, thought Boomer . . . tinkling tunes played on harps. A parade of servants, in white aprons and curious white headdresses, (half-cap half-veil) brought in tray after tray of food.

Sulking, Boomer turned down the drinks that the golden servant girls were pouring so generously, and the food that was still being passed around, standing off to one side scowling at other people who were enjoying themselves, watching Garland dancing with Timon, swaying and spinning to the harp music. Treachery! Treachery, even in the Fantasia. Nothing but treachery. Boomer spun away impatiently, then found himself staring down into a tray that was being held out to him. Horror froze on his face as he recoiled. The food in front of him was alive with worms, the whole tray was crawling with them. He looked left and right. On either side of him he saw the Fantasia people choosing cakes and savouries, all of which were writhing. Slipping sideways, Boomer worked his way across the room, glancing wildly from side to side until he found Garland helping herself to a little pie. Boomer grabbed her arm.

'Don't eat it!' he cried. 'Just *look* at it! It's full of worms . . . maggots!'

'Worms?' Garland said. 'Don't be mad. It's delicious.' And she took another little pie. 'Just because they took your drum.' she said. 'Never mind. They'll give it back to you tomorrow.'

'You're eating *maggots*!' cried Boomer, and then, looking incredulously at Garland, had the strange feeling that he was looking at someone who was wrapped around in a deep dream. But who was doing the dreaming? Was he in Garland's dream or was Garland in his?

Garland yawned. Timon yawned, too.

'I think it's the best meal I've ever eaten,' he said, 'and those drinks – they're just – just delicious. So let's party on and just have a good time while we can.'

And as the harps began their tinkling flow once more he and Garland hooked arms and danced off together. Boomer looked after them, feeling his face crumpling up with amazement.

For now, looking around, it seemed to Boomer that everyone in the room was entranced . . . that he was the only person there with any ordinary feelings . . . the only person who was able to recognize a maggot when they saw one.

'Why would anyone want to leave this place?' Yves was saying to Maddie and he put his arm around her. She did not shrug it away. Garland danced by and saw this, but she did not seem to notice it, or, if she did, she was not angry about it. Boomer would have expected her to be furious. Running up to Timon, Boomer grabbed his arm, pulling him out of the dance.

'Hey! Wake up! Can't you see what's going on?' he cried. 'Everyone's – everyone's sort of entranced.'

'Forget it! Enjoy yourself,' said Timon, and at that moment Boomer felt hands close around his upper arms. Brewer had come up behind him and had listened to his cries of warning. He gestured to one of the other servants and they seized him. Kicking between them he was bundled backwards out of the middle of the dancing circle. Boomer stiffened his legs so that his heels dragged on the ground then screamed desperately, so that some of the Fantasia people looked over at him. Yet not one of them made any move to help him. They simply laughed and talked and danced on.

Shouting and kicking out, Boomer was pulled away from that enchanted dancing circle, dragged and tumbled sideways down one passage, then along another, and then, abruptly and bruisingly, pulled downstairs into a huge kitchen. And in a way it was not too different from being in the upstairs room, for here in the kitchen everyone was laughing and whirling around as if cooking and filling trays was an entertainment in itself.

'What have you brought me here for?' he yelled. 'Are you going to turn me into a slave?' A sudden more alarming thought flew through his head. 'Are you going to *cook* me?'

Brewer laughed.

'A slave? Of course not. It's just that you seemed to be one of us. You weren't touched by the mind-weed were you, and most people are. Perhaps you're one of the chosen. Here! Try this!'

And then the man on his left side twisted his arm up behind his back with one hand while slipping the other under his chin.

'No!' shouted Boomer, but Brewer was already advancing on him with a cup of green fluid.

'No!' shouted Boomer again and then coughed and spluttered as the man who was holding him tilted his head and Brewer tried to force the green fluid into him. Boomer was determined not to swallow a drop of it. He could not escape but he could spit, and he spat the whole mouthful into Brewer's face. A kindly woman who had been busy at one of the tables whirled around and handed Brewer a towel. Brewer began to mop his face carefully.

'You know what, Missy,' Brewer said to the woman. 'I reckon this one here is one of us. He seems to resist the mind-weed. Look after him. I'd better get back to the big hall again.'

Mind-weed? Still held fast, Boomer stared as far as he could around the kitchen and at the pots simmering over the wood-stove. Turning his head sideways, stretching a very little, he found he was able to peer into the pot closest to him and to see that it contained a sort of greenish soup. And now the strange sharp scent of it edged in at his nostrils. The green-soup smell filled the room and almost against his will Boomer felt a peculiar lifting of his spirits . . . it came out of nowhere and he found himself breathing it in . . . breathing it quite eagerly. Missy saw him staring at the soup and smiled at him.

'Breakfast tomorrow,' she said. 'It's wonderful stuff, that mind-weed isn't it, pigeon? Changes the world for us.'

'I've never tasted it,' Boomer said uncertainly. And Missy laughed.

'I should think not, little eagle. We don't eat it ourselves, do we? But them that *does* eat it, they thinks they're getting exactly what they most fancy. They thinks they're breakfast-ing off eggs, say . . . pancakes . . . porridge . . . That lot up there – they think they run things, but really it's us down here that has the power. They can play their games, but in the end they do what they're told – which you'd better do too, if you've got any sense, robin. I mean if you join in with us you'll be one of the powerful ones. You'll run the whole world. And your friends – the ones out there – they'll patter along after you and do everything you tell them to.'

'What if they don't want to?' Boomer asked.

'Oh, they'll want to,' said Missy. 'Once they drink a bit of the mind-weed dew they'll gambol around us like lambs. Do this, do that, we'll say. And they'll do it. Do it to the end.'

'The end,' said Boomer apprehensively.

'It's very quick,' Missy said. 'No one feels anything. We wouldn't want anyone to suffer.'

As she spoke she was opening a big oven door and pulling out a roasting dish filled with a huge joint of meat. Boomer clapped his hands over his mouth feeling that the mere sight of Missy basting that flesh was going to make him sick.

'I felt a bit queasy in the beginning, mind you,' Missy was saying. 'But the world's that crowded with people isn't it, chook? Might as well use up a few of them.'

Fortunately at that moment something happened which took all of Boomer's attention. A door opened and two men came into the room, escorted by about half a dozen Greentown men. Maska and Ozul.

17

The Mind-Weed Dream

Missy looked over at the newcomers. The man who had held Boomer released him, distracted by Maska and Ozul. Boomer immediately seized the chance to slide into an alcove on one side of the biggest stove. Heat came off the bricks but, temporarily forgotten, he half-hid himself among the cloths and dusters that hung from wooden hooks set into the gaps between the bricks, watching and listening, while Ozul and Maska asked to be taken to some place where they could see the circus people spinning and dancing . . . watching and listening as the men who had brought him down answered them in soothing voices, speaking with authority. It suddenly occurred to Boomer that these men were more than servants. Even though he was down here in the kitchen, surrounded by people who fetched and carried, he was suddenly certain he was listening to the true masters of Greentown, to people trying to put Ozul and Maska at their ease. Plenty of time, the chief cook was saying. No one, not even the travelling Fantasia, was going anywhere at this time of night.

And suddenly Brewer was there once more, dancing around them, rubbing his hands together. Would they like a meal? Maska seemed indifferent to this suggestion – but Ozul suddenly looked extremely hungry. Boomer watched as they sat him down, quickly setting out a meal in front of him. Ozul began to eat greedily, and as he did so, every eye in the room swivelled to watch him, and behind him or over his head secret smiles were exchanged, shooting from one person to another, picked up and passed on.

Attention was so focused on Maska and Ozul that Boomer saw an opportunity. He pulled one of the cloths hanging on the hooks over his head, and tried to arrange it so that it looked roughly like one of those odd caps the kitchen people were all wearing. Then he stepped out . . . stepped right . . . stepped left . . . paused as if he had no intention of going anywhere, and then slipped towards a door on the other side of the room. People looked past him – over him – all of them concentrating now on the two men at the table, so Boomer reached the door unchallenged. It was slightly open. He pushed it a little wider and stepped out of the kitchen.

Boomer found himself in a long corridor with other passages branching off from it. Just for a moment he paused, utterly uncertain of just which direction to take, but then, hearing footsteps coming up behind him, he marched ahead, slid into the first of these passages, and then dived into the first room he came to. Footsteps! People were hurrying past, though whether or not they were looking for him he could not tell. The footsteps retreated; others advanced and then retreated too. Boomer listened, and at last, believing he was hidden and partly safe, he turned and looked around him.

He thought at first he was in a pantry and that there was some dark stranger with a pale face standing at his elbow and checking his every movement. He clenched his teeth violently but, though he was trying to be brave, a curious high squeak of terror forced its way out between them. A moment later he realized that the dark stranger was nothing more that a tall clock, standing rigidly against the wall and looking out over his shoulder.

He had hidden himself in a sort of museum room. Shelves and shelves of objects, none of which seemed to have anything to do with one another, rose around him. A line of hats stretched out at shoulder level. On the shelf below lay a sword in a gilded sheath, a silver birdcage, and an old brown photograph of a forgotten family celebrating a birthday back in the days before the Chaos. On the shelf opposite him, Boomer made out a red bust, hung with necklaces, sitting firmly under its glittering ornaments, and watching him closely – or so it seemed, though its smiling oval face was quite eyeless – was the carving of a cat turned a little away from him. On the shelf below that cat, he made out half a dozen frames with ragged threads of canvas winding like brown worms from between them . . . pictures piled on top of each other. The mere suggestion of worms however made Boomer shudder and look rapidly at the next things. There in a slot beside the door a fur coat hung next to a series of dresses, rich with golden braid, and on the far side of the door those crowded shelves began again, seeming to stretch out for ever. The marble statue of a unicorn . . . a polished bell . . . on and on, on and on. But there – there – in a space between the wall and the shelves was his drum. It could only have been there for a few minutes, must have been pushed in carelessly . . . and yet it seemed already to belong there simply because it fitted in with nothing else, partly because it fitted in with nothing else, and nothing else there fitted in with anything.

Boomer struggled with the strange contradiction of everything around him. The sound of a voice came towards him, a faint distant chatter to begin with, growing louder and louder, echoing in that main corridor just beyond the door. Boomer did not like to close the door in case the sound of it clicking shut caught someone's attention. Instead he hurriedly stepped back into the shadow of the great carved clock. But the voice whisked past and its chattering faded into the distance.

Wrapped in shadows Boomer relaxed then, taking a breath, tightened himself up again. He was about to reclaim his drum – he hated seeing something that seemed so much a part of him at home in this alien setting, but something else caught his eye. Opposite him at the front of the shelf below the shelf that held the unicorn he made out two brooches side by side . . . brooches set in delicate frames . . . brooches that did not glitter so much as smoulder in the shadows, looking like jewels from a fairy tale. Boomer studied them, suddenly feeling, in a defiant way, that Greentown owed him something . . . that they had stolen his drum and that, even though he had found his drum again, it wasn't because Greentown had given it back. He hesitated, then stepping past the door quickly snatched up both brooches, sliding them into his pocket before slipping himself into his drum harness. And, suddenly, feeling the weight of his drum . . . the friendly tug of the harness over his shoulders . . . he was himself again . . . not quite a Maddigan, perhaps, but a true member of the Fantasia for all that.

As he stood there he heard, off in the distance, the sound of doors opening and, once again, an echoing voice. And then – not just one but many voices advancing towards him.

'You'll sleep well tonight,' he heard someone say. 'We've some comfortable rooms for you.'

And then – no doubt about it – he heard Yves's voice, though not sounding as sharp and determined as it usually did – sounding a little blurred and indistinct as if Yves was talking into a pillow.

'I won't deny we're tired,' Yves was saying, 'but we do have our own beds out in our vans.'

'Give yourself a change,' said the first voice. 'We make things luxurious for visitors.'

'We'd love a bit of luxury,' said another blurred voice . . .
Maddie.

'I'm so tired,' agreed a third voice . . . Garland, pushing in as
usual, but sounding sleepy.

Once again the voices and the footsteps died away.

Boomer squatted there in the semi-darkness, testing the
silence. At last he stood up, thinking he must somehow get out of
this cupboard . . . find his way back among his own people . . .
back where he belonged. But then, for the third time, he heard
voices in the main corridor, though coming in the opposite
direction this time.

'Good numbers there,' someone was saying. 'It's good to
collect a few more workers. It takes more and more people to do
everything there is to do around this place.'

'And this lot – they're clever in their own way,' said another.
'They'll be able to entertain the two great ladies and . . .' The
words were lost. Somewhere a door opened and shut. Silence
rushed in on Boomer for a third time, and he squatted down,
cuddling in behind his drum, trying make sense of all the different things he'd heard.

'And this is where you will be able to sleep,' said the servant
to Garland. 'It will be a change for you.'

Garland found herself in the most luxurious bedroom she
had ever seen. Fantasia people sighed in wonder. The beds
were piled with furs and pillows, and the one which was pointed
out to her invited her to flop and fall in it and dream sumptu-
ous dreams. She looked left and right – saw Maddie collapse
among the cushions two beds away . . . saw Yves fall opposite
her, and Lilith cuddle down beside him . . . saw Timon and others sink down, while Eden on the other side of the room seemed
to be already asleep . . . asleep within about ten seconds.

'Thank you,' she said. 'Thank you so much.' Then she hesitated. 'Where's Boomer?'

'Boomer? Oh, he'll be here somewhere,' said the servant. 'He'll be safe.' Something about this did not seem to match with Garland's own memory of the last few minutes, and she stood there blinking uncertainly. But she was tired, so very tired and the bed was so amazingly inviting. All she had to do was collapse forward and be engulfed in comfort. Which she did! Which she was! The servant smiled a smile Garland did not see and backed out of the room. And within the next few moments Garland was asleep. She did not even hear the key turn in the lock behind her.

But Boomer – who had at last slipped out into the silence of the main corridor, who had run on tiptoe, his drum shivering in front of him – Boomer, who had hidden in the dark arch of yet another branching passage – watched around a corner, half-hidden by shadows. He saw the servants who were really masters come out into the main corridor, saw one of them turn and saw the key twitch in the lock.

'Done!' he heard the servant say. 'Sleep well,' he added, though anyone hearing him say this would also have heard the mockery in his voice. Footsteps came towards them from further down the long corridor.

'Are they shut in for the night?' someone asked, and a grandly dressed figure appeared . . . a tall man dressed with scarlet trimmed with gold lace. He loomed over the two servants standing by the locked door, and they all stood there, hesitating for a moment, but at ease with the world.

'Let's hope they sleep well,' the scarlet man remarked at last. 'It might be a while before they get the chance to sleep quite so well again. There is a lot of work that needs to be done around here.' Then he took the key from the lock and hung it on a brass hook to the left of the door.

'I was just saying that it's not often that we get the chance to get such good numbers,' said the second servant, and they moved off, side by side. If any of them had glanced to the right as they passed the arched entrance to the little passage in which Boomer was hiding they would certainly have seen him, but they looked neither left nor right, not so much walking as marching. He listened as their footsteps grew fainter and fainter. Silence.

As soon as he was quite sure that the main corridor was empty Boomer slipped out, drum and all, stood on tiptoe to flick the key from its brass hook and (looking nervously left and right) and put it in the lock. The lock was stiff; he had to use two hands to turn that key. All the same he did turn it at last, then carefully sliding the key into his pocket he opened the door and stepped into the room beyond.

Boomer found himself bathed in an eerie half-light. Several old lanterns shone faintly from the walls allowing him to make out a room full of vague lumpy shapes and filled with the sound of heavy breathing. He reached up and, taking one of the lanterns from the wall, swung it right, swung it left in a semi-circle. There they were . . . all of them. There were his friends, his Fantasia which was mother and father to him, lying around on piles of straw, and all apparently asleep. There was Garland, smiling as she slept; there was Maddie, her mouth partly open as if she was about to eat the straw she was lying on; there was Lillith, lying off to one side like a deserted doll flung away by an impatient child.

'Hey!' cried Boomer, softly at first. 'Hey! Wake up!' Something about their sleep was intimidating and he dared not speak very loudly. Then, with relief, he saw movement. Timon! Timon was sitting up . . . sitting up and blinking . . . rubbing his hands down over his face . . . standing up . . . staring around . . . then moving across the room towards Eden.

'Timon!' Boomer exclaimed, grateful that he was no longer alone.

But Timon did not turn. It seemed he had not heard him. Boomer slipped around Garland's feet and ran towards Timon, planning to grab his arm and show him (triumphantly) the stolen key. But Timon walked past one of the lamps, and the lamplight, though soft and dim, briefly lit up his face. Boomer stopped abruptly, for Timon's expression frightened him. The eyes, open but narrowed, flickered with a greenish light. Timon's mouth had thinned into a rigid line and its corners were not so much turned down as *dragged* down as if by some strange muscular spasm. There in the shadows of that cold, straw-filled room Timon had become an evil alien, reaching out towards his brother's throat as if he might strangle him.

'Don't,' said Boomer, reaching out too . . . reaching out, though he was terrified again, to drag at those taut, crooked fingers. Timon half-turned, swinging out his right arm as he did so, striking Boomer's side just below his waist. It was as if he had been hit with a plank of wood. Boomer toppled sideways as Timon struck again but this time he thumped not Boomer but Boomer's drum which sounded a single beat . . . a curious signal . . . an announcement of some kind. At the sound of that single beat, the dreadful set expression on Timon's face seemed to melt away. For a second Boomer, now writhing on the floor with his drum on top of him and the lantern flung out to one side, saw the softer Timon, the one he was used to seeing, push its way into the world again. This altered Timon stood there looking around in bewilderment. Then his expression tightened again, and hardened once more as if strings had been pulled somewhere inside Timon's head establishing a different order. His eyes narrowed. The corners of his mouth were tugged down as before and Timon bent over Eden again, reaching for the silver medallion that lay, reflecting the lamplight, on his brother's thin chest.

A sudden sound, a throb in the air around him, intruded

again. Timon hesitated, for the beat seemed to be altering him, calling him. Blinking he slid the medallion chain up and over Eden's sleeping head and, as he did this, Timon saw his own hands and paused . . . for surely those hands were not *his* hands. Those hands in front of him holding the silver chain seemed to be green – green and covered with scales.

Timon dropped the medallion and crouched down, feeling a confusing battle inside his head, but not sure just who was battling with who.

'Timon!' a voice was hissing at his elbow, and Timon thought he could hear, not only the voice, but a beating heart as well. Someone seized his shoulder and shook it desperately. 'Timon! What's happening, man?' the voice cried. Timon turned and saw Boomer, standing beside him, one hand pushed forward and grabbing at him, the other thumping his drum with one clenched fist. 'What are you doing?' asked Boomer.

'I don't know,' said Timon, sounding dazed. 'I was – I must have been dreaming.' He looked down at the medallion in his hands, then bent and slipped it back over Eden's head once more. 'I was . . . I don't know . . . taken over. Having a nightmare.'

'You were scary,' Boomer muttered, 'and this whole place,' he looked around him, 'I think that everyone's been drugged or something. Everyone seems to be dreaming.'

Timon looked down at his own hands – perfectly ordinary hands – and then stared around him at the dim lamps, the straw and the sleeping Fantasia.

'Let's wake everyone up,' he said. 'This isn't the place we went to sleep in.'

He made for Garland.

Garland was dreaming. She dreamed about her diary and ran to seize it, eager to write in it, but it rose like a wild moth, flapping its pages like dark wings. It flew . . . it flew . . . and as it flew from somewhere between the flapping pages of that dark-moth-diary Ferdy slid like a lost bookmark and advanced towards her smiling, happy to see her.

'Ferdy,' Garland cried. 'Ferdy! Oh Dad!' And she ran to meet him, but as she ran a curious beat sounded in the air beside her . . . boom! boom! boom! and Ferdy seemed to retreat, stepping back in time to that sound. 'No!' cried Garland. 'Ferdy! Dad! Don't leave me!' But he faded . . . he dissolved, and Garland woke up to find Boomer beating his drum in one ear and Timon singing in the other, humming the Fantasia theme and shaking her awake.

'Why did you wake me?' she cried. 'I was in a – in a happy place. Soft, all soft! I was in a wonderful bed.'

She looked around at the straw, finding it hard to believe in what she was now seeing.

'It's nothing,' said Boomer, shaking her shoulder. 'It was a trick. They're tricking us. You all ate and drank things, but I didn't, so I wasn't tricked. I looked at those cakes and things and all I saw was worms.'

All around them there was movement now, as people, driven out of their dreams by the drumbeat, began to blink and stir. To the right and left of them Fantasia people now sat up blinking incredulously and began to shake the people next to them, saying their names urgently, waking them up once more. There was Penrod, stretching. There was Bannister yawning and running his fingers through his hair. There were Byrna and Nye, blinking and staring as if they did not quite believe in each other.

'Why do they want us?' Garland asked the air around her. 'Do they want us to be slaves?'

'Maybe!' said Boomer. 'Or . . .' his eyes grew round '. . . or maybe we're to be like cattle. Maybe they were planning to eat . . .'

'Let's get out of here,' Timon said urgently, just as Maddie helped Yves to his feet.

'Let's get out of here,' Maddie agreed, sounding like an unsteady echo.

'If we can,' said Yves, staggering a step or two forward, looking towards the door as he did so.

But Boomer now drew the key from his pocket and waved it around, like a man in danger drawing a gun that will hold enemies at bay.

'Let's go!' he cried. 'And we've got to stamp and shout and sing. That sort of breaks through the power of the mind-weed. That why they took my drum away from me.'

'My hero!' said Maddie, snatching the key from him. 'Wake up Tane! Bannister! Hey, Nye! Stop dreaming! Someone's pulled a fast one on us. But we're waking up again. Hey! Hey! Hey! We're on our way.'

'Lilith! Wake up Lilith!' cried Yves, but Lilith slept on, dreaming that she was being hailed as the greatest dancer in the Fantasia. Boomer beat the drum close to her ear, but she slept on, and in the end Yves lifted her and carried her against his shoulder as they clustered around the door . . . as Maddie unlocked it, then flung it wide, leading them out into the corridor beyond. It was only an empty corridor and yet it felt like being out in the real, wide world again.

In the Greentown kitchens Brewer and Missy were entertaining Ozul and Maska. Ozul lifted a great glass of the green mead and drank it with relief and pleasure.

'And you?' Missy was holding out a similar glass to Maska, but Maska pushed it away.

'That's not very polite, chicken,' said Missy reproachfully, but Maska ignored her.

'They have the children,' he said to Ozul. 'And that means they must have the medallion too. Let us take advantage. Let us go and get them while they sleep.'

'Just a moment,' said Ozul. 'We're entitled to a little entertainment . . . a little rest . . . a little luxury.'

'Indeed you are, sir,' said Brewer, topping up the green mead. 'And Greentown is the place for pleasure.'

He slid a plate of delicate food in front of Ozul who exclaimed with pleasure at the sight. Seizing the knife and fork he began to eat greedily. But Maska, watching with his own strange way of seeing, saw the food on the plate writhing and twisting in and out of itself. He drew himself up and, for a moment, though he did not quite know it, Brewer was in great danger.

But there was an interruption. Distant music made itself heard – not the mere twangle of the Greentown harps this time, but the sound of a trumpet, revelling its own triumphant sound with the solid thud of a drum beating below it. Brewer stiffened, then rushed from the room.

'Delicious,' said Ozul. 'Bring me more.'

The Fantasia moved through the corridors of the Greentown cellars, playing their music and singing their songs, opening doors as they went. Other people, bewildered strangers, staggered out, blinking and confused at first but then joining in with more and more confidence. They marched up the stairs. Bannister escorting the band and brushing aside any servants who tried to stop them . . . for, after all, Bannister was the strong man. The Fantasia marched along yet another corridor, climbed yet another stair and came out at last through great arched doors into that same main square in which they had performed earlier in the evening, cheering as they came, victorious, welcoming the rush of fresh air and the light of a half-moon. Their familiar vans were there, unpossessed and empty. They marched on. There was no way of stopping them.

From one doorway Maska saw them and cursed to himself. He wanted – he desperately wanted to charge across the square, to snatch Jewel from Goneril's arms and overpower Eden and Timon, but he was encumbered by Ozul, limp and smiling, babbling of happiness, even though he was slung across Maska's iron shoulder.

All Maska could do was to watch the Fantasia people crowding into their vans, singing and cheering as they did so. The motors started. The whole Fantasia shouted. Those not yet on board threw up their arms, before leaping into those vans, hanging out from doorways and waving out through windows. Wheels began to turn. While the Greentown people stood around helplessly, the Fantasia made for the road beyond the town.

In the leading van crammed in between Maddie and Yves, Boomer took from his pocket the two brooches he had stolen from that room full of strange objects and set them out in front of Yves.

'I saw these brooches down there,' he said. 'I thought they looked – sort of important in some way. And they'd stolen my drum, so I stole their jewels.'

Yves shot a glance down at the brooches, then looked hastily at the uncertain road again. At first he frowned, but then his expression changed.

'Take a look,' he said to Maddie, suddenly (it seemed) possessed by a sort of fury.

'They're Solis badges, aren't they? I reckon they're the badges of that other lot,' he said 'the lot that were sent out from Solis before us . . . those men that vanished and were never heard of again.' He shot a sideways glance at Maddie. 'Aren't they?'

'I'd say it's a dead cert that the last party Solis sent to Newton – the ones that never made it to Newton, wound up in Greentown,' Maddie said.

'It was my fault that *we* almost wound up there,' said Yves in a quiet bitter voice. 'My fault.'

'Forget it! It's part of the risk we take, isn't it?' Maddie answered. 'But we set a lot of people free from those rooms there down below the kitchens . . . a lot of people, and Boomer left them with the secret of freedom. They need a good drumbeat. So I'd say the ones that were set free might take over, wouldn't you? I'd say the Greentown people were well and truly outnumbered by their slaves.'

Sitting behind Maddie, Garland stirred restlessly.

'Boomer saved us,' she said a little blankly. 'He was the brave one. The clever one. The one who beat the drum.'

Tane's van edged up beside them, and Boomer found he was staring across at Timon. Timon looked back at him and smiled.

'Great work there, Boomer!' he shouted through the open window, sounding as if he meant it.

All the same there was still something in that smile that reminded Boomer of the savage mouth, its corners dragged down, of the face that Timon had worn, as he bent over Eden. Boomer gave Timon a rather weak smile, and a wave then looked away in a hurry. He really had been clever, he thought, but without meaning to. And now he was frightened of Timon, without being sure just why. It was hard to be sure of anything in this life, thought Boomer. That was the great thing about machines. Things happened because something else happened, and if you thought about it you could understand why and how. And he was one of those who really longed to be sure of everything. He sighed deeply. Perhaps that was the way it was when you were a Fantasia man. Things were always twisting into other shapes around you. In the end, there was nothing much you could do about it, except to march boldly ahead, beating your drum and singing.

18

The Children of Newton

So yet again the Fantasia rolled on, zigzagging up through a familiar mountain pass, then struggling to wind their way along a rutted track strewn with rocks . . . struggling even more to ride the road, when it reared up, trying, it seemed, to flick them into space. Once or twice they stopped because they had to stop, and Yves, Tane and Banister unpacked long, interlocking boards and rods of steel from the roofs of the vans and built bridges over deep clefts in the road. Then, when the vans had crawled safely across . . . when they had dismantled and packed the bridges up again . . . the Fantasia inched onwards and came, at last, out from between the sharp, almost perpendicular slopes, and onto a high plain they knew well. Once, during the Chaos there had been battles fought here and even now, so very many years later, the damage and the left-over signs of battle survived. There they were, those big machines left behind to rust . . . to flake away . . . almost melting into the land, yet rearing up defiantly every now and then, like natural sculptures of rock. But now spring came to meet them, draping the remains of the old battle with blue and pink flowers – flourishing periwinkle and fumitory.

And Yves, taking a turn to drive Maddie's van, tried to talk to Garland about it all.

'I never get used to it,' he said. 'It's more like the setting for some old story than a real countryside, isn't it?'

'I suppose so,' said Garland and, though she was secretly agreeing with Yves, she heard herself sounding guarded. She did not want to get too friendly with Yves . . . she wanted to keep him at an arm's length, even though she was simultaneously remembering all the times he had been brave and hard-working and brought the Fantasia along its difficult road. But perhaps trying to talk to her, trying to be nice to her, was just part of his way of working himself more deeply into Maddie's life. Perhaps he was trying to take her over, just as he was trying to take over the Fantasia, and make it his own.

Yves might have detected her caution, because after a while he stopped trying to talk to her and simply drove, looking ahead. Then suddenly he seemed to see something in the far distance . . . something he had been hoping to see.

'Look!' he shouted. 'Newton! Newton at last.'

Garland looked eagerly, but at first she could not make out any sign of the city. The horizon was smudged as if huge, dark thumbs had somehow rubbed along the edge of things, blurring them forever. Determined to see what Yves was claiming to see Garland screwed up her eyes, squinting at the horizon and then suddenly she recognized a different sort of smudging . . . a darker mark against the clear sky. Newton! It wasn't the biggest city in the world – not as big as Solis, anyway – but it was supposed to be the cleverest. It had inherited the wisdom of the men who founded the city and and enclosed it – wisdom which included a way of drawing the power of the sun out of sunshine, a way of imprisoning that power, a way of compressing it and locking it into cells, which other cities with the right technology could then use to turn wheels and drive pistons. Men and women who understood such things, or who *longed* to understand them, all made for Newton, and often found work there. However they had to swear oaths of secrecy, so that Newton could stay ahead of other cities. Once you became a citizen of Newton you had to be loyal to Newton alone.

'Will they actually trade a converter?' asked Garland suddenly doubtful. 'I mean will Fantasia's performances be enough to buy one?'

'Oh, a performance wouldn't buy the fraction of a converter,' said Yves. 'We'd have to perform for years, and even then they'd probably shrug us off. But Ferdy brought stuff from Solis . . . some old discs – ancient, really – that contain records from the past, *and* a few clues about the way things fit together. Newton doesn't know everything when all's said and done. People want to know their histories and Solis has a thousand histories. And then there's the whole question of how parents pass things on to children. Ferdy had red hair and you've got red hair. Boomer's dad used to be a great drummer and Boomer can beat out a good rhythm too. The wise men of Solis know how things like that are passed on and we think Newton might be glad of the knowledge. They've always been fascinated with their children in Newton. So we're hoping to trade wisdom for wisdom . . . history for mystery.'

Garland began to grin a little, then hesitated halfway through her grinning. In spite of herself she was enjoying her gossip with Yves. Quickly she pinched the corners of her mouth back into seriousness, determined not to be entertained by anything he might have to say.

'Of course Newton's got its own dangers,' Yves went on. 'It's bang on the top of a fault line.'

'A fault line?' Garland asked curiously.

'It has a lot of earthquakes,' Yves explained. 'That's why their buildings are so close to the ground. Apart from their old tower of course. Goodness knows how that has survived the quakes and shakes.'

'Are there any sweet shops?' asked Garland. 'We'll have to watch Lilith all over again if there are.'

Perhaps Yves thought she was criticizing Lilith.

'Well, make sure you do watch her,' he said. 'She's an impulsive little thing.'

So the Fantasia jolted forward, along one of those roads that kept dissolving and disappearing, and then struggling out of nothing once more, but even when the road vanished it did not much matter. Now they were able to see their goal . . . and, as they travelled on, ever on, Newton slowly took shape before them . . . a city of tall glassy buildings . . . stretching up out of the wild country around it, but spreading out too, as if determined to make certain it was in charge of the world.

KNOWLEDGE IS STRENGTH said the great words over the city's old arching gate.

'Just bear in mind,' Maddie was saying to Timon and Eden, 'that this city is devoted to the pursuit of learning.'

'Bear in mind that they are as mad as cut snakes,' said Yves, but in a quieter voice.

'As we go through that gate, they'll have us checked out,' said Maddie. 'They'll turn the lights on us and they reckon they can read our minds, so – pure thoughts everyone.'

They were there at last – ready to enter the city. The band assembled and the performers put on their costumes, as Newton's own sounds came flowing towards them . . . the sound of many voices shouting, arguing, it seemed. Rather an anxious sound.

'Some crisis!' said Maddie sounding dubious. 'Some huge argument! Shall we wait?'

'March on!' said Yves. 'It's our job to make people forget their arguments!' And the rest of the Fantasia agreed with him.

So they began their great Fantastic March, and came in through the gate. Suddenly long arrows of light appeared, aiming themselves at the band . . . the vans . . . the horses. Garland blinked as the lights passed across her face, imagining the light soaking into her through her eyes and reading all her secrets. She tried to keep her thoughts as pure as possible.

They moved on between the first houses and sheds, dancing and spinning, then moved triumphantly up the main road only to find themselves dancing and spinning between lines of children, who suddenly treated them as no other children Garland had ever treated the Fantasia before. Usually it was children who welcomed them with the greatest excitement, the strongest happiness, but the children of Newton seemed challenging – even hostile. They shouted, pointed derisively, made aggressive darts at the jugglers and acrobats and even threw rotting fruit at them. One girl ran at Garland, grabbed her arm and tried to swing her out of the Fantasia line.

'Join us!' she shouted. 'Don't be a traitor! Don't let the Biggies boss you around!'

But Garland was strong. She twitched her arm free quite easily, then pushed the girl back into the crowd she had come from. Something struck Lilith, who screamed, putting her hand to her head. She stared unbelievingly at fingers stained red.

'I'm dying,' she called. 'They've killed me.'

'You've just been hit by a rotting tomato,' Garland said, but she sympathized with Lilith, thinking that she too would have been terrified at finding her fingers stained scarlet like that.

'I haven't been here for ages,' Garland heard Maddie saying. 'I don't remember children – certainly not children like this.'

The Fantasia persisted. And then, quite suddenly, it seemed they had worked their way through the mocking hostile crowd behind them. The children peeled away into side streets and Garland heard one of them, a tall boy, shouting 'To the Fort!' 'To the Fort!' as if he were the one in charge of this wild band.

A few minutes later the Fantasia found themselves marching

towards the offices of the ruling council. *Knowledge is Strength!* said the words over the door, which opened cautiously, and then was flung wide. At last they were being welcomed, greeted by white-robed adults, quiet and courteous. Bowing a little, they walked alongside them, escorting them to the centre of the town which spread out like a great green lawn edged with tall buildings, some of them very old.

'Scrimshaw!' announced their leader holding out one hand to Yves while patting his own chest with the other.

'Maddigan's Fantasia,' said Yves, shaking the held-out hand.

'Of course,' said Scrimshaw. 'You were here some years ago. I loved the juggling . . . the arcs through the air. And I loved the way you whirled and danced on the trapezes . . . like strange irregular planets. We're so glad to see you.'

Almost at once they were being offered food and drink. 'We need distraction. We need a lure,' Scrimshaw was telling Yves. 'Come through into the Cortex – our centre of government, that is. I am sure our elders will welcome distraction every bit as much as the children will.'

'Oh we're not just a distraction on this occasion,' Maddie said, determined not to be left out, 'we're traders as well. We've got something to trade . . . our treasure for yours . . .'

Garland tried to hear what was going on, but she was interrupted.

'What are you doing?' Boomer asked coming up, drum and all, on one side of her. 'Look! They're giving us a party.'

'You and your mother don't have to do the deals any more,' Lilith said, bouncing up on the other side. 'My father will work it out. We can just eat stuff and leave it to him.'

'But something's happening,' said Garland impatiently. She could see Eden and Timon drifting towards them. 'Why did all those children attack us as we came in? That's never happened before.'

'Hey!' said Timon, almost like Garland's echo. 'Why did all those children throw things and shout at us? You'd think they'd be thrilled to see a show like ours.'

'Ours' he had said as if he were part of the Fantasia. Garland found herself looking at him with a kind of soft longing though she did not quite know what she was longing for. Company perhaps. The company of someone her own age or maybe a little older . . . someone who was certainly older than Boomer and Lilith, those jiggling irritating children dancing around her.

'They must be jealous of our cleverness,' Lilith was saying, while Garland, sternly shaking herself out the unexpectedly soft mood that had sneaked out of nowhere and taken her over, tried to listen past Lilith's bouncing cries to hear what Yves and Maddie were saying. She edged towards the adult group, working out who was who. She knew the Fantasia people of course and she knew Scrimshaw by now, but there was also a thin serious-faced man called Doppler and Doppler's wife, Rosalind, listening gravely to Maddie.

'. . . these records we're bringing you are unique,' Maddie's voice came drifting across to her, sounding rather taken aback. 'They're treasures.'

'I well remember your past visit,' Doppler said, totally ignoring Maddie's offer of records. 'I remember your clowns. I imagine children must love the clowns. That is a fact, is it not?'

'Oh yes, children love clowns,' agreed Yves. 'Adults do too. But if you don't mind we'd like to discuss the possibility of buying a solar converter from you. Trading knowledge for knowledge, because, as you know, knowledge is power . . .'

'But we are already committed,' said the deeper voice of one of the Newton officials. 'We have sold the only available converter.'

'And the prices we have already agreed to may be even better than anything you have to offer,' said another, and then there was a mixed-up mumble of talk, the voices weaving backwards and forwards. The deep voice suddenly emerged again.

'. . . besides we also have problems at the present. We are having to cope with a curious chaos of our own. Our children are in revolt. They say they are tired of being told what to do by their parents. They say they want to run their own lives.'

'It seems they are desperate to have their own way,' said another official.

Boomer and Lilith were arguing about just where a drummer should march in a Fantasia band. Garland turned towards them in astonishment.

'Did you hear that? Shut up you two. Did you *hear* it?'

They stood staring at her, their mouths hanging open.

'Hear what?' asked Lilith.

'I heard,' said Eden. 'The children are revolting.'

'They are not! They're just kids like us,' said Boomer indignantly.

'No! He means they're having a revolution,' said Timon. 'There's a mutiny against parents. The children want to take the world over.'

Behind them Maddie's vice rose, sounding both astonished and indignant.

'Well, *make* them! Make them do as they're told. I mean children should have a lot of freedom . . . I agree to that . . . but they shouldn't be in *charge*.'

'You don't understand,' said Doppler. 'These children – *our* children – are our treasures. You know that back before the Remaking the people who lived in Newton couldn't have children . . . the war had poisoned the land . . . poisoned the water. Of course the earthquakes didn't help. But then the trace element was sourced.'

'The helix was unravelled,' put in Rosalind. 'The contamination was contained.'

'Nature was allowed to be natural,' Doppler said rather smugly. 'The first child born here – well, it was a blessing – an occasion for celebration. Huge celebration! And slowly, slowly we worked our way back to a time when children could be born here. We treasure them.'

'We don't oppose them,' said another voice. 'Opposition might damage their certainty of self. All the same . . .'

'Well, as we came in they met us, and *self* was the only thing they seemed to be certain of,' said Maddie. 'And any self has to fit in with other selves . . . the selves of friends and neighbours and visitors . . . even parents. Now, did you say you have only the one solar converter that you are free to trade?'

'. . . and that you have just sold it to someone else?' finished Yves.

'There is another delegation in town you see. A small delegation from Solis,' explained Rosalind. 'Their offer is not perhaps as elegant as yours but they were here first and we agreed . . .'

'They *can't* come from Solis,' Maddie cried. 'We represent Solis. Where are these traders?'

'They did tell us you would be here,' said Scrimshaw, 'and they did say you would put on a show for us. We do need something to distract us. Our minds have not been focused on manufacture . . .'

As she tried to listen in to the words of this debate, Garland suddenly became aware of other voices and turned to find a group of children had moved in around their edges and that Lilith had started talking to the boy who seemed to be at the head of the group.

'Kaanaana?' she was saying, screwing up her face as if she couldn't quite work out what he was saying. 'Bol-ek-kana! Is that your name?'

'Everyone calls me Kaana. Well, that's what I call myself, and what I say goes,' the boy replied, strutting a little. 'What were you doing marching along like prisoners, letting the Biggies go first?'

Careful thought Garland. *Lilith's going to be in trouble again if we don't watch out. She'd love the thought of being in charge of herself.*

'Kaana!' exclaimed Eden as if it were a name he recognized.

'We always let the Biggies go first,' said Boomer. 'People can see them – the Biggies that is – from way off. And if there's a crowd they can make out the Biggies over the heads of other people. They can hear my drum of course, but they want to actually *see* things as well.'

'Don't you ever do what grown-ups tell you to do?' asked Lilith. There was a dangerous note of admiration creeping into her voice.

'No! Never!' said a girl at Kaana's elbow. 'We don't eat what we're told. We don't go to bed when we're told. We've broken off from that lot. We live a free life.'

'I am Kaana,' declared Kaana once more, thumping his chest in a boastful way, 'and what I say goes. Anyhow, what are you doing in my city?'

'*Your* city?' exclaimed Garland.

Timon and Eden were staring at Kaana as if he utterly fascinated them.

'They do whatever we tell them to,' said Kaana grandly.

'But with us the Fantasia works because our parents work it,' protested Garland. 'We're part of the Fantasia . . . we're right in it . . . but it just wouldn't work without Maddie . . . or Yves,' she added reluctantly glancing over at Lilith. 'If your father wasn't there to be ringmaster and to help with shifting the heavy stuff . . .'

'We could probably do most of it by now,' Boomer interrupted her, obviously impressed with the ideas of the Newton children, and Lilith leapt in to agree.

'These kids are right,' she said. 'We could do the Fantasia on our own.'

'Hey! Look!' Garland exclaimed. 'You! You for example. When you hurt yourself you run straight to Yves, wanting a hug. When the weather's bad, he's the one who stands out in the wind and rain, tightening the ropes and making sure things don't fall off the roof-racks. You're just going along with this lot because you're a brat – and they're brats too.'

'And you just say that because you think you're the boss of the Fantasia,' yelled Lilith. 'You're always on about how you're a Maddigan as if just having that name makes you so wonderful.'

'Forget her,' Kaana cried to Lilith. 'Leave her to be a slave. Come with us!'

And, suddenly, as if they had exchanged a secret signal, Kaana and Lilith and the three other children took off, Lilith waving her arms in the air as if she were indeed shrugging herself free from secret and invisible bonds. The ribbons on her looped, brown braids flapped like butterflies keeping pace with her.

'Lilith! Don't be stupid!' yelled Garland. 'Come back!' But Lilith did not so much as turn her head. 'Lilith! Don't get lost!' She did not want Lilith getting lost for a second time . . . it had been so complicated . . . such a problem . . . back in Greentown. Not only that Garland was suddenly filled with concern, for, though Lilith really annoyed her, she certainly did not want her lost out there in the unknown streets of a city that was seeming almost hostile. Lilith was part of her own life . . . she could just remember when Lilith had been born, could remember the death of Lilith's mother, something Lilith could not remember herself. Memories like that grew into you and became part of what you were.

'Are you just going to let her run off like that?' asked Eden, looking suddenly concerned.

'It's what she wanted to do,' said Garland uncertainly. 'Any-how she'll be back.'

'But she can't zoom away with a lot of aliens,' said Boomer.

'Oh, all right!' said Garland, a little impatiently. She looked around and saw the grown-ups were talking with one another . . . wheeling and dealing, Maddie would say. Garland sighed. 'It looks like we've got a bit of time. Let's find out where they were taking her.'

So, followed by Boomer, Eden and Timon, she turned her back on Maddie and Yves still talking with the grave Newton men and women, turned her back all that adult discussion, to follow Kaana, Lilith and the other children, running through a crowd who made way for them, smiling indulgently as they jostled past. They ran down a street set with long, low shops, hard for a Fantasia person to pass by. At the other end of the street Garland could see Lilith trying to slow down so that she could look in at the windows. But Kaana was grabbing her arm and tugging her forwards. Lilith had certainly wanted to go . . . had certainly wanted to run and leap after sitting in a van for so long . . . had definitely wanted, in her Lilith way, to be one of the ones in charge of the world, and yet, as she ran with the children of Newton, she suddenly seemed like a captive, taken over by those wild children. And the wild children seemed to be waving her like a sort of captured flag as they ran.

Turning a corner they came into yet another street of shops, with narrow houses built above them. At the end of the street rose a tall grey building, plain, square and somehow aggressive, the tallest building in Newton. Standing around its black, blank front door were a few adults looking as if they were waiting to be let in. Directly above the door was a large window. Another slightly smaller window was set above that first and a third blinked out above the other two. Each had a small balcony curving in front of it. Apart from these three glassy eyes the wide face of the building was entirely blank except for a large official symbol painted to the left of the windows, a sign that Garland recognized in a vague way, though she couldn't remember what it stood for.

As Lilith, Kaana and their companions ran towards this curiously sinister building, the front door, which had seemed so tightly sealed, swung open. Garland could see other children crowded in the space behind it, holding it wide so that Kaana, Lilith and their companions could run through. The adults also moved, darting towards the door, shouting some sort of appeal, as if they, too, wanted to be allowed in. But the door slammed quickly behind the children. Those anxious adults were shut out once more.

Garland came up, panting and puzzled, and listened in. It seemed the adults were pleading with the children inside.

'Do come out,' a woman was calling. 'We're your parents, not your enemies. We can work something out. And we miss you. We really miss you. Do come out.'

The window over the door suddenly opened and a girl looked down at them.

'No!' she cried. 'We're not coming out. You think you're the bosses of this town, but we're the important ones really. We're the future, we are, and this is our fort. You're nothing but a lot of Biggies and Oldies.'

'But it's dangerous in there,' called another woman. 'You know what they stored down below there in the old times.'

'Ages ago! Out of date!' another child shouted, looking over the shoulder of the first.

'Still dangerous,' the woman pleaded.

'It never goes out of date,' said another.

'We want to be in charge,' shouted a boy from somewhere in the shadows behind the girl. 'Children can run the world.'

'We won't get Lilith out of there in a hurry,' said Boomer

dubiously. 'She'll be really keen on ideas like those. And that door's shut and guarded. Hey! We'd better get back and tell Yves.'

'We should have grabbed her,' Garland said. 'But she was off that quickly . . .'

'Let's go back,' begged Boomer. 'Yves might have some ideas.'

'Maddie might too,' Garland said quickly. 'She's the one for good ideas.'

'Yes, but Yves is taller,' said Boomer, and they began to run back down between the shop windows, suddenly anxious that they might have been missed, and that there might be trouble in store for them.

19

Human Pyramid

They came back to find the Fantasia people staring angrily across the city square at a group of men sitting outside a tavern, drinking what looked like ale, laughing and toasting one another, while the Newton people flitted around Yves and Maddie, obviously trying to make peace with them.

Garland stared not so much at the ale-drinkers as at the familiar figures sitting with them. Ozul and Maska, looking battered and damaged but triumphant. Seeing them smiling smugly over at the Fantasia she felt she understood everything and was filled with desperation.

'But who *are* they?' Maddie was exclaiming. 'Why are they haunting us? Why have they got it in for us?'

'It's to do with Timon and Eden, isn't it?' Tane put in. 'Maybe if we offered to swap the boys for the converter . . .'

'Never!' cried Maddie. 'They're Fantasia people now and Fantasia people are true to one another.'

'I know that,' Tane cried back. 'I didn't mean it. I was joking.'

'Let's take them on,' Yves was saying. 'Let's march over there and suggest . . . just suggest . . . that they withdraw their offer. We've come all this way to get the converter for Solis. We're not going home without it.'

'Are you implying violence?' cried Scrimshaw, cutting in on

the Fantasia debate, as if he could scarcely believe what he was hearing. 'I tell you we have already come to an agreement with them. Signed and sealed!'

'Yves! Careful!' cried Maddie. But she was not altogether attending. She was looking around as if she had lost something, and Garland sighed knowing exactly what Maddie was looking for.

'Hi, Mum,' she called, trying to sound reassuring.

Maddie had indeed missed Garland and was certainly not pleased with her.

'Why *will* you keep running away like this?' she said. 'You know it drives me up the wall. And we need help with the unpacking and setting up and so on. They want a full performance. They're hoping a circus act might bring their children back into the fold.'

Garland could see that, on beyond Maddie, the group of white-robed Newton people had swollen. There were now several women there, apparently arguing with the men. Garland looked back to Maddie.

'We had to go,' she said. 'Lilith ran off first. She skidded away with some of the Newton kids. We wanted to get her back, but we couldn't.'

'What!' cried Yves, swinging around. 'Did you say Lilith has gone away with those – those ruffians? Why weren't you watching her? Where did they go?'

'There's a building a few streets away . . .' began Garland, 'and . . .'

'Oh yes,' said Scrimshaw, pushing in quickly. 'The children have taken over a space for themselves in an old building. They call it "The Fort". Of course we're not happy about the militaristic element in their games, but . . .'

'Where is this fort?' asked Yves, entirely forgetting the converter for a moment.

But one of the Newton women cut in.

'That Kaana – he thinks he knows everything!' she cried. 'And that old building . . . We should have got rid of it years ago. I know it's part of our history, and some people think history's important. And I know it's stood up against the earthquakes over the years. And of course it's hard to know what to do with what's down in the basement but . . .'

Other people joined in and the end of her sentence was lost. A crowd of Newton people began moving down the street as if something was going on and they didn't want to miss it. Maddie and Yves, suddenly alarmed, began to move with them.

'Why didn't you stop her?' Yves shouted at Boomer and Garland. 'This is the second time you've let her get away on you. Heaven knows she's smaller than you. You could have grabbed her . . .'

'She was gone so quickly,' said Timon. 'I mean Garland and Boomer were arguing with her and then these other children somehow . . .'

'Kaana made her feel she'd have a great time if she joined in with them,' said Eden. 'And they – they sort of whisked her off.'

Soon Garland, Timon and Eden were looking up at that square grey building once more, but this time they were surrounded by a mixed crowd of Fantasia performers and Newton people. And there, on the balcony that stuck out like a pouting lip over the door, Kaana stood, legs astride, looking scornfully down at them as if he were king of the world and they were his humble subjects. Mothers and father gazed up at the balcony, trying to reason with Kaana or shouting pleadingly to children who (they knew) were somewhere behind him. Kaana turned. They could see him tugging something and a moment later Lilith was standing beside him, like some treasure he wanted to display. Garland thought Lilith might be looking a little unsure of herself, but it was hard to be certain. And now Yves was pointing up at the painted symbol.

'That's a bio-hazard sign!' he exclaimed incredulously. 'Are you letting your precious children play in a building full of toxic waste?'

'It's quite safe,' Doppler said. 'The waste is shut away in sealed cellars under the building. There's a layer of lead in that ground floor.'

Doppler fell silent, but now unexpectedly Rosalind wheeled on him.

'He wants his daughter and I want my Kaana!' she shouted. She spun round to face Maddie. '*I* don't believe it's safe. Drums of poison . . . waste from the old days. We can't bury it. We can't empty it into the rivers. It's been kept there in the bottom of that old house. So there are two risks for the children . . . the risk of falling out of the windows and the risk of being poisoned. They've been warned over and over again. But you know what kids are. They think they can do anything . . .'

'. . . get away with everything,' called another woman. 'Doppler, you're a deep thinker. Work out a way to bring those children down . . .'

'. . . down and out . . .'

'I'm sure it is safe,' said Doppler feebly.

'Don't the children realize?' Yves cried angrily, ignoring Doppler. 'Don't they care? Lilith! Lilith! Come down at once. It's dangerous up there.'

Kaana nudged Lilith.

'I don't have to listen to you any more,' she piped back, her voice sounding thin and not entirely certain of itself. A chorus of childish voices cheered somewhere behind her.

'Yes, you do,' called Yves. 'Come down at once.'

'Kaana says we're the future, not you,' Lilith called.

'Lilith, I mightn't be the future, but I *am* your father,' Yves called back, but by now unseen children were making such a row Lilith probably did not hear him. If she did she gave no sign of it.

Garland had been staring upward too. But now she glanced over at Timon and Eden. They were standing off to one side, talking rapidly to one another. And, thought Garland, there was something odd about their expressions. They were looking strangely startled, as if someone had given them surprising news. Leaving Yves to argue with Lilith, she wandered towards the boys.

'You look as if you've got ideas,' she said as she came up to them. 'Anything useful?'

'Nothing useful,' said Timon. 'Just something weird, weird, weird! Because we suddenly remember something about Newton.'

'Okay! What?' asked Garland.

'In the future there are floods – it's in the history books – and the city sort of *subsides* . . .' Timon began.

'. . . sinks . . .' put in Eden. 'And it becomes poisoned too. So the Newton people make for Solis.'

'Of course they take their knowledge with them,' said Timon, 'and they get work there. But it's partly their knowledge the Nennog uses to – well, to become the Nennog. It's like a family story to us because . . .'

Eden interrupted him again.

'. . . because Kaana up there – he's our great great great-grandfather. I mean he seems pretty dumb now, but once he hits Solis he becomes a great geneticist, and it's partly his work the Duke of Solis used to turn himself into the Nennog. If it wasn't for Kaana, we wouldn't exist. Weird!'

Voices broke in on them. Yves had begun shouting at Doppler again.

'Oh, I'm sure they'll come out in good time,' Doppler said in a soothing voice.

'Lilith will get bored,' said Boomer. 'She'll start whining. She always does.'

'Or maybe they'll throw her over the side,' said Bannister. 'You never know your luck.'

And then something happened that somehow changed everything. The ground began to quiver.

At first Garland thought it was something that the children were bringing about, perhaps by stamping and beating the walls, but the quiver grew stronger. It took over the whole world around them. The town around them began creaking and rattling. The very earth under their feet somehow rippled as if a huge wind was blowing up from the centre of the world to twist the land around them.

'Earthquake time!' yelled Yves, tilting this way, tilting that way, trying to keep his balance. 'As if we didn't have enough to cope with,' he groaned as he tumbled over.

Garland tilted this way and that as well and then she, too, fell on her back. At last the shaking stopped, but Garland found herself staring into the sky and dancing with a sudden idea.

'Mum! Yves!' she cried. 'We could put on an act down here. Those children up there might quieten down and watch. They might come down to get a better view of us.'

'They might throw tomatoes at us,' said Boomer suspiciously.

'I mean if they were interested they might come down,' Garland persisted, 'and . . .'

'Worth a try!' exclaimed Yves. 'It's worked before.' He turned to the men and women around him. 'And if we solved your problem . . .'

Maddie cut in.

'If we solved your problem,' she said, 'you might see your way to solving ours. You might pay us with the converter.'

'Either way I want my daughter out of that building,' said Yves.

'Who else wanted that converter?' asked Timon. He asked quietly but the women heard him.

'That lot over there,' said Scrimshaw's wife, Barbara. 'They've offered a good price but . . .'

She was pointing towards the back of the crowd, and looking back Garland could see, and knew Timon could see as well, those two tall dark figures watching them.

'Do what you like!' Kaana yelled. 'Be as clever as you can. But you won't get us out.'

Grown-ups called up to the children above them. The children yelled down, enjoying their power. Garland listened to them and suddenly found she was wondering about herself.

'Do you think I'm too . . . too . . .' she began, turning to Eden. 'Too bossy?'

'OK, you can be a bit too Maddiganish at times!' Eden said, speaking absent-mindedly. 'And you treat Yves as if he were some sort of spy from an alien world.' But he wasn't looking at Garland, he was staring after Timon. 'What's up with Timon?' he asked her suddenly. 'Why was he talking in that sort of voice?'

But Garland was not interested in Timon just then. She thought about the possibility that she had been somehow unfair to Lilith, and stared up at the narrow window. 'Hey Lilith!' she called. 'Lilith! Sorry! Sorry if I . . . anyhow, come on down again. We miss you.'

'I miss you,' Yves called, taking a cue from Garland. 'You're part of the Fantasia. Come back to us.'

From where they stood they could see Lilith smiling. She looked down at them with a grin that was half-defiant, but also a little ashamed. And then she turned, and it seemed as if she might successfully climb down the stairs and come running out through the front door to join them, laughing and pleased to have worried them. But as she turned, Kaana grabbed her arm.

'No deserting!' he was yelling at her. 'If you want to go down there we'll push you off the balcony.'

'We'll *catch* you,' called Boomer. 'We're champion catchers.'

Maddie turned to Eden. 'You!' she said. 'You're the magician. Do something – something to get their attention.'

Eden immediately flung his arms wide, juggling stars and bells. As he did this a curious ghostly forest grew up around him. Trees green with leaves, chattering with birds, yet somehow woven out of cobwebs and moonlight arched over his head. Inside the fort a sudden silence fell. The runaway children were fascinated. Kaana felt the fascination too and it made him angry. He bent and picked something up from the floor of his balcony, drew back his arm and threw it furiously at Eden, but Eden was ready. The stone – if indeed it was a stone – broke into two pieces – pieces with wings. One bird flew left. The other flew right. They flew into the cobweb trees and vanished.

And now, at last, not only the children at the windows but Kaana himself grew silent, touched with the wonder of what he was being shown. Eden danced and clapped his hands. Flowers began to fall over the children on the balcony. Eden flung his arms high and suddenly he was holding a rose – a huge white rose which he tossed up to Lilith, who leaned over to catch it and then began waving it triumphantly.

Eden called up to the balcony and the windows above it. 'This is nothing!' he cried, panting just a little, 'this is just a bit of a taste . . . come down and see the rest of us.' Then he leapt into the air, flung his arms wide and seemed to drift back to earth like a leaf, while the children at the windows disappeared, and some of the children on the balcony, Lilith among them, turned making for the door behind them. The walls around them seemed to quiver and breathe out dust.

'Go carefully!' shouted Yves. 'Good work,' he said sideways to Eden. 'Get to work on that drum of yours!' he told Boomer.

And within a moment or two the Fantasia band began leading the Fantasia back away from the building with a crowd of Newton people following. And in twos and threes some of the rebellious children began pushing through the arched door and began following the crowd, keeping their distance to begin with, but then relaxing, becoming part of it all as they looked for and found their anxious parents.

'Stop!' shouted Kaana furiously. 'Everyone stop! Come back.'

Lilith twisted around and watched him critically. 'You're not really much of a boss are you?' she said.

And then she screamed – everyone screamed – for the balcony, the building, the whole town of Newton suddenly began rocking again.

'Just hang on!' Kaana yelled.

This time the town did not merely groan and rattle. Somewhere behind them there was a huge crash. Somewhere a building had tumbled. And as the people of Newton and the people of the Fantasia were flung from side to side, sometimes crashing to the ground again, the concrete cube of the Fort began to crack in two. A jagged line, fine as a thread to begin with, suddenly ran down from the roof to the top window, then down to the second. Glass shattered. That jagged line widened as it moved to the window above the door and then seemed to stab into the ground. Dust puffed out into the air, fragments of concrete fell around them.

Garland was one of the people bowled over by the earthquake. She sprawled on the ground for a second time, bruised and blinking, then bit by bit, a leg here, an arm there stood up, wobbling, though she wasn't quite sure if the wobble was a wobble in the world or a wobble in her own bones.

'Look! Look!' screamed Boomer.

Billowing out of the ground, forcing its way out through the crack that had run down to the ground, came a cloud of green-ish smoke like a blurred monster anxious to devour anything in its path. Rosalind screamed, and she was not the only one. As the cloud rolled towards them, many of the Fantasia people fled before it.

'Don't breathe it in,' Doppler was calling, but it was hard not to, as it flooded the air around them. 'Stand back! Stand back!'

'Kaana!' Rosalind was sobbing.

A voice came from somewhere above them – from the balcony, thought Garland.

'Dad! Dad!' Lilith was calling.

'Mum!' called Kaana. 'The stair's broken. Get us down!'

His confident voice had changed. The great green serpent of smoke could not be ordered back into the ground and anyone could hear that bold, determined Kaana was frightened.

'Lilith,' muttered Yves, taking no notice of Kaana. 'We'll never get in at that main door now. We'll need to bring them down from above.'

'Logical. Yes, logical,' said Scrimshaw. 'Perhaps the helicop-ter . . .'

'You have a helicopter?' cried Maddie.

'We have plans to build one,' said Scrimshaw rather compla-cently.

'We won't be able to wait for you to fit one together . . .' yelled Yves. We need to do something *now*!'

Green smoke billowed out of the door, but the balcony was still clear . . . easy to see up there above them.

'Human pyramid!' Garland yelled. 'Human pyramid!'

'Good idea,' Maddie said in a quiet but commanding voice. 'Human pyramid!' she shouted.

Bannister, Yves, Byrna and Nye ran forward and dropped onto their hands and knees directly under the balcony. Tane, along with two shy young acrobats – Lattin and Moira – leapt up onto them and knelt on their backs, Maddie and old Shell leapt first onto Bannister then up onto Tane then up yet again to kneel partly on Tane and Lattin, partly on Lattin and Moira, while Garland leapt from Bannister to Tane to Maddie and stood there holding out her hands to Lilith, who was already lowering herself over the balcony rail and down into Garland's arms. It was easy with Lilith. She had had practice with human pyramids, but Kaana, who was to come down after her, was much more difficult. For one thing he was bigger and heavier. For another he was desperately afraid.

'I'll fall!' he was screaming. 'I'll fall! I'll fall!'

'Quickly!' said Garland. 'I'll catch you. I can. I know how to.'

'If you stay there you'll be poisoned!' yelled Boomer.

'We're here to catch you!' shouted Timon and he and Eden stood on either side of the pyramid, arms raised.

'For heaven's sake hurry!' yelled Yves.

Kaana was hanging, terrified, from the balcony. A line of green mist lazily curved out and over his head. He hung there kicking and screaming like a little child.

'I've got you,' Garland told him – though she hadn't quite.

'No, you haven't,' Kaana cried, but his fingers were slipping. He dropped into Garland's arms, so desperate and so heavy that they both tumbled sideways. Everyone around them yelled out. Then Garland found she was rolling on the ground, her own fall broken by old Goneril of all people, while Kaana was being hugged by Timon. He and Timon were nose to nose for a moment but curiously enough Kaana did not seem to be grateful. He let out a wailing cry as if he was being terrified by something totally new and unexpected, and Timon immediately dropped him on his feet and let him go.

'Away! Away!' someone was shouting as the Fantasia's pyramid fell apart, as Bannister, Tane, Byrna, Nye and all the others bounced onto their feet again.

And then they were all running, Kaana actually crying as he ran.

And then – only a few minutes later it seemed – the whole population of Newton seemed to be gathering around the Fantasia people exclaiming with gratitude and hugging their children.

'The converter is yours,' said Doppler. 'You've bought it in more ways than one.'

'We didn't arrange the earthquake,' Maddie said. 'We can't take credit for that. But we do what we *do* do . . . what we *can* do. We can help you tidy up a bit . . . and then we can offer you a performance.'

And this is what they did.

And meanwhile, out of town, off in the deepening shadows, Ozul was taking things from one of the black packs which he had faithfully carried, suspended from his shoulder or strung across his chest.

He pressed a lever. A screen sprang up . . . or perhaps the shape of a screen, for though it had a shape this screen seemed to have no surface. Ozul and Maska both looked deep into a spinning void. Green light suddenly flared from within the void, falling on Maska and Ozul and appearing to sink deep into their skins. A sound made itself heard, incoherent to begin with but gradually forming words . . . furious words.

'. . . and you have achieved nothing . . . nothing . . .' the voice said. 'The fools of that past time have tricked you over and over again.'

'Sir and Master,' Ozul replied. 'They *are* fools, these Fantasia people, but they are *tricky* fools. They are whimsical. They have minds that go off at an angle. They have not been properly subdued and you did tell us not to subdue them in case our own time is too – too *changed* by their submission. You told us to be very, very careful.'

'No excuses,' said the voice, coming and going as if its reality was not quite certain. 'This is a final warning. You must not let that converter get back to Solis. And you must find the Talisman and bring it home to me. Otherwise you face deletion. Enough!'

The curious spin within the frame stopped and disappeared. Ozul sighed, and touched the lever. The frame closed itself down again. Ozul looked at Maska, and then looked over at the bright lights marking the place where the Fantasia and the people of Newton were actually dancing and singing together. The performance had turned into a party.

And the Fantasia people partied with great pleasure, glad to be at ease with the world. Garland danced with Timon, and thought that she could not remember a time when she had even felt so light-hearted. 'I'm happy!' she thought. 'Happy *now*! Tomorrow will be a *usual* tomorrow . . . full of questions and arguments. But right now, dancing with Timon, I'm happy.'

On the edge of the celebration Boomer moved to sit beside an extremely subdued Kaana.

'We'll be off tomorrow or the next day,' he said. 'We never stay long.'

'Good,' said Kaana, but he said it in a curiously listless way.

Boomer looked left and right, just in case there was anyone listening to them, and then he said in a low voice, 'That boy Timon . . . the one dancing with Garland . . . he isn't one of our tricksters, not like his brother. But he – he seemed to frighten you. How did he . . .'

Kaana interrupted him.

'He isn't a boy,' his voice rose. Suddenly he was filled with a terror he dared not express. 'He's . . . not a real boy! He looks like one, but I looked into his eyes and a – a – a sort of demon looked back at me.'

'I know,' said Boomer. 'It's looked out at me, too. But no one would believe me if I tried to tell them.' And he stared across at Timon, knowing for sure that something was wrong but quite unable to give a name to it.

20

The Tunnels of the Dead

Dear Ferdy, we moved on . . . but it is different now.
We have the converter and we are on our way to Solis
again . . . on our way home. Of course the Fantasia
itself with all its vans and wagons is our true home, but
Solis is our resting place. It's really spring now . . . flowers
growing up out of the grass and the fruit trees blossom-
ing. And the mountains which we crossed earlier –
those mountains which often look like a sort of scribble
across the edge of the sky, now look like real land once
more . . . scarred land . . . like teeth biting into the
blueness. I danced with Timon at Newton. We danced
and danced together and somehow or other our steps
seemed to match. It was the best dancing I have ever
done. It just shows. If you want to dance really well you
need the right partner.

Spring or not the weather was not good. In the morning
Yves called for a brief parley.

'I think we might have to go through the tunnels this
time,' he said. 'And that means it will be quicker to take that
other road home. We'll check out the pass, but this weather is
really dicey!'

The Fantasia moved on.

'The tunnels were once the roads to old mines,' Garland told Timon and Eden, 'and the roads branch out under the mountains. It's slow going underground. Exciting though!'

But at that moment there was rumble and then cries from somewhere ahead. Garland, followed by the two boys, ran to see what was going on.

'It's blocked,' Yves was saying.

'A slip,' said Tane. 'The road into the pass is blocked.'

'At least we weren't caught in it,' said Yves. 'But it'll take us weeks to move this lot. We will have to take the tunnels.'

'Oh no!' exclaimed Timon which was so unexpected that everyone turned to look at him and he shrank back into himself. 'I've heard they're – they're sort of poisoned,' he mumbled. 'And Eden hates underground ways.'

'They press in on me,' said Eden. 'Even if I shut my eyes I can feel the world pushing down on me, trying to squash me flat.'

'It could be like an adventure,' Garland said. 'We'll help you.'

'We can't shift those rocks,' Yves repeated. 'Maybe Newton could help. They've got those big earth-moving machines there. But we don't have anything like that.'

Maddie stood, frowning over the map which flapped as if it were trying to escape from her.

'Urupokainia . . . the underground road,' she read, and then looked around at them all. 'I promise it's not too bad. Ferdy and I went through there once. On our first tour together.'

'Regular tunnel of love as I recall,' said Goneril. 'Let's just get on with it. That baby kept me up all night cutting teeth. And you two,' she looked at Timon and Eden, 'you don't look twice at her. You don't offer to mash her food or change her nappies.'

'Look!' said Yves. 'I'm going to have a closer look at that

blocked road.' Leaning sideways he grabbed Boomer's bike and leapt onto it, and set off up the road. He was rather too big for the bike and looked extremely odd, like some sort of Fantasia clown . . . but the faithful motor carried him well enough.

Lilith shrieked, 'Don't, Daddy! Don't, Daddy!' terrified that she was going to see him fall over the edge.

'There's nothing to be worried about,' Yves yelled back to her, then swung around still shouting as he did so. 'It's perfectly safe.' But, even as he was telling her how safe it was, there was a sudden violent explosion. Yves and the bike flew into the air, torn apart from one another. Yves went in one direction and Lilith's shrieks seem to go with him. The bike went in another followed by Boomer's cries of alarm. Yves smashed into the ground and lay there gasping. The bike hit the ground and promptly blew up.

'Daddy!' screamed Lilith and would have run to him, but Maddie caught her by the collar.

'No! No, Lilith! The track must be mined. It'll be a Road Rat trap. They must have tracked us and set up a trap so that they could get us on the way back from Newton. And there might be other mines . . . stay here.'

Through the dust and grit and smoke they could see Yves slowly sitting up. Even sitting seemed as if it was rather too much for him.

All the same he dragged himself onto his feet, swaying like a tall tree in a wind that no one but he could feel.

'What a surprise,' he said croakily. 'First bad weather and now explosions.'

'Follow the trail your bike left,' called Garland, and everyone looked at her as if she were speaking in some foreign language. 'Well, he got that far up the hill without being blown up,' she said rather defensively.

Maddie nodded, then turned back towards Yves.

'Can you see the trail?' she called.

Yves looked around in a vague way. 'I don't know,' he said sounding lost. But then his voice sharpened. 'Yes I can,' he said. 'Just!'

'Follow it back to us!' Maddie told him. 'Go carefully!' And they watched, all terrified as Yves gathered himself together and jumped for the track the bike had left behind it only a few minutes earlier. He walked along it rather like Garland walking a tightrope, carefully, carefully, just as if there were a thousand feet of empty space below him. When he stepped out among them, there was a curious puffing sound – the sound of held-in breaths being set free, and Lilith hurled herself on Yves with such force she almost knocked him back into the dangerous ground once more. But Yves was looking over Lilith's head . . . looking at Maddie. Garland felt her face taken over by a frown. After all *she* was the one who had pointed out the bike tracks. *She* was the one Yves should be thanking.

'Let's press on then,' Goneril said in the voice of someone who wanted to put a lot of unnecessary rubbish behind her. 'Urupokainia! Tunnels of the Dead, here we come!'

'My bike!' Boomer was saying as if he could hardly believe himself. 'My bike! It was the best thing I had – that bike – and now it's all smashed up.'

And off we went Garland wrote to Ferdy, but writing this time on some page that existed only in her head. She could see the imaginary pencil leaving imaginary silver words behind it. *You know how it is. If one road does not work we have to try another, so we turned around, which was really hard and then went back down the mountainside. The sky is clearing now, and now we can see the roads branching out down below and winding . . . winding . . . and of course we are winding too. I am uncomfortable about it because we did not want to go this way and yet it seems as if we haven't got any choice. Cattle must feel like this when they are being herded. And who knows? Those enemies Ozul and Maska are probably watching us from somewhere, watching us come . . . watching us go . . .*

She could not see them but in a curious way she had come to feel their presence. And indeed they were watching, battered but implacable – watching the Fantasia retrace its way down the road that would have taken them through the pass, and then swinging off along a narrow but sweeping road to the right.

'There they go!' said Ozul in his voice stumbling and impeded now. His lower jaw did not seem to be moving easily. 'We must follow.'

'. . . follow . . .' said Maska like a grating echo, speaking with even more difficulty than Ozul.

And when the Fantasia was well launched on its new road Ozul and Maska did indeed follow, moving rapidly but carefully too, moving through the shadows which seemed to greet them and take them in as if they were old friends.

Timon, Eden, Boomer and Garland walked beside the slowly moving vans, Garland and Timon just a little ahead, Boomer and Eden following. They could hear Lilith's voice coming from inside the nearest van.

'Dad, why are they called the Tunnels of the Dead?'

She had asked this several times and Yves had always given the same answer.

'It's not important, love. Forget it.'

But Lilith could not forget it, and neither, it seemed, could Eden.

'I don't want to go through those tunnels,' he said to Timon.

'Do you want us to leave you behind?' Timon replied, but Garland thought Eden deserved reassurance.

'Ferdy once told me that there was something sort of calm and beautiful about the tunnels. He went through them several times. Sometimes we have to, because the pass gets blocked with snow.'

'And this time it's blocked with mines,' said Boomer. 'The tunnels will be the best way.'

Eden wasn't convinced. 'But we'll be miles underground in the dark with thousands of dead people,' he said. 'Maybe radioactive dead people.'

Garland stared at him as if she could hardly believe what he had just said.

'Radioactive? No way! Just simply dead,' she said at last.

'In our time . . .' began Eden, but Timon took over.

'In our time we mine radioactive material from the Silica Mountains . . . these mountains, that is.'

Up in the slow-moving van they heard Lilith's voice again. 'Why are those tunnels called the Tunnels of the Dead? Why won't you tell me?'

Yves might have answered this time, but there was an interruption. Maddie's arm came out of the window of her van signalling a halt. Yves signalled to the van behind him, then put on the brake of his own van. Gently but firmly it came to a quiet stop. He turned to Lilith.

'They're called the Tunnels of the Dead because rich people from the towns down below use them as crypts. They bury their dead here. Happy now?'

Garland felt sure that Lilith might not be happy with this answer, but she did not wait to check on Lilith's response. Instead she pushed ahead, Timon and Boomer behind her and Eden coming last of all.

They reached a small group of buildings with peaked roofs standing on either side of a great cave in the flank of the mountain.

The cave looked like a great dark eye and the rocks around the eye were carved with strange symbols and messages which Garland could not read. As they walked towards it, staring doubtfully, there was a sudden gentle eruption in the ground in front of them. Everyone jumped back as a hand came through to wave at them . . . a strange hand with a thumb and a single nail and the fingers fused into something like a little shovel. Something worked under the thin soil. The earth parted like a curtain and, as they stared, a Tunneller – a small stunted bald figure – suddenly seemed to leap out of the ground to stand, rather challengingly, in front of them.

'The radioactive waste changed them . . . mutated them,' muttered Garland to Timon.

'But we have very good hearing,' said the Tunneller, staring at her through lenses like a shadow balanced on its stubby nose. Beyond him other Tunnellers were advancing out of the cave, all wearing those dark goggles to protect themselves against the sunlight.

The whole Fantasia came to a standstill. Yves and Maddie looked at each other and sighed. Then they marched forward briskly to meet the Tunnellers, planning to bargain for a passage through the mountains and to bargain for guides as well . . . for they would certainly need guides.

'My dad is going to deal with them,' said Lilith smugly. 'People do what he tells them.'

'They'll just want a performance,' said Garland loftily. 'Everyone does . . .'

She broke off suddenly, looking towards the black tunnel mouth in consternation.

'What's the matter?' asked Boomer.

'Nothing,' said Garland. 'Well, I don't think – I just thought . . .'

'You said "thought" when you didn't think!' cried Lilith. 'But anyway you're always thinking, thinking, thinking. Too much thinking and not enough doing.'

Garland shrugged. 'I thought I saw an enemy,' she said carefully. 'I thought I saw one of those men who – who have been following us. But I can't have. I mean they were behind us and we've moved on pretty sharply. I must have been wrong.'

Ozul had stepped quickly back into the darkness of the cave.

'They think they will buy their way through with a performance no doubt,' he said. 'They have nothing much to exchange except the so-called wonder of their skill. Once they get into the darkness surely – surely they will be ours.'

'We should have had them days ago,' said Maska. 'But we will have them this time . . . the two boys, the baby, and maybe the converter they gained back in Newton. Why not? It must be something of a treasure and the Nennog would probably reward us if we brought it back to him. And once we have the children we will force the boys to surrender the Talisman, whatever it might be. We will carry all that we can home to the Nennog.' He grinned. 'Lucky there are just the two of us. That lot there couldn't take the short cut that we took.'

Outside the cave, in a small stone circle, the Fantasia had begun to assemble itself for a cramped performance, and the Tunnellers, each one moving it seemed in a private cloud of darkness, gathered around them.

Once again Maddie threw her knives around Garland with elegance and accuracy. Garland stepped away from the board, waving to the crowd, leaving her shape behind her, marked out with sharp, gleaming stars and moons. Yves shouted and gesticulated, punishing the air with his flicking whip. Tane clowned and tumbled with Boomer, as Garland walked haughtily over their head, balancing on her tightrope while Byrna and Nye stalked around, like strange long-legged birds on their stilts. All went well. The Tunnellers gasped and clapped. The band played and at last Eden did his remarkable magic show. The Tunnellers gasped again and surely, behind their dark glasses, they goggled too. And they wanted more.

'Singing! Singing!' they shouted, and began to sing themselves, just to show what it was they were now longing for. And suddenly a well-known voice . . . a Fantasia voice joined in. Garland turned, scarcely able to believe it. Lilith came dancing on, singing as she came. She sounded terrible as she always did . . . shrill and squeaky like some machine needing oil.

> Follow your rainbow. Follow it far
> A rainbow road to a shining star.
> The shining star that hangs above
> A shimmering sign of rainbow love.

Garland groaned softly, but to her amazement the Tunnellers joined in. They all knew the words of the song and sang it along with Lilith. And every Tunneller was a terrible singer – worse than Lilith, if that were possible. All the same anyone could tell they loved singing and bouncing around to their own squawking voices. Anyone could tell the Tunnellers thought this was the best act of all and that the Fantasia would be allowed to pass into the tunnels beyond.

'They won't let my van through,' said Yves with a sigh. 'It's the biggest van and it's weighed down with equipment. They say it might be too heavy for some of the bridges in there.'

'But what are we going to do then?' asked Tane. 'We can't leave you behind on this side of the mountain.'

'Bannister and I have been going over the maps,' Yves said. 'It seems there is a bush road that curves around the side of the mountain and it would be strong enough to take one van,' Yves said. 'I doubt if the Road Rats even know it's there, so it's probably not mined. I should be able to inch around that way and meet you on the other side. A group of Tunnellers have promised to keep pace with me in case I run into any difficulties.'

'I'll come too,' said Tane. 'An extra pair of hands is always useful.'

'Hey, Eden . . . do you want to go with Yves?' asked Garland. She could see Eden was torn in two ways. He hated the thought of the tunnels, and yet he did not want to leave his brother.

'Make up your mind!' Timon said. 'We don't have much time – or much choice.'

'It might be a trap,' said Eden. 'Tunnels always look like traps to me.' Nevertheless, as he spoke he moved to Timon's side.

'I'll go with *you*, Dad,' cried Lilith. 'I'll be able to sing to cheer you up.'

Yves did not look altogether thrilled by this suggestion, but Lilith scrambled in beside him, as the line of smaller vans edged into the underground darkness with a crowd of Fantasia people walking after them. Tunnellers gave them lamps to carry and once they were inside they found the tunnel dimly lit with torches burning in brackets on the walls.

'Looks mysterious doesn't it?' said Timon. 'I'm going to walk for a while.'

'Me too,' said Garland, thinking it might be rather romantic to stroll through deep shadows with Timon.

'Me too,' echoed Eden. 'It's bad enough being in a cave, but being shut up in a van which is shut up inside a cave would make me feel the world was really squashing me flat.'

'Walk then, but stick close,' Maddie ordered Garland. 'It's so easy to get lost down here. One tunnel is exactly like another.'

'We'll be able to hear one another, won't we?' Timon asked.

'Oh yes,' Maddie agreed. 'But it's not quite as easy as that. Down in the dark voices seem to come from every direction. Working out just where the sound's coming from can sometimes be tricky. Stay close.'

And so the Fantasia began its long trek through the mountain tunnels with certain Tunnellers bobbing along beside them. However they proved to be a difficult crowd to talk to, for they spoke an early language of the Remaking, and spoke it with a strange accent too. It seemed to Garland as if Tunnellers somehow communicated with one another with cries and gestures rather than with words.

In the beginning the paths they followed were long straight paths . . . well cared for and well lit, though the light was eerie . . . coming at times not only from lamps but also from swarms of fireflies moving overhead in wild spirals as they were disturbed.

'This way! This way!' called the head Tunneller, dancing and gesturing, irritated by their slow progress. Young Lattin drove Goneril's van for her, for her sight in the semi-darkness was not good, and Goneril stumbled behind everyone else for a short distance, holding Jewel who began to grizzle. And then to cry. Wailing echoes came at them from all directions.

'Wretched child!' grumbled Goneril blaming Jewel for her own slow progress.

'I'll take her for a bit,' offered Eden. 'I'd like to.' And as he took Jewel she fell silent.

'Well,' said Goneril sounding grumpier than ever. 'There's no gratitude in life. Next time she wakes at two o'clock in the morning, you can get up to see to her.' And Goneril made for her own long van, which was being driven by silent Lattin. Although it was long, her van was just narrow enough to squeeze along the underground road.

Every now and then the ceiling above them suddenly seemed to vanish and they would find themselves in some high-roofed space from which roads seemed to go off in all directions. They laughed and talked rather defiantly for, in spite of the solid road underfoot and the glimmering torches, the tunnels were strangely threatening to outdoor people and the Fantasia people needed to invent light-heartedness in order to be sure that things were going well.

And they were being followed. A tall black figure was coming behind them, certainly walking with more judgement than Goneril. Ozul was not quite at home in the dim passages, but the fireflies shone on the walls and ahead of him he could see the moving lights as the vans (with Garland, Timon and Eden, the baby Jewel slung against his chest, following them) retreated deeper and deeper into the heart of the mountain.

Back in the outside air, another tall black figure inched along a narrow road watching a single big van creeping between trees and ferns, a green bank on one side, a fall into green nothing on the other. Every so often there was a turning space tunnelled into the bank or built out over the drop, but Yves did not want to turn. His van crept onwards while Maska followed, pausing if the van paused, standing back among the ferns himself, trying to look like a log tumbled down from above and propped against the side of the track. But perhaps he need not have worried, for Lilith's singing was attracting almost all the attention of the Tunneller guides.

At last they came to a place where the track stretched out long and straight and with no turning bays in sight. Maska smiled grimly and pulled something from his belt. It gleamed like a thin dagger, but it was a metal tube. He put up a hand to his right ear and wound it around and around as if he were winding up a musical box, then put the tube to his lips as if he were planning to play a tune on it and hissed into it. Suddenly a dart shot out of the tube, twisting and glittering as it flew, fast as a bullet, to strike one of the back tyres of the van and bite deeply into it. Almost at once the van began to sag, and, as he watched it, Maska's smile grew wider and possibly even grimmer.

21

The Elegant Stranger

'**H**ow are you feeling?' Garland asked Eden.

'Don't ask,' he whispered back. 'It's better if I don't have to think about it. Does it go on for much longer?'

'I don't quite know. I've never been this way before,' said Garland. As she spoke it seemed she, too, could feel the mountains towering above her, pressing down on her and understood something of what Eden must be feeling. Ahead of her the voices of the walking adults and the lights of the last van disappeared around a corner.

'We'd better not let them get too far ahead,' said Timon quickening his step. 'Here, let me hold Jewel for a while.'

Suddenly a strange soft voice spoke to them. It came from a little way ahead of them, and though it spoke gently and rather plaintively Garland quivered all over at the mere sound of it. Timon and Eden came to a sharp stop, as a woman appeared out of the darkness. She seemed to feel their surprise even though she couldn't have seen their faces clearly. 'Hello,' she was saying. 'Hello, Can you help me?'

She was very tall and was looking down at them — not through those dark glasses that the Tunnellers wore, but through the slits in a black mask embroidered with golden threads and with tassels of gold dangling down from between the eyes and ears. Even in the dim tunnel her clothes had a luxurious shine to them. The faint lamplight caressed her shoulders and illuminated the fall of her skirt, so that her surface seemed somehow rich, velvety and elegant – and entirely out of place. As they stared at her, alarmed and suspicious, she moved towards them with a curiously wobbling step, almost as if she were just learning to walk, then suddenly, wobbly or not, towered over them.

'Thank the stars,' she said. 'I thought I was lost and all alone here. I can't find the group I was with . . .' Her voice trailed away. Garland felt sure this velvety stranger was waiting for an invitation to join them. Then she spoke again. 'My name's Morag,' she said. 'Who are you?'

Garland looked at Timon and Eden, and they began to walk forward again, the stranger walking rather quickly beside them.

'It's easy to get lost down here,' Garland said, half apologetically. 'Walk with us. Follow our lot, and we might find yours.' (*Who on earth is she?* Garland was secretly wondering.)

Unexpectedly fireflies suddenly took off from the walls to dance madly around Morag's head, so that, for a moment, she seemed to be wearing a curious halo of shifting light. Halo or not, it certainly seemed to annoy her for she struck out at it almost as if the fireflies were frightening her.

'Garland?' called a faint, echoing voice somewhere on ahead of them . . . Maddie being an anxious mother, checking to make sure she hadn't run off to explore one of the side tunnels. Garland was horrified to hear just how distant Maddie's voice was sounding.

'Hey! We're getting left behind!' she cried, hurrying after Timon and Eden, while Morag followed closely on her heels, wobbling after her in that curious velvety way.

'Have we lost them?' Eden was saying.

'Have they lost us?' asked Timon.

The tunnel in front of them divided.

'This way,' said Timon. They turned a corner and found themselves looking into darkness.

'Where are we?' Eden cried, panting a little.

'I heard them only a moment ago!' Garland cried. 'Oh look! I think there's light along there. That'll be them.'

They hurried towards that distant gleam which grew a little stronger as they stumbled towards it.

And suddenly, unexpectedly, they found themselves coming into an arched chamber, whirling with fireflies. Peering into the shadows Garland made out a track leading to the right.

'There!' she pointed.

'Or there!' said Timon, pointing in another direction. There, sure enough, was a second dark slot, but this time on the left.

'It must be a sort of crossroads. Which one do we take?' asked Garland. 'Hey Maddie!' she shouted. 'Maddie!'

The ghost of an answer came out the darkness. Maddie was shouting back from somewhere, but now sounding very distant. Her voice was so confused with its own echoes that Garland had no idea of just where it was coming from. As she stood there, peering left and right, trying to work out just which path they should take, Eden tugged at her jacket and pointed ahead to yet another dark arched doorway – three possible pathways, all full of shadows and all alive with echoes.

Morag's soft, elegant voice, speaking from behind them, cut into their confusion. 'It was this way,' she said. 'The voices definitely came from this tunnel here.'

Turning back towards the stranger, so soft and velvety there in the dim light, Timon, Eden and Garland stared at her with a mixture of hope and doubt.

'But you said you were lost,' she said suspiciously.

'So I am, but I know how sound travels,' Morag declared. '*This* is the right road. Follow me.'

'Well, I don't know,' said Timon, pulling a doubtful face as he put Jewel over his shoulder. 'We have to be sure. Who are you? What are you doing down here?'

'What are any of us doing down here?' asked Morag. 'I am trying to find my way through the mountains. But I lost my friends, and if we don't hurry we will lose yours too. Every minute we hesitate they are getting further and further away from us.'

'But my mother will come back for me,' cried Garland. 'I know she will.'

'In that case we'll meet her halfway,' Morag said. 'Follow me.'

And they did follow her. At the time it seemed the best thing to do.

After a moment a shadow glided out of the darker shadows to stand in the middle of the crossroads, but it was not Maddie. Ozul stood there grinning right and left, though not from any sort of happiness. He paused, then set off down the tunnel Morag had chosen. A few moments later he dropped something on the floor of the chamber, then moved on even more quickly, bearing his yellow teeth at the darkness.

'I hate this,' he could hear Eden saying somewhere on ahead of him. 'Something's wrong.'

'How true,' said Ozul, nodding to himself in the dark. 'But wrong for who?'

And then the world exploded. Feeling her way along after Morag, Garland felt as if she had been lifted off her feet and smacked violently against the wall. The tunnel lamps went out. It had been dim before but suddenly it was truly dark. Rocks tumbled and crunched against one another. The world seemed to be grinding its teeth with fury. As the first rumble of rock on rock died away Garland could feel someone beside her shifting around in the darkness. Then a familiar voice broke in on her. A baby cried out furiously.

'Me!' said Timon. 'It's me. Us!'

'Is Jewel all right?' panted Eden faintly.

'She's fine,' Timon said. 'Just frightened! But I think the tunnel has collapsed behind us. We're not going to be able to go back that way – not easily anyway.'

And Maddie – who had left the other Fantasia people, coming anxiously back through the tunnels to look for Garland – opened her eyes. She could feel a slow beetle of blood trickling down the side of her face, and she could see that she was not quite alone. Several Tunnellers had appeared out of nowhere to cluster around her. They had taken off their dark glasses and their eyes shone in the darkness with a phosphorescent light.

Maddie picked herself up and looked around her. 'What happened? What was that?' she cried. 'Garland? Garland?'

'Surprise!' said one of the Tunnellers. 'Big surprise. Shock! Us too!'

Moving as quickly as she could, Maddie now stumbled back into the crossroads chamber, holding her lantern high. She could make out the strange walls and the arched mouths of two tunnels. And she could see rocks still trembling where there had once been the mouth of a third tunnel.

'What happened?' she cried again.

'Rock fall!' said one of the Tunnellers as if he were speaking to a young and very foolish child.

'But there was an explosion!' Maddie cried. She pointed at the rocks. 'Dig!

'No dig,' said the Tunneller. 'Risky. Need support. Need allies. Get help!' And immediately the Tunneller set off up the tunnel through which they had just come.

'Wait! Wait!' Maddie called. 'Don't leave me. I've got to get our children out and . . . listen to me! Wait!' She ran after the Tunneller, determined not to be left behind.

By sheer coincidence, Yves was almost immediately above that underground crossroads when he felt the explosion, felt the van rattle and heard Tane, who was checking the back tyre, cry out in alarm. Picking himself up from where he had been thrown, Tane flung out his arms in confusion.

'What's going on?' he shouted. 'What next?'

'Change the tyre,' called Yves grimly and Tane bent over the back tyre once more, frowning as he saw it was almost entirely flat. This wasn't the only thing filling him with dismay. The bush around him was ringing with Lilith's voice. She finished one song and mercilessly began another. Even Yves, peering out of the van window, was looking like a man who had had enough.

'Lilith, love, maybe you should rest your voice,' he called back over his shoulder. Lilith broke off and smiled at the back of his head.

'No, I'm fine,' she said, and began a new song.

'Just a bit of a break,' Yves suggested.

'But they love me,' said Lilith. 'These Tunnellers really love my singing.' She looked at him suspiciously. 'Don't you like it?'

'Darling girl, I love it too,' said Yves. 'Of course I do. It's just – just echoing in the van and –'

Tane came around to Yves's window holding something in his hand.

'Hey, look at this!' he said. Yves looked at what he was being shown and frowned.

'It's – it's like a dart,' he said blankly, and then stared at Tane with sudden alarm.

'It *is* a dart,' Tane agreed, 'and it was sticking out of our back tyre. Not an accident. No way!'

'Sabotage?' asked Yves. He turned to Lilith, 'Listen, love, we're going to have to jack up the van and change a tyre. You go into the back of the van, get yourself something to eat. Have a rest.' He swung himself down and moved towards the back. Lilith liked the idea of a small snack. She shifted sideways and made for the door that closed off their living space. Swinging the door open, testing a few notes as she did so, Lilith entered the back of the van happily enough. After all, this door was the door to her home – her safe place in a dangerous world.

But then she stopped still, staring in amazement and horror, for there in the centre of the living space . . . there at the tiny table between the bunks . . . was Maska himself, with the solar converter on the table in front of him. He looked up and gave her a smile of hideous triumph.

'So happy to see you again,' he said. 'I'll give you some good advice, even if it is a bit late for you to make use of it. Always lock the back door of your van when you travel through dangerous territory.'

But, as he reached for her Lilith screamed the loudest scream in the world.

To Yves outside, just beginning to work on the tyre, it seemed as if that scream filled the whole valley around them. To Tane it seemed as if it might split trees and cause birds to fall, stunned, from the sky. And as they staggered, staring wildly at each other in a moment of shocked bewilderment, Maska jumped out through the back of the van, swinging the package that held the converter in one hand and holding Lilith high above the ground in the other. Yves sprang towards Maska but Maska hoisted Lilith, kicking, screaming and struggling, even higher in the air and shook her at her father.

'If you come after me she will be terminated,' he said. Though his voice was broken it was still ruthless. He shook Lilith at them yet again, and then took off up the road, carrying Lilith under one arm as if she were nothing more than a small pillow stuffed with feathers. He was even able to carry the converter, which Yves knew to be a great deal heavier than Lilith.

Yves stared after him, panting, stunned and helpless. Tane looked over his shoulder, his face twisted into a helpless grimace. A chorus of voices arose around them, coming out of the green edges of the track, coming through tiny cracks and wormholes in the ground.

'The songbird! He has taken the songbird!' the Tunnellers were shouting.

'What shall we do?' Yves shouted at Tane. 'What shall we do? I can't just let him carry her off.'

'If we leave him he might – well – he just might let her go,' Tane stammered. 'I don't know what to do. And he's got that converter.'

'Forget the converter! What about Lilith!' Yves yelled. He turned from side to side, staring wildly into the air around him as if the banks of the road or the trees might suddenly give him an answer.

Neither of them noticed that all the Tunnellers had disappeared. There, where they had been only a moment earlier, shouting about the stolen songbird, was an empty track, thick with fallen leaves, dead twigs, but suddenly marked, along the bank on the right, by a line of holes in the ground.

Meanwhile in the tunnels winding almost directly under Yves's van, Garland, Eden, Timon, Jewel and the mysterious Morag inched along their chosen passageway. They stepped out, at last, into another great underground hall, its walls set around with huge carved shelves. Their edges were inlaid with metallic symbols and runes, which flashed in the light of the lantern as it swung a little in Garland's hand, and on those shelves were laid long boxes . . . hundreds of them, it seemed, retreating into a distance quickly blurred with darkness.

'Coffins!' exclaimed Garland.

'Sarcophagi,' said Morag, no longer speaking like that lost velvety stranger, but like a guide who knew the place by heart. Garland and Timon looked at her with startled suspicion, then peered up and down the walls for possible doors between the shelves, but there were no doors to be seen.

Garland turned back to Morag, only to find Morag was moving confidently over to a sarcophagus – an open one – and looking down at the man in it. Garland looked too. He looked fresh and at ease with the world . . . as if he had only just fallen asleep.

'Who is he?' she asked, suddenly sure that Morag would have an answer.

'He's the gravedigger,' Morag answered, and this time there was something curiously familiar about her voice . . . familiar and terrifying too. 'Imagine his surprise when, just as he was about to fasten a lid over me, I sat up and smiled at him. There are not many men who can resist my smile.'

Then Morag turned . . . turned slowly, and looked at them out of green, suddenly glowing eyes. Her face stretched sideway in a horrible grin. Eden screamed, 'The Nennog!'

'Uncle!' hissed Timon. As the two boys backed away from the transforming figure of Morag, Garland backed with them, wondering how on earth the Nennog, that ruler of a future time, could possibly be down in the dark under the Silica Mountains, grinning that dreadful grin. How they could possibly escape anyone who had such power? She shot a quick glance behind her. And now, entirely blocking the way they had come, stood Ozul, arms outspread as if he were longing to embrace them all.

No hope! Garland thought. *Not here. Not this time.*

'Time to go home, boys,' she said – the Nennog said – still speaking with the tongue of this recently dead woman. Garland realized Morag must be dead . . . she was an empty body the Nennog had been able to possess. As she thought this, Morag reached out an arm that seemed to stretch further than any true person could stretch, to grab the silver chain around Eden's neck, and to twist it into a strangling halter. Eden made a dreadful choking sound as both Timon and Garland leapt to rescue him. The Nennog loosened his grip and flicked the chain over Eden's head. The medallion dangled from a hand that suddenly seemed to Garland to be covered in green scales.

'Mine! Mine at last!' Morag's lips moved but now it was entirely the voice of the Nennog that came out between them. 'You certainly won't be needing it any more. Get them!' he commanded. And Ozul obediently moved in on them.

Garland, Timon (holding Jewel) and Eden were being herded back onto an empty shelf among the sarcophagi. Ozul stood over them, guarding them, and now began passing metal units drawn from the pack that swung at his hip, to Morag who fitted them together slowly constructing a device all too familiar to Timon and Eden. Garland, looking over Ouzel's bent shoulder, watched it grow.

'What's that?' she whispered to Timon.

'A slider. It's the machine we used to ride a time-pulse back here, to you.'

'You said the Nennog couldn't move through time,' she whispered to Timon, but it was Eden who answered her, his lips barely moving.

'He can't. Not in the way we can. But he can put out tentacles of power. His power can move in on certain people.'

'He can sometimes *possess*!' said Timon. 'When the circumstances are right it seems he can possess empty people, *dead* people, and take them over. And I think there might be radioactive links here under the mountain that he can ride on . . .'

'He's been able to take over a body . . . a fresh body,' muttered

Eden. As he said this the Nennog looked across at them and smiled. Using Morag's hand with its elegantly painted finger-nails he held up the medallion, waving it mockingly at the boys.

Then two fireflies appeared, and began dancing around his head. For some reason this seemed to annoy him, and he struck them away with more that ordinary irritation.

'You're giving off radiation,' Timon said. 'They want to feed off you.'

'It is I who will feed off them,' said the Nennog, plucking one of them from the air and sliding it between Morag's painted lips. Morag chewed and swallowed, still waving the Talisman before them. 'How about a magic trick, Eden? How about a little miracle? But I forgot. I have the Talisman. You will be powerless now.' He hung the medallion around his neck – around Morag's neck – then touched it tenderly.

'It *is* beautiful,' he said, and went back to building the unit that would transport Eden, Timon and Jewel back to their own time and to some fate Garland could not imagine. And perhaps she, too, would be carried away with them, away from the Fantasia . . . away from Maddie, and Boomer and Lilith . . . away from all the people and all the things that suddenly seemed infinitely dear to her.

Even as she watched the device suddenly came alive between Morag's elegant hands. It was hard to say just how. There was light of course, a pulsing blue light and a continual soft beep, but there was more than that. It was as if some entirely new element was revealed in the aura that extended around it. It was, thought Garland, as if actual seconds had become visible – almost like fireflies of a different kind.

Morag turned, looking over at them with the Nennog's eyes, then turning towards Ozul.

'Contact Maska!' he said. 'Tell him we have the children and that solar converter too. It is a great source of power and I long for all the power in the world. Tell Maska to join us. We will soon be home in our own time.'

'Let me go!' Lilith was screaming, up on the mountain track. 'Let me go!'

But Maska took no notice of her furious cries.

'Let me go!' she screamed again and began kicking wildly.

They were negotiating a dangerous curve in the path, and perhaps her furious kicking annoyed even Maska, for he stopped and held her up so they were nose to nose, looking into each other's eyes.

'Quiet!' he said. 'Quiet, or I will consume you.'

'Let me go or else . . .' Lilith was sobbing with fear, but with fury too. She aimed yet another kick at him.

'If you are good, I just might let you go in due course,' he said. 'If you annoy me I will bring about ultimate termination – then throw you like rubbish over the cliff.'

Something caught between Lilith's panting body and Maska's iron chest began to utter a shrill peeping sound. Reaching up with his free hand, he twisted his left ear slightly. Something in his throat shifted. Lilith stared unbelievingly as a narrow jointed rod with what looked like the head of a tiny microphone unfolded from that ear and quivered in front of his lips. Maska spoke into it.

'Yes?'

'At last,' said the Nennog. 'Ozul will meet you, accompanied by the shape I am controlling. It is hard to maintain. I may have to retreat. You have their converter and we have the Talisman.'

Silence.

Maska twisted his ear once more, and the communication device folded back into him. And as he did this there came a sound far down the road behind them.

'That's my daddy,' Lilith wept. 'He'll show you!'

'No! I will do the showing,' Maska said. 'After all, I do have his treasure don't I?' He slung Lilith across his shoulder and set off down the road swinging the converter in his left hand as if it were a big box of thistledown.

But all at once the path ahead of him erupted. Maska hesitated, then found himself confronted by about twenty Tunnellers. The road on which his feet were so firmly planted suddenly seemed unreliable. It crumbled at the far edge. Maska leapt back towards the centre of the road, stumbling as he did so.

'What now?' he cried furiously.

One of the Tunnellers jumped out in front of the others.

'You are threatening the songbird!' he cried.

Yves, desperately chasing after Maska, paused as he saw the way the road was breaking up and twisting in the middle.

'Set the songbird free!' the Tunneller was shouting. 'Restore her.' And Yves was filled with a strange, wild hope.

'Lilith!' he yelled. 'Stop screaming. Sing something! Quickly! Sing!'

And Lilith, being Lilith, did sing. There wasn't too much difference between her squealing and her singing, but the Tunnellers began swaying in time to her song.

I am dancing, dancing a rainbow dance,
Singing a rainbow song . . .'

The ground under Maska's feet suddenly subsided, and his left leg sank into earth. In shock and surprise, desperately trying to keep his balance, he dropped both Lilith and the converter.

A singer has to take her chance . . . Lilith sang in her screaming fashion, rolling away from Maska while the ground beneath him crumbled even more dangerously. He tilted, flailing his arms as if they were the blades of a propeller, and staggered towards the space on the other side of the road.

'Lilith! Lilith!' cried Yves, terrified that she would fall too.

A singer must be strong! sang Lilith, trying to pull the converter to safe ground. It was much too heavy for her to carry but all the same, like a true and unexpected heroine, she struggled to drag it back towards Yves.

'Protect the songbird,' cried a chorus of Tunneller voices, and the whole track under Maska suddenly disappeared. With one of his strange metallic cries, he toppled out of sight and they heard him crashing down, down, down through the bush below them. The converter wobbled dangerously and seemed as if it was about to tumble after him.

'Oh, Lilith, darling!' cried Yves embracing her and pulling her back to a safer part of the road. 'Thank goodness! Thank goodness. Now just stand there against the bank.' He reached for the converter and pulled it back to safety.

'Daddy, I saved that converter thing,' Lilith said proudly. 'I saved it by singing.'

'You did,' said Yves. 'You surely did! And you can sing as often as you like from now on.'

22

Dancing Fireflies

Far down below Yves and Lilith, hemmed in by the sarcophagi, Garland, Timon and Eden faced dead Morag who looked at them with the eyes of the Nennog. Timon was crying out in out in protest.

'But if you destroy the converter you'll release all that energy – it could destroy everything . . . everyone . . . for kilometres around . . .'

The Nennog interrupted him.

'Why should you care? You will be safe with me. You will be hundreds of years on ahead of this cursed time.'

'The time lines will twist!' Timon shouted.

'But no one here is of any importance,' The Nennog said. 'Believe me I have read about this stupid circus very carefully. I have followed a thousand time threads and, though there will be alterations for a great many other people, none of them will be changes that dislodge me. That is all that matters. Ozul. Bring the boys and the baby over here.'

Ozul moved in on them. Timon passed Jewel to Eden then jumpt to his feet, prepared to defend Jewel, and to defend Garland, too, perhaps, but it was Eden and Jewel that Ozul seized, only to drop him and leap away uttering a cry which was certainly a cry of pain.

'What?' cried the Nennog. Ozul turned towards him.

'Lord,' he began, crying out in agony and confusion, 'my arm . . . my arm . . .' He clasped his right shoulder with his left hand, while his right arm dangled beside him as limp and useless as an arm plaited of wet string. 'I can't feel my arm,' Ozul said.

'Must I then . . . ?' cried the Nennog. 'Must I . . .'

And the shape of Morag, still with something of the elegance that had once belonged to a live woman, advanced towards them. Behind her the device pulsed with light . . . pulsed with time. Garland shrank away. She could not help herself. It was a curious comfort to find Timon also shrinking beside her. Only Eden, hoisting Jewel rather clumsily, stood firm. He stared at the Nennog-Morag figure and suddenly fireflies surged in on them, not so much flying from the walls of the cave around them as dissolving out of the air, and flying directly into those eerie green eyes, crawling into Morag's ears and up her nose. Incredibly that terrifying figure began a sudden dance of desperation, but more and more fireflies appeared swarming all over the figure of Morag. Now the Nennog who possessed her and moved her began to roar with fury and fear. Eden jumped to his feet to gaze intently at that dancing roaring shape, concentrating on it as if by mere staring he would wipe it out of existence. The tall figure writhed, flailing at the air to drive away the glowing swarm that was slowly enveloping it, then stepped back again, while the time unit behind flashed continually with its own strange light. Ozul yelled out in sudden consternation . . . and then there was a flash . . . a furious flash, not only of light, thought Garland, but of time itself, as if minutes hours and years – centuries even – had suddenly exploded around her. She heard her own voice screaming. She heard Timon call her name – felt him grab her arm and pull her backwards. She heard Ozul saying something that was perhaps a curse.

And then it was over. The huge dazzle died away and after a while – a few seconds, a few minutes, she could not say – she was able to see again. The lamps they had brought with them still shone with that faint and faded light that was the light of these tunnels, but the carefully assembled time unit lay like a heap of metallic sticks on the floor, disconnected and dead.

'Gone!' cried Timon. 'What happened?' But, before anyone could say anything there was a growl from the shadows. Ozul was picking himself up, glaring over at them. No time for questions let alone answers. No time for anything but running away, even if there was nowhere safe to run to. Timon snatched Jewel from Eden, and grabbed Eden's arm as he and Garland jostled past Ozul who had not quite regained his feet, making for the crossroads once more, Eden flopping beside Timon in a confused way just as if he had forgotten how to run.

'But it's blocked . . . it's blocked . . .' panted Garland. Within a minute they were once more confronting the fallen debris that had shut them off from their friends . . . from the Fantasia who were somewhere on the other side of those stones, no doubt looking for them, desperate to find them again. Jewel's grizzles turned into a loud bawling.

'Now what?' cried Garland, swinging around to face Ozul, thinking that there were three of them and that Ozul, whatever else he might be, was not that terrible Nennog any longer. They might be able to beat him off.

'I will take you back myself,' Ozul was shouting above Jewel's racket, but now Eden began to pull himself together.

'No way! Ever!' he shouted, and flung out his hand in front of him. The jagged roof above Ozul suddenly crumbled. Rocks poured down on Ozul. He crouched down but one rock stuck him powerfully on the head just as if it had aimed itself at him, and he fell unconscious at their feet.

Timon and Garland stared at their enemy brought so low,

and then looked, with uneasy astonishment, at Eden, who had suddenly slumped down beside them and was sitting there with his head sunk down between his knees. 'Okay, Eden,' said Garland, scarcely recognizing her own voice. 'The Talisman's gone with the Nennog. How did you do that?'

Eden looked up, as bewildered as they were.

'Yes,' said Timon, and his voice was shaking too, 'you've got some explaining to do. But escaping first, explaining later. We've got to work out a way of getting out of here, and we'd better do it now.'

'I didn't do anything back there,' said Eden. 'I called the fireflies, but I can't quite work out why. And I don't know what happened to the Nennog after that.'

Timon was staring at the blocked passage in front of them. 'These rocks going to be hard to shift,' he said.

And at this very moment, just as if a wish were being answered, a voice broke in on them . . . faint, a little broken, but definite. There it was again.

'Garland! Garland, where are you?' Maddie's voice. And though it was blurred anyone could tell it was just on the other side of those fallen stones.

'Garland!' shouted another voice – Bannister's voice – and then a whole chorus of voices joined in, all calling her name. Suddenly the whole tunnel (rock fall or not) seemed to be ringing with it.

'Here!' Garland shouted back. 'Here we are.'

'Thank goodness! Just stay where you are. We'll have you out in no time,' Maddie called. 'Our strong man will manage two or three of these rocks easily. You will, won't you, Bannister?'

And indeed Bannister did roll a few rocks to one side. And in next to no time there was a space they could climb through, and join their Fantasia once more.

Goneril ran to grab the grizzling Jewel from Timon's arms.

'What sort of brother are you?' she cried. 'How could you take her off to dangerous places? Oh, I've been so worried about her. I'm never letting her out of my sight again.'

So the Fantasia set off once more, trekking back down the tunnel road to the place where the vans were waiting patiently for them. And, after that, it seemed no time at all before they were coming up from under the mountains, just as Yves arrived, driving his van out of the bush, so that they were reunited – all together once more with alarming stories to tell as they sat around the campfire in the evening. 'I saved us with my singing,' Lilith boasted over and over again.

But Garland found herself wondering . . . wondering about how it was that suddenly she owed so much to Yves . . . and wondering about other things too.

'That Talisman vanished with the Nennog,' she said to Timon. 'But Eden still – well, he still did magic things. He made fireflies come. How could the Nennog be frightened of fireflies?'

'I think the fear of fireflies belonged to Morag,' Timon said. 'I know she was dead and the Nennog was using her, but something of her was still there and still working and the Nennog couldn't altogether control it. And there was more to it than that, wasn't there, Eden? I mean they weren't just ordinary fireflies were they?'

'I tried to make them radioactive,' Eden sighed. 'These tunnels are quite radioactive.' He sighed again. 'I tried to draw radiation out of the rocks . . . the Nennog couldn't stand up against it.'

'The Nennog fell – and that medallion of yours fell with him. So how could your magic go on working?' said Garland.

Eden was silent and Timon shrugged and shook his head.

'I just don't know,' he said at last. 'We don't know everything. I mean we don't even know for certain what the Talisman is. We always thought it must be that medallion, and the medallion's gone. But Eden says he can still feel it . . . feel the power of the Talisman, I mean.'

'Does that mean he's – well, he's sort of in touch with it even though the Nennog's carried it off with him?' asked Garland.

'I don't know,' said Timon again. 'I only know that Eden says he can still feel its power – just as if it was close to him and connecting to him. And, like I said, there's a lot about the Talisman that is a real mystery – even to us.'

23

A Pointing Arrow

'I just don't *know* this road,' Maddie was saying. 'I don't recognize *any* of it. Bannister . . . get your nose out of that book and tell us where we are.'

'Tunnelling through the mountains in the way we did has thrown us off course,' Bannister said, laying his book aside in a guilty fashion. 'I think we're on a road *here* . . .' he placed his forefinger on the map spread out over his knee '. . . but I'm just not *sure*.'

'What you really mean is we're *lost*,' said Yves accusingly.

'Maybe . . . just for the moment,' said Bannister, looking up and down the map in a distracted way. 'Just for the moment!' he repeated, making his voice sound brisk and capable, though his hands were flapping like a couple of lost birds. The map flapped between them.

'You don't really know, do you?' Maddie declared despairingly. 'Oh, Bannister – listen! We must . . . we absolutely *must* . . . work out the right thing to do. Just think of what's happened to us over the last week. Even if we manage to get along without losing ourselves in caves or anything like that we don't want to find ourselves in some deserted unknown place without fuel of any kind, and no one who might pay for a performance.'

Garland listened to this, feeling increasingly nervous. They were Maddigan's Fantasia. Of course they couldn't stop. Of course they had to keep going. But what was the point of keeping on going if you didn't know where you were going *to*? You might be moving closer and closer to despair. The roads of the land were the strings that held it together and once those strings were lost everything might fall apart. A wandering Fantasia might somehow slip away between those strings and tumble into nothing. In Garland's mind the world shredded. Bits of it peeled away. Roadless, it crumbled into useless scraps between the stars.

'What shall we *do*?' cried Maddie, sounding wild with despair. 'Here! Let *me* see that map again.'

She snatched at it. Bannister would have happily surrendered it, but Yves stopped her.

'Take a breath,' he told her, 'and don't tear that map any more than it's torn already. We've got through worse things, haven't we? Remember that storm almost a year ago? Remember being caught by the flood? All right! We've lost our usual road, but we can't be too far away from it. We've just got to think things through and work it out.'

Maddie took a deep breath. 'You're right. Sorry! Just a wild, black moment.'

'Part of the adventure of things,' said Yves, smiling across at her.

Garland was angry to think that Yves was able to comfort Maddie in any way. And she was angry because, before she could stop herself, she found herself agreeing with Yves. *It's the sort of thing Ferdy would have said, but he's just pretending to be Ferdy*, she thought scornfully, and swung down from the van deciding to walk away from everything . . . from Timon and Eden . . . from Boomer . . . but most of all from Yves.

The track they had been following since they came out of the tunnels was well worn. People must use it; it must lead somewhere but it was an eerie road for all that, creeping slyly as it did through ruins . . . and not just ordinary ruins. There was something about the disintegrating peaked roofs that rose out of the scrub, tilted at odd angles to the land below, which suggested that lives touched by mysterious ceremonies had once been lived under them.

And now they were confronted by a huge broken pillar lying across the track. But not one that had been deliberately placed there . . . sections of other pillars lay in the long grass on either side of the road, and stone blocks lay scattered as if some giant child had been carefully constructing temples and castles but then, getting bored, had kicked its buildings to pieces and had then walked away, leaving scattered fragments behind it. Garland left the adults arguing about what to do next, and wandered off among these ruins, frowning at them as if they were puzzles she might fit together again. At first her exploration was of the stumbling, bumbling kind, but suddenly she found that walking had become easier. Looking down at her feet she found they had cleverly discovered a hidden track – yet another of those little strings that tied the land together . . . thin as a thread but quite distinct. It was not a track that the vans would consider, for it was only about as wide as her feet and wound upwards in an absent-minded way to wander among savage rocks. But, as she stared down at her feet, Garland felt yet again that strange tingle that always seemed to be both a hunger and a warning. Of course she knew what she was going to see before she saw it – that faint but determined gleam, that twist in the air, announcing the presence of the silver girl. As she watched, the silver girl took form, fluctuating a little as if she was riding on ripples in the air which nobody else could feel.

Garland took a breath. *This time* she thought. *No hanging back!* This time she walked boldly towards this strange ghost, determined to speak directly . . . determined to ask questions.

But even as she did so, the silver girl began her wavering as if Garland's approach was somehow sapping her power. Fainter she grew, then fainter once more, and still fainter, dwindling to a mere silver smudge – a sort of mistake in the air. Garland stood exactly where the silver girl had stood and looked around her. Nothing! Nothing and no one!

And then, just as she was turning away, she saw something on the rock next to her. Words. A short sentence. A pointing arrow. Those words – that arrow – had been there for a long time. The letters and the head of that arrow were barely visible. Moss had almost filled the crevices. Still they could be seen if one looked at them closely. The words could even be read. *A book is like . . . is like . . . A book is like a garden carried in the pocket.* The arrow pointed up the hill.

Garland turned and ran back to the place where her mother, Yves, Tane and Bannister were still arguing over the best thing to do next. She felt she had been given a sort of clue, even if she didn't know what it meant or quite what that arrow was pointing to. Books! Well, a place that had once had pointed roofs, temples and pillars might once have been filled with enthusiastic readers too.

'Mum!' she cried, interrupting Yves who was laying down the law about what sort of road the vans could cope with. 'Mum, I know the way we must go. I've had a sign.'

Maddie turned with something of a sigh. 'What sort of sign?'

'I sometimes see this silver ghost . . .' Garland began, only to see Maddie immediately turn away, hoping to hide her impatient expression.

'Don't *look* like that!' cried Garland. 'Mum, there are words on the rock over there and an arrow pointing the way . . . it's the way we must go. I'm sure of it.'

'Garland,' said Yves, trying to speak gently. 'You know that's impossible. There's no track over there that's wide enough for the Fantasia vans even if we drove very slowly. They just wouldn't cope with those rocks.'

'You know he's right,' said Maddie. 'That slope's impossible for the vans.'

'But there's a carving on the rocks and an arrow pointing the way,' Garland persisted. 'We have to take notice of it. That's the true way.'

Maddie sighed.

'Garland, we're going to haul that pillar away, and take off in *that* direction. It's decided.'

'You never take any notice of things I tell you!' Garland yelled. 'You just don't! Yves is the only one you ever listen to.'

'He's a driver!' Maddie yelled back. 'Forget that slope! It's impossible. Just get over to our van and . . . and make us a big pot of tea. Shell's making one but we could do with another.'

'You do it!' Garland cried furiously. 'You think you know everything. You do it.' And wheeling away she ran back towards the rock with its strange inscription, scrambling up the slope and then hiding herself behind it, planning to sulk for a while. But almost immediately a shadow fell across the grass in front of her and she looked up to find Timon standing over her.

'Go away!' said Garland.

'Don't be cross,' said Timon. 'I'm on your side. Let's set off and just see if this skinny little track goes anywhere.' He touched the mossy inscription on the rock. 'Must have been carved by someone keen on reading! Someone like Bannister.'

'We'd better not go too far,' said another voice, and there was Boomer coming up behind him. 'They won't take long to unblock the road and . . .'

But Garland was already on her feet, taking off up the track, glad to have Timon, at her heels, glad to think that someone believed in her visions. Boomer watched them go frowning. He looked rather longingly back at the Fantasia gang struggling to put chains around the pillar on the road below. He looked up the slope at Garland and Timon, following that thin track and walking away from him. And then, at last, making up his mind, he began to follow Garland and Timon. From back beside the vans Maddie called Garland's name, but she pretended not to hear.

They climbed and climbed, the three of them, winding in and out of rocks until, suddenly, Garland stopped and pointed triumphantly. Another arrow! Worn letters marching in a line! *Any book you haven't read is a new book.*

'That's two arrows and two messages about books. You're right. Bannister should have come with us,' she said. 'Shall I go back and get him?'

'They'll only grab you and put you to work,' said Timon, grinning.

'Funny to think that someone has cut book-talk into the rocks,' said Boomer. 'There's no one here to read it.' They climbed on – then abruptly the rocky track came to an end, seeming to fall away into nothing. Garland, Timon and Boomer found themselves standing on an unexpected edge.

'Well, that's that,' said Timon rather blankly. 'I can't believe your track leads on into the air.'

But Garland was already pointing to one side of the drop.

'No! Look! It goes down there,' she said. 'See?' And she was right. The track had doubled back on itself, beginning again a little to the right of them, but taking on a different form, for there, climbing down the side of the cliff, was a zigzagging line of old steps.

'I suppose you're determined to go down there,' said Timon, rather apprehensively.

'I've told you. I had a sign,' Garland reminded him.

It wasn't easy. Garland had to lower herself over the side very carefully indeed. Panting and frowning, she kicked with her feet, feeling for the first step, angling herself so that she could lower herself down safely.

'Be careful!' yelled Boomer. 'Careful! There's no hand rail.' But Garland was already inching herself around so that she faced outward and downward. Then she began feeling her way, very carefully indeed, step after step, down that strange stair. Timon followed her and Boomer followed Timon, beginning a tuneless whistle as he did so . . . a whistle of fear rather than pleasure. After all, that stairway was terrifying. A few steps down and Boomer stopped whistling. He just had to complain. 'This is just mad,' he said plaintively.

'Go back then,' suggested Garland, but turning around on those stairs seemed even more risky than simply going on. Boomer followed doggedly . . . down and down . . . trying not to glance down into the space that seemed to be beckoning him . . . jump! Go on! Jump! I dare you! Dive! Dive into nothing!

And, after all, walking down so very carefully, with their right hands against the cliff and their left hands waving out over nothing at all, they all reached the bottom without falling, and immediately saw words cut into the rock.

Books are a finer world within the world and then, below these words, yet a third arrow. And below the arrow a single word. *LIBRARY.*

'Library!' exclaimed Garland incredulously.

'Library,' Boomer echoed her. 'Who'd want a library out here in the middle of nowhere? I mean . . . there are libraries in places like Solis and Newton, but there's no one out here to borrow books. I mean rabbits and hawks don't read. Anyway, won't your mum be looking for you? Let's go back.'

'No way!' said Garland. 'Well, I mean *you* can. I'm going on. I think I've been *told* to go this way. And those people – the ones that once lived with those tilted roofs and pillars and things back there – might have wanted to read.'

They began to pick their way along the bottom of the cliff.

'You tell her,' Boomer said to Timon. 'She does what you say.'

'But I want to see the library too,' said Timon, and looked sideways at Boomer. And Boomer immediately fell silent for these days it always seemed to him there was something sinister in Timon's expression, even though he could not quite work out what it was.

The cliff curved suddenly to the right. As she turned the corner, Garland came to such a sudden standstill that Timon ran into her, and Boomer ran into Timon. They had found themselves staring across a sunny meadow, and in the middle of that meadow stood a tall arched gateway – a gateway with no fences on either side of it, just a gateway, looking grand, yet completely senseless too. Beyond the gateway, on the far edge of the meadow, rose a tall building, its grey stone gilded by bright sunshine. *The Library* said words cut into the gateway's stone arch. 'Look!' whispered Garland. 'It's there. There! It really, really is a library.' And she moved towards it, worked on by a sudden enchantment.

24

Into the Library

'**S**omeone's watching us,' said Boomer suspiciously. 'Let's go back again.' But Garland advanced confidently Timon beside her. Unwillingly Boomer trailed after them, mumbling and grumbling to himself, as they worked their way across the meadow that sang with the buzzing of bees. It felt strange to be going under that arch when they could just as easily have gone around it, felt strange, only a few minutes later, to find themselves climbing cautiously up three worn steps and in at an open door.

A great hall, lined with shelves and shelves of books, stretched ahead of them. For some reason this seemed stranger to Boomer than if the walls had been filled with windows opening out on planets and distant suns. 'Books!' he said.

'Well, we were warned,' said Timon.

'Hello!' called Garland. 'Anyone here? Any librarians?' she called again, joking a bit to hide the fact that the strangeness and silence of the place were scaring her.

'Anyone here?' Timon called too.

Here . . . here . . . here their voices echoed but there was no reply.

'Come on,' said Garland, advancing towards the door at the end of the hall. 'There must be *somebody* here. Somebody to do housework anyway! There aren't any cobwebs on these books, even the top ones.' She rubbed her finger along the edge of, a shelf. 'No dust! Someone must keep things dusted. There must be some sort of librarian lurking somewhere. Hey! What if Bannister was here? He'd melt with happiness.'

'I don't want Bannister to melt,' mumbled Boomer.

Moving slowly through that entrance hall, then through the door at the far end of it, they came into a big room, dimly lighted by a series of candles. Books and more books. And there in the middle of the room a wide desk, and big square cabinet filled with drawers beside it. Spread out on the desk was a flattened piece of paper. Sunshine, struggling weakly through a deep slot of a window high in one of the walls, illuminated the paper as if some magical, pointing finger was determined they should not walk by.

Garland looked down at the paper. Just for a moment its surface seemed alive with words – printed words and words that had been scribbled on top of them so that the paper seemed to be crawling with lines that were impossible to read. The messages, the arrows, the steps down into the canyon had all been scary, but for some reason the sight of that piece of paper with its words crawling all over it was more scary still.

Meanwhile back at the Fantasia there was fuss and fury.

'Where have they all *gone*?' Maddie was shouting.

And Yves, still panting and wiping his sweaty forehead, said, 'Knowing Garland I expect she took off up that track, just to get her own back. She probably wants you to worry.'

'Well, I *am* worrying,' said Maddie. 'I'm still cross but I'm worrying at the same time. We Fantasia people can easily do two things at once.'

'You can follow them, perhaps,' suggested Bannister, frowning over his map. 'Look! There seems to be a big camping place just ahead of us along this track . . . at least I think

it's a camping place. I can't quite read what it says, because
the letters have faded and the map has been folded through
the middle of the word so the print's worn away a bit, but I'm
fairly sure it says *Camp*. So the rest of you could push on, and
Maddie and I could shoot up to the hilltop and look around . . .
give them a call.'

'Well, I suppose so,' said Yves. 'We do need to be on the road
again and it's well into the afternoon. Perhaps Tane should go
with you too. But that Garland of yours . . .' He shook his head,
frowning darkly.

'Oh, it's partly my fault,' said Maddie. 'Off you go, and
when you get to the camping place wait for us. I mean there are
three of them aren't there – Boomer and Timon have gone with
her.'

'What happens if you don't find them?' asked Tane.

'Oh, we'll find them,' said Maddie crossly. 'Of course we
will. Come on Bannister. Let's go!'

25

Gabrielle

In the echoing library Garland, Timon and Boomer stared at the paper trying to read what it might have to tell them. Then Garland's face cleared. She looked up and laughed then bent over the paper once more, pointing at something written on it.

'This is a map,' she said. 'Look! It's got the library marked on it in big black letters. It *is* a map and I think it's a better map than the one Bannister works with. His is all blurry – it's really ancient – but once you get all these lines worked out this one is clear enough.'

'It's not clear,' protested Boomer. 'The words are all crawling about.'

'No they're not. It's just that someone has written all over it,' Garland said. 'The actual printed words are underneath and the scribbled words are on top. This is where we are now, isn't it? And look! Away over here on this empty piece. Doesn't it say "Solis"? And this line must be the road the vans are on. Look! There are drawings of those houses and temples and things. The buildings that have turned into ruins. That road out there – it might be some sort of holy road.'

Timon bent over the map peering at it in the faint light. His expression changed.

'I think we'd better get back and warn them,' he said.

'What about?' asked Boomer, trying desperately to peer over Timon's arm at the map. 'What does it say?'

'It says "swamp",' said Timon. 'Right here in the middle of that road we're on. We wouldn't want to find ourselves driving the vans into swampland, would we?'

'Let's go,' cried Garland, completely forgetting her quarrel with Maddie. 'Go now! Quickly!'

'That's what I've been telling and telling you to do,' said Boomer.

'We'll take the map,' said Timon. 'It's a good one. Look! There, just before the swamp begins there's another road marked in. I think it swings out around the swamp, but I can't be sure.'

He swept the map from the table. But as he did this an echoing sound surged in on them from every direction. The doors of the big room swung shut. A moment earlier they had been able to look out of those doors, along the hall, out though the front door to the strange gate, and the sunny meadow. Now, suddenly, there was no way out.

A section of bookshelf swung open, creaking as it did so. As they watched a dark, crumpled shape edged towards them from behind the books. Some goblin, candlestick in hand, was coming out through the wall. Boomer made a strange groaning sound . . . the sort of sound people make when they find themselves facing a ghost. It was no ghost however. A moment later they could see that it was a woman – a strange, oblong little woman who seemed almost like a book herself . . . a book filled with creased pages caught together in a bent cover.

Even in the twilight of that badly lit bookroom they could see she was old – very old. Very old. And yet she was somehow powerful too. Timon and Garland were certainly both taller than she was and even Boomer towered over her by a full inch, but for all that there was something formidable in her advance across the room towards them. And there was something about her that Garland immediately recognized, though she had never visited that library in her life and had certainly never met the old woman before.

'Borrowers,' this old, old woman said to them. 'Borrowers at last. I'm the librarian. Now, what can I do for you? What do you want to read?'

Garland was staring at her as if she had seen a ghost . . . indeed she thought she *was* seeing one. It wasn't so much the old woman's face (though by now she was sure there was something very familiar about that face). It was those earrings – those long earrings set with blue stones, tumbling from the lobes of the old woman's ears almost to her shoulders. Garland had seen those earrings in drawings and had even been told about them in family stories of the old times.

'What are you doing with that map?' the old woman suddenly asked sharply, staring at Timon who was standing with the map rolled in his hand. 'That map belongs to the library.'

'We were only looking at . . .' Boomer began. But Garland interrupted him with an incoherent cry, and then: 'Gabrielle!' she exclaimed incredulously. 'Gabrielle Maddigan.'

The old woman started. She came to a standstill, then leaned forward, holding out her candle and peered at Garland carefully.

'No one has called me that for years,' she said. 'I almost forgot I actually had a name. But who are you?'

Garland could not believe it. There before her was the actual, amazing Gabrielle . . . Gabrielle the great reader! Gabrielle the great rider! The very Gabrielle who many many years ago had invented Maddigan's Fantasia and turned it loose to wander the dissolving roads of the world. Somehow, though she had always known that Gabrielle was a real person, she had never quite believed in her.

'I am Garland Maddigan,' Garland said. 'I'm the daughter

of Ferdy who was the son of Cosmo and Cosmo was *your* son.'

It was the old woman's turn to look incredulous. She stood very still once more, staring at Garland as if she were a closed book filled with some remarkable story.

'Such a long time ago,' she said at last. 'Such a very long time ago. And oh – I loved that Fantasia. But first my husband died, and then my dear Cosmo, and then Ferdy took over. It seemed it was time for me to move on.' She looked at Boomer and Timon. 'Are you Maddigans too?'

'I almost am,' said Boomer.

'I'm a friend,' said Timon. 'Actually I'm not born yet.' Gabrielle showed no surprise at this strange statement, but moved forward a step or two still studying Garland.

'Welcome then, you Maddigan you. Welcome to the library – my library. A second Maddigan's Fantasia. Books and stories can be fantastic journeys too, you know. You stand still and yet you go . . . *everywhere*!' She flung her arms wide, and though she was so small and old, excitement flowed out of her.

Garland looked around her. She had a curious feeling of contradiction.

'Do many people come here to borrow books?' she asked cautiously.

'This library is a place where books are defended,' said Gabrielle. 'Somewhere along the line their time will come again, and then, because I've saved them, this place will be the starting place for a thousand new journeys. And those people who will read them some day . . . will start their travels here, will spin and somersault and cartwheel and swing and clown and balance as they dance a thousand feet up in the air. And you –' Gabrielle peered intently at Garland '– you can tell me – is my old Fantasia still going?'

'Yes, it is!' cried Boomer, not wanting to be left out. 'And I'm the one who beats the drums. And I'm learning to be a clown, too. Tane is teaching me. And Garland there – she does a bit of everything . . . a bit of magic . . . a bit of juggling . . . but mainly tightrope walking. She's an amazing tightrope walker. And Timon doesn't do anything, but his brother, who isn't here, is a wonderful magician and . . .'

Garland felt so overcome with the strangeness of things that all she wanted to do was sit down and hold her spinning head in her hands, but there was no time to do that. She had to fight her way through the great confusing cloud of astonishment that had closed in around her. Somewhere beyond those closed doors was the world, and in that world the Fantasia just might be driving towards the swamp.

'The thing is,' she said, interrupting Boomer, 'we've got to get back and warn the Fantasia. This map here shows that the road they're on – *we're* on –' she added quickly, for after all, even if she was confronting a remarkable ancestor in a strange library in the middle of a forgotten wilderness she was still a Fantasia girl '. . . this road runs into a swamp and I'm scared Yves and Maddie won't see where the swamp begins and our vans will get stuck and we might lose a van. And we've got to get back to Solis because . . .'

'Solis? Is Solis still standing?' asked Gabrielle. She sounded genuinely surprised. 'I thought it would have tumbled over long ago. So many places tumbled. The world out there often fell to bits around me as I travelled through it. Mind you, for all my flipping and cartwheeling I always wound up on my feet. Not everyone did. Believe me, I came to understand just how savage the world could be. Oh, I stood up against it, but it wore me down, bit by bit. Years went by and I grew too old to live easily in such a shifty place. Then Ferdy took charge of the Fantasia, and for some reason I felt that passing it all on to Ferdy set me free. So I live here now . . . have lived here for a long time now, with my friends around me.'

'Your friends?' asked Garland.

'My books,' said Gabrielle. 'I always loved reading you know, and when I found this place – it's marked in on that map you've been looking at – it seemed made for me. So I take care of the books . . . and some day the right time will come and, as I said, this will be a treasure house. There *is* one difficulty however.'

As she said this she began looking rather sternly at Garland, almost as if Garland herself were the difficulty.

'The difficulty is that the Fantasia might get stuck in swamps,' said Boomer. 'Hey! We've got to go.'

'The difficulty is that I am getting old,' said Gabrielle, speaking now in rather a pathetic voice, and holding out a limp, wrinkled hand to Garland who took it obediently. Gabrielle's hand tightened on hers, and though Garland tried to shake herself free, she found it impossible to escape the vice-like grip. After all, Gabrielle had been an acrobat for years and years and somehow or other she had stayed very strong. 'I need you,' Gabrielle said. 'You have come to me at the right time. It must be a sign.'

Garland's mouth fell open. 'But I'm part of the Fantasia,' she said. 'I mean, I do love stories and reading, but I have to travel on with the others.'

Gabrielle's grip did not loosen. It tightened if anything.

'It's so astonishing that we should meet like this,' she went on, as if Garland had not spoken. 'There are reasons for everything. You must stay with me. It's meant! You're needed here. And it's wonderful work – caring for the books, helping them to last. True life lives on through the librarian. You'll love the work.'

'No way!' cried Boomer, 'we've got to go *now*! We've got to warn the Fantasia. And we must take this map to them. It's a miles better map than Bannister's.'

'Oh no!' said Gabrielle. 'That map is a treasure. It stays here. But I'll open the door for you.'

She must have touched some button somewhere – under the edge of the table perhaps – with her left hand, for the big doors swung open again. There was the entry hall with its open door . . . there was the strange gate with the sunny meadow stretching around it. In the distance Garland could even make out the steps cut into the face of the cliff. And somewhere beyond the cliff, out of sight, the Fantasia might, even now, be scrambling around looking for its lost children. Or it might even be setting out without them. She sighed and licked her lips.

'I'll stay,' she said. 'Well, I'll stay for a while but Boomer and Timon have to go . . . they have to take that map too . . . take it to my mother. Because if the Fantasia is saved, then it's like a part of you has been saved. And a part of me. And as long as we get the message to them we can stay here and argue about the rest.' As she spoke she scooped up the map with her free hand and held it out to Timon who snatched it away from her and quickly began folding it.

'Hey! No way!' cried Boomer, dancing with impatience and fury. 'No leaving Garland behind.'

Garland turned to look at him

'Go!' she hissed. 'Go now! Run! Run and warn them.'

'It's a bargain I suppose,' said Gabrielle. 'Believe me, I wouldn't hold you like this, but I do need someone. I need you.' She hesitated. 'If I let you go you must promise me you won't run off. Yes. Give a promise. A Maddigan promise. A Maddigan promise, one Maddigan to another.'

Garland stared at her through the gloom. She thought about the Fantasia . . . she thought about the old woman facing her . . . her great grandmother. She knew Maddie wouldn't desert her, but she might send the Fantasia on ahead. Garland thought of the swamp that might be lurking there, possibly hidden from sight.

'All right. I promise,' she declared in a serious, promising voice. Gabrielle relaxed.

You're a Maddigan,' she said. 'Maddigans don't lie to each other. I trust you.' And she let Garland's hand fall to her side.

For some reason Garland now felt more tied to the library than she had felt when Gabrielle's old fingers had been clasped around her wrist. Boomer and Timon who had been standing, half-turned towards the door, turned back again, staring at her.

'You're free,' yelled Boomer. 'Run!' But Garland was already sighing and shaking her head.

'Maddigans don't betray other Maddigans,' she said. 'You're the free one. Quickly! *Now!*' she suddenly yelled, and, at last, after all their hesitation they did run. Garland watched them leap side by side through the great door out from the shadows and into the sunlight. She watched them tearing across the meadow transformed into golden boys by the late afternoon glow.

'You've done the right thing,' said Gabrielle. 'And now – would you like a glass of milk? Fresh milk? I've got cows out the back. And hens! And a garden! There are not many libraries that have a farming section like ours. Let me show you around.'

But Garland was watching Timon and Boomer run, racing towards those dangerous steps. She watched, and Gabrielle watched with her, as the boys climbed up the cliff and vanished over its rim.

Once they had edged themselves up those stairs and over the rim of the cliff, Timon and Boomer jogged up the track, winding between the rocks as quickly as they could, making for the place where, only an hour ago the Fantasia had been struggling to shift the pillar across the road and arguing about their next direction.

The boys came over the rise and stopped in dismay for the Fantasia vans were gone. It had moved on without them.

'But they wouldn't leave us,' said Boomer. 'Even if Maddie was furious with Garland she wouldn't just . . .'

Timon interrupted him.

'Maddie's van is still there,' Timon said. 'Look! It's half hidden by those bushes. Come on.'

They were about to jog off through the stones as speedily as they could when they heard a scrambling sound and Maddie, Tane and Bannister burst out from between the huge boulders, almost colliding with Boomer. Maddie seized him, swinging him off his feet and shaking him, while shouting angry questions over his head at Timon.

'Garland!' Maddie was crying. 'Where's Garland? Where is she? Where is that wretched runaway girl?'

'Back there!' Timon shouted, pointing with the map, which he then held out towards them. 'She's all right, but she made us leave her there. The Fantasia's in a bit of danger and she wanted us to warn you.'

'Danger?' Maddie slowed down and looked around. 'Where's the danger? Is the sky going to fall in or something?'

'There's a swamp!' yelled Boomer. 'We found a map and it shows a swamp.'

Timon spread the map. At first it blew out like a flag and wind continued to billow in under it as Maddie, Bannister and Tane crowded around it. Timon held it down rather like a fisherman holding a flapping fish and pointed at the road and the printed warning.

Bannister struck his forehead.

'"Swamp!"' he exclaimed. 'I couldn't make out the word on our map. I thought it said "Camp"'!

'Oh Lord!' cried Maddie. 'They've gone. Well, *we* haven't. We were waiting for you and Garland. But . . .' She turned to Tane. 'Tane . . . the key's in my van. Run down the hill and take off after them. Warn them! But don't go clowning off on your own.

Remember to come back for us. Run!' Tane took off down the hill without asking any questions. Maddie watched him go, then turned to Timon. 'Now! Where's Garland?'

'In the library!' Boomer said interrupting. 'She promised to stay and . . .'

'The *library*?' exclaimed Maddie, sounding as if she'd been told that Garland (being a Fantasia girl) had vanished into a magician's top hat.

'The *library*?' echoed Bannister, but in a very different tone of voice.

'We found a library,' explained Timon. 'A whole library full of books – and with a librarian too.'

'Old Gabrielle!' Boomer interrupted him. 'Your old Gabrielle is in charge of the library, but she grabbed Garland and . . .'

'The thing is,' said Timon. 'Garland promised to stay there as long as Gabrielle would open the doors and let us free so that we could warn you . . .'

'. . . about the swamp!' finished Boomer.

'Gabrielle wants to keep her,' said Timon. 'She wants – well, a sort of assistant librarian I suppose. A Maddigan. And Garland's a Maddigan. Anyhow Garland promised to stay there and help her.'

'And she told us that Maddigans keep their promises,' Boomer added.

Maddie gritted her teeth and shook her head. 'Maddigans *do* keep their promises. But only when their mothers let them,' she said. 'I'll have a word or two to say about Maddigans making promises without their mother's permission.'

'We'll show you the way,' said Boomer eagerly.

'No! You kids go back to the road down there with Bannister,' Maddie ordered.

'Maddie!' said Bannister. 'You're not leaving me behind. A library. And I'm the Fantasia reader! Of course I'm coming too.'

26

The Great Maddie

Garland and Gabrielle sat opposite one another at a small table. Shelves of books rose up on either side of them, the spines looking like a thousand narrow doors, each one leading to a different kingdom. Garland glanced around at those books with apprehension thinking they might suddenly leap out of their places and fly around her, flapping their pages like wings. However they just sat there, shelf upon shelf of them, closed and silent, keeping themselves to themselves. Deep down Garland knew she was struggling not to cry. Gabrielle had said the library was its own sort of Fantasia, but Garland found it hard to see how this could be, for the library stood still, while the Fantasia danced and spun and cartwheeled along the highways and byways of a dangerous world.

'You have no idea how happy I am to have you here,' Gabrielle was saying. 'I mean the library is what I wanted . . . it's what I *chose* . . . and yet I have felt so lonely for another voice sometimes. I've longed for another book lover. The books are comfortable friends in a way . . . and yet sometimes even the best reader longs to talk about what they've just read with someone else. It's a way of understanding it all even more . . . of making what you have read truly real.'

'I do like reading,' said Garland carefully. 'I've read our books over and over again. Of course we don't have many of them.' She paused. 'But what I really want to do is to spin along with the Fantasia,' she said. 'After all the Fantasia was your invention. And it's got our name. I want to keep on walking the tightrope. Walking the tightrope is like being alive. It's dangerous but if you're clever you stay on the wire.'

'You can do things like that here,' said Gabrielle.

'But you need to do them in front of a crowd . . . a different crowd each time,' explained Garland. 'The crowd watches, and their watching turns into part of your cleverness.' An idea came to her. 'I mean a writer writes a book – OK – but somehow or other that book isn't truly finished until someone reads it. And a trick isn't really a trick unless someone is surprised by it. And anyway,' Garland added, 'I want my mother. I had this great fight with her and now I'm sorry. I want things to be fixed up between us.'

'You might have to live through that,' said Gabrielle. 'It's impossible to have everything we long for in this life. It's too late to begin now, but tomorrow I'll begin to show you the books. You'll be amazed . . . simply amazed . . .'

Then, far off but clear, they heard a voice calling. 'Garland! Garland!'

Garland leapt to her feet.

'Mum! Maddie!' she yelled back. 'She's here,' she told Gabrielle. 'It's my mum. We had this fight but she's forgiven me and I've forgiven her.'

'But remember your promises,' said Gabrielle in her creaking voice. 'You did promise! And a Maddigan keeps her word.'

Garland sat down again. Maddie! she was thinking. Maddie would find a way out of this. Maddie would just break the bonds of that promise and sweep her back into the heart of the Fantasia.

'Where are you?' cried Maddie, sounding much closer now. 'What is this place?'

'It's a library,' Garland said, speaking through the door into the hall full of books, certain she didn't have to shout any longer. Maddie was close enough to hear her.

Another voice made itself heard, a man's voice, quiet yet carrying.

Bannister.

'A library!' Bannister was exclaiming, as if the word 'library' was another word for 'treasure'. 'Boomer said it was a library. I didn't believe him. I just had to see for myself. And it is. It really is. A library.'

And with these words Bannister and Maddie came into the room, Maddie leading the way, ignoring the books and looking only for Garland, while Bannister came after her, walking vaguely, almost strolling, staring at the shelves like an astronomer who has just focused on a new universe.

Garland jumped up, pushing her chair over, and flung her arms around her mother.

'Darling!' cried Maddie, hugging her back. 'Thank goodness you're all right. I'm sorry I was so bad-tempered back there, but you know – life gets so complicated in patches . . .'

'Did you drive into the swamp?' Garland cried back. 'Did Timon and Boomer warn you?'

'Look at this,' Bannister mumbled in the background. 'I've never seen anything like it. It's heaven.'

'Tane's on the way now to warn them,' Maddie said. 'And when you look at that new map there's a road that veers off . . . it's probably overgrown, easy to drive past, but I think if we follow it we might find ourselves on the road we usually take.' She looked over at Gabrielle, and her expression changed. 'Who are you?'

'Mum, it's a Maddigan – the *great* Maddigan!' exclaimed Garland. 'It's Gabrielle.'

'Good heavens,' said Maddie weakly. She picked up the chair

that Garland had been sitting in and sat in it herself, staring across the table at Gabrielle. 'I thought – well, to put it bluntly, I thought you must be dead.'

'I am very much alive,' said Gabrielle stiffly. 'And I must inform you that your daughter has promised to stay here with me, and to inherit my library. She has given the word of a Maddigan.'

'And let me tell you, even if she'd promised ten times over, she is coming with me,' declared Maddie. 'I'd never let her give herself up. I've lost her father and I am not going to lose her.'

Gabrielle stared into space for a moment. 'Ferdy?' she mumbled rather as if she were trying to remember just who Ferdy was. But then something like a glassy beetle crawled down her cheek. Perhaps in spite of herself Gabrielle was weeping a little. 'My son dead. My grandson dead. And I'm still here.' Then she stiffened. 'She has *promised*,' she said. 'And that promise is a promise I expect to be kept.'

And suddenly the doors shivered and closed once again, as if the library were both a place of safety and a trap . . . anxious to keep something it had won from the outside world.

Tane was driving Maddie's van rather more speedily than it was used to being driven. The path ahead was deeply corrugated and full of jagged stone, and the van not only rattled, but jumped into the air, all four wheels off the ground. Inside, its tins and boxes leapt and danced and rattled in a little fierce Fantasia of their own. Tane swerved around one stone large enough to be called a boulder and then accelerated. 'Careful! Careful!' cried Boomer.

'There's a time to be careful and there's a time to live dangerously,' said Tane. 'As long as we don't wind up in the swamp ourselves.' The van bounced across great gaps in the road rather like a horse leaping ditches then spun around a corner, its brakes screaming.

'I don't want to leave Garland with that Gabrielle, even if she is a Maddigan,' said Boomer.

'We won't,' replied Tane, speaking through his teeth. 'Garland belongs with us. Just trust Maddie.' Timon toppled sideways in his seat as Tane swung the van around yet another bend in the track, and then they were leaping and jolting over fiercely uneven ground. Up and over a rise and Tane gave a shout. 'There they are! There they are.' He leaned on the horn. One long toot. Three short ones. Another long one. They charged towards the distant vans of the Fantasia.

'Stop!' Boomer and Timon were shouting together though nobody except Tane could possibly have heard them. 'Stop!' They were shouting to the Fantasia and to Tane as well, thinking the van was about to break into pieces.

Tane tooted madly yet again. But then he suddenly relaxed back into his seat. 'They've heard us. They are stopping. Well, I think they are.' The van slowed down.

Fantasia people were certainly leaping out of those other vans on ahead, and were peering back down the track. They began jumping up and down and waving wildly.

Tane leaned sideways, still steering a little incoherently, and waving back through the side window. 'Hey! It's all in a day's work,' he said, in a trembling voice. 'We'll stop and explain. Save the day and the Fantasia too. And *then* we'll go back and get Garland even if we've got to besiege that library you keep going on about, and shake that Gabrielle until her teeth rattle. If she's got any teeth left that is.'

'She's got teeth,' said Boomer. 'She looks as if she could bite hard with them. And the thing is Garland promised. She *promised*. And she couldn't cross her fingers because Gabrielle was holding her hand.' He thought about this. 'Does it count if you cross your left-hand fingers?'

Tane did not seem to know the answer to this. 'Well, Maddie's probably there by now,' he said comfortingly. 'And you know what Maddie is. She's tough too – Maddigan-tough! Though maybe it would be a good idea if we got back and gave her a bit of support now we've saved the day here.'

Someone was running fast towards them.

'There's your little brother,' Tane said to Timon. 'Must have been worrying about you. Nice to be missed, isn't it?'

'Open the doors,' said Maddie. 'Open those doors at once. Or it will be the worse for you . . . and as for your library. I'll pull the books of the shelves and tear their pages out of them. Because you might be the great Gabrielle, but I am the great Maddie and no one is going to take my Garland away from me.'

There in the eerie shadows of the closed room, Maddie and Gabrielle faced each other, both glaring, both unyielding. And it seemed to Garland that, because they were both being obstinate about things that mattered to them, there was a curious likeness between them . . . fists clenched, eyebrows drawn in, the corners of their mouths turned down.

'But you must understand. I *need* someone,' said Gabrielle. 'I must have someone. This library has grown to be like another Fantasia to me . . . and I am not going to last forever. Ferdy took over the Fantasia out there and this child here, his daughter she tells me, did give me a Maddigan promise, and . . .'

She was interrupted, but not by Maddie or Garland.

'It *is* a Fantasia,' declared a delighted voice. Bannister came striding across the big room towards them. 'Maddie, this is just astonishing. There are all the stories in the world here . . . all the histories and mysteries . . . I've never seen anything like it.'

Old Gabrielle looked sideways at him with some surprise. It was obvious she had forgotten he was there. Her expression altered.

'They mean something to you, these books?' she asked. 'Just seeing them changes you?'

'Transformation! I'm transformed,' Bannister exclaimed, flinging his arms up into the air, a book in either hand. 'I didn't think there was any place outside of Solis that had a library like this one. And this one – Maddie, just think – this one is actually owned by a Maddigan.'

'To be honest I don't own it,' said Gabrielle. She had straightened and looked suddenly sharper. 'I *care* for it. That's a different thing. But, as I was saying a moment ago, I'm getting old . . . to be honest all the taking care of it is getting a bit too much for me.'

And now Bannister turned to Maddie. His mouth opened, then shut again. He took a long, slow breath. Anyone could tell his mouth was full of words trying to put themselves into some order before he let them out. Staring at him through the dim light of the closed room, Maddie looked startled, like someone who has just seen the solution of a puzzle, but does not quite like it or dare to believe in it. 'Maddie . . .' Bannister began, and then fell silent, struggling with his mouthful of words.

'Bannister,' said Maddie. 'We need you. We need every working man we can get. You know that, don't you?'

Bannister nodded. 'Yes,' he said. 'Oh yes! It's just that . . .' And he looked up at the shelves of books with such enchantment . . . such longing . . . that suddenly Maddie began to laugh.

'Oh, it's an answer,' she said. 'I'll admit it is an answer. I can see we have to set you free,' she said. 'We'll pay tribute to Gabrielle here, and we'll buy Garland out of her promise by offering *you* to the library in Garland's place.'

Bannister's expression changed again. He looked somehow younger . . . so eager as he peered through the shadows first at Maddie and then at Gabrielle. 'It's not as if we would need to say goodbye forever,' he said softly. 'Not now you know that these roads exist. Not now you know the way here. You can go in one of your Fantasia circles and wind up here again . . . drop in for a cup of tea.'

'Indeed we could,' said Maddie. 'But Bannister – you know how it is with the Fantasia. We have to move on. No choice! Garland and I will go now . . . we *must* go . . . and join the others.' She looked at Gabrielle. 'I wish there was time,' she said, 'because meeting you is like meeting someone out of a fairy tale. And there is so much to tell . . . so much to ask about . . .' She looked around at the books. 'But . . .'

'But the Fantasia must move on,' said Gabrielle. 'I know. I *do* know. Because, after all, I invented it and I was the one who used to drive it on. But I – I grew tired of all that moving on, you see. I wanted to stand still which is what I am doing in a way. Though I feel I am still moving on in my head, you know. There is no such thing as stillness for some of us.'

Then Garland and Maddie hugged Bannister who hugged them back, but in such a distracted way Garland felt he was trying to read the titles on books across her shoulder. And, after a moment of hesitation, Garland and Maddie hugged old Gabrielle too, which was like hugging a legend.

Around them the walls creaked and rustled. The room opened its doors, and through one door Garland saw the hall and that other open door at the end of it. She saw the meadow beyond it, now an evening meadow, still light but no longer sunny. There in the middle of the meadow was that strange gate without walls and there, if they looked hard, dim in the distance, the cliff, its narrow zigzag scribble of steps hidden in the shadow.

'Be very careful climbing that cliff,' said old Gabrielle.

'Don't worry! We will,' said Maddie. 'We know how to be *very* careful. We've had a lot of practice.'

And hand in hand she and Garland set off together . . . back through the gate, across the meadow, up the steps and along to track . . . back to the road where they found Yves parking their van, preparing to set out with Tane and Timon to bring them home once more. Found! Found! All together again.

Maddie and Garland climbed into their van. Maddie jumped into the driver's seat, sighing with relief, started the motor, then swung the van around and moved off down the road, moving, always moving, for, as they had reminded old Gabrielle, the Fantasia always had to move on.

27

Night Wings

Dear Ferdy . . . On we go, on and on. You would be proud
of us because we're going so well. Of course we miss
Bannister. We keep expecting to see him loping from one
van to another, with a book in his pocket so that he
can snatch a quick read when he thinks no one is
looking. Penrod has become our mapreader, and that
new map makes a great difference. Its print is so much
clearer and the lines don't fade out in the way they
did on the old map.

Garland paused, sitting back and looking at her page. It
was true . . . that new map worked well . . . just having a map like that made you feel you were in control
of life, which meant you were in control of yourself too. Taking a deep breath, Garland grinned at the world around her.
'This way,' she could hear Maddie saying. 'Cross this field . . .
this space . . . and we find a really good road. We've been making great progress over the last day or two. Just as well. The solstice is bearing down on us, but – Solis – here we come.'

'And the converter with us,' said Yves. 'They should send
out a city procession to welcome us in. They should pay us too.'

Garland, listening, found confusion creeping in on her. She
longed for a Fantasia triumph. She loved to imagine the gates

of Solis swinging wide and people bursting out to mill around them, welcoming them in. She wanted that triumph, but she did not want the triumph to belong to Yves. Maddie must be the one who led the Fantasia into Solis and she herself – Garland – should be up there, too – riding Samala beside Maddie, waving to the crowd, blowing kisses and letting them flutter away from her like wild butterflies into the Solis air. She wanted that entry to be a true triumph of Maddigans.

The vans were moving steadily, but so slowly that she and Timon, Eden and Boomer were still able to stroll side by side, looking forward and sometimes back over their shoulders at the little line of vans crawling through the wilderness. When they were crossing open land they looked as lonely as if they were the only living creatures in an empty echoing world. 'I hope we get there before the solstice,' she said.

'At this rate we will,' said Timon with such certainty that Garland looked at him with surprise.

'How can you tell?' she asked curiously.

Timon named the number of miles to Solis and the number of miles they were making each day.

'But how can you tell for *sure*?' asked Garland again.

'What's really interesting is why *you* can't tell,' Timon said, half joking and half serious. 'Look! We're taking steps of a certain size, and those steps add up to the distance. And each time the wheels go round they move us on a certain distance. Add those little distances together and they make up a big distance . . . all the way from here to there.' He looked sideways at her as if he were looking at her with someone else's eyes. And then, as if he did not want her glimpsing the person looking out through him, he looked away and began to joke. 'We are three million worm's lengths from Solis . . . unless the worms are at full stretch of course. Then it's probably – oh – say about two million and a half.'

Garland laughed, and laughter somehow lightened her.

'Worms' lengths,' grumbled Boomer on her other side. 'How could you get enough worms to measure a mile?'

'You'd have to pay them,' said Timon, and as he looked over at Boomer that strange glint was in his eyes once more. Garland could not see it, but Boomer, about to snap back with a smart answer, caught his breath, then fell silent.

'Yves is taking all the credit,' Garland grumbled. 'But he didn't find that map. We did.'

'But really he's the leader of the Fantasia now,' said Boomer, bending forward a little so that he could speak around Timon.

'He isn't!' cried Garland. 'No way! A Maddigan has to be the one to lead Maddigan's Fantasia. Maddie's the leader, and Yves has to do what she tells him to do.'

'Boom! Boom!' muttered Boomer. 'That's drum language for Ha! Ha!'

Garland suddenly felt she just had to be on her own. She peeled herself away from the others, then made for her home van, irritated to see that Yves was now driving it, something he did from time to time.

'Where's Mum?' she asked, swinging herself onto the running board.

'She wanted to have a break. She's been behind the wheel all morning,' said Yves.

'Well, who's driving your van?' asked Garland, and was cross with herself for sounding so grumpy.

'Tane's in charge of my bus,' Yves said. 'But, anyhow, while you're here just let me ask you something.'

Garland waited. Yves was silent as if he were thinking out what to say next very carefully indeed.

'Why are you always so bad-tempered with me?' he asked at last. 'I'm working my guts out to keep this show on the road . . . pushing, pulling, hauling, driving, performing . . . and all I get from you are dark looks. Honestly, Garland, it wears me out. And it's just not fair.'

'But you're taking over . . . bossing everything!' cried Garland. 'This is *Maddigan's* Fantasia and you're turning it into something else.'

Yves was silent for a moment.

'Look,' he said at last. 'We lost Ferdy . . . that was a dreadful thing. Ferdy was ringmaster and he was the sort of man who could do anything. And believe it or not he was my best friend. You don't ever think about that, do you? Losing him – it was a disaster. And I feel grief, just as you do. But it's like Maddie says. We have to keep on. And though she can do most things, she just can't do them all. She needs someone to move into Ferdy's place . . .'

'No one can move into Ferdy's place!' cried Garland quickly.

'Maybe not – but we've kept going, haven't we?' Yves cried back. 'We've done what he would have wanted . . . we've kept going. We won through to Newton. We've got that converter. We'll get back to Solis – well, we'll probably get back. Nothing's certain, even now. Nothing's ever certain. Your mother – believe me, she misses Ferdy every moment of the day. But she's just too brave to sit around moaning about it.'

Garland and Yves rode on in silence, Garland balanced on the running board while Yves steered the van very carefully in and out of wild broom bushes, spiking upwards into the clear air. Rabbits leapt up and ran in front of them, vanishing into long grass, and the Fantasia dogs that were having a run set off after them, barking excitedly, glad to be simple dogs set free from performing. Ahead of them the scrub and tussock parted to reveal a road once more. Yves settled back into the seat and wriggled his shoulders.

'You probably know this already, but I'll tell you anyway,' he said. 'I really admire your mother. And you! I think you're a great girl. Bad-tempered and a great nuisance at times, always running off and holding us up, but for all that I think you're a bit of a heroine. You're like your mother in a lot of ways. Of course all you two can think of at present is grieving for Ferdy. But down the track a bit . . . I mean things could change . . . nothing stays still forever and . . .'

'Don't!' cried Garland. She jumped away from the running board, not wanting to hear what Yves might be about to say, and dropped down into the tussock, falling flat on purpose and rolling over and over like a tumbleweed. Then she pulled herself into a sitting position and glared after the van. She suddenly felt she had driven and walked too much. She suddenly longed to be on her own, riding Samala once more, but as she half turned in the direction of the floats that carried the horses, someone spoke to her.

'What was all that about?' asked Timon, coming up beside her.

'Him!' said Garland. 'It's like I said. He's planning to take everything over . . . the Fantasia . . . *and* my mother . . . and even me.' She picked herself up, brushed herself down, and then began walking on, just a little unsteadily to begin with. Yet after a few steps the old familiar rhythm took over. Smoothness came back into the world. Timon walked beside her, saying nothing at first. Then he took a breath. 'Perhaps you should find some way of getting rid of Yves,' he said.

Garland was shocked . . . shocked in such a mixed-up way that, for a moment there, she could make no sense of anything, not even herself. She was shocked not only by what Timon had just suggested, but by the strange silky quality that had crept into his voice. Suddenly it had seemed like a stranger's voice. And though, only a moment earlier, she had been thinking that she would happily get rid of Yves, hearing Timon actually suggesting it frightened her.

Timon laughed. 'Just joking,' he said. 'Though anyone can tell Yves is out to take over anything he can get.'

'Yes,' mumbled Garland. 'I mean I sort of hate him at times. But I don't really want to – to hurt him or anything.'

'Well, there we are then,' said Timon cheerfully.

So they moved on towards Solis, sometimes walking and sometimes riding on into the late afternoon with their backs to the west. The day deepened and darkened, the setting sun pushing their long shadows out in front of them, and the road, battered but constant, finally led them in amongst trees and then into a full forest. They made camp in a clearing which Garland thought she recognized. Yes! They had certainly been there before. Food was cooked and shared. A few stories were told. Songs were sung and then the Fantasia, with Byrna and Nye setting themselves up as guards for the first part of the night, felt comfortable enough to make for bed. Wind sighed in the trees around them, and somewhere between the roots of the trees, crickets sang busily.

Worn out by capering and carping Garland hugged Maddie, then flopped into her own bunk and fell into dreamless sleep while Maddie worked on by lamplight, sitting at the table that folded out from the wall. After a while Yves looked in on her. 'Anything I can do?' he asked.

'No thanks,' Maddie said. 'Just updating a few records. And then I'm off to bed like everyone else. I'm really tired, but we've got to be up and away in the morning. Before sunrise would be good.'

Yves paused, staring at her, tangled but still beautiful in the candlelight. Just for a moment he looked as if he might have something important to say, and Maddie looked up questioningly. 'Anything wrong?' she asked him, smiling and frowning at the same time.

'No,' said Yves. Maddie looked at him, sighed and then laughed.

'How about a small drink?' she said. 'I think we've earned it.'

A short time after that, when Yves had gone to his own van, Maddie rolled herself into her bunk. And she did sleep well, breathing deeply . . . perhaps so deeply that the sound of her own breathing filled her sleeping ears and stopped her hearing anything else.

For, slowly, slowly the door handle edged down. Slowly the door opened, its small creaking sounding like yet another cricket in the night. Darkness filled the van, but the figure sliding in through the door and between the bunks was even darker. It moved slowly and very softly, holding a hand in front of it, fumbling just a little with something it held. Suddenly a thin, pale wand of light struck out into the midnight of the van, waved from left to right accidentally touching Garland's face so that she mumbled and turned over in her bunk-bed. The light immediately vanished. If Garland had been aware of that light at all, it had simply seemed like part of her dreaming.

Silence. Like a pointing finger the light appeared once again, but neither Maddie nor Garland stirred as their visitor moved to the back of the van. That bright thin finger swung left and right, pointing out a few things to the shadowy shape behind it. The hand advanced to pick some of the things up . . . and then to replace them quickly and quietly. There at the back of the van the finger . . . ran left . . . ran right . . . and then went out again. Moving very slowly and carefully the black figure, almost indistinguishable from the blackness of the van, reached out ahead of itself.

Its fingers closed on something, struggled to pick it up, but did manage, at last, to hoist it silently off the ground, and then carefully . . . carefully . . . inched down the van with it. Still moving, very slowly and quickly, though weighed down on one

• 300 •

side by a heavy package, the figure edged towards the open door. The outside air breathed in, as the figure slid out, taking whatever it had stolen along with it.

Once again the silence took over . . . but, after all, the silence and the darkness had barely been disturbed.

And then!

And then, suddenly, something wild screamed in the night. Suddenly the whole Fantasia seemed to tremble with a series of thumps! Maddie sat upright in her bunk. Outside a figure, stooping and alert, had dropped out of the trees and onto the roof of the food van . . . another dropped beside it. Nye, the wakeful guard, swung around staring up into the night, while Byrna, the drowsing guard, jumped up and out, staggering and trying to work out in a jumbled way just where the sound was coming from.

'Up there! Up there!' shouted Nye, pointing. There on the roof of the food van someone – some*thing* – was standing . . . a huge bird, wings spread wide. Nye shouted wildly, and then, as he reached for his gun, the van shivered and began to roll forward . . . the lights came on and shone ahead of it. At the same time a motor began a soft but powerful purring, and the figure on the roof took off upwards. Nye fired his gun, Byrna his bow and arrow, without quite knowing just what they were shooting at. But the van moved faster and faster, racing past the camp-fires out of the camp and into the night.

The sound of the shouting and the gunfire had wakened the whole Fantasia. People tumbled out of their tents and vans, confused and alarmed, and came stumbling towards Byrna and Nye shouting. 'What is it? What's wrong?'

'They've stolen the food van!' shouted Byrna.

'What? More Road Rats?' yelled Tane, coming up to join them.

'Not rats! Bats!' Nye shouted back. 'Great bats swooping out of the air.'

'Bats?' Tane said. 'No way! Think of where we are. We've been set on by a gang of Birdboys.'

'Birdboys?' cried Yves, coming to a stop, and clapping his hands to his head. 'Of course. There was that great thump on the roof of my van.'

'Who are the Birdboys?' Eden asked Garland.

'They're not boys,' Garland answered. 'Not often. Mostly they're grown-up. We just call them Birdboys. They're almost like flying gypsies.'

'Flying!' exclaimed Timon incredulously. 'Do you mean they've grown wings?'

'They found a way to make wings and when they have to swing upward they run them from little motors,' Garland explained. 'They do a bit of robbery. They swoop down on travellers – not to kill them – just frighten them and rob them.'

'And that's enough, isn't it?' growled old Shell.

'Pity you didn't remind us we were in bat territory,' Nye said. 'Hey, Maddie! Did you hear? The bats have stolen our food van. We're always losing it.'

'More than that,' said Maddie standing in the door of her van. Her voice was filled with such grim despair that everyone around her fell silent, staring back at her, waiting for some terrible announcement. 'The solar converter was in my van. But it seems to have vanished. I checked first thing and it's not there any more.'

'Gone?' shouted Yves. 'How can it have gone?'

'Where? Which direction?' asked Goneril.

'How can I tell?' asked Maddie flinging out her arms and then letting them flop down at her side despairingly. 'Does anyone have a clue? Byrna? Nye?'

'They took off in *that* direction,' said Byrna, pointing, 'I could see the lights for a few minutes, and then nothing. And they *flew* up and away. Well, some of them flew. Flew up and away. There must have been someone driving the van.'

'Flying? That might make it complicated,' said Maddie. 'Unless we've got someone who can read tracks in the air. How on earth could a Birdboy carry off that converter? It was really heavy . . . Okay! Is there any point in setting off after it right now?'

'Wait another hour or two,' said Yves. 'Even if we set off now with torches, the wheel tracks will be almost impossible to see.'

'But we can't let them get away with the converter!' cried Garland.

'We haven't very much choice,' Yves said. 'Just think about it. They know the forest by night and we don't. Anyhow it's not much use to them. With a bit of luck they'll sling it out somewhere along the track.'

Looking at the faces around her as well as she could Garland could see other Fantasia people agreeing with Yves.

'We'll never sleep now,' she said, and Yves sighed, then smiled wearily.

'Sleep? What's that?' he asked. 'It seems to be something I remember from this time last year . . . ages ago. Never mind! Let's just do the best we can.'

28

Hunting the Birdboys

As soon as the first light of day slid a transparent grey finger down between the trees Yves was up and about, calling everyone together.

'Straight ahead,' he said. 'They'd have wanted to get free of the trees wouldn't they? And a food wagon's not the sort of thing you can fly off with. It can't be far away. We're probably too late to save the food . . . but you never know. There might be a bit left. And somewhere someone has that damned converter which we've suffered so much to acquire.'

'He's guessing,' Garland said, talking sideways out of the corner of her mouth to Timon. 'And anyhow once we get free of the trees how are we going to tell which direction they've taken? They could have gone anywhere.'

'We just have to guess right,' said Boomer, bouncing in his Boomerish way beside her. 'And there'll be tyre tracks.'

But as it turned out there were plenty of clues, for, as they spread out and wandered through the trees on either side of the road, they found things thrown out of the van . . . cartons and crates, torn or splintered and always empty.

'A lot of this isn't our stuff,' said Penrod, kicking at some of the rubbish. 'It's been here for days.'

'Shows we aren't the only travellers along this track,' said old Shell.

This had already occurred to Garland. And later, as they hunted on, she sidled up to Maddie, hunting beside her. 'Did you dream of *hearing* anything?' she asked trying to make her question sound almost accidental.

'Not a thing!' said Maddie. 'I could kick myself. Of course I was tired . . . well, we're all tired . . . but I made things worse for myself. I had a little nip of whiskey before I went to bed. I haven't done anything like that for weeks and weeks and it must have really knocked me out.'

'Did Yves have one too?' asked Garland suspiciously.

Maddie laughed.

'No fooling you!' she said. 'We did clink glasses . . .' She looked at Garland. 'We were just talking,' She said, rather defensively. Garland felt that familiar surge of suspicion once more.

'You talk to Yves all the time!' she said. 'And I think he wants to marry you . . . he wants to take over the Fantasia and have it all for himself.'

'Oh, Garland darling,' said Maddie. 'You really are impossible. You keep on saying that. Now listen! Yves just tries to help me and that's understandable. Remember he makes a living for himself and Lilith through the Fantasia. Remember he's worked with us for years. And as for me . . .' She hesitated. 'Garland, I still feel totally married to our darling Ferdy. But we can't talk about it now. We have too much else to worry about.'

'You always say that,' said Garland.

'And I'm always right!' declared Maddie.

And of course she was always right. There was always too much to worry about. Garland hurried ahead, anxious now to catch up with Timon and Eden.

The three of them moved together, picking their way carefully through the ferns that fell away in banks under the trees.

Off to the right and ahead of them they could glimpse Yves, Tane and Nye also picking their way between the trees. And suddenly Garland saw Yves stiffen, holding up one finger signalling silence. They all listened and all heard, faint but distinct, voices laughing and talking. They were too far away to hear the words.

Yves turned and beckoned everyone in around him.

'Now,' he whispered. 'It is our turn to move quietly . . . to sneak up on them if we can. Remember we don't know if they are wearing their wings or not . . . we don't know anything about them, really. But what we do know is that we might have a chance to get back a few of the things that were ours in the first place, mainly that converter. At least they won't be able to eat that. So off we go . . .' His words were very soft. 'Spread out! Spread out widely, and let's work our way inward.'

Yves moved away to the left, disappearing among the trees. Tane moved to the right. Timon and Garland edged together following Tane. Boomer stood nervously trying to work out how he could seem brave without taking any risks. At last, making up his mind, he simply went straight ahead, pushing through the ferns and sneaking almost silently up and over a series of little ledges, softened with green and gold mosses.

Almost immediately he found himself looking down into a hollow filled with a green tangle of saplings and ferns like arrowheads of lace. And there, sitting with his back to Boomer, was a Birdboy – a young one who seemed to be almost Boomer's own age. He could easily have heard Boomer coming up behind him if he had been listening, but he was concentrating on the bag he was eating from greedily, one biscuit after another. Even as Boomer crawled towards him, he was impressed with the desperate way the boy was eating those biscuits . . . impressed, too, with how thin he was and the way his shoulder blades stuck out. But, after all, the Birdboys needed to be thin, thought Boomer. Their wings would not lift anyone too well fed. And, on the ground those wings were a problem. This boy had taken his wings off. They were lying beside him, neatly folded on top of one another, and there on top of them was the little motor that drove them. Boomer found himself staring at them with longing. Since his little motorbike had been ruined he had missed having a machine in his life. Horses were all very well, but there was something about turning wheels and busy pistons that thrilled him.

He must have made some sort of a sound. The Birdboy began to turn. Boomer leapt, caught the Birdboy and bowled him over, at the same time hissing: 'Shhh! Shhh! You can have the biscuits. Shhh!' Because after all biscuits were not nearly as valuable as the lost converter.

Perhaps his words had some effect, or perhaps the boy was frightened of being caught with his secret plunder. They rolled over and over together, struggling and tussling, then sat up, both dizzy, both unsure of just which way up they were.

The boy opened his mouth to shout.

'Biscuits!' hissed Boomer again. 'Just shut up and you can have the biscuits.' He reached out and grabbed a biscuit from those that had spilled from the pack then crammed it into the Birdboy's mouth. 'Stick that in your beak and peck it!' he said. The boy coughed, then struggled to cough silently, rolling from side to side on the ground, and suddenly Boomer was completely sure of what he had only suspected. 'You stole them, didn't you? Your lot stole them from us and you stole them from your own lot! OK! You can have them all. I don't want them back. Can you hear me? *You – can – have – them!*' he whispered.

The boy stared at him, slowly closing his mouth. He certainly seemed to understand what Boomer was saying.

At that moment a wild shouting began from somewhere in

the bush beyond. Boomer relaxed. Out of a curious goodwill he helped the boy to his feet, then passed what was left of the bag of biscuits over to him. 'Something's happening. Quickly!' he said. The Birdboy began to run through the trees to find out just who was fighting who, and who was winning.

'Hey! Wait! You've left your wings behind,' Boomer shouted, but the Birdboy took no notice of him. Boomer hesitated. He just could not run away leaving that set of fascinating wings on the grass behind him. He just had to pick them up and try to run with them, which proved extremely difficult. They flapped and slapped and though they were very light they somehow managed to tilt him this way and that, and though the motor was small it was somehow complicated to carry. All the same Boomer managed somehow to scramble along, carrying the wings with him.

Bursting out through the trees, he found himself on the side of a forest road with the food van parked to one side of it. In a neat and orderly fashion the older Birdboys had been break-fasting around a small campfire, but now they were confronted by Tane, Nye and Yves. Yves was yelling at them.

'OK! So you've eaten our food! Forget the food! But the con-verter! Where's the converter?' He was sketching the shape of the converter in the air as he shouted.

The tallest of the Birdboys, a gangling young man who seemed to be their leader, frowned as he tried to follow what Yves was saying. He looked at his friends and shrugged, hold-ing out his hands to either side of him. Copying Yves, he also sketched the shape of the converter in the air. But his compan-ions just shrugged as he had shrugged.

'One of you went into one of our vans . . . not the food van, one of the other vans, and stole a box from it,' Yves declared. 'Where is it?'

'Something to eat?' asked one Birdboy carefully. 'To eat?' He mimed putting something in his mouth and rubbed his stomach.

'No!' said Tane. 'Nothing to eat! A box . . .' he broke off and turned to Yves. 'You know,' he said, frowning. 'I don't think they did take our converter. I just I don't think they'd be interested. All this lot wanted was food.'

'They might have thought the box had food in it, though,' suggested Byrna.

The search began, but the clearing was simply a place where the Birdboys had stopped off for a small feast. And, as Tane had said, the boys themselves were just not the sort of thieves who would have looked for anything other than food. Rather reluctantly Boomer put the wings down with the motor on top of them and began hunting along with his Fantasia friends.

As he searched he felt someone pull at his sleeve and, turning, found himself face to face with the biscuit Birdboy once more.

'What do you want?' he asked. 'We have to find our converter?' And he found himself sketching a square box in the air.

The boy frowned, shaking his head and fighting to find words.

'Not just us,' he said at last. 'One other.' He held up one finger.

'What do you mean? One *other*?' asked Boomer.

The boy pointed back towards the Fantasia camp, pecking at the air with his forefinger. 'Someone *else* there,' the boy said, watching Boomer, trying to work out if Boomer understood him. Boomer nodded his head. The boy struggled on, anxious to tell Boomer something. 'Someone . . .' he walked his fingers through the air. 'Watching! I was watching from . . .' He pointed upward. 'In the branches,' he said at last. 'I was . . .' he took a breath '. . . in the branches. Saw him. Not you! Not us! Another one. Moving very hush.' He mimed someone tiptoeing.

Boomer looked up, and saw that Yves was listening.

'Where did he come from?' Yves asked.

The boy shrugged. 'Just there. Moving!' he said. 'Moving into the . . .' he hesitated, and then drew in the air once more.

'What's he drawing?' asked Penrod. 'It looks like a . . .'

'A van!' cried Boomer. 'He's drawing a van.'

'The food van?' asked Yves. He pointed over at the food van, just visible through the trees.

The boy looked towards the food van, frowning. Then his face cleared and he shook his head.

'Another!' he said, holding up two fingers this time.

'Did you see him come out?' asked Yves sharply.

The boy kept shaking his head.

'Dark!' he said, and made a sweeping gesture at the air around him 'Dark!' he cried, 'and he – he very dark too.'

'Let's go,' said Yves wearily, and indeed he had every reason to sound tired.

'Go?' cried Timon, sounding as if he could not believe what he was hearing. 'Are you going to let them . . .' he gestured vaguely at the bird boys. '. . . are you going to let them get away with stealing the van and robbing your food?'

Yves looked at them and then at Timon. 'What's the point?' he said shaking his head and sounding even more tired than he had sounded a moment earlier. 'Look at them. There's no point. Of course we'll take the van back and anything left inside it. But I believe this kid. They didn't steal the converter. Someone else did that.' He paused, and then added bitterly, 'We'll arrive in Solis soon and even if we don't have the converter, well, we can always put on a show.'

'Punish them! It might stop them next time,' said Timon.

Yves looked at Timon, then over at Tane and Penrod who both shrugged, puffing out their cheeks, then shaking their heads slightly. Yves looked back at Timon. 'No point now!' he

said. 'Let's just pile into the van and get back to the Fantasia . . .
go back home.'

And he was right. There was nothing more to be done. The
van was recovered and, though a lot of the food was gone, there
was no point in trying to punish the Birdboys. Tane looked over
at Penrod who understood Tane's astonished expression and
who shrugged and shook his head. Wasn't it strange to think of
Timon, that good-natured Timon, insisting that the Birdboys
should be punished? Then they forgot everything except the
van. It was going to be hard work, guiding that food van back to
the Fantasia camp and there were places where it would have to
be pushed. Lucky there were so many of them there to push it.
Turning towards the van Tane saw Boomer at its open door. He
seemed to be sliding two huge kites into it . . . at least just for a
moment they looked like kites, but then he realized that they
were wings – Birdboy wings. Boomer saw Tane watching him
and looked back at him defiantly.

'Well?' he said. 'They stole stuff from us. We deserve a bit of
payment don't we? And I wouldn't mind learning to fly.
Wouldn't you?'

He was talking to the right man. Tane felt a flame of interest
run through him. He had always wondered just how the Birdboy motors worked and now, thanks to Boomer, it seemed he
might have a chance to find out.

Garland had wanted to hunt with Timon, but in a different
direction from Yves. She quite liked the idea of being the one to
find the converter. She set off on her own. However she could
not find a single Birdboy clue, and in the end, she turned and
picked her way carefully home again. Back at the Fantasia
camp, Garland moodily watched Eden and Lilith, who seemed
to be getting on well together. Eden was teaching Lilith how to
shuffle cards, and how to make certain mystery cards vanish

and then turn up in someone else's ear. Garland knew that if she moved over and asked to join them they would be pleased to show her the tricks too, but she felt too discouraged for company. She certainly did not want Lilith teaching her how to do anything. And something puzzled her. It seemed Eden was actually avoiding his brother, and there was no reason for this as far as Garland could see.

And suddenly – there it was again . . . that tingling that she knew so well by now. And sure enough, there before her the air was rippling. The silver girl was trying to take form. But this time, for some reason, there was something hesitant about the way she was emerging . . . and though it was hard to be sure, her wavering expression seemed to be one of anxiety. Still at last, there she was, struggling, drifting a bit on one side, but *there* – stamping her foot and then fading immediately as if she could not make herself as real, as true, as she needed to be. Then she was gone.

Garland stared up . . . stared down and then seeing nothing began to turn away. Why? She was asking herself. There must have been a reason . . . there was always a reason . . . but what could it be? The girl had not pointed out any direction. She had done nothing but stamp her foot.

Stamp her foot. Garland paused and stared at the ground where the girl had stamped, and now she was looking carefully, she noticed the ground over there was somehow disturbed. Clods of earth made an uneven patch – a freshly turned patch only vaguely visible among the grass. If it had not been for the stamping of that silver foot she would certainly have missed it. Feeling suddenly alert, sure she had been given a clue to something, Garland looked down at the turned earth, kicking some of it away. The soil, soft and loose, surrendered; the clods lifted easily. And then, suddenly vivid, a little scarlet tongue licked up out of the ground at her.

It wasn't really a tongue of course. It was the corner of a red scarf or something similar. Garland, stared, bent down and tugged at it, but though the soil had yielded the scarf (if it was a scarf) it did not give in. It was wrapped around something further under the ground, something that would not yield . . . something that seemed to ask her to discover it. She looked around and saw the Fantasia busy around her, then set off looking for the van Tane often travelled in, because there she was sure she would find a spade.

Yves, looking tired and deeply worried, drove the food van back to the Fantasia camp, with other Fantasia men wandering after him. Boomer trotted along, thinking about the wings. In a way he had stolen them, but after all, he argued all over again, the Birdboys owed them something. They had stolen Fantasia food.

'I might fly,' he was thinking, and was filled with secret excitement, as he imagined himself looping through the air and maybe beating his drum as well. 'It might be useful to have a sort of Fantasia Birdboy. Tane could help me.' To his secret astonishment he found he was rather missing that Birdboy, and he could not work out why. They had known one another for about ten minutes. There had been no time for them to become friends. Perhaps it was simply that he had a vague feeling that, in other circumstances, at some other time, they *might* have been friends.

Boomer ran a little way to catch up with Timon. 'Pity not to get the converter,' said Timon, strolling easily beside the van, and it seemed to Boomer that, although Timon was looking concerned and anxious, there was a strange mocking echo at the back of his voice.

'What could they have done with it?' Yves cried sideways through the van window. 'And what would they want it for?

They can't use it in any way. A converter just couldn't mean anything to the Birdboys.'

'Perhaps they thought they might trade it or sell it to someone,' suggested Timon, and now Boomer thought he could see a faint suggestion of a smile at the corners of Timon's mouth, as if he were having a private joke at the expense of the Fantasia.

'He's making fun of us,' thought Boomer, but he knew he could not prove it.

'Sell it?' asked Tane, a few steps ahead of Boomer. 'Who would they sell it to? Do you think Birdboys would buy a converter? No, the Birdboys were after food – that's all.'

'But the converter *has* gone,' persisted Timon.

'Don't remind me!' groaned Yves. 'Here we are! Home again. Because this is home for the next hour or two.'

Boomer charged forward, happy to see the Fantasia once more – glad to see it was intact and getting around things in its usual way. But, as he went ahead, he saw . . . he thought he just glimpsed . . . out there among the trees a familiar figure ducking from view. He thought he had seen Maska . . . Maska so close to the Fantasia that any stranger would have imagined he was yet another Fantasia man.

'Hey,' he began, but the van was stopping and people were crowding around it. There was Maddie . . . there was Garland both pelting towards them. Garland had a strange look on her face as if she were about to burst out with exciting news.

'Did you find the converter?' she shouted with a strange smile on her face.

'Did you find the converter?' Maddie asked too, just a word or two behind Garland.

'No!' snapped Yves. 'I didn't!'

'I know you didn't!' cried Garland. 'Because I did!' She waved a scarlet scarf at him. '*I* found it.'

'You found it? *You?* I can't believe it!' yelled Yves. He jumped from the van. He flung his arms around Garland and hugged her. 'Did she really?' he cried to Maddie.

'She did indeed. Our heroine!' Maddie said.

'Where on earth did you find it?' Yves asked Garland.

'*In* earth not *on* earth! It was buried – buried over *there*!' cried Garland waving the scarlet neck scarf over towards the trees. 'It was buried, and *this* was tied around the top of the box.'

'Hey! That's mine,' Yves said, sounding as if he could scarcely believe it, and stepping back as if he were afraid she might flick him with it.

'I suppose anyone who steals a converter could steal a scarf,' said Tane. 'Let's make for Solis before we run into more trouble.'

'Yes, but wait a moment,' said Yves. 'This makes it look as if one of us took it. But who would do such a thing?'

'Your scarf, mate,' said Nye.

Yves whirled on him. 'Are you suggesting I did it?' he cried incredulously.

'Not seriously,' Nye said, throwing up his hands. 'It's just that . . .'

'No one's suggesting such a thing,' said Maddie. 'We're only saying that it's strange.'

'Why would I even think of doing it?' asked Yves, still angry.

'You might want to sell it secretly,' suggested Garland. Almost immediately she was ashamed of herself for suggesting such a thing even in fun. Yves glared down at her.

'Or *you* could have done it,' he said. 'Everyone knows you've got it in for me. You were in the same van as the converter, weren't you? And you were the one to find it. Oh, very convenient!'

'I wouldn't do anything like that!' shrieked Garland. 'Anyhow that box was really heavy to carry.'

'So what!' Yves yelled back. 'Really wanting something you could blame on me might have made you extra strong.'

Maddie stepped in. 'Stop! Stop this rubbish!' she cried. 'We're wasting time and energy. No one imagines for a moment that either of you did it, so stop tormenting each other. We won't solve this mystery over the next few minutes so let's just press on, and get ourselves away from this infuriating place. Come on. We're the Fantasia. We have our troubles and mysteries, but we don't give in to battering one another – even with words.'

So that is what they did.

As Garland moved to help with the winding and packing of ropes, Boomer edged his way up to her.

'I was talking to that Birdboy,' he said. 'And I'm pretty sure they didn't have anything to do with taking the converter. I don't think you did either. Or Yves.'

'But someone did,' said Garland. 'Someone took it from our van and buried it.'

Boomer looked somehow shifty and yet determined too.

'The Birdboy says that when they were up in the trees he looked down and saw someone sliding around the camp and go into Maddie's van,' he said. 'And then he saw the person come out again. And the person he pointed out was . . .' Here Boomer fell silent. Then he pointed over at Timon who, together with Eden, was over by Goneril's van fussing over Jewel.

'Goneril?' said Garland. 'No way!'

'No!' cried Boomer softly, jabbing impatiently with his finger in Timon's direction.

'But that's crazy,' said Garland angrily. 'It's just as crazy as Goneril. I mean why would Timon do such a thing?' Boomer shrugged. He had no idea. 'I can imagine Yves doing it. I can imagine him having plans to bring the Fantasia down and then to take it over. But Timon wouldn't do such a thing. We've been his protection.'

'Well,' said Boomer, 'I think he's changed. I mean he was OK to begin with, but I think he's gone a bit spooky. And just now I think I saw one of those two men who have been following us sneaking around.'

Garland was silent for a moment.

'You're wrong,' she said at last.

Boomer shrugged and then said, 'I might be, but I'm right about some things. I *did* see that man.'

'But he's Timon's enemy,' said Garland. 'You know that. I suppose he might have – he might have ganged up with Yves or something. He might have bribed him. He might be working out a way to ruin the Fantasia. Then Yves could take it over, and those men, Maska and Ozul, could get Timon and Eden as a sort of reward.'

'You just don't want to believe me,' said Boomer. 'You're making up mad things, because you want Yves to be the villain.' And he walked away.

29

Timon Astray

Moving on! And it's great when things are going well.
You know what it's like sitting in the van and watching
the world sort of unwinding itself. Trees make forests,
and then the forests fade away and suddenly it's all
wide space ... water perhaps ... some river ... some
lake. Unwinding, unwinding. And then we spin around
and go back, winding the world up again as we go.
Winter has turned into spring and now spring has turned
into summer. We move slowly but we do move, on and on,
on and on.

So the Fantasia moved on just as it always did.
Through all sorts of weathers ... all sorts of troubles
... they moved on. There was relief in moving on
more or less smoothly – almost *gliding* along, Garland thought.
And yet these days nothing except the road was smooth. Sitting
together in their van, Maddie and Garland looked sideways at
each other with a sort of sad suspicion.

And these days Lilith was practically always furious with
Garland. It shouldn't have mattered. Lilith was only a little
kid. Yet Garland found it did matter. Lilith and she had their
fights, but Lilith was part of her world and, rather to her surprise, she found she was missing Lilith and thought Lilith

might be missing her as well. Though they were deliberately riding or walking apart from one another, their eyes kept meeting, then swinging away as if they were both pretending they had looked at each other by accident.

At one break, for eating and stretching, they found themselves standing side by side. *I won't say anything*, thought Garland, gazing into the distance, pretending to be wrapped up in a private dream. Lilith, on the other hand, was anxious to say a lot. She was bored and longing to entertain herself with a bit of fighting.

'You said it was my dad who stole that converter,' she burst out. 'But he didn't. He couldn't have. He was in the van asleep. I woke up to have a drink and saw him sleeping there.'

'You probably weren't awake for long,' replied Garland, 'and anyway you could be making it all up. You make up a lot of stories.'

'I do make up a few,' said Lilith rather proudly, looking down at herself as if she half-expected to see stories printed on her skin. 'I like inventing stories.' She preened herself then went back to being fierce again. 'But I'm not inventing this time. And anyhow my dad would want to *help* the Fantasia. You know that. He's brave and he pushed us on to get to Newton. And now he's pushing us back to Solis.'

This was true. Garland felt a little ashamed of herself. Lilith went on. 'My dad would never betray the Fantasia . . . he likes Maddie too much. He'd like you if you let him.'

Garland felt herself toughening up once more. 'I don't have to be liked,' she said loftily. 'And you're only a little kid. You don't understand anything.' Then she turned away.

On the far side of the campfire Boomer was bent over a great pair of wings. He seemed to have no time for anything else over the last few days. As he stretched them out, checking the harness and the way the motor connected to them, Boomer

imagined himself lifting his feet from the ground and flying . . .
actually flying . . . up, up out of the Fantasia, leaving all its grey
troubles behind him as he soared into the blue. He imagined
himself stretching up to the sky, rising and falling in the clear
air, making fun of gravity. Flapping a wing-tip in front of him,
fanning himself with it, he dreamed of flight. But then Timon
walked past and for some reason the mere sight of Timon spoilt
Boomer's blue, drumming dream.

'Hey, I'm watching you,' he blurted out and then wished he
had stayed silent. Timon turned half-grinning. The grin would
look friendly to anyone passing – just two boys having a bit of
fun together – but Boomer knew there was nothing friendly
about it.

'What did you say?' asked Timon.

'I said I was watching you,' mumbled Boomer. 'I *know* about
you.'

'What do you know?' asked Timon.

Boomer took a breath. 'I know the *truth*,' he said.

Timon laughed. 'Clever you!' he said. 'But what's truth anyway? It's too mixed up for anyone as little and simple as you are.
And you need real imagination to get any idea of truth. You'll
never get anywhere near understanding it.'

Then he turned and walked away. Just for a moment Boomer
felt something he had never really felt before. He had had lots
of arguments with people in and out of the Fantasia, and sometimes on his travels he had met someone he really disliked, but
he had never actually hated anyone. However in that flash of
time he hated Timon.

Looking across to the other side of the fire he saw Maddie
and Yves talking together, heads almost touching as if they
were discussing something particularly secret and serious. He
looked over at Garland and saw that she was watching Yves
and Maddie too, staring darkly at them before standing up

and, deserting Fantasia friends and warm fireside, making for her van.

Once in the van, once the door had clicked shut behind her, Garland felt herself relaxing, the world growing easier. Sighing deeply she turned towards her bunk. There had never been a time when the Fantasia had felt like this . . . so uneasy and strange . . . so brittle, as if it were about to snap into pieces. Yet after a moment she knew that, though there was great relief in shutting that door and being on her own, it was not enough. She longed for her mother to come in – to give her a hug and then relax and gossip with her, just as she used to gossip in the old days. The old days? It was really only a few weeks ago . . . day after ordinary day, unravelling those tangled roads left by the Remaking . . . ordinary days melting into one another and adding up to ordinary weeks filled with unpacking and packing, planning and performing, yet such terrible and tormented weeks too.

When she had tried to write in her diary last night, telling Ferdy what was going on, her sentences had twisted and lashed like tormented serpents, filled with helpless fury. Thinking about all this Garland felt under her pillow and snatched her diary out into the soft air of the caravan. Her pencil marked the last night's ending place. Quickly, quickly she began to scribble her fury.

I don't know what to think. Maddie is right. Rightrightrightrightright. We do need Yves, and I don't really suppose he wants to bring the Fantasia crashing down crashcrashcrashcrash, though I do think he wants to take it over . . . be its great master. And, deep down, what is Yves? What is he? He's a cheat, that's what. A cheat and a nothing! He's a miserable ghost trying to fill the space my father left. And he mustn'tmustn'tmustn't. He can't. Can'tcan'tcan't. Now the Fantasia is mine. Minemineminemine! I am a true Maddigan. The only true Maddigan left in the world.

The door opened and Maddie came in. 'Keeping track of the days?' she asked, smiling.

'I don't want a single day to get away from me,' Garland said, quickly closing the book. Maddie sat down on her bunk-bed just as Garland had imagined her sitting only a moment ago. She sighed deeply . . . so deeply that Garland looked across at her apprehensively. That sigh seemed like something she had sighed herself. It was hard to believe the sigh had come from Maddie.

Maddie must have felt her gaze. She looked up. Their eyes met. It was a long time since Garland and Maddie had shared such a deep, pure stare.

'I'll tell you something,' Maddie said at last. 'I don't know if I should or shouldn't, but I will. Yves has just suggested that when we get back to Solis we might marry. Now then . . .' she cried, raising her hands as Garland opened her mouth, '. . . don't you dare say a word until you hear what I have to say. It wasn't because he loved me in the fine old way, but because he said life was getting complicated what with you being so hostile and people taking secret sides and so on. He said . . . and it's true . . . it would make everything settled and straightforward. But I said no. I said it would hurt you too much, and I told him what I told you . . . that I still feel married to Ferdy.

'Now, bearing all that in mind, do you think you could bring yourself to be just a little friendly to Yves . . . to be grateful for what he does, which is to work very hard for the Fantasia. Do you think you could work *with* us and not *against* us? Be a true Fantasia girl?'

Garland thought she was about to cry. 'OK,' she said gruffly, looking down at the ground. 'I'll try. I'll try to be a bit more friendly.' She turned around and stared out of the nearest van window. 'I just hate seeing him prancing in Ferdy's place.'

'So do I,' said Maddie, 'but what I would hate even more is seeing that place empty.'

Through the van window, Garland could see the last flames rising up from the campfire like bright trembling blades, and by their shifty light Garland also saw Timon walking past it, not much more than a black shape and looking as if he might be making for her van, coming to see her perhaps. Beyond him she could make out Eden and Boomer sitting side by side, slinging off at one another, but in a friendly way, not like enemies. Eden and Timon had seemed rather separated over the last few days, Garland thought, but perhaps that was because they were settling down in the Fantasia and were no longer dependent on one another in the way they had been. She sent a thought out to Timon. *I'm in here. Here I am.* But, as she watched, Timon swerved off to one side, and the light shifted on his skin which seemed to shimmer.

Once out of the sight of her window, he paused, clapping his hand across his mouth as if he were about to be ill. He glanced over at Garland's van again, making a movement towards it as if that was really where he wanted to find himself. But then he turned yet again, moving in a jerky, lopsided way, as if he were a puppet, and an invisible puppet master was twitching his strings. Walking off into the forest, he followed the scrappy road at first, then turned off to the right and began picking his way in between the trees, breathing deeply as if he was enjoying the scent of damp leaves and moss. However his expression wasn't the expression of someone who was enjoying anything at all.

'There you are,' said a voice.

'There you are,' said a second voice, echoing the first, but the second voice sounded like a voice cranked out of a damaged machine.

'Here I am,' Timon whispered, stopping then smiling into the shadows as he turned.

Ozul and Maska slid towards him.

Ozul was holding his small power book device open, its greenish light playing on his face. He looked deeply into the screen, then raised his dazzled blank eyes to stare at Timon, nodded, and then looked back at the screen again.

'What am I doing here?' asked Timon softly. He was refusing to look directly at either Ozul or Maska, and his question seemed to be one he was asking himself, looking around as if an answer might come to him from the air.

'You came so that you could speak to a member of your family,' Ozul said. 'Your dear guardian the Nennog is not – well, let us say he is not pleased with you. Nevertheless he is about to suggest a way you can make it all up. Look! Let me show you!' He turned the screen of the power book towards Timon who shrank back, wincing at first, but then slowly moved forwards as if there were something deep in the screen he must see whether he wanted to or not. Taking the power book from Ozul, he bent towards it as if the green light flooding out from it was somehow drawing him closer and closer to a hidden heart of green fire.

A voice spoke . . . a slow, thick voice, rich in menace.

'I am not pleased,' the voice said. 'I am not pleased that converter was found again. I have checked on it and it is an astonishing thing. I don't want the wise men in Solis to get it or it might change the past too much. And if the past changes I might cease to exist. And you and your brother might cease to exist. Do not forget that.'

'I did my best,' said Timon. 'They had their guards out – actually their people are everywhere. It is not easy. Ask Ozul. Ask Maska.'

'You must do better,' the voice said. The light pouring up out of the power book made Timon's skin look green. Scales seemed to be forming on the fingers holding the power book; scales began creeping up from under his collar taking over his neck. 'The solstice is close and the Fantasia is nearly home,' the voice whispered.

'I *will* stop them,' said Timon. His voice was soft too, but somehow strong as well. 'I will find a way.'

'Oh, I know you will,' said the voice suddenly filled with an unpleasant irony. 'You will find a way. Your existence may depend on it. You must bring me the converter so that I can keep it safe. And you must find the Talisman and bring it to me as well.'

Timon's face seemed to be altering as he looked into the screen, taking on quite another appearance – the appearance of someone – something – not quite human. He smiled and nodded.

'I will find a way,' he repeated, and his hand, scaly and green, on the power book seemed not unlike the hand of the Nennog himself.

30
Strange Possibilities

They were under attack. And they were being beaten. Garland propped herself against rocks, looking out desperately and seeing Goneril, Tane, Shell, Nye and Lattin lying there in front of her, flung around like broken dolls. Her bow was beside her but she had no arrows left and she knew – she just knew – that over there, beyond that wall of scrub and rock, the enemy was gathering itself, ready to charge again. This time there would be no stopping them. And where was Maddie? Wandering off with Yves no doubt, leaving the Fantasia to its doom. Garland picked up her diary which lay in the dust beside her and began scribbling once more.

> Ferdy! We tried to make it without you. We did try. But it was too hard. It will soon be over which means that perhaps we'll meet again ... Ferdy ...

But then another voice broke in. Someone was calling her name.

Garland woke up.

Dreams were astonishing. All in a moment the world could change. She was not lying on a battlefield surrounded by Fantasia dead, but was asleep in Goneril's van which was jolting slowly along in the Fantasia train. Opposite her was another bunk closed in with wooden slats, more of a cage than a bunk really, and there, under the cover, Garland could see Jewel, calmly sleeping. Goneril was nowhere in sight, but Timon was leaning in the doorway, turning his head towards her as if he knew she was waking up. And he had seen the book lying half under her pillow – not her own reliable diary. But the crumbling volume from the future.

'Why were you reading my diary?' asked Timon.

'It's my diary really,' said Garland. 'I was babysitting Jewel, and I saw it there and thought I would try and get some idea of the difference between – between the things that might happen and the things that *are* happening. And I tried to read it, but I just – well – I just sort of went to sleep. This *time* thing of yours is so – so weird.'

Timon sat down on the edge of her bunk.

'It is strange,' he agreed, 'but I'm glad Eden and I came backwards. I'm glad to have ridden with the Fantasia.' He looked at her. 'I'm glad to have met you.'

Garland felt herself blushing.

'I'm glad to have met you too,' she said, meaning to sound offhand, but her words sounded much more shy and mumbling than she had meant them to. Being firm with herself, she cleared her throat and said, 'If you'd arrived here at the right time . . . if you'd saved Ferdy . . . we might be back in Solis right now and everything would be happy ever after.' The caravan gradually slowed and stopped. 'We must be going to camp for the night,' Garland said. It looks dark out there already.'

From somewhere outside they heard Maddie's voice. 'Everyone out,' she was crying. 'Everyone! Look at this.'

Timon and Garland did not move immediately, but sat there staring at each other. The door rattled and swung wider. 'Hey!' Maddie called. 'Come and see. Now!'

Garland sprang up rather guiltily. Something was happening

. . . some Fantasia excitement . . . and she was just sitting there, staring at Timon as if he were some sort of boyfriend. It seemed disloyal.

'Come on,' she said. 'Something's happening.' Squeezing past Timon she made for the door. As she jumped into the outside air, she heard him following her rather more slowly.

It was late evening. The Fantasia vans had all drawn up on top of a long rise, and were all pointing in the same direction. Miles of clear darkening space stretched ahead of them. Yves was out there dancing and gesturing as if he were taking credit for the whole evening, and pointing excitedly into the distance.

'Solis!' he shouted. 'Ladies and gentlemen – I give you the lights of Solis!'

And there, from behind a line of distance hills Garland could see a glow rising up into the air.

'The lights of Solis!' Yves repeated, flinging up his arms, and a ragged cheer went up from the Fantasia people.

'A week!' cried Maddie. 'Maybe sooner. Within a few days we'll be home . . . we'll have juggled and cartwheeled our way home again, and all errands will be done too. We're not quite there yet, but . . . but . . . hey, what about a party?'

The whole Fantasia stamped and clapped and hugged each other.

'Great!' cried Garland, clapping and stamping too. She turned to Timon. 'A party!'

'Great!' he agreed, and yet looking up into his face she was suddenly sure that he was not really pleased. The fire burned up and the band tuned up. Boomer marched in and out of the vans, beating the drum with his usual abandon. Eden danced by with Jewel in his arms. Tane swung by with Goneril though it was hard to tell just who was holding who. Lilith moved in on her father and Yves cheerfully twirled her around, but then, after a moment, he left Lilith, crossed the dancing space and swept a deep bow to Maddie and they set off on their own together. Garland had wanted to enjoy the party, but the sight of Maddie and Yves dancing so cheerfully caused a sour smile to creep over her face.

'Maddie's having a good time,' said a voice behind her. Timon! He took her hands and they danced as they talked.

'Nothing I can do about it,' Garland replied. 'She's allowed to.'

'What if there was?' he asked. 'What if Eden and I could take another shot at it . . . at going back into the past. We might be able to warn your father? Save him?'

Garland came to a dead standstill.

'But you said you didn't have enough – enough energy in that slider thing. You said there wasn't enough power to go forwards to your time and then backwards to mine again.'

'We've got that converter now! I think I could work out a way to – I think I could use it to recharge our slider.' He smiled. Looking at that shadowed smile Garland thought it was not a warm smile – not quite a comfortable one. 'We might risk it. But I'll have to talk it over with Eden.'

'Now!' cried Garland grabbing his arm. 'Get him now!'

Timon looked over at his brother, dancing like a stick-boy, holding Jewel high for a moment, then hugging her. Timon's strange smile did not disappear. It seemed to deepen.

'Later,' he said. 'Later when things have quietened down and we can concentrate. In the meantime – let's party.'

So they partied on, and then partied on again, while in the distance the glow of Solis seemed to creep higher and higher into the sky, swallowing the stars that had shone out briefly above the hills.

But even a celebrating Fantasia has to slow down and sleep. Goneril began yawning and, at last, took a sleeping Jewel from Eden. Tane, Byrna and Nye, Penrod, Shell and all the others made for their vans. Yves picked up Lilith and smiled as her head flopped down onto his shoulder. Maddie called Garland. 'Time for bed, love!'

'Coming!' called Garland but she did not come. Worn out as she was, she was still trembling with excitement – with possibility – as, sitting on the edge of the Fantasia, she listened to Eden and Timon arguing.

'It feels wrong,' Eden was saying.

'It didn't feel wrong when we jumped back the first time trying to save ourselves so why should it be wrong to jump back again and try helping Garland?' asked Timon.

Eden was silent. 'Can we do it from here?' he asked at last. 'I mean when we made our jump we had the Nennog's energy unit to plug into and now . . .'

'Wake up!' said Timon rather impatiently. 'We've got that converter now. I think there's enough energy to do it. We co-ordinate with a time pulse, then plug the slider into the solar converter, and I think it will recharge enough to carry us back – not to our own time but to a time that's just a bit earlier than the time we focused on last time we jumped. Then we can warn Ferdy, so that Ferdy survives, right? And if he survives and makes his mark in Solis that means the Nennog might not move into power the way he has done . . . which means a lot of people in our time will survive, maybe even our own parents among them.'

Eden was silent.

'You mean you might – you might rescue your parents as well as Ferdy if you do this – this sort of time jiggle?' Garland gasped. She looked at Eden as if she could hardly believe he was hesitating. 'Why are you even thinking twice about it? I might get my father back, and then future time would be change and change and keep on changing, and somewhere on ahead you might get your parents back too. It would be all happy endings.' She hesitated. 'But then you – you would probably have to go back and stay in your future time, wouldn't you? It would be just as if I'd never met you.' She looked at Timon. 'It's so complicated. I don't understand it all.' Then she took a breath. 'But I want you to do it if it means saving my father.'

'Tomorrow morning then,' said Timon. 'Very early. Everyone will sleep in after all this dancing, and I'll be able to do a few calculations . . .' He fell silent.

Garland drifted back to the van which was her home.

'Where have you been?' asked Maddie. 'Partying with the boys?'

'No! Just talking!' said Garland indignantly, and Maddie laughed.

'It's great that you've got company,' she said. 'I mean there's always Boomer, but it's terrific to think you've got someone like that Timon . . . someone around your own age. Handsome too! Now get into bed and sleep. Because tomorrow – Solis, here we come!'

Garland quickly undressed and climbed into bed, but though she was weary she found it hard to sleep. Broken bits and pieces of thoughts and dreams kicked up their heels, took hands and danced around with her ideas . . . the memory of Timon's blue eyes, eyes that could look so warm at times and so strange and somehow frightening at others linked into the possibilities of tomorrow's journey on towards Solis. But stronger and stranger than anything else was the eerie thought of that other possible journey. Ferdy might somehow be born again. No! Not born again. Just not *dead*. She was longing to see him, and yet, to her horror, she found that she had somehow got used to the idea that he was dead. She wanted him back – of course she wanted him back – yet felt that she would never ever quite believe in him again. How could that be? Garland thought of Yves and Maddie dancing together and clenched her teeth. At last, in spite of her swirling thoughts, she slept a little, woke, and then slept again. Waking for a second time she saw morning lightening the sky out beyond the van. It was time. It must be time.

Garland climbed out of bed very carefully, not wanting to disturb Maddie, dressed quietly and slid out into that new day. At first she could see nothing but the same old circle of vans and the smouldering ashes of last night's fire. Then, looking between Goneril's van and Penrod's, she saw the boys, Eden with the baby Jewel slung against his chest. As she jogged across the circle towards them Timon looked up, and smiled with strange relief and beckoned to her urgently.

'What are you doing?' she asked in a low voice as she joined them. They had dug a hole and set up the instrument they called the slider. It was emitting the small but determined electronic cry, and the pulsing blue glow that she remembered from their terrifying encounter with Morag.

'They left the converter in Yves's van last night,' Timon said. 'But Yves was sleeping soundly. He had a few drinks at last night's party. Anyhow I sneaked in and sure enough I found some possible connections. They worked well. Mind you it's complicated. This converter takes in light, and as you know light travels fast . . . a hundred and eighty-six thousand miles in a second. That's a lot of energy. Somehow – but I'm not sure how – I think this converter takes in the light and manages to convert its speed to accessible energy and save that energy in a whole series of little cells.

Anyhow I've powered the slider up from the converter – at least I hope I have – and I've set it up, and according to the dials there's enough power to guide us back again – if we need to come back that is. We might not want to.'

'We hope,' said Eden rather darkly.

'What does that mean?' asked Garland apprehensively.

'It means Eden should do something about his negativity,' said Timon.

Eden looked across at her. 'It depends on the convergence of time-lines,' he said. 'We need to connect with what we call a pulse and sort of ride the pulse to . . .'

'Yeah, yeah we know,' said Timon, impatiently. 'I've told her all that.' He was adjusting some tiny dial on the rod.

'I just thought of something,' said Garland. 'What happens if we meet ourselves back there . . . I mean will there be two of me or what?'

'Can't happen!' said Timon. 'As soon as we appear, we just sort of melt into those other selves.'

'Or there's another theory which is that we can't occupy the same space/time as ourselves, so we might explode all over the universe,' Eden muttered.

'I like Timon's theory better,' said Garland.

'Well, we're about to find out,' said Timon. His hand moved on the slider. 'It's about to establish a power field . . .'

31
Sliding Through Time

Garland could never quite tell what happened next. She felt herself changing. *This is what sugar feels like dissolving in tea*, she thought wildly. *I'm coming to bits ... more than bits, I'm coming to bits of bits. No! I'm changing to some other sort of stuff. But how can I still think?*

What have I become? She floated and seemed to spread out like a cloud blown apart by winds moving in from several directions. *I'm nothing*, she thought, then somehow felt herself being pulled together ... rushing back into herself once more.

And then she found herself on her hands and knees in long wet grass. Somewhere a baby was crying,

She knew that cry. Out of the air in front of her a shape was forming. A log? No. It was Eden, lying face downward, but turning onto his back immediately so that he could gasp in a lungful of air. Jewel lay beside him, furious to find herself apparently lost among fallen leaves, needing to feel a strong arm around her. Or perhaps she needed to be fed.

'We're here,' said a voice behind and above her. Timon!

Eden slowly sat up, feeling his own arms and knees. The Slider stood there between them, pulsing as if it was a living thing with a blue, beating heart.

Garland could not believe it. There, below her, lay the Fantasia, set out like a strange game on that little curving plain that had reminded her of a cupped hand. Looking down on it, she knew that this was exactly how it had been that other time . . . the time she would never forget. As the brothers quickly disconnected the slider and packed it into one of Eden's boxes she looked to the right, staring madly, expecting to see herself right there, writing on the first pages of her diary.

But the light was just different this time. There below her she could see Bannister . . . Bannister walking around, keeping guard, peering in the early morning light at an open book in his hand. It must have been hard to read, but he was trying. Somewhere ahead of him in time was Gabrielle's library. But Gabrielle's library was definitely in the past for Garland. No. This was another time. It must be in the future for her, too, even though she found herself remembering it.

'Right!' said Timon, patting Jewel in a reassuring way. 'We're back in the right place but a few hours ahead of ourselves. The Road Rats are probably asleep too. Let's go!'

The two boys began to slip and slide down the slope and Garland followed them, but as she did so she felt a familiar strangeness.

'Wait,' she cried but they took no notice of her. 'Wait!' she cried again, and as she did so, saw the air rippling and there was the silver girl, gesturing and waving her arms forbidding her to go forward. In that other earlier time, Garland remembered, the silver girl had not taken shape. She had been nothing more than a strange ripple in the air.

'I must!' Garland shouted at her. 'I want Ferdy back.'

And she ran onward . . . right up to the silver girl, right *through* her, immediately feeling an explosive shock running from her heart out to her fingertips. The whole world burst into silver sparks but Garland shut her eyes and stumbled on. When she opened her eyes again the silver girl had entirely disappeared and the brothers, further down the slope, had turned and were staring at her.

'What happened?' asked Timon.

It was too complicated to tell him. 'I don't know,' she cried. 'Well, I'll try to explain later. Just run on.'

So they ran on into the wide embrace of the Fantasia – and there before her – there was Ferdy, up early. Just for a moment she thought she saw herself, hoisting up a bucket of water for her horse Samala. The sight of that ghost of future time terrified her, but she closed her eyes, ran on, only to feel herself, with a sort of horror, somehow dissolving into that other early self and taking her over. It was a sickening sensation. It felt wrong. Nevertheless she struggled to ignore it. Instead she flung her arms around her father, leaning against him. 'Dad!' she cried, hugging him hard, over and over again.

'Steady on,' he said, sounding surprised and a little impatient with her. He shook himself a little free of her. 'What's brought this on? What's wrong?'

But Garland could not tell him. 'I just love you,' she said, 'that's all.' She hugged him again.

'Butter me up all you like,' said Ferdy, 'you're not getting out of taking water to your poor horse. And then it's practice. You know that.' It was exactly what he would have said, back then in those happy days. But those happy days were not back then. They were now.

Ferdy looked past Garland and she felt him stiffen – grow angular and strong within the circle of her hug. 'Where did you two come from? Who are you?'

'They're friends . . .' Garland began, just as Timon said:

'We've come to warn you . . .'

'Road Rats!' cried Eden getting in first. 'Road Rats are creeping in on you.'

Ferdy pushed Garland to one side. Suddenly he had become

quite a different man from the one he had been only a moment ago. He looked around, he listened.

'How did you know?' he asked.

'My brother and I heard them,' Timon said rapidly. 'We saw them. They're after your food and fuel.'

'It's true,' Garland cried. 'I heard them too. They've got motorbikes.'

Ferdy looked at the brothers, then back at Garland. She could feel him trying to work things out. The brothers were total strangers – could they be trusted? They might be telling the truth, but after all they could be Road Rats themselves and Garland might have been tricked. But the Fantasia did not take chances. Ferdy made up his mind.

'OK you lot!' he shouted, and the whole Fantasia, watching and working around him, stopped whatever it was doing to listen to him. 'Attention! Attention! Listen up! Parley!'

Garland now saw the ripple of a different sort of movement spreading out through the Fantasia.

'Get your bow!' Ferdy told her. 'You boys . . . have you got any sort of gun? Bows and arrows? No! Right! Well, you just keep your heads down, and heaven help you if you're having us on.' And then he was gone, racing over towards their van, shouting to Maddie, talking to her urgently, then giving her a hurried kiss. Garland watched, overcome with a sort of enchantment, while around her the Fantasia organized itself, as people somehow switched themselves from one activity to another . . . ran to arm themselves and pull the vans together. It was like watching one of the plays they put on in Solis.

Garland turned to Timon.

'Thank you! Thank you!' she cried under her breath. Yet as she said this she found she was not grateful in the way she had expected to be. There was the Fantasia: there was Ferdy, but . . .

'Forget it,' said Timon. 'Just get ready! The Road Rats'll be on their way.'

'Wait and see what happens this time round,' mumbled Eden, but he was talking to himself rather than Garland or Timon. 'Where's Goneril? I'd better ask her to hold Jewel for a bit. I think life's going to get dangerous.'

And when, only a few moments later (or so it seemed), the sound of motorbikes suddenly filled the air and Road Rats roared into the Fantasia, the space in the circle of vans was completely empty. Their bikes reared back like noisy horses. This space was not what the riders had expected, and within moments they had all come to a standstill, their bikes snarling under them.

Looking out from the darkness under her family van Garland saw them, in a way she hadn't before. There had not been time. Now she noticed the different shapes of the bikes and the men astride them. The bikes which had made them seem so powerful and threatening then, now seemed like noisy encumbrances. Some of the men wore their hair and beards so long they looked as if they must have had goats or bears for fathers. Not that they were all hairy. That huge man there didn't have a hair on him. And he must be their king. She remembered him from the last time . . . he had a crown tattooed on his bald head . . . a bald head that shone as if he had just polished it.

Peering out from her hiding place, Garland could see not only bulging Road Rat shoulders and forearms, but a whole range of weapons too – the bikes were slung around with swords and clubs, clubs and sling-shots. However the shuddering motorbikes were rather hard to control and the Road Rat warriors were using all their energy to hold onto their precarious machines. But that tattooed chief had managed to draw out a club made of greenstone, and was waving it in the space around him. Garland knew this sort of club was ancient – a treasure really – and wondered how the Road Rat King had come by it.

After those first arrested moments the King made a sort of beckoning movement with his club, and his followers moved again, but wheeling forward very carefully this time.

Suddenly, Ferdy leapt out in front of them. Then the whole Fantasia burst out of hiding and closed in around the Road Rats, knives in hand, arrows drawn, guns aimed, courage strong. Garland remembered how once they had been taken unawares. Now, she was thrilled with a Fantasia that was armed and ready.

Ferdy spoke.

'You have one chance and one chance only. Drop your weapons! And get away while you can! Get away.'

The Road Rats looked around the circle . . . looked at the drawn arrows, the knives and the guns.

The King hesitated, swung himself off his motorbike, holding out his club as if he were about to surrender it, then swung it around and dived at Ferdy.

'Attack! Attack!' he yelled.

All at once everything was rattle and battle. And all at once everything was exploding too fast and fiercely for Garland to be sure of just what was happening. She saw blows falling, saw Bailey tumbling backwards. No escape for Bailey, even in this other time. But then she saw another man falling. The King of the Road Rats stopped abruptly, an arrow in his throat, and, as Garland stared, her mouth hanging open, another arrow came from somewhere to strike in beside the first. Those Road Rats that were close to the King spun around, screaming, but unable to do anything except to watch him tottering. They half-leapt to catch him, but then let him fall for they had to guard themselves. Those further away were fighting blindly on. Penrod struck his opponent to the ground, Byrna and Nye closed in on either side of a wildly whirling Road Rat, and Nye half-lured him while Byrna smashed in on him. Old Shell suddenly flung up his hands and tumbled sideways. But now, in spite of themselves, most Road Rats were staring down at their leader, convulsing in his death throes.

'Go! Get out!' Ferdy was shouting. 'Get out while you can. Get your miserable hides out of here. Go!'

As he yelled this, Nye and Byrna both fired arrows, both aiming at the same man, who fell sideways, his bike shooting away from under him. And indeed the Road Rats did not really need to be told again. They turned. Some Road Rats screamed away immediately. The men on their feet dashed for their bikes and kicked them into life once more. Engines roared. The Road Rats fled.

Garland could not restrain herself.

'We did it. We did it! And you're all right!' she screamed, dancing madly in the sunlight and shadow of that Fantasia camp.

'Well, it would take more than a few Road Rats to bring your old man down,' said Ferdy, grinning. 'Those motorbikes – they're more trouble than they're worth when it comes to hand-to-hand combat.'

He turned to Timon and Eden who were coming out of hiding. 'You boys were right on the money. I won't forget it.'

Over by the fallen body of Bailey, Goneril was shouting.

'He's in a bad way. Give me a hand over here.'

Ferdy, Maddie and Bannister rushed over. Garland hesitated, and then turned to Timon.

'Bailey's not supposed to die just yet!' she exclaimed, hearing herself sounding indignant. 'And old Shell – Shell's dead this time round.'

'But Ferdy's alive,' said Eden. 'We managed to change what we wanted to change. But we can't change everything.'

This time Bailey was dead almost immediately and would

have to be buried along with old Shell. Garland was having to go through Bailey's funeral for a second time.

Standing among the Fantasia people, all familiar yet somehow oddly strange to her, Garland finally had time to think about what had happened, and found she was not as happy and grateful as she had imagined she would be. The people around her were real . . . they must be real. There they were and there was not one of them she did not know. Her father, Ferdy, was standing just over there saying the last words over Bailey, and he was exactly as she remembered him. But to her dismay she suddenly found she did not *believe* in him. She did not believe in any of them . . . she did not believe in this different time. She turned to Eden.

'What now?' she asked him. 'Do we go back? I mean forwards.' She shook her head. 'You know what I mean?'

'Do you know what you mean yourself?' asked Eden, rather gloomily.

'You're such a downer,' Timon said to Eden. He looked at Garland. 'Hey, you've got what you wanted, haven't you?'

Garland did not want to meet his blue gaze in case he read the doubt in her own eyes. She turned her head, and there – there riding openly in on them – were Ozul and Maska. Of course! Back then – that back then which had become right now – Maska and Ozul had been watching them. How were they going to fit into this changed, present time? Ferdy stepped forward to intercept them

'What can we do for you?' he asked. 'Probably not much. This is a bad time for us. We're burying one of our people.'

'Deepest sympathies,' said Ozul, using his friendly voice, and indeed he did manage to sound sympathetic. 'I don't want to intrude, but we absolutely must. You see you have our runaway rascals with you . . .' He aimed a finger at Timon and Eden almost as if it were a loaded gun.

'Those boys?' Ferdy turned in bewilderment to look at them.

'They're runaways,' said Ozul. 'You know how it is with youngsters. A little family fight and they took off. Their mother, our poor sister, is in a terrible state over it all.'

'He's lying, Dad, he's lying!' cried Garland. 'He wants to kill them.'

Ferdy turned and stared at her. 'How on earth do you know?' he asked her in a low voice, and Ozul interrupted.

'The child is mistaken . . . is lying herself,' he said, sounding rather less friendly. Ferdy looked up at him.

'That's my daughter there,' he said. 'She might make a mistake or two, but she doesn't lie.' He looked over at Timon and Eden. 'Well, you kids. Do you want to go with these – these gentlemen?'

'No,' said Timon.

'No way!' agreed Eden. 'They're our enemies. They do want to kill us.'

Ferdy turned back to Ozul and Maska.

'That's that then,' he said. 'Simple! On your way.'

Ozul smiled again.

'I should mention that there is a reward,' he said. 'A large reward . . .' and he took out the bag, that very bag which Boomer had stolen from him at the booth outside Gramth. But that was in that other time. It had not happened yet. It might never happen now.

'Clear off!' Ferdy said. 'It wouldn't be much more work for us to have another funeral right now. We're geared up for it.'

Ozul and Maska looked around and saw the Fantasia rippling a little, filled with excitement because, after all, Timon and Eden had warned them of the Road Rats. Thanks to that warning they had beaten the Road Rats, and were still feeling they could take on any enemies. They edged in towards Ozul and Maska, preparing to defend the children.

'You will regret this,' said Maska in his metallic voice. 'You will be sorry.' But having promised this, those two servants of the Nennog turned and rode away.

'Dad, you were wonderful!' cried Garland. 'You believed us.' Of course she meant it, and yet at the same time she found herself wishing she could really believe in this altered time. Somehow there was no room in her head for the things that were now happening around her, for her head was already filled with that other version of things. Ferdy was looking rather sternly at Timon and Eden. 'But you boys, you *do* have a story to tell, haven't you?' he said. 'No time to listen to it now, but later on I'll want to hear every little bit of it.'

And later on, after Goneril had taken over Jewel, after the Fantasia had packed up and travelled on down the road and then camped in the Horseshoe yet again, the boys did tell their story – or part of it, how they'd come from the future, that they knew about the Fantasia's quest for the converter and how they wanted to help. Eden juggled, whirled and turned the flames of the fire into animal shapes, making them dance around the Fantasia. But they did not mention to Ferdy that in an alternative time in which they had also lived and danced, Ferdy had died, and that the Fantasia had gone on without him . . . had gone on without him and had done well.

Garland watched in silence as Goneril cuddled Jewel, complaining about her, but holding her tight. Goneril said the same things that Garland remembered her saying, wearing the same expression on her face as she said them, and yet Garland did not really believe in what she was seeing. Of course Yves was there, being a background man, a second-in-command, just as he had always been. Maddie was there too, but quieter in this time, letting Ferdy talk for her as well as for himself. Ferdy was just as he had always been . . . out there in the front of things, setting the Fantasia's world in order. Garland joked with him and hugged him tightly. And yet – and yet, even when she had her arms around him, and was able to feel his muscles and bones under his red jacket, she could not, she just *could* not, believe in him.

32
Saying Goodbye

hen . . . WHOOSH. They all jumped up. Only inches away from them, a flaming arrow quivered in the ground. WHOOSH! There was a second one. Suddenly the air seemed full of them. Yves came running towards them shouting, 'We're under attack! We're under attack!' although they could all tell that already.

'Dad!' Lilith was screaming from somewhere.

'To the vans!' Ferdy shouted, leaping up. 'Move it up! Let's go!'

Everyone was already heading for his or her van. 'You boys, take your sister and cram into the van with Goneril! Ferdy cried over his shoulder. 'Go! Go! Go!'

And within minutes it seemed the Fantasia was bumping along the narrow track, pursued by Road Rats on their curious motorbikes and other more fantastic machines, put together from thousands of pieces of junk. Garland rode in the family van (Maddie at the wheel saying 'Don't worry! We've got through worse than this.'), while Ferdy kneeled on the roof of the van, his own bow in his hand. *But this can't be true . . . it just can't* she was thinking. *This is me, but those people out there can't be the real Maddie, can't be Ferdy. These vans can't be the vans of the true Fantasia.*

Goneril's van rattled along with the rest. Eden kneeled at

one window, Timon at another, watching a strange version of a motorbike drawing alongside them. The rider clapped a weapon to his shoulder. A ball of fire came spinning towards the van then shot across its roof, narrowly missing them.

'A gun! He's got a gun,' said Timon, turning towards Eden. 'A sort of cannon. Do something!'

'I'm trying,' said Eden, 'but it's hard to focus like this.'

They hit yet another bump and bounced up in the air. Jewel began to cry.

Another fireball shot towards them. Eden closed his eyes. The fireball swung around, curving like a burning boomerang and headed straight for the fantastic motorbike. The driver and the man behind him shouted and threw themselves off, one to the right one to the left. The fireball struck the machine and exploded. Behind them the other Road Rats set up a cry of 'Utu! Utu!'

'Garland!' Ferdy shouted, hanging over the edge of the van and shouting in through the window 'You're quick on your feet. Can you slide back to the van behind us and tell Yves we're going to climb that ridge on ahead, and make a stand there. Run along on the far side of the vans. There's good cover there.'

Garland grabbed up her bow and her quiver of arrows and slotted an arrow onto the string.

'Now!' Ferdy cried. 'Quickly, while there's a bit of a gap.'

'Quickly! Quickly, darling!' screamed Maddie.

Garland kicked the far door open and was outside, being splashed with mud as the van rattled on by.

'Quickly!' yelled Ferdy yet again, and Garland began to run, bow at the ready.

As Ferdy shouted yet another Road Rat came swerving in at them. 'Utu! Utu!' he was yelling, and threw an axe that narrowly missed Garland and buried itself in the side of the van.

Garland wondered why she was not terrified, then realized yet again, that she just did not believe this was really happening. And, thinking this, she spun around and fired the arrow from her bow which struck the Road Rat in the leg. He let out a howl as his bike veered away to the side.

'Run!' yelled Ferdy yet again from somewhere behind her. 'Run!' And Garland did what he told her to do, thinking as she galloped on ahead, how strange it was to be following the orders of a father she loved, but could not quite believe in, and thinking, too, that the Ferdy of her own time would not have asked her to do anything quite as dangerous as this.

He's Ferdy but he's not quite my Ferdy. I'm in this other time and I asked to be here.

Horses were being driven past, but the Road Rats would not fire at the horses. They were hoping to take the horses over as part of their loot.

Where was Yves's van? Where was it? There! There was his van! A moment later Garland was shouting Ferdy's message in at the van window. She had lived through dangerous moments. She had done what Ferdy had told her to do. Yet none of it was real. Her truth lay in another version of this time, and there seemed to be nothing she could do to make this time believable.

Only a little later, they had managed to ride up successfully onto the rise, to spin the vans into a wide circle and to entrench themselves almost safely, and, while Tane and Bannister peered over the rocks, watching the Road Rats below them, Ferdy and Maddie were holding a Fantasia parley, working out what to do next. Garland, Boomer, Timon and Eden stared out between the vans and down over the rocky sides of the rise, watching the Road Rats circling and shouting. There were so many of them . . . many many more than there had been during the first attack. They were a Road Rat army.

'Wrong! It's all wrong!' said Garland suddenly.

'What?' said Eden.

'It's wrong,' she repeated. 'In that old diary – the one that you brought back from your time – there was an ending when we didn't make it. We were trapped with the Road Rats, picking us off one by one.'

'Like this, you mean?' asked Eden.

Timon said, 'Ferdy might still find a way.'

Their heads turned in the direction of the adults.

'Bailey gone! Shell gone!' Goneril was saying in the voice of a sad witch. Other voices joined in saying other names.

'We'll never outrun them,' said Ferdy. 'Where did they all come from?'

'We'll fight them off,' said another confident voice . . . Byrna perhaps.

'We can't fight them all,' Yves declared. 'This time there are far too many of them. What do we do?'

Maddie spoke.

'Surely they can't think we're worth the trouble. Look at them out there. They've got our food van . . . they've got our fuel . . .'

'But it's more than that this time,' said Ferdy. 'It's "Utu".'

'Tane,' said Garland. 'I don't understand that. What's "Utu"?'

'It comes from an old tongue,' Tane told her. 'It means "Revenge!" An eye for an eye.'

'An eye for an eye!' Ferdy was saying slowly. 'A king for a king.'

'Oh, Ferdy,' cried Maddie. 'Don't even think of it.' She seized his arm.

'You didn't have to kill him,' Yves said.

'I didn't have to, but I did,' said Ferdy.

Maddie suddenly burst in with a little flood of words.

'But listen! Listen! Who knows how many of us would've been hurt back there – hurt or killed – if Ferdy hadn't done what he did.'

'Right,' agreed Yves. 'I was just saying . . .'

'Road Rats are unpredictable,' said Ferdy. 'If we hold them off long enough, most likely they'll get bored or discouraged and go off, looking for easier pickings. So! Let's get organized. What we must have is rest – good rest if possible. So! First watch – Tane and Bannister. Four hours, right? Then me, with – say with Garland to keep me awake! After that Nye and Byrna. How does that sound?'

Nobody argued.

'Right then!' said Ferdy 'Off you go. Sleep! Those are my order to everyone – except you and Bannister, Tane. And Bannister – no candles! No reading! You're a watchman this time round, not a reader.'

Garland felt so screwed up with the strangeness of everything that she was sure she would not sleep, and yet, when she looked back, she could not remember when it was she had last slept so soundly. It was just that, lying there in the dark (puzzling, puzzling, puzzling), quite suddenly she just somehow *was* asleep. Afterwards it seemed that all the time she slept she was also hovering somewhere up in the air watching herself sleep and thinking *Yes! That's me, but it's not really me. The real me is up here watching everything as if I were reading an invented story.* All the same she did not stir, until somewhere in the night a hand fell on her shoulder. Blinking awake, she stared up into Ferdy's face. He patted her shoulder again.

'We're on, kid,' he said. 'Our turn.'

They began to move quietly out of the van. Ferdy paused by Maddie's bunk. He smiled at Garland then leaned towards Maddie.

'My love!' he murmured and kissed her. Maddie did not wake, but in her sleep she smiled and turned her face towards Ferdy, who looked down at her, smiling back, rather sadly, Garland thought. Together they slid out of the van, silent but somehow watchful. An old moon was hanging like some sort of pendant against the dark skin of night.

'A talisman!' said Garland pointing.

'What?' asked Ferdy on ahead of her. 'There they are, thank goodness. Both awake.'

Bannister was sitting by the campfire, legs stretched out in front of him. He drew up those long legs and stood as they approached. *But of course he's not here – not really here*, Garland was thinking. *He's back with Gabrielle, saving books, and reading, reading, reading.*

'All quiet!' Bannister said, sounding real enough to be believed in as he gestured down the hillside. There, smouldering in the darkness below them they could see a Road Rat fire and Road Rat shadows moving around it. Tane yawned as he stood too. 'I can do another shift if you like,' Bannister offered.

'Heavy day tomorrow,' Ferdy said. 'Goodness knows what's going to happen, but it won't be easy. I didn't know there were so many Road Rats in the whole world. Off you go. Get what sleep you can. And, Bannister – sleep! Don't read!'

'Right!' said Bannister, grinning in the dark.

Ferdy slowly sank down with his back to a rock and Garland sat down beside him. The heat of the fire came out to somehow polish them with its heat. Garland could feel her skin beginning to shine. In the darkness Ferdy sighed.

'Funny how things go,' he said. 'I mean, men struggle and God laughs.'

'What?' Garland felt her forehead wrinkling.

'The solar converter,' Ferdy said. 'This is not just an ordinary Fantasia adventure. We have to win through to Newton.'

He was talking to her, but somehow he was talking to himself even more. Garland longed to tell him that they had been through all that . . . that they had won the converter . . . that the lights of Solis were glowing up into the night air and that they would soon be marching triumphantly into the city, but she kept her silence. None of that was true here.

'When I say we've got to win through to Newton I mean the Fantasia has to win through,' Ferdy went on, 'and those Road Rats down there . . . well, I did kill their king. They won't let up. They haven't many rules, but I've heard that revenging a king is one of them. So it's up to me to put things straight.'

'How will you fix things?' Garland asked, somehow not believing in him, though he was sitting there beside her, looking down at the fires and shadows below them.

'Well, here we are . . . besieged,' he said. 'We've got better weapons than they have, but they outnumber us. There's just – just too many of them. Too too many! I think we have to offer a sacrifice. Buy them off. I'm telling you this because I have to tell someone, and you're a Maddigan.'

For a dreadful moment Garland wondered if Ferdy was planning to offer her to the Road Rats as payment for their dead king, and then almost at once truly understood what he was telling her. Ferdy was planning to sacrifice himself. How could it matter? He was already dead. Dead – but dead in another time. Garland turned in the dark. She seized him frantically.

'No!' she whispered.

His hands closed gently but very firmly on hers.

'But that's what being the boss is all about,' he said. 'From Gabrielle on we've learned that lesson. In the end, and in a lot of different ways, the boss is always the sacrifice. And when in a few years you're the boss of the Fantasia . . .'

'I don't want to lose you all over again,' Garland cried.

'Again?' said Ferdy. Garland fell silent. She knew that if she began to tell her story she would not be believed. It would all be treated as something she had dreamed up half an hour ago.

'Come sunrise,' said Ferdy, 'they'll be in on us. I know that, because it's what I'd do if I were their leader. And there are just too many of them out there. Too many! We might put up a good fight but we'll be wiped away . . . the whole Fantasia gone, the whole mission to Newton failing and Solis threatened unless I give them what they want. It's too much. Garland, let me go,' he said for she was clinging to him desperately. 'Listen! You're the last Maddigan. It's up to you from now on. Make your mother strong. See that you all get through to Newton and back to Solis again. Maddie will try, but you'll need to help her. Be like Gabrielle. Be like me! Be strong.' He stood up. '*Become* the Fantasia!' he said, then released her.

But none of this is true. You're not the real Ferdy,' Garland thought to herself, though suddenly he was. He was Ferdy, that old Ferdy she remembered, stalking off into the night ready to die for the Fantasia like a true Maddigan. Garland sat stunned and then, very cautiously, she picked herself up and began to follow him, creeping down the slope, down, down, then down again, moving from rock to rock. As she came towards the bottom of the hill she could see the Road Rat camp . . . tall figures on guard . . . their strange machines standing silently, waiting for the morning attack. Suddenly there was movement. Voices hissed and echoed. 'Who's there? What's that? Stand where you are!' The dark figures of the sentries moved towards the dark figure of Ferdy, King of the Fantasia, and Garland heard his voice then other voices, something almost like ordinary conversation, though she couldn't hear the words. Then she heard a sudden cry, punctuated by thumps and blows. What she did see was her father's dark figure, bending first to his knees then pitching forward, exactly as he had fallen in that other time, even though in that other time it had been an arrow in his chest that had made him tumble. What she did hear was the distant soft thump as he hit the ground.

And at last this other time seemed real . . . real all over again. Garland clapped her hands over her own mouth to stifle the cries she felt rising up within her. But she was a Maddigan, and sometimes silence was a form of strength. Turning there in that terrible sad darkness she began to climb back up the hillside – back to the Fantasia which, regardless of time, was her home and her responsibility too.

And this time of course she was the one who had to tell Byrna and Nye, had to wake Maddie, who cried when she heard what Garland had to tell, weeping wildly, had to leave Maddie weeping and tell the others as morning flowed in over the land, and the Fantasia awoke to the echoes of a Road Rat retreat. 'Utu! Utu! A King for a King!' the Road Rats were shouting. 'A King for a King!' and, mounting their strange machines, they rode away.

Timon looked at Garland. 'I'm really sorry,' he said. 'I suppose some things happen – well, they happen *across* time in different ways. We can't escape them.'

'Maybe he just had to die . . .' said Eden. 'Maybe there's a sort of deep-down pattern to things we can't change much.'

'And what happens if you go back to your time – back to the future and check it out?' said Garland. 'Things might not have changed for you.'

'They will have changed,' said Eden, sounding rather apprehensive. 'But maybe not in the way we need them to change.'

'Don't sound so negative,' Timon ordered him in a scornful voice.

'Hey!' said Eden. 'What's up with you? You've gone all bossy in the last few days, and I don't like it.'

'OK! OK!' said Timon turning away from him. 'Chill!'

'It's not OK!' yelled Eden. 'Sometimes I'm not even sure of you any more. And I want to be sure of you.'

And Garland thought that in some ways Eden was right.

Timon had changed, though it was hard for her to work out just how. Even though he was there, standing squarely in front of them, giving advice, telling them what to do, he no longer felt in tune with them. She interrupted the arguing brothers.

'Stop it!' she yelled at them. 'Things are bad enough. Because, thanks to you and your time-shifting, I've had to lose my father twice over.' She felt she was going to burst into tears.

Timon ignored her, still scowling savagely at Eden. 'Good one, Eden! See what you're doing!'

What was going on? Was this the Timon of this time they were living in or was it the same Timon of that other time, that time she still thought of as her true time, but changed in some way. It was a relief when Boomer came riding by, obviously feeling safe enough to ride on his little bike once more. Lilith was chasing after him. Boomer slowed. He stopped, and Lilith stopped too, staring at them.

'Garland,' he said gently. 'Hey, Garland. Sorry. Sorry about your dad and that –'

Garland worked to put herself together inside her own head. She smiled at this version of Boomer who somehow seemed familiar and safe and a true part of the Fantasia. Why did Boomer seem real to her when she felt like a ghost to herself?

'Yeah, I know. Thanks!' she said. Boomer looked over at Timon and Eden, standing with their backs to one another, and looking in different directions.

'They reckon you're joining up with us,' he said to them, almost but not quite asking a question.

Timon half-turned to look at Boomer. 'Could be!' he said. 'Would you like that?'

But before Boomer could answer there was a shout. Yves! Yves ordering everyone to gather and to listen to what he had to say. A parley after Ferdy's death rather like that other parley in that other time. She was going to have to live through it twice.

'Gather round! Gather round!' Timon grabbed Eden's shoulder but Eden shrugged it away.

'Coming?' asked Boomer, setting off himself.

'That's *my* dad, telling them what to do,' said Lilith proudly, and she went too. Garland did not move. After all she already knew everything that would be said. Yves would be wanting them to go back to Solis and Maddie would be telling them that they had a task, that they must bargain for the solar converter and bring it back from Newton. And then they would take a vote on whether or not Timon and Eden could be part of the Fantasia. She knew all of it – *all* of it – already. She could feel it swirling in her head – and she clapped both hands over her ears anxious to hold everything still.

'I can't go through it all again,' she cried to Timon and Eden. 'Can we – can we go back – go back to the other first time. I can't go through it all again. Because mostly I just don't believe in this time any more. Not the way I believe in the other time. Let's go.'

'Yes,' said Eden. 'Let's go. If we can read a time pulse that is.'

'Right!' said Timon. 'And if there's enough power,' he added doubtfully. 'They don't have the converter yet. And in this time line they mightn't get it.'

Garland stared at him with horror. 'You mean we mightn't be able to go back to my own time?' she asked him.

'But this is your own time,' Eden said. 'I mean this is the time you asked to be in. You chose it.'

Timon was silent then turned away. 'Back in a moment,' he said over his shoulder.

Garland and Eden stood together, not quite sure what to do next. But Timon was back a few minutes later.

'Okay! I've checked, and I'm pretty sure there's enough power in the converter to make a jump. And it's not so far into the future. Let's go to Goneril's van. We can set up there.'

So they skirted the crowd, hearing Yves say some of the same things he had said earlier in another time and place, slinking along behind Maddie's van and slipping into Goneril's van, where Jewel slept. Eden scooped up Jewel and put her against his shoulder. Garland sat on a bunk watching as Timon adjusted the slider.

'All set,' he said at last.

Garland saw Timon's long hand go out to the slider. All at once there was another of those exploding moments. She felt herself dissolving again – and then they were living through those moments of frozen confusion. Days and nights flicked past them as if somewhere a finger was flicking the pages of a diary far too quickly for any word to be read.

Sunshine . . . rain . . . wind . . . calm . . . lightning . . . thunder . . . sunshine again . . . faster and faster. The frozen children rocked in a storm of time. Then everything slowed down once more . . . slowed and stopped.

33
Back Again

There they stood . . . Timon, Eden and Garland . . .
unfreezing, moving cautiously at first and then with
more and more confidence.

'Whoah!' said Timon, looking at the slider. 'Spot on. Well,
almost spot on.'

'What do you mean, "almost"?' exclaimed Garland.

Timon was moving his finger on the slider.

'Funny!' he said. 'We're here in the right time . . . but there's
been a hiccup! It's later – about a week later.'

Garland's head spun. 'But how can that be?' she asked. 'It
doesn't make sense.'

'It's what we call the butterfly effect,' Eden said. 'We didn't
do much back there – I mean we didn't save Ferdy – but we did
change things a bit, and so the place we've come back to isn't
quite the same as the place we left.' He looked over at the Fantasia. 'It does look a bit different, doesn't it? Not much, but a
bit.'

'A week later!' cried Garland. 'But that means . . .' she
paused working things out in her head. 'We've only got a few
days to get to Solis before the summer solstice.'

'Let's get going then,' said Timon. He sounded remote – not
friendly in the way he had sounded only a few minutes ago in
that earlier time. As he stared out into the Fantasia Garland had

the feeling that she and Eden had stopped existing for him except as useful tools – tools which he might need to call on at any moment.

'A week,' Garland repeated. 'People could have died in a week, or – or got married!' She began to run, and Eden ran after her.

Timon looked after them with a superior smile. He started to follow them, but then stopped abruptly, taken over by some invisible force. Spasms wracked him from head to foot, but he did not cry out. There on the edge of the Fantasia he silently gasped and struggled, turning his face this way and that, shutting his eyes as if there was something he was refusing to see. Greenness glowed through his closed lids and even crept out onto his cheeks. He gasped, then gasped again. Then, finally, he spoke.

'Yes, Lord Nennog, I hear you,' he murmured. 'You're inside my head, and every word is coming in truly. What is it you want me to do?'

Garland had already forgotten Timon. It seemed at first that the Fantasia camp she was running into, Eden at her heels, was just as she had left it, though as far as she could tell everyone was more or less the same as they had been. There was Penrod (alive! alive!) taken aback by the rare hug Garland was giving him in passing. There were Byrna and Nye, those wild twins. Goneril was carrying an armful of wood towards the fire, grumbling on . . . grumbling on . . . always being Goneril.

And there was Maddie, seeming even more astonished at being hugged by Garland than Penrod had been. 'What's come over you?' she asked, laughing and hugging Garland back. 'You haven't been running off again have you?' she asked.

'Not far,' said Garland, lying, for she had been further than she had ever been in her life before. Garland could see the familiar vans, but all looking strangely worn – certainly more battered than she remembered them. Or perhaps they had always been like that. There was no way she could trust things in the way she had once trusted them.

'Another day,' said Tane, ladling out bowls of something from a pot over the fire. 'I'm not sure that it's going to be another dollar though. Not today.'

'We could put on a show,' said Penrod, but there's no one here to pay us. We'd have to pay ourselves.'

Somewhere behind them people, tasting the meal, began to exclaim with distaste.

'Is this soup or porridge?' someone asked.

'Don't ask,' said Tane. 'Just eat it and be very, very grateful.'

'I'm going to throw up,' grizzled Lilith.

'Well, do it away from me,' muttered old Shell.

'If whining was meat we'd all be full up,' said Goneril stoically. She turned to Eden who was cuddling Jewel. 'Give that bairn to me.' And she took Jewel tenderly in her arms. 'I've got just a wee bit of milkies back in the van for you,' she whispered.

'A bowlful of these rare delicacies for you?' asked Tane ironically, passing a bowl to Garland, who took it, though she was not hungry.

'Thanks,' she said, and turning to Maddie she asked, 'Mum, we've got to keep going, haven't we?'

Maddie nodded wearily.

'Right! We've absolutely got to push on. But we do *have* to sleep as well. We'll push better with a little bit of sleep. Don't worry. We'll be up and off again before dawn.'

Saying this, she took a few steps towards the van. Garland saw Yves touch Maddie's hand as she passed him. Once the sight of that little caress would have made her furious, but now she felt nothing but a sort of calm sadness. She must be getting tired too. Or perhaps, deep inside herself, she was admitting that Yves was not so bad after all.

'I hate this stuff,' Lilith was still whining behind her. 'I want something nice to eat.'

One thing was certain, Lilith was always Lilith. Turning, Garland gave her such a warm smile Lilith stopped in her tracks, shocked into silence by being suddenly liked. The very bows in her hair seemed to flap with astonishment. Boomer shot past on his bike wearing a pair of huge bird wings that flapped wildly around him. *So*, thought Garland, *the Birdboy adventures must have happened more or less as she remembered them.*

Timon walked past looking eerily calm and composed. 'Still think you can fly?' he asked Boomer derisively.

'I might get a chance to practise tomorrow!' Boomer cried.

'Dream on,' said Timon contemptuously, 'dreams are free.' As he said this his eyes met Garland's. *He's changing!* she thought. *Why did he speak in that scornful voice? He didn't have to. Timon's changed in some deep important way. Why? How?*

'But those wings are amazing,' Tane shouted at Timon's back, and sounding rather indignant at having the wings dismissed. 'I've spent a bit of time looking at the motor too. I think I've worked out a way to power it up.'

But Timon was making for Goneril's caravan. He climbed into it, and shut the door behind him.

Garland turned away. She was tired, but not tired in the way that everyone else in the Fantasia seemed to be tired. Somewhere there would be a corner where she could sit in restful silence and work most of the confusions and contradictions out of her head before she went to bed. Tane was moving by, collecting the bowls, joking with people as he went.

'We'll be back in the land of milk and honey soon. Boomer might even be able to fly there,' he told her. Garland looked between the vans towards Solis.

'The Solis lights don't seem quite as bright tonight as they – they used to be,' she said uncertainly, and Tane paused, looking towards Solis too.

'We're so close to the summer solstice,' he said, 'too close. Maybe they're running low on power. Never mind. We'll put a bit of speed on.' He waved a bowl in the direction of that glow. 'Hey, Solis . . . don't worry. We're on our way. Maddigan's Fantasia will save you.'

Garland gave a bit of a grin and sat down beside the fire, hoping that she would have time to stare, without interruption, into the smouldering ashes but there was a rustle as Eden (that stick boy) crouched down beside her. There must have been something of the way she gathered herself in that worried him.

'Do you want me to go away?' he asked cautiously.

'No,' said Garland. 'Just for a moment I – well, I thought you were someone else.'

'Timon?' asked Eden, staring into the fire. 'He has gone all strange hasn't he? You see it too, don't you?'

Garland nodded. There was something she suddenly had to say. 'I've really stuffed things up, haven't I? By wanting Ferdy back.'

'Not your fault,' said Eden. 'I'm pretty sure it's nothing to do with you. Probably us. Maybe we shouldn't have come here in the first place.'

'No need to try being nice to me,' Garland told him. 'I don't deserve it. I was the one who wanted to go back and change things. But nothing important changed, did it? Bailey still died. Dad . . . well, I just didn't *believe* in him, not until he set out to die. And then I did believe in him for a few minutes. And somehow shifting from one – what did you call it? Time stream? – shifting from one time stream to another has changed things here a bit, hasn't it? Maybe we won't get to Solis in time.'

'He frightens me,' he murmured. 'Timon, I mean! He really, really frightens me.'

Eden and Garland looked at each other, both of them struggling with strange worries almost like dreams, and with no way of waking up from them.

Out in the darkness, some distance beyond the firelight and the ring of vans, Timon was sitting with Ozul's power book set up in front of him. He *had* gone in at the front door of Goneril's van only to slink secretly out through the back door and to vanish into the night. Though he had no torch of any kind he walked as if he knew exactly where he was going and ten minutes later found himself with Ozul and Maska, who stared through the dusk at him, then bowed their heads as if they were recognizing their master.

Timon spoke. And now, across time and space, it was the Nennog's eerie voice that came out from between his lips, speaking not only to Ozul and Maska but to Timon himself.

'Very good, Timon,' the Nennog said. 'Most creative. You are doing well.' And the laugh that then came out through Timon's quivering lips was the Nennog's laugh. In spite of himself Ozul shivered at the sound. Maska remained totally still, staring out over Timon's head into the darkness.

'Can this mere circus ever succeed?' asked the Nennog.

'They might,' Ozul muttered. 'Might! They're very tough . . . very determined.'

'Timon?' asked the Nennog.

'They won't,' said Timon, seeming to answer himself. 'I'll see to that.'

Maska broke out, speaking in a decaying but urgent voice.

'If there's a chance they might succeed . . . even a small chance . . . we should kill them.'

'Then we might never find out just what the Talisman was . . .

is, and I might – that is to say the Lord Nennog – might be in another sort of danger,' said Timon.

'Exactly!' the Nennog said through Timon's mouth. He laughed again. Ozul hid his face in his hands. 'Ah, my boy what a team we are. Which of us is which? Shall I delete these unnecessary idiots?'

Ozul looked up desperately.

'My Lord,' he cried softly. 'We have worked for you – been true to you . . .'

Timon squirmed as if he, too, were wrestling inside himself. He began to pant slightly.

'No!' he said at last, speaking in his own voice. 'They still have their use.'

His expression changed, and the voice that struggled through Timon's lips was the Nennog's once more.

'What is it?' asked the Nennog sharply. 'I can feel doubt in you.'

'It's – it's nothing,' said Timon, still twisting. 'It's hard to make room for you. My head is splitting in two.' Maska moved sideways to stare at him, and Timon raised his head to stare back at Maska. His eyes glowed that blank and horrible green. Maska stepped back again.

'I will find the Talisman,' Timon announced in his own voice. 'I will work out what it is and bring it to you. I promise. You can trust me. After all I *am* you.'

'Exactly,' said the Nennog smugly. 'Exactly and excellent. At last I have made a true connection. So, Timon, go about my business! Go now!'

Tane, stirring the embers of the fire and putting fresh wood on it, looked up to see Timon stalking towards him out of the shadows.

'Hey! You should be resting,' he shouted, and then, 'are you all right?'

Timon was just a little unsteady. 'Fine,' he said remotely. 'Fine! Just tired . . . very tired.' And suddenly he was racked with another ferocious spasm. 'Fine!' he repeated, but clutching himself and rocking himself back into the world.

'You don't look it, mate,' said Tane. 'Get some rest. Will you be okay? Do you need a hand?'

'I'm fine,' said Timon. He walked over to Goneril's van for the second time that evening. The door closed behind him once again.

And now the Fantasia was wrapped in darkness, except for the fire and for a single light burning in the back window of Maddie's van. Writing secretly by candlelight Garland saw a tear splash down on her page.

She was crying. *Ferdy, Ferdy, Ferdy*, she wrote, *I thought all the crying was over. But in a way, over in that other time at least we did have a chance to say a sort of goodbye. We Maddigans like things finished properly don't we? We don't like straggling ends. Here's a promise. We will get to Solis in time*, she wrote, *and Solis WILL SURVIVE. I promise you. I promise you. Which means I have promised you twice over. Pretty powerful promising.*

She looked at what she had just written and shook her head.

It's strange to have two diary entries for the same thing . . . the same but different, she thought.

And then she closed the cover of the old diary and settled herself to get some sleep.

34
Boomer Flies

Those trees, which had been bare when the Fantasia passed them on its way out, were deeply green. Their leaves rustled in a light warm wind. It was two days before the solstice, two days before mid-summer, and Garland was waking into yet another morning's sunlight angling through the van window and striking remorselessly into her face. The sun out there was determined that she should wake up and get going. Garland felt under her pillow for her diary, but she did not begin writing in it straight away though lines were scribbling themselves out in her head.

> Do you remember the lake, Ferdy. Of course you do. We're on the edge of that lake and we have to cross it. It takes ages to go around it. Late winter into mid-summer. Four months' travelling and we're racing to keep our promise and to get to Solis just when we said we would.

But she had said goodbye to Ferdy even if she had said it in another time, and now it was as if her life with Ferdy was – well – still important – still part of what she was in a most secret, central way – but somehow closed down. She no longer felt obliged to tell him where the Fantasia was, and what it was getting up to.

She leaned against the side of the van and looked out of the window, cupping her hands on either side of her eyes like a passenger at sea staring out of a porthole. The van was parked on the edge of that lake, and there like a strange ship in the middle of the lake was a curious island – almost a floating city – a centre for holidays and trading. The rich people of Solis came here to relax . . . to lie around, staring into the blue above and the blue below. Garland leapt from her bunk, stretched, and then in a few minutes dressed and made for the outside world planning to stare into the blue herself. After all the blue belonged to everyone.

The whole Fantasia seemed to be up and about ahead of her. She thought she could see them all. Boomer was shifting some anonymous boxes, his Birdboy wings still strapped to his back and making even the simplest job difficult for him. How he loved those wings. Maddie was helping Nye yet again to straighten the stilts on the roof of his van and Yves . . . Garland stopped. Yves was sitting at a little table talking vigorously to a man she did not know, a man wearing a shirt with a large sun printed – or possibly embroidered – on it. As she stood wondering, the man moved and she saw that, directly below the great yellow sun his shirt sported a blue patch – a picture of the lake. No doubt about it he was a lakeman and he and Yves must be talking terms.

Garland skipped over to Maddie. 'You should be with him,' she said, but no longer sternly. She spoke with resignation.

'Come off it,' said Maddie. 'You know the lake people don't deal with women, not officially that is. They're a lot of dreary old Destruction leftovers, and dealing with women is against their leftover customs.'

'What do the lake women do? I mean what do they talk about?' asked Garland.

'Clothes. Babies. Shopping,' said Maddie, grinning.

'How dumb is that?' asked Garland. 'Mind you, shopping would suit Lilith.'

Another man in a matching T-shirt came towards the small table, carrying racks of fish and steak and a woman followed him carrying a tray laden with brown bottles.

'They're setting up a bit of a barbelay for themselves, complete with stubbies. It's their custom. I mean they *were* from the Golden Coast before the Destruction took their beaches away from them.'

'We haven't time for any barbelays,' said Garland. 'We're in a hurry.'

'It'll be quicker to go across the lake than around it,' said Maddie. 'I think Yves will manage to arrange something. We'll probably have to buy our way in with a show, so get yourself ready.'

The thought of a show was wonderful. It was almost as if over the last few days the Fantasia had lost touch with its real purpose. Now it might have a chance to win itself back. As Garland spun towards the van a voice she knew all too well called out to her.

'Hey! Hey, Garland. Look!' and there was Boomer, now high in a tall tree, still wearing those Birdboy wings.

'Come down!' yelled Garland. 'We might have a show to do.'

'This could be my act,' Boomer said, and he actually strutted along the branch, clucking and flapping those wings in an extremely important way. Garland couldn't help grinning.

'You want to see me?' asked Boomer, spreading his arms and his wings along with them. But suddenly Lilith rushed up, screaming and calling for help.

'It's an emergency!' she cried. 'Help. He's gone mad.'

Garland immediately thought of Timon . . . thought of his strangeness over the last day or two. It was not impossible to believe she might follow Lilith into Goneril's van and find Timon gibbering and rolling on the floor, his mouth full of green froth perhaps. But it was Eden who had upset Lilith. It was Eden who was madly searching for something, lifting not only pillows but mattresses, flinging things around him.

'The diary!' he shouted to Garland when he saw her in the doorway. 'The one we brought with us. It's gone.'

'OK! OK!' said Garland. 'But don't tear the van to bits or Goneril will absolutely tear you to bits too. Just be . . . just be systematic!'

She was pleased with herself for thinking of the word 'systematic' and Lilith was delighted with it too.

'That's right!' she said. 'Be systematic and then we'll find it.'

But out in the reeds and rushes on the side of the lake someone was holding that diary . . . someone was turning the pages carefully, passing over the recent entries, going back into it a bit. Someone was reading the words, hearing them spoken in Garland's voice.

Will there be room out there for a grown-up me? Will I ever get married? Of course I'll never leave the Fantasia but there's no one in the Fantasia I could marry. Well, there is Boomer of course. But I could never fall in love with Boomer – he's only a kid, and anyway he'd only love me if I was a clockwork girl with wheels instead of feet.

Though the book was closed very gently, there was still something about its closing that seemed to suggest Timon had slammed it shut. 'Are you the Talisman?' he said aloud. 'I don't believe it. The medallion's gone, but Eden's still got his power. So the Talisman must still be close to us somehow. But how? The Talisman! What *is* it? *Where* is it?' He stared down at the diary's faded cover in a sort of angry puzzlement, then lifted it as if he were going to throw it as far as he could out into the lake. 'What's going to happen to me?' he mumbled. 'What am I becoming? Give me a clue! Give me a clue!'

But, though his arm went back, for some reason Timon could not throw the diary away. Instead he brought his arm back again, paused and then, very carefully, settled the diary inside his shirt once more. As he stood there his expression changed. He was in pain. He doubled over, writhing as if he was being torn in two, clutching his chest, vaguely trying to protect the diary as he bent, while his narrowed eyes began to give off that strange greenish glow. Timon struggled with something that was in the outside world and in an inside world too. He was struggling to be himself.

At last he seemed to get himself under control once more. The anguish flowed out of him. Slowly, he stood up, then – slowly, slowly – he walked off back towards the busy Fantasia.

Nobody was particularly thinking of Timon – wondering where he was or *how* he was. Over in Goneril's van Garland and Lilith were putting things away, though Lilith was not being particularly helpful. Eden sat slumped between the bunks, his face buried in his hands.

'Just tell me,' said Garland. 'Tell me why it matters so much. I mean you can just steal another version of the diary, can't you? Just whip it away into some other time in between mine and yours and grab the diary from back there and let the people of that other in-between time worry about losing it.'

'You know it doesn't work like that. Those other in-between people are *us* too,' Eden began, but he was interrupted. Somewhere outside someone began a hoarse screaming.

'Goneril!' exclaimed Garland. 'Something's wrong – really wrong. Come on.'

Lilith was already at the door. Garland followed her almost falling over her. Eden, distracted from his own despair, leapt out after them.

Outside the Fantasia people were all staring incredulously up into the air at Boomer – Boomer flying and tumbling. Tane ran beneath him, looking up at him and shouting instructions. At any moment it seemed Boomer might actually crash to earth again. His hands moved wildly as he tried to work the controls of the motor strapped to his chest, but anyone could see those wings were really too much for him, though every now and then it seemed he was almost in charge.

'Change gear-mode,' Tane shouted.

'Land! Land!' screamed Goneril and Boomer tumbled towards her, then swooped up. 'I can't,' he shouted over his shoulder, speeding upwards into a high curve, only to come rushing down, down once more. Lilith's scream blended with Goneril's. But once again Boomer managed to save himself, zooming upwards, this time straight towards a tree. It seemed he must smash himself against one of the bigger branches, but he somehow managed to swing out past it, and grab a smaller one. He hung there, swinging and panting, high above the ground.

'Whoah!' they hear him exclaiming, and the Fantasia burst into a chorus of advice. 'Down! Come down! Turn it off! Shrug those wings away.'

'Pull yourself along,' Garland shouted, perhaps more clearly than anyone else. Timon came up to join the group. Looking sideways at him, wondering where he had been, Garland thought she saw an expression of satisfaction on his face. But before she had time to wonder about this, Boomer reached for the next branch which bent and snapped in his hand.

'Whoah!' he cried again, now swinging by one arm high above their heads.

'Hang on,' called Garland, running over to the tree and beginning to climb.

'Get the safety net!' she heard Goneril shouting, and thought it was good advice, while Boomer dangled, perfectly still now, frightened that any sort of struggle might break the branch he was clinging to.

'Stay cool, Boomer!' Garland shouted, though she had no

idea just what she would do when she reached him. She was close enough now, to see that his fingers, locked around the bending branch were slipping. In another moment . . .

'Do something! Do something magic!' she could hear Lilith shouting to Eden.

And then Boomer finally lost his grip. He screamed out as he fell, and Lilith screamed too. Garland saw him tumbling past her. His fall seemed endless. But then he did hit the ground. Garland longed to clap her hands over her ears imagining that she might actually hear the crunch of Boomer's bones.

But something entirely unexpected happened. Boomer bounced. The ground somehow rebounded beneath him as if he had fallen onto a trampoline. Boomer fell again . . . bounced again. 'Whoah!' he cried. 'Whoahhhhh!'

And the Fantasia people burst into laughter . . . laughing with huge relief. Goneril embraced Eden, their saviour-magician, then ran to help Boomer to his feet once more and hug him too.

'Your magic is still working,' Lilith was shrieking at Eden who stood looking as surprised as anyone else. 'Show me how to do it. Show me!'

Boomer was standing up again, staggering a little. He looked down at the ground under his feet, then stamped hard on it. It seemed perfectly solid. There wasn't an atom of wild bounce about it.

'Accidents will happen,' she heard Timon calling across to Boomer. 'Lucky you!'

She swung down from the last branch and ran towards them, shouting as she ran. 'Are you OK?'

'Think so,' said Boomer. 'I thought I had worked it all out but . . .' He shrugged and began to examine his wings carefully. 'When I got going it was all sort of scary,' he muttered. 'I suppose you have to practise. Birds do.'

Tane came hurrying over. 'Thank goodness you had a bit of help with that one,' he said. 'And now I'm going to help you a bit more. You got that gear sequence wrong. And I think you're heavier than most of the Birdboys. We must try to come up with a way of injecting a bit more power into that system.'

'Wonderful!' Maddie was calling in her bossy, head–of–the–Fantasia voice. 'A happy end to a stupid adventure! And now back to work!'

'Back to work!' repeated Yves and the adults, spreading out and around, began their lifting and folding and packing once more.

'Garland,' Maddie was yelling. 'Give me a hand here, will you?'

'But Mum . . .' Garland began.

'Garland!' Maddie shouted. 'The solstice is galloping towards us. We've got to go.'

All in a moment Boomer found himself on his own, trailing one wing and staring down at another. After a moment he hitched the wing over his shoulder again. It felt almost as if he were wearing his drum. And he felt that his Fantasia family was behaving much too casually about what they had just seen. He had just had a terrible fright, but, after all, he had flown . . . he had actually flown, even if he had found it hard to fly in the right direction. 'Hey!' he called, but already people were getting to work. Only Timon was still standing around, and Timon was turned away from him, watching Garland who had done nothing but climb a tree in a perfectly ordinary way.

'Hey you! Timon!' And Boomer, gathering courage, leapt forward and grabbed Timon's arm only to fall back and down as if he had been struck. For he had felt something like an electric current rushing through Timon . . . something quick and furious. Boomer had never been bitten by a snake but this is what he imagined a snake bite might feel like, as if the snake itself, along with its poison, was twisting through his whole body. As Boomer lay on the ground rocking to and fro, Timon looked down at him and then, glancing left and right, leaned forward.

'Are you OK?' he asked, but the blue eyes staring down at Boomer seemed totally chilly.

He held out his hand, but Boomer rolled himself up, like some sort of chrysalis, in his own flexible wings, shouting, 'Get away! Stay away from me! Leave me alone.' Then he relaxed. The wings somehow unwound themselves flicking him back onto his feet, and without looking left or right Boomer tore off toward Goneril's van his wild wings flapping so powerfully that every step he took was like a leap into the air.

Timon watched him go, a little smile touching his lips, that greenish light flashing briefly at the back of his eyes. Then, instead of joining one of the work crews, he walked on past the vans, making for the edge of the lake. He stood there staring out at the great blue spread of the lake and then looked sideways, his eyes looking from one patch of reeds to another until in the middle distance he made out two figures. They were small – insignificant – too far away to be recognizable and yet Timon felt sure he knew exactly who they were, and set off, as casually as if he were merely going for a lakeside stroll. All the same he knew just where he was making for, and who he was going to meet.

35

'Don't Trust Him'

Maska saw him approaching, and looked across at Ozul who was busy setting up the power book. 'He is on his way,' said Maska. These days his surface looked more like flaking rust than true skin.

Timon came marching towards them, his steps sterner and much more purposeful than they had been when he strolled away from the Fantasia. 'Is it ready?' he asked, looking past Maska and focusing on Ozul who was now kneeling trying to make some small connection. The screen suddenly blipped and burst into life. Green light sprang out from it, dyeing Ozul's forehead and cheeks for a moment. Timon stepped up to him and pushed him away. Dropping to his knees in front of the screen, he spoke to it.

'The diary – it's not the Talisman,' he said.

'What then?' asked a croaking voice, savage with irritation.

'I don't know,' said Timon. 'I just don't know. And it's not so easy to find out. It's hard to ask the right questions. My brother doesn't trust me any more.'

'Do you think he has it? That he's hiding it?' asked the Nennog.

'I can't tell,' Timon replied. 'And it's not so easy to sneak away from the Fantasia either. They are struggling. They need all the help they can get, so they notice if I'm not there.

I need a communication device. This one.'

Beside him Ozul let out a sound of protest.

'But Master . . .' he began.

The Nennog spoke again.

'Give it to him. And, Timon, search for it! *Search!* Find it! And report back to me directly.' The screen went blank and the green glow faded. Timon stood up slowly and turned to Ozul.

'Well, you heard him,' he said, and gestured towards the power book. 'Pack it up and give me the case.' Ozul stared at him briefly and then, obediently, began folding the device into itself while Timon looked over his shoulder, staring at the distant Fantasia. When Ozul wordlessly handed him the case, he simply snatched it and, without another word, made off around the edge of the lake.

'He will betray us,' Ozul said.

'The Nennog does not think so,' said Maska in his struggling voice. 'And the Nennog is always right.'

Timon strode on towards the Fantasia.

By now the Fantasia was ready . . . poised and ready to move on once more. Off to one side Boomer was talking to Garland who had her bow slung over her shoulder and was hanging a quiver of arrows from her waist.

'Don't trust him. Please. Don't trust him. Truly he hates me, but I think he hates the whole lot of us.'

'He doesn't. He can't!' said Garland. 'You're just jealous.' She turned away but Boomer caught her arm. Strangely enough he sounded less like Boomer to Garland than like a sort of grown-up guardian.

'He doesn't even feel like a person. Try grabbing his arm the way I'm grabbing yours. I grabbed him back there, and his arm felt like wires. Burning wires. They burnt me! And they made me – you know – *jump!* Like electricity jumps you.'

The strange thing was that Garland half-believed Boomer.

But she did not want to find herself admitting that what he was telling her might be true.

'Oh, get away, Boomer,' she said impatiently. 'That's just mad. Not possible.'

'I don't make things up,' said Boomer. 'I'm not a making-up sort of person.'

Garland knew this was certainly true. She half-turned towards Boomer again . . . half-opened her mouth with no idea at all just what was going to come out of it. And then beyond him she saw Yves and Maddie marching towards them, both looking grim.

'Oh-oh! Trouble!' she said quickly, worried by their expressions but secretly glad that something was distracting her from thinking about Timon. 'What's wrong?' she called to Maddie, and Goneril, behind Garland, interrupted in her Gonerilish way.

'What did they say, those lake people?'

'They don't want a show,' said Maddie. 'What they *do* want to do is to buy the converter. And of course it's just not for sale.'

Goneril gasped, clapping her hands over her head.

'They *know* about it? It means something to them?'

'Word must have got around. Anyhow they're prepared to pay a fortune,' said Yves. 'You know what they're like here . . . they depend on Solis, and yet in a way Solis and the lake people are rivals. They don't want Solis to become too powerful. But we won't sell, and they won't take us across.'

'Won't take us across?' exclaimed Penrod. 'Do we have to trek all the way around the edge? We'll never get there by the solstice.'

'No. Not quite as bad as that. They've agreed to hire us rafts, so that we can find our own way over,' said Yves. 'We'll have to be very very careful indeed, and it's taken our last actual money, but if we get the converter to Solis . . .'

'If we get the converter to Solis, Solis will pay us very well,' said Maddie. 'But we've got to get it there first . . . and we've got to get it there by the solstice. The rafts are over by that little wharf there. So . . . let's go rafting. Nice day for it.'

As they set off, marching after Yves back into the heart of the Fantasia, Timon sidled in and joined them, smiling at Garland, the smile of a friend who has been away for a long time. Indeed he seemed to be, once again, that old Timon, the tall prince who had first joined them, all those weeks ago. 'Have you hurt your arm?' she asked, for there was a bandage wound around his wrist and in under his sleeve, but Timon looked down at his bandage, shrugged as if it was something he couldn't be bothered talking about, then gave her a grin that was almost mischievous. Lilith's voice floated back to them.

'Dad, how will we get past the Guardian? We don't know the password the way the Lake people do. Dad, what about the Guardian?'

'What's the Guardian? asked Eden from somewhere off to the left. He had not been walking with them, for over the last few days he had seemed to be edging away from his brother, finding other company whenever he could.

Lilith looked at him with astonishment. 'The Guardian is the *Taniwha*,' she cried. 'Everyone in the world knows that. It lives in the lake. Dad, how will we get past it without the lake people helping us?'

'Look!' said Yves a little desperately. 'We're the Fantasia. Right?'

'We can do anything,' Maddie put in with fantastic confidence. 'We can out-monster any monster. Now, first of all we'll edge the vans onto those big rafts. Easy-peasy! And then those of us who are left over will split into small groups and we'll go, quietly and politely, onto the small rafts. Hey! Look, there's the magician's table lying in the grass. How did that come to be left out here? Fold it up and pack it away, Garland.'

'What happened to your arm?' Garland asked Timon again, as she made for the magician's table lying in the grass just outside Maddie's van.

'Burnt! Putting out the fire. Clumsy!' said Timon. But when Garland put out her hand towards him he shrank away from her touch.

'Hey, it's fine. Thanks for asking and all that, but it's fine.'

Immediately uneasiness edged back into her.

'Did you know Eden had lost that diary?' she asked, longing for everything to be friendly and understood between them.

'Fuss over nothing,' said Timon. 'I'd borrowed it. I wanted to check up on something. I've put it back now.' Then, on the steps of Goneril's van, he paused. 'You know *your* diary will be worth a fortune in a few hundred years.'

'Yeah, right!' said Garland laughing. 'But then my diary *is* that other diary, isn't it? I mean that diary you've got is a future ghost of mine.'

'Hard to work out, isn't it?' said Timon. 'All we can do is to laugh and keep on going.'

He did laugh, but his laugh was not a comfortable one. Garland could not work out just what was going on with Timon. He was OK at the moment but maybe she would begin feeling uneasy about him again the next time they met.

And she might have felt even more uncomfortable if she had seen Timon's expression as he shut the van door behind him. Once he was *inside* and on his own, he became something entirely different from what he had been *outside* with the powerful forces of the Fantasia working around him, helping him to hold himself together.

'Where is it?' he asked the air. '*What* is it?'

Green light flooded his eyes, and under the force of that

green glow the interior of the van underwent a curious change. Certain things suddenly shone out as if they were being forced to respond to Timon's gaze. Other things seemed to lose their shape and somehow shrink into insignificance. A book concealed under Goneril's mattress suddenly lit up and became as visible as if it were lying on the top of her quilt. Timon pulled it out and stared at it briefly, but it was nothing he wanted – *How to Get a Man and Keep Your Independence.* He grimaced scornfully, then pushed it back under the mattress again, before turning to study Eden's bed, putting his head close to it and running that strange green gaze – up and down it . . . up and down. Something shone out vaguely, not under the pillow, but hidden inside it.

'Gotcha!' muttered Timon. Then, almost carelessly, he ripped the pillow open. Feathers flew up around him, drifting and swirling. Timon groped among the feathers and pulled an object out from the nest, staring down at it with a triumph that was not entirely his own. 'Gotcha!' he said again, but staring down at what he had found as if it were something in which he could hardly believe. Straightening, he looked left and right, then, almost unwillingly it seemed, he moved back to the door of the van, opened it and leaned there, looking out wearing the expression of someone who was working out just what to do next.

The shoreline of the lake curved in front of him . . . blue water, a thin edge of sand crossed every half mile or so by a series of boat ramps which thrust out into the water like wooden commas in a long, liquid sentence. A daytime mist was rolling in across the lake, but the shoreline in front of them was clearly visible, and in the middle distance, on one of the bigger ramps the Fantasia vans were drawn up in a line. Once out on the water, the rafts became invisible in that mist, the vans seeming to float above their own reflections in an unnatural way. Two vans were already being poled away towards that mist. Meanwhile a third van – Yves's van, the heaviest van of all – was being driven, it seemed, straight onto the surface of the lake. Of course, Timon knew, there must be a raft drawn in by that jetty. He hoped it was a very big one.

After a moment Timon closed his eyes in a purposeful way. His eyelids still glowed for a few seconds, but slowly that eerie stain faded, and when he opened his eyes they were, once again, the eyes of the good prince, ready for adventure. He set off confidently towards the jetty, watching as the third van now floated away, following the other two. Judging from the way Tane, Yves, and Penrod were bending and hauling, yet another raft was being drawn alongside the jetty and yet another van was no doubt being prepared for a voyage into the mist.

Crossing the Lake

Timon was not the only spectator. Boomer, Lilith, Garland and Eden clustered a little way along the jetty, beyond the point where it began stepping out into the water, all watching anxiously as the vans edged out and on and then away. 'Are they going to make it?' Boomer asked. 'I mean it looks really . . .' He broke off. 'It looks sort of impossible,' he said at last.

Timon came up and stood beside them. Boomer glanced sideways at him, then edged away, pretending he wanted to look over the jetty railings and into the water below.

'It does look impossible,' Timon said, 'but you're the experts.'

'Of course we'll make it,' Garland declared. 'We have done this sort of thing before. Boomer will tell you. Boomer, remember the time before last . . . or was it before that . . .'

'He's being a bully,' Lilith suddenly screamed out. 'I hate him. I hate him.'

And Eden was shouting, 'You give that back to me. It's mine.'

Garland turned. The two brothers were wrestling on the ground, struggling to snatch something from one another.

'Why were you hiding it?' Timon yelled.

'It was mine,' Eden yelled back. 'I just wanted to look after it. Anyhow, I'm allowed to have a few secrets.'

'Shut up! The Taniwha will hear you,' screamed Lilith, making far more noise than either of the boys.

'What's the problem?' asked Garland.

'He's stolen my cameogram,' Eden said rather more calmly, speaking past Timon to Garland and Boomer. 'I wanted to remember them.'

'And I just wanted to look at it,' said Timon, stepping back. 'They were my parents too.'

He certainly looked innocent enough as he held up a little round frame from which a man and woman, three dimensional and somehow real although they were so small, gazed seriously out at the world. 'It's nothing much – except to me, that is. See?'

'Weird clothes!' Lilith said critically. 'Really weird! They look as if they're dressed in silver paper.' A sudden thought came to her, the same thought that had already come to Garland. 'Hey! Is that the Talisman thing-y you keep talking about?'

'No way! It's just a private picture I carry around with me!' cried Eden, jumping and snatching it from Timon, who gave it up easily enough.

'You'd better not be lying,' he said. His voice was light-hearted, but Garland, staring at him, saw with dismay that his mouth was thinning and the corners were being drawn down in that way that always frightened her. Eden must have seen it too.

'You want proof?' he cried. 'OK! Look!' And, abruptly, he hurled the picture into the blue waters of the lake. 'It's gone. I wouldn't throw the Talisman away, would I?'

Timon froze, then seemed to go a little mad. 'Idiot! You didn't have to do that!' he shouted, rushing to the jetty rails and staring down into the green, while Eden, sad and bewildered now, subsided on the thin grey boards. Timon vaulted over the rails splashing down into the sea. He stood there, water lapping up above his knees, staring down into the water as if he were trying to read words in the foam on the water.

'Hey!' Lilith shouted at Timon. 'Come out of the water. I don't want to see you eaten by the Guardian.' Eden and Timon both looked over at her, and she added, 'The Guardian will really truly hear you if you yell and splash like that.'

'The Guardian will hear *you* a mile off,' said another voice, cutting in on the argument with authority, and there was Yves bearing down on them. 'Get out of that water. There's a history of people who paddle in this part of the lake just disappearing.'

'You're making that up', Garland said doubtfully.

But at that moment, looking beyond Yves to the jetty, she saw something that drove Timon and Eden and their wild argument out of her head. Out on the jetty Tane was delicately unpacking the solar converter from one of the vans and putting it onto a small raft. Somehow she knew that Yves was planning to be captain of that particular raft and to have the solar converter under his own particular authority.

'*You're* taking it!' she cried. 'You're taking that solar converter thing – on one of the little rafts.'

'Of course I am,' said Yves. 'And I'm taking it separately. I'm sure the vans are going to be all right, but if we *do* have trouble with any of the rafts it will be one with a van on it. I don't think that converter would enjoy a dip in the lake, do you? Salt water wouldn't improve it. We can't take any risks. Anyhow, come on you lot. Stop your stupid fighting and get on one or other of the little rafts. It's *our* turn to go.'

Maddie had carefully driven their van onto the last big raft and was stepping on herself, along with Goneril who was cuddling Jewel, and with Penrod. Yves herded Lilith after them. Then Yves stepped on his own raft with the converter firmly lashed in the centre and beckoned to Garland and

Boomer to follow. Standing boldly beside the converter, he took up the long pole almost as if it were a sword of glory.

Timon and Eden hesitated for a moment, and then moved to get on the raft too but Tane, one raft further on, called out to them, 'Over the weight limit for *that* raft,' he said. 'You boys come with me.'

Yves was already bending and pushing. His raft hesitated, as if it were rather reluctant to leave the shore, then curved out onto the still waters of the lake.

'Now, quiet, you lot!' he said in a stern voice. 'No fighting! I feel that even a bit of shouting might upset the balance. Anyhow, I need to concentrate.' He bent and pushed again. Side by side the small rafts began to follow the big ones towards that thin, hovering fog. Somewhere ahead of them Garland could hear a regular subdued splashing. Mist, like shreds of pale silk in the air, began to drift around them, and they, too, became part of the mystery of the lake.

'Do you know which way to go?' Garland asked Yves doubtfully.

'You bet I do,' said Yves softly, poling on. 'I've done it before. And your dad – the great Ferdy that is – he knew this lake by heart. Well, he was the one who first showed me. I took lessons from him.'

Timon's voice carried across the water. 'How big is that Guardian – that monster you were talking about?' he was asking Tane.

'Big,' Tane said. 'Big and old. It's a mutant they say. The mutant spawn of mutants formed way back in the Chaos.'

Everyone fell silent. Nobody wanted to attract the monster mutant of mutants. And (perhaps because they were poling along so very quietly), Garland heard, somewhere in the fog behind them, subdued splashing. She nudged Yves, and pointed silently back into the mist. But Yves had already heard and so had Tane. They stood straight in the middle of their rafts listening, the poles poised in their hands. The splashing went on. And then, there behind them, smudged with the mist, two shapes — both unfamiliar and yet familiar too — came sweeping towards them, seeming to glide effortlessly over the surface of the water. Timon's voice came whispering over the water for a second time. 'Ozul! Ozul and Maska!'

'Oh no!' groaned Garland. 'Quickly! Yves quickly!' And, as she spoke, she was letting her bow slide from her shoulder and into her right hand while blindly drawing an arrow from the quiver hanging from her belt.

Yves on his raft and Tane on his both bent and pushed powerfully, but Ozul and Maska were like machines. They would be overtaken and there in the heart of the fog they, the Fantasia children, along with Timon, Eden and Jewel might vanish for ever.

An arrow came flying out of the fog, missing Timon by inches. He shrank down, but the next arrow seemed to drive right into him. Garland saw him fall flat on the raft, but heard him cry, 'Don't stop! Don't stop. It just went into the shoulder of my jacket. I'm trying to hide, that's all.'

'They're firing at Timon,' said Boomer, as if he could hardly believe it. Garland thought he even sounded a little jealous because Timon was getting all the attention. Of course he wouldn't really want the arrows that went with it.

But now it was Garland's turn. She set her arrow free, only to see Maska take one hand from his pole and catch it in mid-flight just as he had done before.

'You will have to do better than that,' he called across to her, in a voice that sounded as if it were forcing its way out through a throat filled with dirt and rust.

'They're gaining . . . gaining . . .' muttered Yves.

'Eden,' Timon was saying. 'Do something.'

Garland could not see Eden well enough to be sure, but some-how she could feel him gathering himself together there in the mist . . . she could feel him struggling and then going limp.

'I can't,' he said. 'I just can't.'

'You fool,' Timon cried. 'You threw it away. You threw away the Talisman.'

'It *wasn't* the Talisman,' Eden shouted back. 'It's just that – just that – I don't believe in myself any more.'

But by then Ozul and Maska had propelled their raft along-side Tane. Maska lifted his pole to strike at Tane who swung up his own pole to counter the blow. That blow fell, and fell so strongly that Tane's pole snapped cleanly in half. Yves, mean-while, had swung his raft around, and now came in from the side with a great, swinging stroke of his own, hitting Ozul, and bringing him to his knees. Maska spun around to face Yves, and as he did so something came in from the side striking him furi-ously on his face. Garland blinked at the strange shape that now stuck out from Maska's cheek. Maska did not bleed but a curi-ous oily liquid sprang from the wound. One of Maddie's edged stars had come at him out of nowhere.

'Mum!' shrieked Garland, spinning around in the act of fit-ting yet another arrow into her bow, and there, sure enough, was a ghost raft, edging through the mist, Penrod poling it and Maddie standing, arm back, aiming yet another of her circus knives – a sharp crescent moon of a blade at Maska. Maska, swayed to the left, then crouched and leapt onto Tane's raft as the moon flew past him. Tane promptly stabbed at him with the broken pole he was still holding but Maska swept the half-pole sideways as if it were a mere straw. Tane swayed, overbalanced, then tumbled backwards into the water, shouting as he fell. But at the same time Yves leapt into Ozul's raft, yelling furiously. 'If you want them you'll have to take me first.'

Ozul, rising up from the logs that made up the raft, seemed

perfectly happy to do this, for he flung himself at Yves. Then Garland, struggling to notch that second arrow, saw the whole raft tilting. Tane was trying to haul himself back on board. Maska moved in preparing to kick him in the face. But now Boomer jumped across the rafts, landing gracefully on Tane's, diving in to clutch Maska's leg like a furious cat-boy, clinging there, biting and ripping as if he had needle-teeth and claws. Maska looked down at him with some surprise, Garland thought, and then thumped his fist carelessly down on the top of Boomer's head, and Boomer immediately fell, limp and unconscious, to the deck of the raft. Maska kicked him into the water, then swung round on Garland. 'You people – you won't – you just won't learn,' he declared, and grabbed the end of her bow. 'You seek destruction,' he said, 'and I am created to deal destruction out.' Saying this he swung her off her feet . . . swung her so easily Garland was filled yet again with the fear that there was something unnatural about Maska's strength. It was a strength which no mere human, no matter how tall and fit, could repel.

Then she was struggling in the lake. The mist was closing around her, the lake water was swallowing her. She had been flicked away from the fight as easily as if she were an insignificant piece of rubbish, getting in the way of the true struggle. She bubbled under the water and then, as her head came up and out, gasped wildly for breath. Looking up through the fog she was able to see that Maska had reached Timon's raft. She also saw with great relief that Boomer was bobbing and gasping in the water quite close to her, and that Eden was reaching out for him.

'Go on! Try to kill me,' Timon was saying, but speaking now in a very strange voice – a voice she did not recognize. 'Try to kill me and you will know final disintegration.'

Maska had been about to deliver a blow. Now he stopped, arm raised, standing there rigidly as if a sudden spell had been cast on him. Timon stepped forward and, placing his fingers almost delicately in the middle of Maska's chest, flicked at him. Maska tottered, arched over backwards, then fell, hitting the water and splashing, just as Tane had done only a few minutes earlier, just as Garland had done herself. But Maska's reaction on hitting the water was like nothing Garland had ever seen. He did not sink immediately. His arms and legs thrashed stiffly but convulsively and huge sparks seemed to leap out from him as if he were exploding. Sparking, then sparking again, he jerked and quivered on the surface of the water, before finally sinking. The lake swallowed him. Maska was gone. Garland found she was clinging onto the side of the raft and Timon, having disposed of Maska, was already holding out a hand, strangely speckled with green, to help her. However, Garland was too frightened to take that hand.

'Quickly!' Timon said urgently. 'Something worse is coming. I can feel it there, twisting under the water. Quickly.'

And he was right. There on the other side of the rafts the water began to seethe and boil. Ozul and Yves broke out of their struggle, springing apart, both staring in amazement and alarm. The water swirled furiously, seemed to quieten down, then swirled again.

And then, at Garland's own shoulder, a great head reared up out of the water. Twisting around she found herself staring into the eyes of something like a horned eel, but huge and somehow old – ancient. Four eyes! Two heads! Garland was looking into double mystery and history too. As if from a great distance she thought she could hear Lilith singing, but of course she was screaming and screaming, and behind that screaming Garland could hear Maddie shouting her name over and over again.

'The Taniwha! The Guardian! The monster!' Lilith screamed as if one name was not enough. And perhaps a monster with two heads, really did deserve two names.

'Garland! Garland!' yelled Maddie across the water as if only one name counted. And then Garland felt herself seized and pulled down.

'It's got her,' Boomer shrieked. 'It's got –' And then all sound was shut off for Garland.

'Garland,' cried Timon, like an echo of Maddie, though Garland was not there to hear him. And he too dived into the lake.

Writhing under the water desperately trying to hold her breath, Garland kicked out at the closest eel head to no effect. Its needle teeth were stitching her clothes wildly. *I'm going to die*, she thought. *Drown and die! Drown and die! I'm going to be eaten. I'll turn into a ghost and haunt the lake.*

Her held-in breath was longing to get out. It began to hurt her. She would not be able to hold it in for much longer.

Then vaguely she saw a shape cutting through the water towards her . . . saw a hand held out to her – a hand with bandage trailing behind it. The lake water was disturbed and it was hard to be sure of what she was seeing, but it certainly seemed that the skin on that hand was somehow scaly. It must be the hand of yet another lake monster, she thought. But there was no way out of it. When you're drowning you can't be choosy. Even a *scaly* hand might be better than nothing

Something like a knife cut through the water. Vaguely, very vaguely now, Garland was aware of it. It was like a blade. It was like a shriek given a shape and an edge. The monster recoiled as if it had been stabbed, then rolled away from her. The scaly hand grabbed her. Garland felt a strange stinging feeling as she was pulled up and up and up, and there she was, gasping hugely in the misty air, between two barges, with Maddie reaching out for her and Boomer, now on Maddie's raft, grabbing at her arm and not a monster in sight. A moment later she was lying on her back on the raft, staring up past Maddie's head and seeing the mist parting a little so that she could glimpse, somewhere up there, a blue, blue sky. 'Garland,' Maddie was shouting and weeping at the same time. 'Oh, precious girl.'

'Get going!' Yves was crying from somewhere. 'Quick! It could come back at any moment. It might be hungry.'

Garland sat up slowly, gulping precious air, but feeling curiously safe. There was Timon, dripping wet, trying to wrap that dripping bandage around his hand again, winding it round and round as rapidly as he could. It was almost as if, rather than wanting to comfort a hurt hand he was trying to hide it. There was Tane, back on his raft, slumped and breathless and there was Goneril, putting a screaming Jewel over her shoulder and patting her comfortingly, so that she would forget the frightening noisy things that had been going on around her in the last few minutes.

Garland sat panting while confusion continued to rage around her.

'Where is it? Where is it?' Tane was yelling.

'Don't be scared!' Timon shouted, hard at work, continuing to wrap his hand with the wet bandage.

'Oh, Garland! Thank God! Garland!' Maddie was crying, entirely forgetting to be tough, forgetting that the show had to go on. Garland was safe, and for Maddie, right then, there was only this wonderful moment.

Suddenly Jewel stopped her screaming, squeaked and held out her arms. And then, suddenly and silently, those huge hideous twin heads reared up out of the water again. Everyone – even Yves, cried out – but Jewel clapped her hands, laughing as if the monster were nothing but a toy hung over that little sideways bunk in Goneril's van. Goneril yelled, and the great head, one with an open mouth, thrust itself towards them. Maddie jumped up and Garland could not see quite what happened next. All she knew was that, as she was still gasping and spitting out bits of water weed, a silence fell – a silence so sudden and so unexpected it was almost like a blow. Then Maddie shifted a little and Garland was able to see that Jewel was patting the monster, and that the monster was arching one of its heads under her touch as if it were enjoying the fuss she was making of it. Jewel gurgled and giggled.

'Is she – is she *talking* to it?' Boomer said.

As Jewel touched that one head, the monster shifted. Its other head ducked under the water, then reappeared and very gently grabbed the edge of Maddie's raft with its teeth. It twisted in the water and began to move.

'For goodness sake!' cried Yves. 'Is it – is it going to *help* us? It's – it's *guiding* us. Here! Tane! Quickly! Let's tie the rafts together if we can.'

'That's just silly,' said Maddie blankly, but they were the Fantasia. They quickly organized themselves, doing as Yves suggested, connecting his raft to Maddie's, then Tane's raft to Yves's, Tane's to the next raft and so on. As they began slipping effortlessly through the mist once more, Garland thought she could feel (almost as if it were an extra chill in the air) that someone was more astonished than the rest of them – more than astonished. Somewhere someone was deeply shocked. Still breathing deeply and thinking what a wonder it was to be able to do so, she looked from face to face, seeing different kinds of amazement. It was when she looked at Timon she felt herself come to a stop. The feeling of deep alarm, that strange arrow of shock, was shooting out from *Timon*. But, after all, it was only to be expected. What would she be feeling – what would anyone be feeling – if she had found herself with a baby sister who could entrance a monster?

'It's *her*,' whispered Eden. He was not whispering to anyone in particular, except, maybe, himself. But they were close enough now for Garland to hear him.

'Her!' echoed Garland, also whispering, without quite knowing what she meant.

Timon was laughing. He laughed with wonder, though there was still something about his wonder that made Garland feel a little uncomfortable.

'Something precious. Yes. Something our mother gave us. Yes! Jewel! *Jewel* is the Talisman.'

They moved on through the mist which began to dissolve like a wild dream. There they were, peacefully crossing the open lake. There far, far ahead of them they began to make out the big rafts with the vans on them . . . the rest of the Fantasia, like a floating mirage.

Behind them Ozul struggled to haul Maska back on board, rather as if he was pulling a dead fish onto the long logs of the raft.

'The baby's got powers,' he said. 'The *baby*!'

'What?' creaked Maska, then jerked and kicked and sparked convulsively once more.

'Come on, you fool. Mend yourself.'

'Can't,' bubbled Maska. 'Bro-ken! Need time. Need space. Bro-ken!'

'Do your best,' said Ozul. 'They're getting away from us. Getting away.'

And indeed the three rafts, drawn by that monster . . . the Guardian . . . the Taniwha . . . were moving steadily to join the rest of the Fantasia. As they came to the shallows within sight of the jetty the monster reared up. It bowed its two heads, looking down at them. Jewel laughed and waved her hands at it before it somehow backed away, sliding down into the blue water of the lake and disappearing. They all stared at the huge ripples it left behind it, unable, now it was gone, to believe it had ever been there.

'He'd have made a helluva feed, that fella,' said Tane regretfully.

'You be careful what you say,' yelled Goneril. 'He might hear you. And we'd make a helluva feed too.'

But Boomer turned to Garland.

'Those men that are after Timon and Eden . . . they're scared of Timon,' he said quietly. 'They didn't used to be, but they are now. Why?'

Garland did not know and could not guess. She stood there dripping, grateful to be alive, but feeling once again that the world around her was a great mystery that she would never be able to solve.

They each took their turn to come alongside the jetty and unload their rafts. When the whole Fantasia and the precious converter were safely ashore Yves shouted, 'Right! We've had a bit of a break. Let's get on with it.'

And being the Fantasia they did get back to work, happy to be safe and doing the things they were used to doing.

As she worked, Garland found her leftover fear and the feelings of deep mystery fading away and being replaced by driving curiosity. She edged closer and closer to Timon.

'How's your arm?' she asked, being careful to keep her voice careless.

'Better,' he said, avoiding her gaze.

'The road'll be quite good from now on. No much walking,' Garland said. 'Do you want to ride with us?'

'I'd better stick with . . . with Eden,' he replied.

'And with your Talisman,' she said.

Timon almost looked at her . . . almost, but not quite. He shrugged.

'Who'd have thought the source of all that power would still be in nappies,' he said at last.

37

Timon Revealed

So we pulled away from the lake, Garland wrote, all tired - so tired - but the Fantasia just can't give in to merely being tired. And after a while as it got dark we made camp as we usually do, and did all the usual stuff.

arland put down her pen and stared around her. There in the distance, visible through branches and leaves, close, so close now, was that faint glow . . . the lights of Solis. Bush leaned in on either side of them, almost but not quite embracing them. Among the trees she could make out strange objects – things that did not belong in the bush, even though the bush was hugging them as closely as if they were rare treasures – the body of a rusting car, an ancient refrigerator, other things that were hard to recognize for time had dissolved so much of them, as it dissolves everything.

Garland closed her diary on her words and on the pencil that had written them. She hid it in its usual place and moved out into the world, joining the Fantasia group. She began helping Tane serve the food, and, as he moved around the circle of hungry people, suddenly realized that she was doing this so she could look at Timon closely and from several angles.

Even though it was a warm night, he had wrapped the red

scarf that had once been buried with the stolen converter snugly around his neck. Eden sat away from him over by the ancient fridge, seeming to ignore his brother and concentrating instead on what Tane was saying to Boomer who was sitting with those wings, spread like the huge, black, torn pages of an open book across his knees. Timon saw Garland looking over at him and gave her a strange smile . . . shy, placating almost, as if he was asking her to forgive him for something. Then he looked away, trying to get Eden's attention, but Eden turned away thumping the ancient refrigerator (which looked strangely comfortable, nestling there among the ferns), and asking Boomer what it had been used for.

'They used to keep clothes in it,' Lilith said quickly, 'socks and things like that.'

Garland moved on a little, offering sausages, only slightly burnt, to anyone hungry enough to take another one.

'Remember the last time we were here?' Yves was asking Maddie. 'The lights of Solis really were so much brighter, weren't they? I mean we can still see them, but they're . . .'

'They're dimming,' put in Penrod. 'I said so last night. They do need us, those city people, don't they? Need us and what we're bringing.'

Garland bent over Yves, passing him the sausages. When he looked up at her, he seemed so battered and tired she felt really sorry for him.

'Hey, thank you,' she said rather awkwardly. It was as if she were practising something for the first time. 'Thank you for – for being so much on my side, back there.'

Yves looked at her with astonishment.

'Of course I was on your side,' he said gruffly. 'We're all . . .' he stopped.

'We're all Maddigans, born or not,' said Garland. She felt she should say more, but didn't know quite what to say. 'Sorry!'

she half-whispered at last. 'Sorry for being so . . .' She stopped. 'Sorry for what I've been . . .'

'Forget it,' said Yves quickly. 'I've probably got things to be sorry for too. It's not been the easiest journey has it? Better luck next time around.'

Garland found herself grinning at him. 'Much better next time,' she agreed, nodding as she spoke. Then she was about to pass on but Yves put out a hand and took her wrist gently.

'Do remember,' he said, 'that I miss Ferdy too. He was – well – like a big brother to me. I know you didn't believe me when I said it before, but maybe you do now. Anyhow it's true.'

Garland suddenly felt her smile quiver. She thought she might be about to cry so she moved on rapidly, only to realize that Timon's place by the fire was empty. He was gone, scarf, bandage and all.

'Where Timon?' she asked Goneril. 'He was over there a moment ago.'

'Putting his sister to bed . . . giving me a bit of a break,' said Goneril. 'You don't know what I have to put up with from that kid. She ought to sleep more than she does, but she's always awake, wanting attention. And as for her nappies . . .'

Garland moved on a step or two, and paused, staring into the bush, listening to the familiar, safe sounds of Goneril's grumbling and the Fantasia chatting. Then she put the tray on the ground and wandered towards Goneril's van, trying to make it look almost accidental – as if she'd lost a handkerchief and was wanting to find just where she had dropped it. In fact it was anything but accidental. No harm in checking, she was thinking.

'Well,' Goneril said, watching her go. 'I don't need my fortune-telling cards to work out who *she's* keen on.'

The door of the van was open. Garland stepped up into it, and looked around, already knowing it would be empty. She walked through the van, touching the bunks on either side, right to the end, then paused to lift the quilts on Jewel's short bunk, knowing again, before she looked, that Jewel had been carried off into the night. The back door of the van was open, swinging slightly as if someone had only just gone through it. Garland stepped down into the dark.

'Where is he?' she was asking herself, moving around the back of van and looking over at the faint, warm light of the distant fire once more. There they were, the Fantasia people, all talking quietly, all tired, all ready for bed but enjoying a little Fantasia gossip before they made for their bunks. It was as if the Fantasia people were telling bedtime stories to one another.

'Where is he?' asked a sudden voice, echoing her own question and making her jump. And there was Boomer, staring at her as if she might know the answer to some terrible riddle. He must have followed her. Garland thought again that Boomer sometimes appeared older than a mere eleven years – that he seemed to be more or less her own age with her own way of understanding the world.

'Gone! And he's taken Jewel,' said Garland. 'OK! We have to find them. You go that way, and I'll go this way. Yell out for me if you find him first. Don't try and take him on or anything like that.'

But she could tell that Boomer did not want to search the shadowy night for Timon. 'We should tell the others,' he said. 'Everyone should look for them.'

Garland shrugged. 'Yes, but what would we tell them?' she asked. 'He hasn't *done* anything, has he? And he's allowed to take his own baby sister for a walk. None of the others really know that he's grown so strange and creepy. They don't see him the way we do. And anyhow they're too flat-out busy to look at him carefully.'

She picked up one of the Fantasia lanterns from its holder by the doorway of Goneril's van and passed it over to him. Boomer looked at her.

'You know he's not just creepy. He's *bad*,' he said, trailing after her as she moved on towards Maddie's van.

Garland unhooked her bow from its slot beside the door, hooked the quiver of arrows onto her belt and helped herself to another lantern. 'Well, I know something's wrong with him,' she said to Boomer. 'Come on.'

And off they moved towards the bush. Boomer chose one track. Garland chose another.

'If I find him I'll sneak back and get *you*,' Boomer said. Garland could tell that, though Boomer was determined, he was terrified too.

Afterwards it seemed to her she had somehow known the right path to take. The trees seemed to make room for her, and then to close around her, but they were friendly trees, brushing against her in a reassuring way, patting her back and shoulders. *Go on! Go on! This is the right way* that leafy touch seemed to be saying. *You're on the right track*. And at last she saw light . . . not the yellow light of the lanterns she and Boomer were carrying . . . not the glowing light of the fire . . . but a greenish light . . . an unpleasant light. She had seen it before. She knew she had found Timon.

There he was, sitting on a fallen tree in the middle of a little bush glade no bigger than the bed compartment of a van, and there at his feet, tucked into her carrycot and wrapped in quilts, was Jewel sleeping innocently. In front of Timon was that green and glowing book she had seen before. He was somehow talking across time and, looking at the eerie light that was shining out of it, beating on his face, sinking into the folds of the scarf around his neck, Garland found it easy to guess who he was talking to.

'The Talisman is revealed,' she could hear him saying. 'I've got it with me – but – but I've no way of transporting it.'

A strange voice suddenly came, grating and horrible, into the mild bush air.

'You are lying. You have the slider. You could bring it home and yourself along with it. But there is no need! No need as long as you are strong. No need as long as you *obey*!'

From where she stood Garland could see Timon's face twist with what she thought must be pain. He tilted his head upwards, as if some agony was burning in every part of him. Shadows shifted uneasily across his tormented face, almost as they are afraid that they might become tormented too.

'I don't understand,' Timon said at last.

'Know me!' said that other voice. 'Look inside yourself and meet my eyes.' Slowly Timon lowered his head. Garland could not tell if the green light was shining into his eyes or out of them. Slowly, slowly she lowered her own lantern to the ground. Swiftly, swiftly she slid her bow from across her shoulder.

'There is one reason we want that Talisman,' the voice said. 'We want it to become part of us. Or we want to smash it out of existence.' Timon looked down at the sleeping Jewel, and, as he looked at her, the voice went on, hideous and implacable. 'Bring her to me or destroy her for me. We are bound, you and I . . . bound together! Destroy her and I will bring you home and you will be . . . not my heir, for I plan to live forever, but my partner. Tell me you understand this.'

Slowly Timon looked up again.

'I do,' he said. And with these words the communicator somehow turned itself off, though Garland could not tell who had done the turning. Her own lantern light fell faintly on Timon and the sleeping Jewel, but Timon did not seem to be aware of it. Instead he looked down at the baby, her thumb in her mouth, one tender foot poking out from her blankets, and

Garland could see his face twist into an expression of such ugliness she couldn't help gasping.

Though, at that moment, she was utterly terrified Garland knew she must do something. She took a breath, preparing to shout at him, to run at him, to smash his communicating device over as she punched him in his horrible face. But within a second that face changed again, and Timon straightened, drawing back from Jewel. He stared around wildly, and a groan . . . the sound some dying animal might make . . . forced its way out. In the same moment he suddenly seemed aware of lantern light falling on him from an unexpected direction, and turned to meet the eyes of Garland, staring back at him gravely along her arrow . . . an arrow trained directly on him. There was a silence between them. Then Timon spoke.

'Go on!' he said. 'Go on! Fire! Do it! Quickly! Quickly, before I change again.'

'What's happening?' asked Garland, holding the bow bent and the arrow aimed.

'You saw it, didn't you?' Timon replied. 'You saw my possession. You know.' He stood up and stepped back. 'Take her! Take Jewel. I promise I won't stop you.'

'How can I trust you?' Garland demanded. 'Your promises are all *spooked* promises. What's happened to you.'

'I'm not what I was,' said Timon. 'I'm changing. He linked into me. He's taking me over. When he moved into me I can't – I can't be myself any more – I become *him*.'

He stepped back even further. 'Take her quickly!'

Garland hesitated. It could be a trap.

'Please,' begged Timon, and this time she just had to believe the pain in his voice. Sliding her arrow back into the quiver at her belt, slinging her bow over her shoulder, Garland took a breath, then darted into the glade. She grabbed the handles of the carrycot, glancing down at Jewel then up at Timon, and then from Timon to Jewel again, as she half-swung, half-dragged the baby back to safety on the edge of the glade. Safety? No! There could be no safety from whatever it was that haunted Timon. Still, at least there was a bit of space between them. She took a breath. She let it out. She took another.

'OK! Let's go back,' she said. 'Let's go back to the fire and the Fantasia.'

'I can't!' Timon cried softly. 'I *told* you. I'm being taken over. I'm turning into – into *him*! And if I turn into him I'll kill Jewel. I'll kill Eden. I'll kill you.'

'No way!' Garland said, as bravely and fiercely as she could. 'I'll kill you first.'

Timon paused. Then he began to laugh. At first it was just a chuckle but it grew louder and longer and turned into a true, full laugh. It was almost as if the laugh was making him feel better.

'It's not that funny,' said Garland indignantly.

There was a movement behind her, a rustle, a deepening of the lantern light. Boomer! Boomer racing bravely out of the shadow, grabbing her arm and trying to haul her after him. 'Come on! Get away. He's awful. Leave him!' he shouted in a great scramble of words.

'No!' Garland cried back. 'He's part of the Fantasia. We have to *help* him.'

'No, we don't!' yelled Boomer. 'He's a monster and we don't have to help monsters.'

'We help *Fantasia* monsters,' Garland yelled back. 'We can't just leave him.'

'No! Because I'll *follow* you,' Timon said, and suddenly his voice had a new rasp in it. 'Go on. Go now! Quickly. It's moving in on me again.'

'Well, we will go!' cried Garland. 'But you follow us. Follow us and fight it! Fight it! Because everyone's still round the campfire. So we'll have a midnight parley and we'll save you. Because we're Maddigans and we can fight any old Nennog in any old time. Come on, Boomer! Grab my lantern and run!'

Snatching up the carrycot, heavy with Jewel's weight, she made off into the bush, running as fast as she could. Boomer ran at her heels with a lantern in either hand, both of them aware of Timon following at a distance. As she clumped along, Garland was both determined and terrified, for somehow she could feel, there behind her, Timon struggling within himself as he ran . . . struggling to hold that Nennog, working within him, at bay. He was running, changing and fighting the change as he ran. It was like having – not a single boy but a whole pack of creatures hot on her heels. '*Maddigan! Maddigan,*' she muttered, running on, trying not to drag or drop the carrycot, trying not to spill Jewel out of it. She burst out of the bush, shouting to the drowsy crowd around the campfire. '*Maddigan!*' The Fantasia leapt to their feet, holding out their arms. Maddie stepped forward to grab her and pull her into the firelight. Goneril sprang for Jewel, who, by now, was startled and crying. Penrod whisked Boomer behind him. And, for the moment at least, there with the Fantasia closing around them, she and Boomer and Jewel were safe.

Timon stood apart from the Fantasia, a ghost on the edge of the bush, as Garland told her story, with Boomer interrupting, pointing and adding bits that Garland did not know about. ('I looked into the power book screen and this – this *thing* looked back at me.')

At the end of it all, Yves looked over at Timon then back to Garland. 'How can you prove any of this?' he asked mildly, and Timon spoke for the first time.

'Look!' he said, and, tugging the scarf away from his neck he stepped forward a little, wincing at the stronger light of the fire and the Fantasia lanterns. Everyone could now see green scales, spreading up from under his collar, covering his throat and neck, creeping up onto his cheeks, and into the hair at the back of his head. Just for a moment his eyes shone green. 'Look!' he said again in a different voice, and they could all see him gritting his teeth and struggling until the greenness died out of his eyes once more. 'Kill me! Kill me quickly,' he said, choking. And the Fantasia burst into one of their great, sprawling arguments.

'Vote on it! Vote on it!' yelled old Shell, but Yves held up his hand. 'We *don't* harm a member of the Fantasia,' he said. He glanced sideways at Maddie. She looked down into Garland's eyes, and then they both looked towards Yves and nodded. 'It's our code!' said Yves. 'But all the same, we've got to protect ourselves. Let's see what we can come up with.'

Amongst the rusting pieces of car, the old refrigerator and the other strange leftovers on the edge of the clearing was an old iron post rising from among the weeds and ferns. Tane and Yves chained Timon to the post.

'It's just to stop this Nennog of yours getting too impulsive with you. And it's not hurting you, is it?' asked Tane, padlocking the chain.

'It's very thoughtful bondage,' Timon replied, putting up his unbandaged left hand, his scaly hand, to touch the scales on his throat. 'They're spreading,' he said. 'They've spread since this morning.' He looked over at Eden, watching him with a mixture of distress and concern. 'I hate to admit it but you've been the clever one,' he told him.

'You'll get over it. We'll save you!' Eden cried. 'At least we can *talk* about it now.'

'Well, I'm in the right place,' said Timon. 'If I turn into some sort of lizard, there'll be work for me in this Fantasia. Maybe people will pay to see me.' And then he recoiled, straightening himself against the post and crying out in pain. 'It's such a fight!' he screamed. 'And he hates it when I try joking.'

Eden took a few steps towards him, but Maddie grabbed his collar and yanked him back again, shouting at him to keep clear.

Eden turned towards her. 'But it might be all right!' he cried. 'We'll get to Solis with that converter, and . . .' he turned back to Timon '. . . and when they get it installed and working it will change the whole future, won't it? There mightn't even be a Nennog any more, and then . . .'

'There mightn't be any of us either,' said Timon. 'Good thing too.'

Garland watched from beside Yves, feeling strangely comforted by his height and strength.

'Are we leaving him here?' she asked.

'Just for two or three days,' Yves said. 'It's what he told us to do. We're leaving food and water, and we're taking all those communicators and things he had with him. We'll reach for Solis, we'll pass over the converter and then we'll come back for him. But we've got to get there first.'

'I could wait with him,' said Garland, but Yves shook his head.

'What if that monster succeeds in taking him over?' he said. 'And we don't know what's ahead of us. We might need every single Fantasia person, if we want to move quickly, and then there's your mum. Maddie wants you beside her every moment of the day from now on. No more sneaking off. No more running away.'

Garland moved cautiously towards the post and to the chained Timon. 'I don't know,' she said feebly.

'None of us do,' said Timon, smiling a little.

Behind her the weary Fantasia people were climbing up into their vans, hooking their lanterns over the van doors, getting themselves ready to set off yet again even though it was the middle of the night.

Timon suddenly twisted and cried out wordlessly, then relaxed again. He looked at Garland, gave her a curious, collapsed smile . . . but she knew it was still Timon who was smiling at her. There was nothing of the Nennog in that expression. 'Will you still love me when I'm a monster?' he asked, and laughed breathlessly.

Garland stepped forward. The scaly hand rose as if to grasp her but he hit it away with his other hand, and it fell to his side once more, the chain ringing.

'Garland!' Maddie was calling from the running board of their van. 'Now! Now!'

'You're not a monster,' Garland said to Timon. 'I can still see you. I know you're there.'

And at that moment there was a sudden scream. Goneril!

'Yves! Yves!' she was calling. Garland turned and saw her scuttling from her van to Maddie's.

'She's gone!' she was screaming. 'She's gone again!'

Boomer came racing over to where Garland stood, staring in confusion. 'Did you know about it?' he shouted. 'Did you?'

'Hey, I don't know much about anything any more,' Timon said weakly.

'What's happened?' Garland cried.

'Jewel's gone!' Boomer shouted back. 'She was in Goneril's van and now she's gone again. It must have been Ozul and Maska!'

Yves came running towards them, with Byrna and Nye at his heels. 'Guard him!' he cried. 'That's all we can do right now. Don't listen to any story he might tell you. Just guard him.'

Garland looked up at Timon, saw his weary face turning towards her and saw, just for a second, the greenness and the convulsion as the Nennog tried to reach back through time and take him over. 'Jewel,' he sobbed, struggling in his chains. 'Jewel.'

'Don't worry,' Garland said. 'I found her once. I'll find her again.' And off she ran.

We have to find Jewel, Garland wrote. But she was not writing in her book. She was writing in her head as she pulled her tough boots on. *I am scribbling my thoughts in my mind – there isn't time to write. We have to go and search again for Jewel. I'll write it down properly later.*

And then she set off into that very early morning.

The Fantasia had never felt as disconnected – as alien – as this. Garland looked over to check on Timon. There he was, chained, and even from a distance she could see his golden princely hair hanging limply down around his ears. Garland felt sure that if he tried to brush or comb it, it would come away with the comb, leaving him completely bald. And then, she thought, the green scales would creep up and cover his whole head. Perhaps they were doing this already.

Nye was sitting at a small distance from Timon guarding him. As Garland watched Boomer came sidling up, looking apprehensive but curious too.

'Don't get too close,' Nye warned him. Timon's eyes opened. He stared at Boomer then grinned a grin which had something of his old teasing grin about it, but was also somehow unpleasant too. At that moment, almost as if it had been called on to take part in an act, a fly began to buzz around Timon.

SNAP! It was over almost before Garland could be sure of what she was seeing. Timon's lips had parted, and a thin green tongue had shot out and flicked the fly into Timon's mouth. Then he looked over at Boomer. 'Hey! Want to join me for breakfast?' he asked.

Boomer stepped back. Garland stared at Timon and he stared back too. 'I did warn you,' he said at last.

'We're having a little parley,' she said. 'And we're going to search for Jewel.'

Then she turned and walked away beside Boomer, leaving Timon chained there.

There they all were – clowns and acrobats, tumblers, trapeze artists, and a tightrope walker – all getting ready to search and shout their way through the surrounding countryside. 'My Jewel,' Goneril was crying. 'I should have fought them harder.'

'You did your best.' (Maddie was trying to comfort her.) 'Face it you're not as young as you used to be.'

'I'm tough though,' Goneril cried indignantly. 'I'm a tough old chook!'

'Listen! Listen!' Yves shouted. 'We can't all set off searching for Jewel. Some of us have to go over there to Solis. We just have to carry that converter to the Duke, now, now, *now!* Tomorrow is the summer solstice . . . the longest day.' And now, within easy walking distance they could see Solis, new towers being built, old ones being repaired, a flow of people going towards the gates, a flow of people coming away.

The voices broke out once more, everyone offering some idea about what to do next.

Garland was, perhaps, the only silent one. She had no idea what the Fantasia should be doing. She knew that Yves was right. The Duke must have that converter they had struggled so hard to bring to him by the summer solstice. He absolutely must have it! Yet Jewel must be found. She absolutely must be found. As she looked from face to face she was distracted once again. Boomer! Where was Boomer?

He was not difficult to find. He was with Timon again, talking to him. Garland could see his lips moving. As the Fantasia voices clashed and blended, she strolled back towards Timon herself.

'At least I don't look like a lizard,' Boomer was saying indignantly.

'Puberty's hard for all of us,' Timon replied. 'Where's Eden?'

'Keeping his distance,' Garland called to him. 'He's really unhappy about everything.'

'. . . and I don't eat flies for breakfast,' Boomer was adding.

'Flies are pests anyway,' Timon said, pushing himself forward against his chains – chains which suddenly seemed as if they might be too fragile to hold him. Boomer quickly stepped back as Garland moved forward. Although she'd seen Timon once already that morning she could not quite hide how alarming and strange she found him. He seemed to read her thoughts.

'I'm the Beast. You're the Beauty,' he said. 'It's all a story, isn't it?'

'How are you feeling?' Garland asked him. Deep down she really anxious about him – anxious about the Timon he had used to be – anxious about Timon she still felt to be lurking somewhere in the mixed-up creature chained to the post.

Timon must have seen this, for he seemed to relax a little, and when he smiled at her, the smile that came though the green scales was truly Timon's smile. 'I feel all the better for seeing you,' he said.

'But watch him!' said Nye.

'Yes, do watch me,' Timon agreed. 'I'm not reliable.'

'Just tell me,' Garland said, 'have you got any idea where they might have taken Jewel?'

Once again, within a second or two, Timon seemed to change.

'I could have a few ideas,' he said. He lowered his voice. 'Look, if you were to let me go . . . or if you distracted . . .' He jerked his thumb sideways at Nye.

'No!' Garland said sternly. 'No way!'

Timon relaxed once more. 'She just might come back to us if we wait,' he said, 'because Maska and Ozul must have taken her. But they won't leave me behind, will they?'

'Things are getting desperate. They might,' said Garland.

'Not now I almost count as the Nennog's child – his son and heir,' said Timon. 'And they can't talk to him any longer. Not without dealing with me first.'

'And if they want to talk to Timon, they'll have to talk to *me* first,' said Nye. Then he pointed to the parley. 'Look! It seems they've got something organized. If I was you, Garland, I'd whisk over there and see if I could find anything useful to do.'

'They'll have worked something out,' Garland told Timon. 'The Fantasia is really clever with tricks – every sort of trick. Don't worry! We'll save you in every way. And we'll save Jewel too.'

She turned and ran back to the heart of the Fantasia parley, anxious to find out what they had decided.

Of course they were being watched.

As Maddigan's Fantasia began to organize once more and the first van began to jolt its way down the remains of an old motorway towards the gates of Solis, Maska watched, grinning to himself. In between the moving vans he glimpsed Timon sitting on the ground, chained to the post. They were leaving Timon behind. Even Nye was going with the vans. Timon's only guardians would be his chains.

So, when the last van had moved on its way, Maska moved too, jittering towards Timon, like a mixture of scarecrow and a damaged toy man. Most of his hair was gone and the skull beneath it looked as if it were made of rusting iron. When he smiled anyone could see his teeth were missing and one of his eyes had turned upwards in his head so that he seemed to be looking out at the world with one eye, and back into his own head with the other. His movements were jerky – a little incoherent – but for all that he still moved quietly, and Timon, singing quietly to himself, seemed unaware of him until

Maska was only a few steps away from him. Then Timon spoke.

'Fresh air, trees, solitude. Hey! What could be better?'

Maska came to a sharp but not altogether tidy stop.

'Enjoying yourself then?' Maska asked. Suddenly Timon turned to look directly at him and Maska stepped back so wildly it seemed that he might topple backwards. 'Sir!' he said. Then he added, 'You cannot *be* the master.'

'Where's my sister?' Timon asked. 'And where's Ozul?'

Maska answered these questions with a question of his own: 'Where is the communication unit?'

'Release me, and I might give it back to you,' Timon answered.

'I am not here to help you,' said Maska. 'You are my master, but without being altogether my master. Not yet!'

Suddenly, in spite of his chains, Timon was on his feet. When he spoke it was in an entirely different voice . . . a voice filled with a savage thunder. 'Release him or feel my anger.'

Then, astonishingly, the bushes at the edge of the vanishing road suddenly swished wildly. Out sprang Garland, confronting Maska with a drawn arrow. Maddie . . . Tane . . . Eden . . . suddenly closed in on him all pointing arrows at him.

'Where is Jewel?' Maddie cried.

Maska stared at her, then looked back at Timon.

'How wonderful it is to have friends who care for you. Do you think their tricks and traps worry me? Well, tell them,' he cried, 'tell these fools. They can fire their darts as much as they like, but they can't hurt me.'

'But I might,' said yet another voice. Tane – Tane followed by Boomer pushing a trolley with a small tank on it, Boomer's great bird wings strapped across the top of the tank and flapping as if they were longing to take off into the air. Tane was armed, not with mere arrows but with a hose. 'We've got a water tank hidden here . . . and you don't like water, do you?'

As Tane said this, Boomer turned on a pump at the back of the tank and Tane directed a sudden stream of water toward Maska. Maska leapt over the jet, jumped successfully enough, but only to land with an ominous crunch. One of his legs seemed to collapse under him, straighten, collapse again but then, finally, to straighten once more.

'I'll get you. I'll get you all!' he screamed at them, retreating in great bounding strides. In spite of his awkwardness he moved at unnatural speed, smashing through the bushes, ploughing right over some of them.

'Quick! After him!' yelled Garland, as they began their chase, Garland, Tane and Maddie leading, and Boomer following behind them all. He did not look as if he was being left behind however. He moved like someone with a secret plan of his own.

Left behind Timon watched them go. Then he bent his head, seeming to struggle with himself yet again. His shoulders lifted and dropped down, his bent head swung from side to side . . . and then slowly, as if he had finally decided just who he was, his head lifted again. There was very little of Timon left in the face that looked out at the world, slitted eyes peering between thin strands of golden hair. Timon stood straighter. His shoulders seemed to broaden. Then he lifted an arm level with his shoulder, paused, looking down at the chain that dangled from it. He laughed. Then, abruptly, he jerked his arm high into the air, reaching for the branches above him. There was a jangling sound as one of the chains that held him broke away from him and fell uselessly to the ground. There was no one there to see Timon transforming – Timon breaking his chains and walking effortlessly away, green in the green world, following the vans, not his friends, and making for Solis.

The Silver Girl

Out in the thin forest, darting from tree to tree, Maska ran, then paused and looked behind him. There was no one following him now. He had shaken them off. Though Maska was not the sort of creature who was able to relax, a kind of ease overcame him. His movements slowed down, becoming rather more controlled as he began to March forward, sure of himself and sure of his direction. If Maska had been the sort of creature capable of showing pleasure, he would have shown it.

Yet suddenly he paused in mid-stride, tottering in a way he would not have done when he first rode into the Fantasia, all those weeks ago. He looked at the ground ahead of him very intently, as if he expected to see enemy tracks, but the leaves and grasses had nothing to show him. Then it happened again. The air throbbed. A shadow, almost like the shadow of a cloud, but moving faster than any cloud shadow slid across the grasses in front of him. Maska looked up. There, circling overhead, looking down on him, was a strange shape, huge wings outspread, bigger than a hawk, bigger even than an eagle.

Boomer.

Giving a wild triumphant cry, Boomer swooped down at Maska who leapt back as if Boomer might indeed attack him with claws and a curved beak.

'Suck on this, robot!' Boomer screamed, but in his excitement he narrowly escaped smashing himself against the top branches of a tree. He veered away, desperate to find space in which to balance himself again. As Boomer wobbled wildly, struggling to regain his smooth flight line, Maska took one step – then another and then, able to run once more, shot sideways to vanish under the trees.

Boomer, swooping and sliding through the air, struggling to work out where Maska might be, suddenly found he had shot out over the edge of the forest and was circling over a wasteland that might once have been a town. There among the rubble below him he could make out the skeletons of buildings, the beetle-shells of things that might once have been cars. Circling again lower and lower, he finally landed in an open space. The motor on his chest had been enlarged. New wires, like brightly coloured worms, coiled out of it. Boomer began to examine these new connections carefully.

'Where is he?' asked a voice . . . and Boomer started wildly, although it was a voice he knew well.

Garland stood, panting and dishevelled, looking around her wildly. Eden came up behind her, staring rather cautiously at Boomer, for in this particular adventure it seemed there was no one who could be trusted. Everything, everybody, might change in a minute or two.

'They're still not quite right,' said Boomer. 'I think it's this one.'

'Hey! Where is he?' Garland cried again.

'Lost him. Sorry!' said Boomer. 'This motor gives me so much more power I can't quite get the hang of it. It's almost like I'm too light for it now.'

'Where are we?' asked Eden.

'It's a place called Outland,' said Garland. 'Solis began here, but moved on over there. These are the scraps it left behind.'

She stared around, searching the ruins, the retreating lines of trees, even the dominating shape of the city, for some sign that Jewel might be close. She listened for crying. It suddenly seemed to her that, even with Boomer there at her elbow, fiddling with his newly powerful motor, even with Eden the magician-boy, the world around her had never been so echoing and empty. The trees had stopped looking like real trees, the sky like a real sky. Instead it looked as if the world had been painted on cloth then set around its edges with a great toy forest, all intended to hide the true world and to confuse someone like Garland.

She found herself longing – not for Yves or Maddie or any Fantasia person, but for her silver girl, the strange ghost who knew all the ways of the world and could point the right way out to her. She clapped her hands across her eyes.

'What are you doing?' asked Boomer, staring at her, but Garland did not answer.

'Shhh!' whispered Eden. 'She's concentrating. She's making something happen.'

'Silver girl! Silver girl!' Garland was muttering into the palms of the hands she was holding over her face. 'I need you. I *need* you! I *command* you.'

Then she parted her fingers, and peered between them.

There on a broken wall ahead of her she saw something move. She could hardly believe it. The silver girl, faint but certain, shifted like a daylight ghost.

'I see her,' Garland cried in triumph, pointing with both hands. Both boys looked in the direction in which Garland was pointing.

'What's she on about?' asked Boomer. 'There's nothing there.'

'Shut up,' said Eden. 'Let's do what she's telling us to do. That silver-girl stuff has worked before, hasn't it?'

'This way,' said Garland, for the silver girl was moving now, sliding from one broken wall to another, rippling faintly across the smashed stones. 'This way!' said Garland. 'Follow me.'

Back in the forest Maska strode along as if he knew exactly where he was going. Trees and bushes caught at him, but he broke through them as if he were the only real thing in a ghost world that deserved to be smashed into nothing. Even the sound of the wind seemed like the voice of a dream rather than a real sound of a real world. And suddenly another sound intruded . . . a sound that was certainly not a true part of the forest. The sound of a baby weakly grizzling.

Maska's steps quickened. Walking with confidence he burst an open glade, and there sitting beside a small fire was Ozul struggling with Jewel, who was waving her arms desperately. Ozul looked up, his face sharp with hope.

'Where is it?'

'I could not get it,' Maska said.

'But we must have it. We must!' shouted Ozul. His raised voice startled Jewel who began to scream. Ozul looked down at a scatter of small objects at his side. He picked up something and dropped it into Jewel's open mouth. 'There!' he cried. 'Take that and sleep!' He looked up at Maska.' I have to drug her. We can't have her making a noise or they'll all be down on us. But we must have that unit back again.'

'I could not get it,' said Maska. 'I have been burned. I have been drowned. I have sparked. I am not what I was. If we do not go back now, I will break down altogether and you will be on your own.'

'But if we go back without the boys as well as the baby the Nennog will be extremely annoyed with us,' Ozul said. 'We might be terminated. You heard him say so.'

'That is true. But if I do not go back I will terminate anyway,' said Maska.

'And what about me?' yelled Ozul.

'I don't care about you,' Maska said. 'I am not constructed to feel affection. You know that.'

Jewel's crying was lessening. Ozul looked down at her.

'She's going to sleep,' he said with relief. 'At least we'll have a bit of silence while we work out what to do next. We could kill her of course. But if we kill her the Master might abandon us – let us die in this appalling time. She's our ransom, if you like.' The crying stopped altogether. 'Silence!' said Ozul gratefully.

And a short distance away, half-jogging, half-tumbling through the ruins of Outland, Garland stopped suddenly.

'She's gone,' she cried. 'The silver girl has just disappeared into nothing.'

'She wasn't ever there anyway,' said Boomer. 'She's just something you dream up.'

'She seems to – to work though,' argued Eden.

'She was there,' said Garland, 'and now she's gone. Though just before she disappeared she seemed to be pointing at something . . . something over there.'

'Her pointing's always meant something before,' said Eden. 'Let's take a look anyway.'

They scrambled across collapsed walls.

'Funny to think that people once lived here,' Eden said, speaking in a voice that was almost a whisper. 'Funny to think of the strangeness of time sort of sweeping things in and then sweeping them out again.' He looked at Garland. 'You live in a land filled with ruins, don't you?'

'That's because of the Chaos,' Garland half-whispered back. 'Anyhow it was about *there* that the silver girl was pointing.' They stood looking up and down what had once been a street, hoping Outland would yield them some clue to its mysteries.

'There!' cried Eden, suddenly pointing almost as the silver girl had pointed.

Behind a tangle of fallen posts and broken wire an unexpected oval dark space could be seen. It looked so much like an eye it was almost as if the ruins were looking back at them without blinking once.

'It's just a hole,' said Boomer rather nervously, but Garland was already scrambling across the posts and through the wires.

'This must be it,' she said. 'Has to be!' The boys heard her hissing words echo as if they were confronted by an army of serpents. 'It's a tunnel leading to – well, leading in the direction of Solis.'

'It'll be too dark for us to crawl along it,' Boomer said even more reluctantly.

'No,' Garland said, as she wormed her way down into it. 'There are patches where the roof has fallen in so it's not too bad. I can see well . . . fairly well.'

'Sounds dreadful,' mumbled Boomer, following Eden who was following Garland. 'It makes me want to sneeze.'

'Don't sneeze,' said Eden. 'You might wake the giant cockroaches.'

'What giant cockroaches?' cried Boomer alarmed.

Garland stopped so suddenly that Eden ran into her.

'Hey, Boomer,' she whispered. 'Listen! Eden was just teasing. Don't shout. Whisper everything. Crawl quietly and don't scrape everything with those wings of yours. You should have left them behind. Remember, I was *shown* this tunnel. It means something.'

'My wings are folded up,' Boomer whispered back. 'They fold well.'

Garland crawled on towards the next patch of light, sure that she was doing the right thing, but entirely mixed up about what she was doing, where she was going or what she might find at the end of the tunnel. And suddenly as she crawled she began to hear voices . . . two voices . . . voices she recognized.

'If we go back without the boys,' Maska was saying, 'the Nennog will surely terminate us. I am engineered to resist termination. That's why I have lasted here and self-repaired myself over and over again in this loathsome time.'

'We must tell him that the Fantasia discovered the boys were traitors and that they were put to death,' Ozul said. 'After all, we do have the Nennog's Talisman at last. And as for the solar converter – well, it would have been good if we could take it home to our own time, but I believe there are – well – let's say *forces* in Solis, who will take care of it for us. Remember, the Nennog has a past deeply rooted in Solis, and I think he has several ways of working things to his advantage. He is working *here* as well as *there*.'

Garland found she was now squatting in deep shadows, at the back of a great cave, its floor covered with rocks and stones. In the daylight at the mouth of the cave Ozul was working desperately putting together some device which Garland imagined might be some sort of slider, some instrument that would carry them back to their own time. There on the far side of the cave, she made out the shape of the carrycot and knew that Jewel was there, needing to be rescued.

'There are friends of the Nennog in Solis?' said Maska. 'I did not know he bothered with friends.'

'Not friends but allies perhaps,' said Ozul. 'More than allies. His great change – his move to power – began back in this time. We were both told.'

'I have suffered damage,' said Maska. 'I do not remember what I was told. I am full of patches of nothing.'

Garland, moving as quietly as she could, slid along the back of the cave. If she could stay in the shadows . . . if she could slide that carrycot, Jewel safely in it, back down the cave to

Eden without waking the baby . . . if she could slide the carry-cot back down into the tunnel . . . so many 'ifs'!

'Hold the light higher,' said Ozul. And Maska obeyed. Feeling the light move across her, Garland froze there at the back of the cave, but Maska and Ozul were intent on putting their device together. They had their backs to her. Neither of them saw her there. Garland took another step and then another. She crept on, and at last found herself looking down at the sleeping baby, somehow knowing at once that its sleep was not a natural sleep. She hoisted the carrycot, remembering how she had carried it before – how to hold it away from her legs so that she would not trip.

In spite of the batwings folded in on his back and the motor strapped to his chest, Boomer had pulled himself out of the tunnel and was holding out a hand to Eden. They were both moving quietly – very quietly indeed – but Garland rather wished they had stayed down below and out of sight.

Something at the mouth of the cave clinked then rattled.

'Did you drop it?' she heard Ozul cry. One step. Another step.

'How I long to be back in my own time again and free from your company,' Ozul said to Maska.

'How I long to be restored,' Maska remarked. 'I have never needed company, but I am badly in need of repair.'

'One more connection . . .' said Ozul. There was a click followed by a hiss and suddenly Garland found herself flooded with light. She stood pinned by it there at the back of the cave, the carrycot swinging from her hands in front of her.

Ozul sighed with relief.

'It is prepared. And it's working. Get the child,' he commanded and then Ozul and Maska, turning to where they believed Jewel to be, saw Garland, almost at the mouth of the tunnel, and stared taken aback. 'You people never give up do you?' said Ozul. Garland dropped the carrycot, and scooped the sleeping baby up into her arms. 'You're not getting her!' she screamed diving towards the mouth of the tunnel and the eager arms of Eden, as Ozul loomed over her, snatching wildly at Jewel. Boomer leapt onto his back, while Eden, quick as a wild cat, dived around the edge of the cave making for the unit Ozul and Maska had put together with such enormous care.

'Get him off! Get him off!' Ozul was choking, reaching back for Boomer.

And then the carefully constructed slider exploded, bright arrows of light shooting out in every direction. Eden! thought Garland. Eden had managed to pull off one of his magical tricks. Or perhaps he'd just kicked it over. Ozul let out a cry of despair.

They had a moment of precious time.

'Go, Garland!' Boomer was screaming, and Garland, clasping Jewel to her chest, and deciding that climbing down into the tunnel was too much of a risk, dodged this way and that, stumbled round the edge of the cave, and raced towards daylight and the outside world.

Once outside she would be able to smell the forest – to see the trees, could run between the leaves and branches.

She looked back over her shoulder and saw Maska holding Eden in one hand and Boomer in the other. He grinned at her, though only half his face was working.

'You'd leave your friends?' he asked her. And, as Garland found herself hesitating, Ozul ran to stand to between her and that wonderful, beckoning freedom. She knew that even if she ran back towards the tunnel at the back of the cave it would take a few desperate moments to squeeze herself and Jewel down through its narrow opening. Ozul would catch her easily.

'Give her back to me,' Ozul said, 'and we just might be merciful to your friends.'

Garland stood there, holding the baby close to her. She could not surrender Jewel to Ozul and Maska. Yet she could not desert Eden, and certainly not Boomer, who had been her friend ever since she could remember, and who, she suddenly realized, was precious to her. And, anyhow, she certainly did not believe that half-promise of mercy.

'Give her back to me,' repeated Ozul, advancing carefully, his hands spread wide.

And then something bounded out of the green forest in front of the cave . . . something that sprang into the cave like some sort of wild creature, crying out, even as it leapt, in a familiar voice.

'Let her alone!' said Timon. 'She belongs to me.' And he struck Ozul a blow that sent him tumbling backwards across the cave and crashing against the wall. Maska immediately dropped Boomer and Eden, and reached for this transformed Timon. Grabbing Timon's shoulder with his left hand, he swung his right hand back to deliver a blow. But the blow never fell. Maska began to convulse once more. Sparks sprang from his joints, and he began a mad drumming dance across the cave.

'Run!' Timon shouted to Garland and the boys, speaking in a strangled voice, as if he were being twisted and tormented by powers that could not be seen. 'Run before I lose myself . . .' his voice faded.

Garland did not want to go near Maska, who was jazzing and sparking. There was time now. Thanks to what was left of Timon there was time. She made for the tunnel, and, holding the baby against her chest with one arm, struggled along it, followed by Eden and Boomer.

'Once we get the converter to Solis,' gasped Garland. 'Once it is installed there we'll be free of all this. We'll go back to being the Fantasia we used to be.'

'Didn't you hear what he said?' cried Eden. 'The Nennog has friends there in Solis. There are people there who might take the converter over. And we don't know who they are.'

They came out of the tunnel into the ruins of the Outland, then walked back through the forest to the old road the vans had taken. Solis seemed close – so close – but they stood staring towards it, hesitating like desolate lost children, confused about what to do next.

'How can the Nennog have friends in Solis if he lives hundreds of years on ahead of us?' cried Boomer, struggling to fasten his wings back into obedient folds so he could stare around them at the city. 'It doesn't make sense.'

'He can't come and go himself, but he could send his servants back through time,' said Eden, 'and they could work for him. And he had his beginning back in your time. I should have thought of that.'

'Let's warn Yves!' shouted Boomer.

Garland looked sadly down at the sleeping Jewel and then at Boomer, shaking her head.

'If we ran all the way we'd still never be there in time,' she said. 'Unless . . .' She looked at Eden. 'Could you magic us there?'

Eden sighed. 'My strongest magic comes to me through the Talisman,' he said looking at Jewel. 'But they've given her something to make her sleep very deeply. I can't get much of a connection.'

'What can we do?' asked Boomer. 'There must be something we can do.'

'There is,' said a voice, and there was Timon, green-scaled and ghastly, yet somehow still partly Timon, struggling to be himself, half walking, half sliding down towards them from the bush.

'Don't trust me too much,' he said. 'I can't be trusted. But I've found I can steal some of the Nennog's knowledge just as he can steal from me. Some of his strength too.'

With an eerie power he hoisted aside part of a tumbled wooden frame, and rolled a rock away to reveal something like a manhole cover in the track in which they were standing. 'There used to be a drain here, back in the old times.' He lifted the cover easily, though it had been jammed closed for perhaps a hundred years.

'When the city stood here it was a city of tunnels,' he said.

'Too many tunnels,' said Eden. 'I just – I just can't do another one. I mean I'd be shut down there in the dark again with the world sort of pressing down on me, and I'd be there with *you*, and you're – well, you said not to trust you.'

'Scared of being shut in?' Timon mumbled. 'Fight it! You have to. I mean I'm fighting this . . .' He touched his green throat, and the scales on his cheeks. 'I'm not doing too badly, am I?'

'Well, I'm not going down there,' said Boomer. He touched a button and his wings unfolded. 'I'm going to fly.'

'You could take Jewel,' suggested Garland, looking at Timon, but he shook his head.

'I can't trust myself,' he said, 'but I think this old drain is the quickest way into Solis. For some reason I seem to remember something – an old plan of some kind. I think it leads to the very heart of the city, so we wouldn't have to wind our way through markets and streets of houses. I'll come with you but I – well, you mustn't give me Jewel.' Then he looked at Garland. 'Do you trust me?' he asked.

'You told me not to, so I don't. But I have to, don't I?' she replied, looking down into the drain. There were steps like old iron staples vanishing into the dark. Eden was already finding his way down. He reached the bottom and held up his arms. Garland passed the sleeping baby down to Eden, then began climbing down herself.

In the ruins of Outland, Maddie, Goneril and Lilith wandered, searching for Garland . . . calling her name but getting no response except the curious mocking reply of the echoes.

'What have I done to deserve this?' groaned Maddie. 'A runaway daughter. And it's not as if we were stick-in-the-mud-stay-at-homes. She gets to see a lot of places.'

'What's that sound?' said Goneril. 'It sounds like some sort of a . . .'

As she spoke an old Jeep suddenly surged out from between two roofless houses leaning towards one another as if they were trying to peer deeply into each other's windows. The Jeep drove down the street towards them and they stood back to let it pass, but instead of swinging by it drew up beside them and a man leaned out smiling broadly and holding out his hands.

'Fantasia people?' asked the driver. 'Yes! I can tell you are. We have been sent to pick you up and drive you into Solis.'

'Well, our own vans have gone on ahead of us,' began Maddie, 'and . . .'

'We would like to give you a ceremonial welcome,' the man said. 'Please get in. The other Fantasia people are waiting for you.'

'Yes,' said Maddie, 'but you see we've lost some children . . . a girl and two boys . . .'

'And a baby!' said Goneril quickly.

'Ah yes,' the man said. 'They are waiting for you too. We picked them up earlier.'

Lilith was delighted.

'They've found Jewel!' she cried, and flung her arms around Goneril. 'They've found Garland and Boomer. We're going to have a great welcome. And we're going to end happily.'

'Thank goodness,' said Maddie, sighing with huge relief. 'Take us quickly before something else goes wrong!' They scrambled into the vehicle. Maddie in the front, Goneril and Lilith in the back.

'All this great struggle and we're back in Solis,' Maddie said over her shoulder. 'It's over. Well, almost over. And then we'll be free to be nothing but ourselves again. Nothing but the Fantasia. Wonderful.'

She did not know – couldn't know – that at that very moment Garland was *not* in Solis but was feeling her way along a drain, followed by Eden, carrying Jewel, who was followed by Boomer. Timon, now walking ahead of them, seemed in a strange way to be as black as night yet somehow casting just a little light around him.

'Nearly there,' Timon said.

'How can you see in the dark?' asked Garland.

'One of my new talents,' Timon replied. 'Look ahead.'

Garland did as she was told, without seeing anything but Timon's shape – a shape which was not entirely his own. *I mustn't trust him*, she told herself. *He said I mustn't trust him. But which 'him' do I believe?* How could he give off light, that light that seemed to be playing around her feet like an affectionate pet?

'I can't see a single thing,' said Boomer.

'Well, take my word for it,' said Timon. 'We're about to climb a staircase and when we get to the top we will be in Solis. Now . . . just kick a bit! There! Can you feel the bottom step.'

Garland kicked, and – yes – she could feel it. It was just ahead of her, a stair shrouded in shadow. She had no idea where it might lead to.

'Hold my hand,' said Timon, and his fingers brushed the fingers of her own hand, which she was holding out in front of her, so that she could feel her way. Garland snatched her own hand back to her side.

'No way!' she cried softly. 'You did tell me not to trust you.'

'Well, climb!' commanded Timon. 'Climb and hitch onto that rhythm. Not much longer now.'

39

The Duke of Solis

High above the city of Solis the Duke of Solis and two of his attendants stood, looking lordly and remote.

At the other end of the room stood a whole deputation of Fantasia people, looking triumphant, distressed and exhausted all at once . . . looking triumphant because though the converter was not in the room with them it was in the city at last and would soon be safely delivered by Maddie and Yves to the experts who would know what to do with it, looking distressed because Garland, Boomer, Timon, Eden and Jewel had disappeared, and looking exhausted as well, because they had worked through the night without sleeping. And they would not be able to sleep again until the others were safely home in the heart of the Fantasia once more.

'To think they struggled and bargained and had so many adventures bringing it to us,' murmured the Duke to his attendants. 'They are heroes. Heroes!' (He spoke rather more loudly, looking up and beaming at the Fantasia people.) Then his voice dropped down once more. 'But of course most heroes are fools as well. All that struggle – all that work – and the result will be very different from one they anticipated and desired.'

'Solis will die?' asked one of his companions, murmuring too.

'Solis will be put out of its misery,' agreed the Duke. 'But it will be reborn in a different form, and I will be its midwife.'

As he said this the door at the other end of the room suddenly swung open. The Duke spun around, looking furious.

'I said we were not to be disturbed!' he barked.

'Oh, but you will want to see us,' said a voice, and Timon came boldly into the room, followed by Garland and Eden.

'Garland!' exclaimed Penrod, and the Fantasia deputation tried to move forward, their faces breaking into smiles of relief. However the Duke's guard moved in on them holding them back.

The Duke stared at Timon unable to believe in him. He glanced at Garland, arms sagging under the weight of a sleeping baby, a strange bedraggled creature with red hair burning out around her weary face, and at the pale and grubby stick-like boy who was Eden. Then he looked back at green-scaled and threatening Timon.

'Why do you think for a moment I would want to see you, you filthy creatures?' said the Duke haughtily.

But it was Garland who spoke first. 'Where's Yves? Where's my mother?'

'They are taking the converter to the technologists,' Tane said. 'In a little while the city will have its power restored to it.' He smiled at the Duke, like a man who expects a smile of gratitude in return.

The Duke frowned. He looked at his companions. 'Do we know an Yves?' They shrugged and shook their heads. 'I don't think we do. Are there more of these gypsies in my city? As for the converter, I want it brought to me personally. I just wanted to look it over – before I had it destroyed.'

The Fantasia people all shouted out in a chorus of astonishment and anger.

'Destroyed!' cried Garland. 'But you *wanted it*. It has to save Solis.'

The Duke smiled again. 'No one tells the Duke of Solis what he can or can't do,' he said, 'least of all an urchin from that gipsy trash they call the Fantasia.'

Garland stared at him in alarm. 'But if you don't make use of the converter,' she cried, 'you'll change. You'll die in darkness. Or you might become something you can't imagine . . . something green and scaly like – like *him* –' she pointed at Timon '. . . only he's kind and strong under his scales. You might turn into the Nennog.' She did not know quite what made her say this. She just wanted to frighten the Duke.

'My dear,' said the Duke. 'I haven't time. I haven't time to play children's games with you. I am Edward, Duke of Solis, and I will remain Edward, Duke of Solis until the time comes for my son to take over. One of my sons. I do have more than one . . .' A door to his left burst open and he turned towards it looking furious. 'This is too much. Too much. I am going to reinforce the guard.'

Garland stared at the newcomer – at Ozul, carrying what was left of his slider, half folded in on itself, and at Maska, now looking more like a huge battered toy than a man – or even a clever robot – sparking a little at his joints, but still terrifying.

Timon stepped forward. 'At last,' he said. 'You have been rather leisurely about putting in an appearance, haven't you? Unplait what's left of the slider, Ozul. Maska, we may need you to locate the technologists and the converter out there in the city power house. The Duke is right. That converter must be destroyed.'

Garland spun around staring at him in horror.

'What's going on?' she said at last. 'You've been on our side. You tricked them . . . damaged them . . .'

'I have been more than one person,' Timon said in a voice that was no longer Timon's. 'He fought against me far more valiantly than I imagined he could. But the battle is won. I am a single entity at last. And my wishes will rule.'

'Boomer said you were treacherous!' screamed Garland.

'That simple honest Boomer,' said Timon. 'He's waiting for you at the main door, isn't he? Those folded wings of his make life a bit difficult for him, don't they, when it comes to going upstairs and around corners. Well, he will have to wait for a long time for you.' He laughed hideously. 'And I have let Timon exercise power. What he did not know was that he was exercising it on my behalf.'

The Duke, who had been too astounded to do or say a thing for a moment, seemed to come to his senses finally.

'Who are you?' he yelled. 'Guards! Guards! Get this monster out of here.'

'You fool,' cried the transformed Timon. 'I am *you*. I am you as you will be in the future, with powers and riches you can only dream of in these primitive days. If your guards strike me down, it is you they will be striking down. If you destroy me, you will be destroying yourself and your own future.' The Duke stared at him, his expression slowly changing. 'You do not recognize me?' the Nennog asked. 'Time brings about changes we cannot imagine.' He leaned forward and whispered some words in a language than none of the other listeners could understand, but these soft words caused the Duke to leap back as if he had been stung.

'Yes!' the Nennog said, speaking through Timon. 'Only you know the meaning of those words. You and your future self. You and me. You see you finally achieved what you wanted, riches and power and immortality of a kind. And I am your immortality. And to achieve all I stand for, you must do as I tell you. Do it now and without hesitation. Do it now, because we are one.'

And only a little later in that the top room looking out over the whole astonishing city of Solis the Duke watched Ozul fitting, slotting, connecting once more. 'Technology! Fascinating!' he said.

'It will all be yours,' promised Timon smiling. Two of his attendants held Eden and Garland but Garland could still shout.

'When you're like *him* . . . a cross between a cockroach and a lizard . . . some of it might be yours!' she screamed. 'Is that what you want?'

The Duke looked over at Timon, and an expression of uncertainty crossed his face.

'Don't be weak!' Timon told him. 'And I promise you unlimited pleasure. So take advantage. Take it now and always.' He turned to Ozul and Maska. 'Time to go,' he said.

'Timon!' called Garland. 'Timon! Please! *Please!* Listen to me.'

'Don't call me by that name,' Timon said, but looking into that green-scaled face that had so little about it that was familiar, Garland nevertheless saw something she recognized and knew that the golden-haired prince was not entirely dead. He was locked somewhere in that monster confronting them, living and listening but also helpless for the Nennog was indeed dominating him.

'Don't destroy that converter,' she cried. 'Let the Solis technologists set it going and maybe you will be cured.'

'Forget the converter,' Timon said. 'Now, pass over that wretched baby. After all, she is my sister.'

'She is *Timon's* sister, not yours!' yelled Garland, clasping Jewel to her. 'Timon! Are you there, Timon? Listen to me.'

'Give her to me before I become truly annoyed with you,' said the Nennog, his eyes glowing ferociously, as Garland, holding Jewel, wrapped in her blankets, backed away from him. The Nennog advanced on her.

'You will be sorry,' he said, 'and so will your whole Fantasia.

Your leader – Yves, is it? – is in my power. All your friends are here in Solis and I only have to say the word any my guards will grind them to powder and bloody paste. The baby is nothing to you – nothing at all compared with your mother, for example. Now give me that Talisman.'

But, still clutching Jewel, Garland did the only thing that seemed possible to her. Suddenly she ran through a pair of double doors only to find herself on a wide balcony. She jumped up on the low wall, and glanced at the great fall into the streets below. There was no escape to the left, no escape to the right. But down below . . . down below . . .

'Why not jump?' asked the Nennog. 'Why not dash yourself and the baby to pieces on the stone below. It is the only way out for you.'

But as he said this Garland *did* jump. The Nennog did not so much scream as howl with fury. The sound rang through the whole city of Solis, springing back at him from the walls as if a whole pack of transformed Timons were howling . . . He ran to the edge of that wall and stared down into the void.

And far below, there on a thick wire, strung as a brace between a ruined tower and a neighbouring block, balanced like a burning candle and still holding a sleeping Jewel was Garland, a true Fantasia girl. She looked up at the top of the wall and saw the transformed Timon, the Nennog, looking down at her. Then she looked ahead of herself, and began walking along the wire as if it were nothing more than a familiar tightrope . . . something she had walked along many, many times.

The hideous figure of the Nennog stared down as if he could scarcely believe it, then whirled on Ozul and Maska.

'Stop her! Intercept her!' he shouted.

They, too, peered down at Garland walking the wire – walking it serenely. Ozul looked up and licked his lips.

'Lord!' he began. 'I can't! And Maska – he can't either. The last few weeks have twisted him, and . . .'

'You are bound to do with I say,' the Nennog declared. 'Do it.'

Maska ran for a back door in his unwieldy way while Ozul made for the door in front of them. But before he reached it, it burst open, and suddenly the room was flooded with Fantasia people. In sprang Yves. Penrod, Byrna and Nye followed him. Maddie came in shouting. 'Garland! Garland! They say she was seen here. Where's Garland?'

Eden sprang forward to point to the battlements and Maddie ran towards the wall, pushing Timon off to the right, without so much as glancing at him. The guards jumped to protect the Duke, but Yves raised his crossbow. He pointed it not at the guards, but at the Duke. 'Put down your weapons, gentlemen!' he shouted. 'Down! Down! Put them down or your master dies.'

'Do it,' the Duke told them. He looked over at the Nennog. 'From, what you say if I am killed you, too, will cease to exist,' he said.

Meanwhile, down on the wire, holding Jewel as if the baby was a balancing rod, Garland stepped carefully. After the first shock she did not feel frightened because, after all, she had walked the wire almost all her life. It was true that the space under her on this occasion was much greater than she was used to, but that wire beneath her feet and her feet themselves were old companions. As this wire ran towards the building it was bracing, it passed a long line of windows on the right-hand side, and suddenly Garland saw a dark shadow moving in one of those windows. Maska. But she must not be distracted. She must not lose her nerve. She walked on almost placidly.

Only a moment later, she felt the wire suddenly shifting under her feet in an unfamiliar way. Carefully she turned sideways on the wire, so that she could look both forwards and backwards. Behind her Maska had climbed out onto one of the windowsills and was now stepping out on the wire himself. Garland smiled. She turned carefully, and walked on, for she had no choice and besides, she *knew* the wire, which was like the same wire she walked in a Fantasia performance, and perhaps Maska did not. Onward, onward!

And then she saw Ozul moving out onto the wire where it connected with the building ahead of her. Garland knew at once that he was filled with terror. She did not know why he was taking this terrible risk, but she was suddenly sure that it was because the Nennog had ordered him to do so, and he feared the Nennog more than he feared a fatal fall.

Things seemed so desperate – so dangerous. She was trapped. Yet, suddenly, Garland had a great feeling of confidence . . . she was at home on the wire, and they, for all their powers, were not.

'So you want to try the high wire act?' she called to Ozul. She looked over her shoulder. 'Can you bounce,' she called back to Maska and laughed . . . a desperate laugh, but a laugh, all the same. Then she bounced lightly on the wire. She had done this so many times, and a wire was only a wire regardless of the space beneath it.

'Don't!' yelled Ozul frantically. 'Please don't! Let's . . . let's discuss this. Let's . . .'

Garland carefully edged around to stand sideways yet again. Once again she could look back towards Maska.

'Do you want to discuss it too?' she asked.

'Discussion is always good,' said Maska in his grating, damaged voice.

'Right! I'll open the discussion!' shouted Garland, and now she bounced wildly on the wire, knowing she could, for she was a child of Maddigan's Fantasia.

Ozul pitched forwards, screaming as he fell. Maska toppled backwards, making a noise like some protesting machine.

Garland watched them fall away from her without a second of regret. Then, very carefully, for even when you knew how to walk the wire you always had to be careful, she turned and stepped forward once more. A few more steps and she would be able to step off onto a balcony of that building the wire was helping to support.

Just then she felt the wire move abruptly and turned to see that, once again, she was being followed. The Nennog, that changed Timon, was moving along the wire towards her rapidly, using both hands and feet, looking like some sort of green spider. He scuttled with the unnatural skill of the Nennog until he was within two or three feet of her. Then he stopped.

'Wherever you go, Garland, I will follow you,' he said.

Garland had been about to step off onto that balcony. Once there she could open a door perhaps, run into the building beyond, lose herself in some way, and find safety for herself and Jewel. Perhaps! Perhaps! But then Timon suddenly moved with such rapidity she could not escape from him. He caught her arm. 'I will follow you!' he repeated in the Nennog's voice and yet with a strange echo of Timon's voice lurking beneath.

There was no hope now, but she would not surrender. 'Then follow this!' she said. Still clasping Jewel with one arm, she jumped from the wire into the abyss below.

In that mad moment she meant to fall even if it meant that Jewel fell with her . . . meant to be free of Timon, both prince and monster and free, too, of the huge wearing puzzle of being alive. But she did not fall far. Timon caught her free hand and held her swinging over that abyss. One of them clung, the other swung like a supreme circus act, Timon now somehow lying along the wire, Garland dangling below it.

And as Garland looked up and Timon looked down, staring incredulously at each other, something struck Garland's face . . . a gleam of light . . . new light. Up on the summits of the tallest buildings, solar panels had suddenly begun to unfold like a hundred silver petals.

'They must have done it!' cried Garland with wild hope. 'The technologists must have connected the converter.'

She felt her fingers slip, just a little in Timon's hand, and suddenly she did not want to die. But she was desperately clasping Jewel with her other arm and could not help herself unless she let the baby fall. And she wouldn't do that – she couldn't! Looking up at Timon she saw the new intense light was falling directly on him, and as it did so, his face began a strange sparkling.

'What's happening?' she screamed, and then saw that the green hand holding hers was sparkling too. The Nennog may have longed for the converter, but he could not stand the light it generated. The scales were falling away from Timon, his golden hair was strengthening. Before her eyes he was changing – becoming once again the boy she had known in the beginning.

But as his true self strengthened and drove the possessing Nennog out of him, his grasp was weakening. It was becoming nothing more than an ordinary human grasp. Timon could not balance on the wire as the Nennog had balanced . . . as Garland had balanced . . . and Garland could not help him without dropping Jewel.

'Garland! Garland! I can't hold you!' Timon screamed, and his voice was now Timon's voice, full of grief and despair. As he cried this she felt herself slip out of his fingers.

They were falling. *This is the end*, Garland thought madly. *Really truly the end!* and as she tumbled and spun down past lines of windows, balconies green with potted plants, down and down again, she hugged Jewel to her chest, her hand covering the baby's head in a last desperate effort to protect her.

And then something seized them. Hands grabbed her collar and the loose shirt in the small of her back. Her fall changed. She was no longer plunging down in that mad, deadly way. Suddenly she was sinking slowly. Then the sound of a small motor revving up came to her ears, and she even began to rise a little, being pulled up in a struggling way, but rising all the same, and being carried towards one of those green balconies she had tumbled past only a moment ago.

Boomer. Boomer flying! Boomer trying hard to fly and manage her weight, sinking a bit . . . rising a bit . . . but managing to stay aloft.

'Want a lift, you great lump!' he shouted in triumph. Then he laughed. Garland laughed too. At least she thought she was laughing but, after all, she might have been crying, as she hugged the drugged and sleeping Jewel to her heart.

They were saved. The converter had been installed. The solar panels of Solis were opening like mysterious flowers, and the towers around them were blooming with light. Solis was saved. And thanks to Boomer and the Birdboy wings, Garland was saved too.

At the far end of the wire Eden helped his brother onto the balcony and then hugged him. Below them, among the pot plants on another balcony, while Boomer hovered above her, Garland unfolded the blanket back from Jewel, still sleeping.

But Jewel wasn't there.

Garland crouched staring down in horror at the empty blanket. Had Jewel slipped out of her grasp after all? Had the baby tumbled away to death in the city below while Garland struggled with the Nennog who had turned back into Timon when the intensified lights of Solis fell on him? Then in the middle of her sudden despair, she heard pounding footsteps, voices crying out, and footsteps again and then the balcony doors behind her opened.

At the same time she was feeling something new – something coming in at her from outside – something entirely familiar as if a note of well-known music was ringing not just in her ear, but through and through her. There it was again, that utter certainty that something magical was about to be revealed. She lifted her head and saw the silver girl, but not as she was used to seeing her. This girl was real. There was not a ripple . . . not a moment of drift about her. She stood in front of Timon and Eden, a girl of about sixteen – still slightly silvery perhaps – but real in a way she had never been real before. And this time she did not point or gesture. She actually spoke.

'When you travel in time,' she said, 'you can sometimes be in two places at once. But you have to ride on the right time pulse.'

'You!' cried Garland, understanding something at last. 'The silver girl.' She looked down at the empty blanket in her arms then up again. 'You're Jewel!'

'Jewel grown-up,' said the girl. 'I'm sorry if I was hard to understand but I was melting this way and that between futures. But now, thanks to you, thanks to your help, things have become certain for me . . .'

High over head the last of the solar panels was unfolding.

'. . . and we love you – me and my brothers, and all those future people on ahead of us, and we're grateful to you. You have saved us. But that future is now forming and settling down, and in that future we were never here . . .' said Jewel, her voice fading.

As she said this Garland understood something else. She

looked almost desperately at Timon and Eden, saw them smiling at her, not simply with friendship but with love as well. A love that would become part of them all, crossing time, strengthening her day by day in her own time, strengthening them in theirs.

'Oh! Don't go!' she called. 'Wait! I want to *talk* to you. I want to ask *questions*. I want to really truly *understand*.'

But they were already fading, melting into that new light. There was Eden, that foresty boy, a child made of sticks and leaves. But he was going. Timon held out his hand once more, his long fingers free of scales. She saw the light shift on his golden hair . . . saw his blue eyes flash at her. But he was going too. 'Garland,' she heard him say.

Then he shimmered just as Eden was shimmering, just as Jewel, the silver girl, was shimmering. Both boys dissolved into light, and light was all she could see there in Solis, the great city of her own particular time.

Garland sat on her bunk in the van, her diary open in front of her, her pencil in her hand. Somehow she found she could not write to Ferdy any more, for she had said goodbye to Ferdy back on that rise, reliving an earlier time which she should never have entered, which she should never have tried to change.

But she wanted to write it all down. Writing it down would give her some power over things that were really beyond her. Of course there was no way she could ever understand them, but all the same she had to *try* understanding them. She had to remember them as well as she possibly could, and somehow build a story out of them, for if she built a story she would be able to learn it by heart and take charge of it and the story would, in time, dissolve into her blood and build itself into her bones.

And so dear Timon, that was how it ended, though I
know it was not a real ending just part of the flow . . .
maybe even a beginning of a sort . . . and you know all
about it anyway. At least I think you do. Do you have
any memory of me in that future time? Maybe yes!
Maybe no! But I remember having you as part of my
story, and I always will.

'Garland!' Maddie was calling her. 'Garland! Garland! Darling
girl!'

Garland walked out of the van and the Fantasia, her dear Fantasia, embraced her . . . closed tightly around her and yet at the
same time seemed to open out like a great glowing flower. A
show was about to begin. In a moment she would be called
upon to walk the tightrope . . . to jump on it, somersault on it.
Nobody could do that better than she could. There they all
were, the people she knew so well . . . all the people who, she
felt, were part of her forever. There was Goneril arguing with
Tane. There was Boomer, dear old Boomer, her saviour, putting his wings on yet again. And there was Maddie watching
Yves who was out in the ring, grand in that scarlet ringmaster's
coat, which he certainly deserved to wear by now.

'Ladies and gentlemen!' Yves was shouting. 'We present
Maddigan's Fantasia . . . the show of amazement . . . the show
of wonders . . . the show that explodes with a thousand
delights . . .

'What a journey,' Maddie was saying. 'There's never been
anything like it. I mean we always have problems, always, but I
don't think there's ever been anything as troubled as this last
time.'

'But we won through,' Garland said.

'Oh yes,' agreed Maddie. 'We won through. I hope for a rest

now, but then we'll hit the road again, and have – I don't know –
a more orderly trip next time.'

'There's always the Road Rats,' said Garland. She found she
did want to travel quietly, but she did not want to travel without adventures.

'You're on next,' said Maddie.

And only a few minutes later Garland was standing in the
ring herself . . . not walking the tightrope yet . . . not juggling
. . . but staring down at the magic cabinet and thinking to herself, thoughts she sent on ahead through the years to Timon.

So I open it, and it is empty . . .

Garland opened the cabinet and it was indeed empty as she
turned down the sides, showing that there was no way there
could be anyone hiding in it. The audience nodded and nudged
one another, preparing to be astonished.

*Life's a bit like the cabinet really . . . a box of wonders. People
climb into it and disappear. Sometimes they go forever. Sometimes
they flit in and out of your life like wild birds . . .*

She looked up as Boomer swooped down overhead dropping
flower petals and little balloons, almost but not quite as Eden
might once have done. Garland put the sides of the box up
again, smiling at the audience, but still sending her thoughts on
ahead to Timon.

*Some people disappear no matter how much you want them to
stay. And some people don't disappear, no matter how much you
might wish them to.*

Boomer beat out a challenging rattle on his drum, and Garland waved her wand, and touched the cabinet.

Its sides fell away. It opened once more but it was no longer
empty. There was her lovely assistant Lilith rising up out of
nowhere in her spangly dress, smiling and blowing kisses to the
people out there, who gasped yet again as Boomer beat a triumphant roll on the drums.

. . . and I guess it would be mean to wish that Lilith might disappear, unless of course you knew, deep down, that she was going to appear again, even if it did mean that you had to listen to her singing.

Lilith jumped down from the magical box, and took Garland's left hand. Boomer took her right and they ran forward to meet the applause, as they might run forward to meet some wave of the sea. They bowed and bowed again while the applause, the whistles, the clapping, rang around them.

So the Fantasia is still Fantastic, and Solis still glows with light, and everyone is happy, except perhaps the Duke of Solis, who is sitting there in the audience, but who is never going to be what he just might have been.

(Up in his box the Duke applauded politely.)

But that, as they say, is another story.